@carolinerobertsauthor

Also by Caroline Roberts

The Desperate Wife
The Cosy Teashop in the Castle
The Cosy Christmas Teashop
My Summer of Magic Moments
The Cosy Christmas Chocolate Shop
The Cosy Seaside Chocolate Shop
Rachel's Pudding Pantry
Christmas at Rachel's Pudding Pantry

Summer at Rachel's Pudding Pantry

Caroline Roberts

HarperCollins*Publishers*

One More Chapter an imprint of
HarperCollins*Publishers* Ltd
1 London Bridge Street,
London SE1 9GF

www.harpercollins.co.uk

First published by HarperCollins*Publishers* 2020
1

A catalogue record for this book is available from the British Library

ISBN: 978-0-00-840194-8

Set in Minion Pro 12/15.25pt by Palimpsest Book Production Limited, Falkirk, Stirlingshire

Printed and bound in the UK by CPI Group (UK) Ltd, Croydon CR0 4YY

This book is produced from independently certified FSC™ paper
to ensure responsible forest management.

For more information visit: www.harpercollins.co.uk/green

For Ken and Pam

'Marriage is not a destination, but a journey.'
Bernard Dsa

Something Old

Granny Ruth's Wedding Cake

Ingredients

350g (12oz) plain flour
1 tsp mixed spice
100g (3½oz) ground almonds
4 medium eggs
225g (8oz) unsalted butter
225g (8oz) caster sugar
225g (8oz) currants
225g (8oz) sultanas
225g (8oz) raisins
100g (3½oz) glacé cherries, halved
100g (3½oz) cut mixed peel
A quality brandy and a nip of whisky
A dash of milk

Method

Macerate the currants, sultanas and raisins in brandy overnight.

Preheat an oven to 150°C/Fan 130°C/Gas mark 2. Grease and line a cake tin, using either a 23-cm (9-inch) round or 20.5-cm (8-inch) square tin. Sieve the flour and mixed spice into a bowl and add the almonds.

Beat the eggs together with a little milk. Soften the

butter. Cube and cream the butter together with the sugar. Slowly stir in the flour and then the egg mixture. When completely mixed, add the soaked dried fruit, cherries and mixed peel. Stir until evenly distributed. Place the mixture into the prepared tin and protect the top with baking parchment paper.

Bake for about 3¼ to 4 hours. Remove from the oven and allow to cool slightly. Turn onto a wire rack. Pour a small amount of brandy and a nip of whisky over the cake whilst warm.

Allow to cool thoroughly. Wrap in greaseproof paper and then tinfoil, store in an airtight container. Store for at least six weeks before use, feeding once a week with a tablespoon of brandy. Decorate as required using an apricot glaze, marzipan and white icing.

For a larger, wedding-style cake, depending on the size of tins, make double or triple the mixture.

1

'*Oh my . . .* that is just beautiful, Rachel.' A tear crowded Jill's eye as she watched her daughter step out from the changing room.

A slow smile spread across Rachel's face. 'I like it too.'

It did feel strange though, being in a 'frock', as Granny Ruth would have called it, and not just any old frock – an off-white, gorgeous, lace-detailed, to-the-floor *wedding* frock. It had a hint of boho chic about it, just perfect for her countryside summer wedding. Rachel did a small twirl in the middle of the shop, then caught sight of herself in the full-length mirror, and paused. Hah, she hardly looked like herself at all; she was usually dressed in old jeans and wellies and could even sometimes be found out on the farm in a practical green boiler suit, which was highly glamorous. Ooh, it was a lovely feeling to be wearing something so special, but strange too.

'I think we might've found the one, Mum.' She had a lump in her throat as she spoke.

'I think so too, love.' Her mum nodded with a proud and happy look on her face.

Rachel had also found *the one* in Tom Watson. Just

thinking about him and their impending marriage made her heart swell, yet there was still a trace of disbelief that all this had happened to her over the past few months. Tom was her long-time friend and neighbour; their relationship had blossomed into something so much more, taking them both rather by storm, a most beautiful, soul-drenching storm.

'Gosh, your dad would be so proud if he could see you now, Rachel.'

'Oh Mum, it'll be so strange not having him there on my special day, won't it?'

'I know, love, but he'd want you to enjoy it . . . to be happy. And he was always very fond of Tom, even before you and he got together. I'm sure he'd have approved.'

'Yeah . . . I think he would have. But he won't be there to walk me down the aisle, will he . . .?' There would be such an empty space beside her on the day, as well as the one that she always carried inside.

'No, love.'

Rachel sighed, then gazed at herself in the shop's full-length mirror, her dark wavy hair falling loose down to her shoulders, her green eyes catching the light. There she was, standing in the prettiest of gowns, which hung and clung in just the right places, as if it had been made for her. The only problem was the price tag. Her mum had persuaded her to give it a try when it had caught her eye, even though it was somewhat over budget, along with a few other gowns that she'd discovered on the sale rack. She'd tried the reduced ones on first, being mindful that this was very much a wedding on a budget. They were very nice, but not quite right.

She looked at the price tag once more, with a sigh. How could she be selfish and go ahead and get this one? It would mean a cut in the wedding budget somewhere else. Maisy, her daughter, and Maisy's best friend Amelia, the cutest of flower girls, deserved lovely dresses, as did Eve (maid of honour) and Charlotte (her bridesmaid). There were flowers to buy, some kind of marquee or tent to organise in case of rain. They could of course do much of the buffet themselves, and they *really* wanted to be able to invite all their family and friends from the village and local farming community to share this happy occasion. So many people had supported them through such difficult times over the years, it'd be a wonderful way to show their appreciation. Rachel really didn't want to have to cut the guest list.

The shop assistant stepped forward from her position near the counter. 'Oh, that looks *stunning* on you, really.' She was smiling softly, the hint of a tear in her eye. 'I see lots of dresses come on and off and sometimes you can just see when it's the perfect gown for the bride-to-be.'

'But I can't . . .' Rachel began.

'Can't what?' asked Jill.

'I can't get it . . . I'm sorry, Mum, I shouldn't have tried it on. We were being silly, thinking we could stretch to this. The others were in the sale, this one isn't. There's so much else we need to pay out on.'

'But I'm sure we could manage, with a bit of careful budgeting . . . if this is the right dress for you. It is your wedding day, after all. A once-in-a-lifetime occasion.'

'Yes, but there's no need for it to make us stony-broke. And I want everyone to enjoy it, not just me.'

'Oh, I suppose . . . but what a shame, love.'

'It's fine . . . There'll be another dress to catch my eye somewhere, I'm sure.' Rachel rallied, despite the nip of disappointment, as she headed back into the changing room. She took one last longing glance at this gorgeous dress before the assistant stepped in to help undo the rear zip, ready for her to step out of it.

'I know it's a long shot . . . I don't suppose there's any chance of a discount on this one?' Rachel ventured. *Well, if you didn't ask . . .*

'Oh, I'm sorry, madam, but we can't reduce this one. It's the new season's range, just come in, and we always try to price our dresses competitively as it is. The others you tried were the remaining few from last year's stock, that's why we could discount them. I'm sorry.'

Rachel gave the dress one last look, the delicate flowers appliquéd on the draped tulle skirt catching her eye, as the assistant began to place it carefully back on the hanger. Ah well, a chance to dream.

'Are you sure?' Jill asked, as she emerged from the changing room.

'Yes, I'm sure. It's lovely, but it's just too expensive. It's not about the dress at the end of the day, it's about me and Tom, isn't it?'

'Yes, you're right,' her mum sighed and nodded. 'Come on then, I don't know about you, but all this dress shopping has just about done me in. I spotted a coffee shop over the road. Shall we go and recharge with a cappuccino?'

'Great idea.'

Settled at a wooden table by the window of the café, Rachel could see the assistant tidying the little wedding shop after their visit. Her dress was placed back on the rail, ready for someone else to try on.

'We'd manage somehow, you know love . . .' Jill's voice trailed off, as if she was a little disappointed too.

'No, it wouldn't *feel* right – even if it looked right – if I blew the budget already. I'm sure I can find something else that'll do just fine.'

How Jill wished she had some secret savings stash she could dig into right now – she'd so love to make her daughter's day. Maybe there was a way she still could?

Whilst Rachel nipped to the bathroom, Jill sketched what she could remember of the dress on a white paper napkin, while it was fresh in her mind: the simple yet flattering bodice with its V front and back, the fine tulle of the skirt with its gorgeous appliqué flower design. She then popped the drawing into her handbag. Well, you never knew . . .

2

TWO MONTHS LATER

'Have you remembered to put the hiking boots in, Mum?'

'Yes, both our pairs are in.' Jill was trailing a couple of all-weather anoraks to the Land Rover. Well, you had to be prepared for all eventualities in Scotland, rain or shine, even in May and at the supposed start of summer.

'Prosecco?'

'Yep, got the essentials packed, of course. The box of six is in the boot.'

'Perfect . . . and I've got the sticky toffee puddings and the Tupperware box of meringues from Granny Ruth right here.' Rachel perused the back of the truck. Cases in, yep, the cool bag of provisions, yes . . . hmm. Rachel had a mental check list but she was sure she was going to forget something. She knew she should have written it all down last night, but she'd been far too busy getting everything ready for Maisy's next two days at school and for staying over at Amelia's. She'd also been flat out organising everything on the farm ready to hand over to their farmhand, Simon, and Tom – her lovely, gorgeous Tom

– who were taking the reins whilst she was away for her hen do. A *hen do*, she could barely believe it.

It felt weird packing up the truck, ready to pick up her best friend and maid of honour, Eve. It was going to be a weekend to remember, Eve had boasted, though she still hadn't spilled on all the details. Rachel was so excited but there were a few nervous butterflies in her stomach too; as a single parent she hadn't had a night away since Maisy had been born five years ago, and with her father's tragic death nearly three years past, and the devastation they had endured in the aftermath, the family hadn't been in the frame of mind to take a holiday.

Dad . . . memories of packing for holidays in years gone by suddenly flooded over her. Long weekends piled into a static caravan near Scarborough on the Yorkshire Coast, fish and chips sitting on the harbour at Whitby, with donkey rides on the golden sands at Filey Bay. Dad's strong hand holding her own as they splashed up to their knees in icy-cold waves that took their breath away, laughing even as they shivered. God, she missed him. Her thoughts turned to her own little girl, Maisy, who had given her an extra big hug at the minibus pick-up that morning before school. Rachel had been left with a solid lump in her throat as she watched the bus pull away, with Maisy waving animatedly out of the window. It felt so strange to be leaving her child behind, even though she was looking forward to these few days of fun and freedom. She'd left a check list for Amelia's dad, Ben, on top of the small overnight case she'd packed with her daughter's favourite outfits, pyjamas and wash bag, and her comforting soft toy sheep. Maisy would be fine, she told herself.

A couple of friends, Kirsty and Hannah, were going to make their own way to the accommodation in Oban and join them there later today, as they had younger children and were sorting out timings with grandparents and dads who were working. Close friend and bridesmaid, Charlotte, was taking a train up after work tomorrow; the best she could manage was an early finish from her Friday classroom shift at the primary school. Honestly, between her and Eve, it had needed military-style strategies to arrange this getaway.

'Right then, Moss is in his kennel, isn't he?'

Moss, their faithful Border collie, herder of sheep and tail-wagger extraordinaire, was going to be looked after by farmhand Simon, and then Granny Ruth when she came over to stay with Maisy for the Saturday night of the weekend shift.

'Yep, and the Pudding Pantry is in safe hands with Jan and Daniel, so it's time to go, love,' rallied Jill.

With that, Dan appeared on the threshold of the Pantry ready to wave them off, calling out, 'Have a wonderful time, ladies.'

Jill gave a small sigh and waved back, looking slightly emotional herself.

Oh gosh, they really were getting fond of each other, Rachel mused. It was still strange to think her mum had a new man on the scene, even if the romance was in its fledgling stages. It was lovely to see her mum with a spring in her step once again. But Rachel couldn't deny it was still hard to balance that against her father's absence. How could anybody possibly step into her father's shoes? But, she conceded, it was so good of Dan to offer to help out at their beloved Pudding Pantry business, and for the next few days he'd certainly be a godsend. He wasn't a bad baker himself, either, and was already getting a name for his cheese and chive triangle scones.

'O-kay then.' Rachel took up the driving seat of their old and slightly battered Land Rover. As she started the engine, she gave a silent prayer that it would make the four-hour journey across the border. She gazed up at the stone farmhouse as she pulled away, feeling a tug in her heartstrings. As they made their way down the farm track, the valley nestled around them, green and lush with fields of sheep happily grazing, she saw little Petie, Maisy's now extremely big pet lamb, munching away. They passed their herd of cattle, Morag and Iona looking over the hawthorn hedge at the departing vehicle with seemingly sad, deep brown eyes. 'Won't be long, ladies,' Rachel called out.

Three whole days away at a cosy wooden lodge near Oban – with her mum Jill, best friend Eve, and close mates Charlotte, Kirsty and Hannah by her side. The lodge had looked so lovely from the images on the internet, with log fires, old beams, all set in woodland beside a small lake. It even had an outside Jacuzzi with a view across the water: very chic.

Pulling up outside Eve's cottage five minutes later, and seeing her friend come bounding out of the front door, Rachel found herself feeling an unfamiliar buzz of freedom.

'Hi, Eve. Are you road-trip ready?' She stuck her head out of the window and beeped the horn excitedly.

'Just about, hun. I'll go fetch my suitcase. Hi, Jill.' She gave a merry wave.

Out she came a few minutes later with a large case – it was big enough for a fortnight, never mind three nights. Rachel hoisted it into the back of the Land Rover. 'Blimey, how long do you think you are going for? What on earth have you got in there, the kitchen sink?' she jested.

'Hmm . . . just a few bits.'

'Hah, are you intending to elope or something?'

A flush of colour blushed across Eve's cheeks. 'Don't be so daft. It's just a few clothes, and well, it could be all weathers. And . . . there's a few extra things to make sure we have a really nice time. It's your hen do, after all. Ooh, talking of which, there's more still to bring from the kitchen . . .' Off she dashed again, returning a couple of minutes later with yet another box of prosecco. 'Essential hen-do supplies,' she beamed. 'Well, we are in the middle of nowhere. We can't be running out of the bubbly stuff.'

'Eve, we're only staying a few miles from Oban. We're not exactly going to the Outer Hebrides.'

'Oh well, better to be prepared,' Eve grinned.

'Exactly,' called Jill from the cab.

'Oh, and there's one last thing, there's a lasagne all

made ready on the kitchen side. If you could bring that out for me, Rach . . .?'

'Really? Oh, wow, that sounds delicious.'

'Well, I was making one for Ben and the girls to have, so I thought I'd double up. So, tonight's supper in our cosy lodge is sorted.'

'Aw, that's brilliant.'

With the back of the Land Rover finally loaded, Eve jumped in, ready for the off.

'Sorted?' asked Rachel. 'Sure you've got everything?' she added wryly.

'Yep, sorted!'

'Great stuff, this *is* exciting isn't it,' added Jill with a wide grin.

'Let's hit the road,' announced Rachel from the driver's seat.

Within twenty minutes, they were over the Scottish border and winding their way along country roads, through rolling hills. The Land Rover climbed and the moorland road peaked to give them a view down over the city of Edinburgh and the wide grey Firth of Forth. The traffic began to get busier as they skirted the city on the bypass heading for Glasgow. The Land Rover was rattling on well – so far so good.

An hour later on the motorway near Glasgow, they saw a services sign.

'Anyone else ready for a wee stop?' chirped Eve. 'I've been holding on for a while.'

'Sounds a good idea. And a nice cup of coffee wouldn't go amiss,' replied Jill.

'Oh yes, a latte is calling,' added Rachel, flicking the indicator on.

The services car park looked busy as they pulled to a stop, with people scurrying in and out of their cars like ants. For a second, Rachel wondered where their varied lives were taking them, what journeys they were making today – the holidays planned, family visits, the trips to work. It was a world away from the peace and quiet of Primrose Farm in the Cheviot Hills.

Jill moved to gather her handbag from the footwell, just as Eve exclaimed, 'Ooh my, eyes at two o'clock, ladies.'

'What?' Rachel looked around frantically. 'Oh, I see.' Rachel's mouth hung open, just as Jill moved quickly to see what the fuss was about, managing to bang her head on the dashboard. The younger girls giggled.

'Ah . . .' Jill had clocked what they were staring at now, taking in the guy in the white van parked opposite them who was removing his T-shirt, oblivious to their ogling. He revealed a rather toned and tanned bare chest.

Jill began rubbing the back of her head. 'Crikey, I haven't seen a body like that in a long while.' She quirked an eyebrow.

'Mu-um . . .'

'What do you mean, *Mu-um*? You two are thinking the same, I'm sure.'

Actually, Rachel had seen a body like that rather

recently, and was very much looking forward to getting married so she could see it every night. Her gorgeous Tom Watson.

The man had now peeled off and discarded one T-shirt to replace it with another.

'Hmm, well, you don't get to see that every day,' added Eve cheekily. 'It's a bit like that old Coca-Cola advert, do you remember?'

'Hah, yes. Probably not PC any more, but guaranteed to put a smile on a girl's face.'

They grinned, grabbed their bags, and got down out of the Land Rover, at the very same time that Mr T made his exit from his van. He fired them a broad smile across the car park, before strolling towards the services entrance. The girls were happy to follow those long legs and pert buttocks, sneaking a glance at each other and then erupting into a fit of the giggles, suddenly feeling like teenagers again.

'And so, the hen do begins,' announced Eve chirpily. 'Not at all a bad start either, ladies.'

After a quick coffee stop, they climbed back into the truck and tucked into the melt-in-the-mouth caramel brownies that Jill had baked as a surprise.

'And, that's not the only secret we have up our sleeves,' Eve said conspiratorially.

'Oh, you can't leave it at that. Come on, spill.' Rachel hated being left in the dark. Much of the weekend planning had been left to Eve and the other hens. What *had* they got in mind?

'Not telling . . .' Eve patted the side of her nose. 'You'll just have to wait and see.'

It didn't seem as if Rachel was going to find out just yet, so she turned on the engine, turned up the radio, and concentrated on the road ahead. Rachel and Jill smiled broadly as 'Islands in the Stream' came on, one of Dad's old favourites, and they all sang along at the tops of their voices.

3

'Are we nearly there yet?' chimed Jill, just like little Maisy might say.

'Well, it says there's only about a mile to go,' reported Eve, checking the GPS on her phone.

They'd passed the quaint coastal town of Oban and were winding their way through narrow country lanes. The woods became denser around them, a little gloomy in fact. Rachel *really* hoped they weren't going to be stuck out in the depths of nowhere like something out of Stephen King's *Misery*. Some hen do that'd be!

But, soon enough, the thick pine trees gave way to open countryside again, and the road became dappled with sunlight, the bracken at each side giving the landscape a moorland feel. A red squirrel dashed across the road in front of them before leaping up into an old Scots pine.

'Ah, look, did you see that? What a cutie,' Rachel exclaimed. She loved spotting wildlife.

And then, as they rounded a corner, they saw a lake shimmering silver ahead, and a wooden lodge – set back from its shoreline – came into view. Wow, what a stunning setting. Rachel's fears were swiftly allayed as she pulled up beside the cabin.

'Oh, what a pretty spot!' called out Eve. 'Even if we are miles from humanity.'

The Scottish town of Oban with its small shops, bars and restaurants was actually only five miles away, but out here it felt as if it could be a hundred miles distant. And with all the ups and downs of recent times – losing her precious father, working like a trojan at the family farm, and the pressures of single motherhood – Rachel reflected that this felt like the perfect tonic right now. And with her best friends, gorgeous mum Jill, a heap of brownies, prosecco and a whole load of wedding plans in tow, what could be better?

'It's beautiful,' added Jill with a beaming smile.

'Come on,' Rachel leapt out of the truck. 'Let's go and explore.'

They climbed the wooden steps up to the balcony. Walking around the lodge, they came to the front deck that overlooked the lake. And yes, there was the fancy hot tub they had seen in the pictures online.

'Wow, what a place for a prosecco moment!' Eve pointed at the Jacuzzi with a wide grin. 'Bubbles in the bubbles.'

'Oh yes.'

'Sounds good to me.'

'A pool with a view.'

And *what* a view.

It was a warm May day, the sky a deep azure with just the odd puff of cloud. The lake was small yet so pretty, reflecting the blue of the sky. There was a cottage nestled on the far hillside, but no other buildings near to their lodge. Nothing to disturb the view, or the noise of birdsong around them. A grey and white heron stood on one leg, concentrating on the waters beneath him. A pair of mallard ducks paddled happily, whilst a coot busied herself at the reeds on the water's edge with three little ones swimming beside her. Rachel wondered instinctively about little Maisy and felt a stab of maternal panic. But it would all be fine, she reminded herself. Maisy was settled at school, and she'd enjoy the sleepover at Eve's house with Amelia tonight, where Ben would be spoiling them with pizza and ice cream. It was time to switch off, Rachel realised.

They wandered back, found the key under the flower pot as instructed, and opened the door on to a gorgeous open-plan living area – all wooden beams, a cosy log fire, a large dining table and chairs, and a characterful kitchen. Perfect. Exploring the cabin with big grins on their faces, they found the four bedrooms: two doubles that overlooked the lake, a twin and a single.

'You take a double room, Mum. Eve and I will have the other. Kirsty and Hannah can share the twin, and we'll save the single for Charlotte.'

'Great. And we get the lake views.' Jill made a thumbs-up sign.

'Absolutely.'

'Me and Rach will be up chatting all night anyhow, knowing us pair,' said Eve.

'Right, well let's go and unload all of Eve's *twenty* bags from the boot then, and get our one case each Mum,' Rachel added wryly.

'Well, I don't know about you lot,' added Jill, 'but I'm ready for a cuppa. Let's get unloaded and I'll get the kettle on.'

'A cuppa, really? This is a hen do, ladies. Let's get the prosecco opened!' Eve grinned.

With a glass of bubbly to hand and swimming costumes on, the girls opened up the French doors and made their way to the inviting hot tub on the deck area. They climbed the three wooden steps, and one by one slipped down into the warm frothing water.

'Marvellous,' said Jill, settling back in the bubbles.

'What a spot,' added Eve, taking in the view of the lake as a gentle breeze rippled over its waters in tiny silver waves.

'Ahh, this is what it's all about,' Rachel said slumping back, just managing to keep her glass above water level as the bubbles rose over her shoulders. 'Oops, don't want to water this stuff down.'

'Bliss.' Eve gave a small sigh.

'Oh, and now we're finally here with time to think, I'll need to talk over some of the wedding plans with you lot too,' said Rachel.

'Absolutely, that's what we're here for, after all.' Eve smiled warmly.

'Can you believe it's only seven weeks to go until the

big day?' Rachel pulled a panicked face. 'It's all creeping up so fast. July will be here before we know it.'

'I know. Time's flying just now,' added her mum.

'And . . . I'm getting slightly worried that I still haven't chosen a dress yet,' confessed Rachel with a sigh. 'I've a feeling I'm going to end up in a white binbag with the arms cut out at this rate.'

Eve and Jill caught each other's eye.

'I know it's not the end of the world,' Rachel continued, trying to convince herself it didn't matter that much in the big scheme of things, 'I'll find something that'll do . . . But that dress I saw back in March has stuck in my mind. Oh well,' she rallied. 'I'm glad we've spent the money on the tipi that we've booked for the wedding day, and we can afford to make a fabulous buffet for everyone to enjoy. Even if the rest of it is on a bit of a shoestring. A dress is just a dress, after all . . .' Rachel took a gulp of her rather lovely pear-drops-tasting prosecco. 'It'll all work out, I'm sure. And I know I'm really lucky, just getting married to Tom's going to be pretty damned special, even if I do end up standing at the altar in a bin bag.'

Rachel spotted another look passing between her mum and Eve.

'*What?*' There was definitely something going on between the two of them.

'Don't be too despondent about the dress, love,' soothed Jill.

Her mum and friend raised their eyebrows at each other, Jill giving Eve a nod.

'It's just . . . we might have something in the offing,' added Eve.

'You do? Well, that's great . . . is there a wedding dress shop in Oban then? Have you booked an appointment?' She bloody well hoped it had a bargain rail.

'Hmm, there might be,' answered Jill, with a twinkle in her eye, not yet giving anything away. She looked at Eve conspiratorially; they were both fighting to hide their smiles.

'Come on. You can't leave me hanging like this . . .'

'You'll just have to wait and see,' concluded Jill, and she clinked glasses with Rachel and Eve with a 'Cheers.'

Rachel hated being kept in the dark. What did this pair have up their sleeves?

Just as the afternoon sun was starting to fade, Kirsty and Hannah phoned to say they were making good time on their journey.

'I can't wait to get there. It sounds amazing. And you say you've been in the Jacuzzi already, you lucky things. No children, no night feeds, no nappy changes for three whole days. Woo-hoo!' Kirsty cheered down the phone line.

'See you soon,' shouted Hannah excitedly from the passenger seat. 'Save us some prosecco, guys.'

'Ah, we've got plenty, don't you worry,' called Eve.

An hour later, with the lasagne warming in the oven and Jill's homemade pudding waiting in the fridge, Rachel sat relaxing on the sofa, settling into the rhythm of the weekend. Just as she thought about closing her eyelids, letting the prosecco carry her into a luxurious nap, a pair of hands were suddenly placed firmly over her eyes.

'What the . . .!'

'Please stand and step this way,' giggled Eve, drawing Rachel to her feet.

'You two are definitely up to something. Tell . . .' Rachel demanded, affronted and excited at the same time.

'We thought the hen might be a good time to give you a sneak preview . . .'

'A sneak preview of what? Would anybody care to enlighten me?' Rachel raised her eyebrows from underneath Eve's slightly clammy palms. After taking several steps together, Eve lifted her hands away with an 'Eek . . .' just as Jill called out 'Ta-dah!'

Rachel found herself in the double bedroom assigned to her mum.

'Mu-um?'

'All will be revealed very soon, love. Oh, I do hope you like it . . .'

There was an air of tension as Eve disappeared from view and there was a rustle from behind the cupboard door.

Eve then appeared with an anxious smile and a heap of ivory-cream material, layered across her arm, that trailed down to the floor. Jill stepped across to help her hold the hanger and then rearrange the material, draping it down to rest on the floor.

It was a dress . . . a beautiful wedding dress! Just like the one in the shop all those weeks ago. And yet as she looked closer, she recognised it was a slightly simpler design. The material of the bodice looked different but it was just as pretty, and the style of the appliquéd flowers was softer somehow; they appeared to be almost floating on the skirt. But wow. Just wow!

Tears started to fill Rachel's eyes and she found she couldn't speak. How had they done this? Was it really for her?

'Do you like it? Oh gosh, Rach, I really hope you like it. I'm not sure if I got it quite right,' Eve started gabbling.

Jill stood smiling, holding the dress aloft, taking in her daughter's reaction.

'I . . . I love it. But *how*? How did you do it?' Rachel was still incredulous.

'I made it.' Eve sounded happy and proud and anxious all at once.

'Well, love, don't you think you should try it on?' prompted Jill.

'Ah, yes . . . of course.'

'I had to guess at the fit,' added Eve, 'but we're pretty similar, and I know your usual dress size. I can always tweak it.'

'But how did you know the style and everything, when we weren't allowed to take any photos?' There had been a big sign in the bridal shop's changing room about no cameras being allowed.

'It's amazing what you can jot down on a napkin,'

explained Jill, with a smile. 'Followed up with a little research and some pictures off the internet.'

'Wow,' Rachel repeated, taking off her jeans and her floral print top.

The dress was now off the hanger and ready for her to step into, with Eve and her mum holding it proudly. Eve's guesswork was pretty damned good as Rachel slipped it on. The delicate buttons up the back drew to a close just about perfectly.

Rachel looked down at the gorgeous gossamer voile-style skirt that had beautiful handmade flowers appliquéd onto it. There was a shimmer too as little sequins, stitched here and there, caught the light. The bodice was made of what looked to Rachel like an ivory cheesecloth material that fitted in a sleeveless V, revealing just the right amount of cleavage, so very like the design from the shop.

'You made this?' It was still hard to believe. 'It must have taken you ages, Eve. It's just beautiful.' Rachel lifted the stunning material of the skirt in awe.

'It's just the prototype, by the way. I've used a cheaper linen material as the base to get the cut and design right. The tulle top layer, I can re-fix. I wanted to be sure you liked it before I made it up in the satin version.'

'What do you mean? This isn't the finished thing? But I *love* it. I love this material . . . it looks kind of "boho" and country, and it's just what I want. Do *not* change a thing on it, Eve. I forbid you.'

'You're sure?'

'It does look gorgeous on her, I must say, Eve. You've made a wonderful job of it,' said Jill.

'Well, we can tweak the final fit, but if you're happy Rach, that's a whole lot of work you've just saved me!' Eve grinned.

'Hah, I can put you to work on other things – bunting for the tipis for a start!'

'Okay, that's fine by me. I'm just delighted that you like it.'

Rachel took a step forward and took her friend by the hands. 'It's perfect, and it means so much more that my very best friend has made it for me. Thank you so much, Eve.'

They fell into a hug, and then Jill joined in, all three of them with happy tears in their eyes.

'Right, well I do believe that this calls for a fresh bottle of prosecco to be opened. We can toast the wedding dress,' pronounced Jill.

'Hear, hear!' Eve gave a happy and relieved wink.

They wandered through to the living area. Rachel gave a little twirl, and then stood by the hearth in the middle of the lodge, staring down at her dress as if she was in a dream. She didn't quite want to take it off yet.

Jill popped the cork and Eve was soon passing her a glass of bubbly. 'Cheers, hun, you look absolutely stunning in it. Tom is going to be one lucky fella . . . but then, we knew that anyhow, with or without the dress.'

'Oh, your dad would be so proud if he could see you now, love.'

For a second or two Rachel stalled. 'Oh Mum . . . how are we going to get through a whole wedding day without Dad there?' Rachel bit down on her lip to stop it quivering. 'And, who on earth is going to walk me down the aisle?'

Jill had to swallow a tight lump in her throat before she could manage to answer. 'We'll be there for you, love, and all your friends. There are so many people to support you.'

'Ah, but it won't quite be the same though, will it? And, you can't *all* walk me down the aisle, can you?' Rachel tried her best to raise a small smile, picturing all her friends and family crammed in by the pews. Aw, this wedding was lovely to be planning, but boy did it keep throwing up new curveballs. Grief and loss didn't just disappear at the happier times, you somehow had to find a way for them to be a part of it.

'We'll always be there for you, Rach. And, on the day, I'll be right behind you, literally,' added Eve, who was so glad to be maid of honour.

'Okay, okay . . . now stop it you two, or you'll have me blubbing, and we don't want this dress messed up with tears and getting all soggy now.' She took a slow breath, before adding, 'Cheers.' Rachel raised her glass with a gentle smile to toast her fabulous friend and her very special mum. 'Thank you. Thank you, both.'

'Here come the gi-irls!' Hannah burst in through the front doors of the lodge, followed closely by Kirsty, sporting a huge grin and waggling a bottle of champagne at them. 'Let's get this party started, ladies.'

The dress was back in its clothes carrier and was now safely stored in Rachel and Eve's bedroom wardrobe, hidden from sight.

'Come in, come on in,' Rachel said, leaping up with a broad smile to greet her friends. 'Welcome to our humble abode.'

'And not so bloody humble,' commented Kirsty, looking around her.

'Oh my, this place is amazing!' Hannah took in the cosy yet spacious log-beamed living room. 'And what is that delicious smell, hey?'

'Homemade lasagne, care of Eve here,' answered Jill.

Eve took a little bow. 'It's warming in the oven, nearly ready.'

'Fantastic. Wow, what a gorgeous place . . . and we get three whole child-free days to enjoy it. I feel like I've been waiting for this for so long.'

'Me too,' added Hannah. 'Don't get me wrong, I love our little Rosie to bits, but eighteen months down the line of motherhood, you start forgetting what it's like to be you.'

'And then there's the husband who needs looking after too,' chipped in Kirsty. '"Where's my work socks/last pair of boxers/my favourite white shirt with the grey stripe?", that kind of stuff. *And* . . . my all-time favourite question: "What's for tea?" As though it's *my* sole domain to be chef as well as housework fairy and baby minder.'

'Hah, don't mind Kirsty. She's just getting it off her chest. I think it was a bit tense on the home front when she was trying to get everything packed and ready to go,' explained Hannah.

'Well, he'll know what it's like while I'm away . . .' Kirsty continued her little rant. 'Callum's into everything just now. You never stop.'

'Well then, absence makes the heart grow fonder and all that,' added Jill. 'I'm sure he'll appreciate you all the more when you get back.'

'Oops, sorry hun,' Kirsty suddenly stopped. 'Shouldn't be moaning on about the other half when it's your hen do, chick. You'll be entering the zone of married bliss very soon, honey. Don't want to put you off or anything . . . Ah, don't worry, I do love him really, but bloody hell he can get on my nerves at times.'

'Well, in all honesty, I can't wait to get married,' Rachel said proudly.

'No wonder, with your gorgeous Tom all lined up.' Eve grinned.

'Hey, a couple of years down the line and he'll be just like the rest of 'em.' Kirsty winked and then broke into a smile. 'Wouldn't be without 'em, mind.'

They all laughed.

'Right then, I think it's time I poured you two out some bubbly. Sounds like you need it!' Rachel grabbed the open bottle from the side. 'And no more worrying about what's going on back home. It's time to enjoy the here and now.'

'Exactly.'

'And . . . what happens at the lodge, stays at the lodge,' Eve said with a wink, raising her glass.

A few minutes later, with the room alive with chatter, Rachel's mobile phone buzzed.

'Hey, Tom.' She took a few steps towards the French doors and went out to the deck area.

'Hi, you got there okay . . . good journey?' Her lovely fiancé's voice was warm.

'Yeah, great thanks, and we managed to find it all right, despite it being out in the sticks.'

'That's good.'

Rachel took in the stunning lake view, with the early evening sun glinting gold on the blue-grey of the water. 'It's beautiful here. You'd love it . . . hey, maybe we can do something like this sometime. Just the two of us.' How wonderful would that be. Romantic walks by the lake, the pair of them snuggled up back at the lodge, the Jacuzzi to themselves . . .

'Count me in, it sounds heaven.'

'So . . . how's the farm faring without me and Mum?'

'Everything's fine. I've just checked on the sheep and cattle – no issues there, so I thought I'd call to let you know so you can relax.' Tom knew all about farming life; he had one of his own right next door to Primrose Farm, after all. Rachel had known him pretty much her entire life, looking up to the boy-next-door who was ten years older, whizzing around on his quad bike and building dens out of hay bales. She had probably been a bit of a nuisance, she mused, trailing round after him as a kid. And now look at them – *engaged*. Somehow, a steady friendship had wonderfully morphed into love over the past year. A beautiful, whirlwind journey. Rachel still had to pinch herself at times.

'Aw, thank you.' It was great of him to help out; he had enough to do on his own patch. But it was a big relief to know her farm was in safe hands.

'Anyhow, it was just a quick check-in to see that you got there fine. Now go and have fun with your girlfriends. Have a brilliant time, all of you.'

'Thank you, we will. And oh, you won't believe . . .' She had almost spilled the beans about the dress – she was so excited about it and overwhelmed with gratitude that Eve had made it for her – but she stopped herself in time. 'No, it's okay,' she told him instead. 'Just something special the girls have planned for me, but I'll keep it as a surprise for our big day.'

'Hmm, sounds intriguing. Can't wait.'

'Me neither.'

Their wedding was booked at Kirkton Church for Saturday 4 July, with a big party planned back at the farm afterwards. Less than two months away.

'Missing you.' Rachel felt a pang at being away from him.

'You too. Love you, Rach.'

'Come on, you two lovebirds, get off the phone,' interrupted Hannah from the door. 'Supper's ready and we're starving.'

'Okay, okay,' Rachel had to smile at her friend's mock impatience. 'Gotta go, Tom. Oh, and Tom . . . I love you too.'

Kirsty gave a wolf-whistle through the open doorway and Eve popped her head out, giving a big thumbs-up. After the tough few years their close friend had gone through, all this hen-do tribe wanted was to see Rachel smiling and happy and looking forward to her big day.

'Oh my, I can hardly move I'm so full.' Eve was sitting back in her chair, rubbing her tummy. The group was still gathered around the dinner table.

'Well, you shouldn't have had seconds of that tiramisu,' Rachel grinned.

'But it was just so delicious. I can't believe that's the first time you've ever made it, Jill.'

'Ooh, you must give us the recipe,' added Hannah. 'My lot would adore it.'

'I think we'd better add that one to the Baking Bible, Mum. A new Italian twist to our good old favourites.' The Baking Bible was the handwritten book of family recipes, started by Grandma Alice, Jill's own grandmother. It had been gradually added to by friends and family over the generations, with new cakes and puddings still finding their way into that hall of baking fame. It had pride of place on the kitchen shelf at Primrose Farm.

'Hmm, I think I might just do that when I get back,' replied Jill with a beam, delighted with its success.

After a quick clear-up of the dishes, Rachel and Eve

made a WhatsApp video call to Ben to speak with the girls before their bedtime. Maisy was chattering on, excited to be staying over with Amelia, saying she had *loved* her cheese and tomato pizza and strawberries with ice cream. They were now watching a movie; Rachel could see them all snuggled together on the sofa.

'Have a lovely time, Mummy. Miss you.' Her little girl's voice and smile were cheerful, reassuring Rachel that all was well.

'Miss you too, sweetheart, and you have a wonderful time too. And make sure you're being good for Amelia's daddy.'

'Of course, we are . . .' She saw Maisy cross her arms and toss her blonde curls indignantly. 'Right, we need to watch the film now, Mummy.' Hmm, sometimes that girl was six going on sixteen.

'Okay . . . Love you, petal.'

'Love you, Mummy. Oh, say hello to Grandma too.'

'Don't you just love 'em,' said Eve with a small sigh, adding, 'Mind you, it *is* nice to be away from all the demands just for a day or two.'

A very relaxed evening ensued, with the ladies sitting out on the deck, chatting away in the fading evening sunshine. Everyone was enjoying the gorgeous lakeside view, with a glass of Kirsty's bubbly to hand, cardis and fleeces on to keep the slight Scottish chill at bay.

It had been the perfect start to the hen weekend, Rachel mused, as she tipped herself into the double bed later on, her fabulous friends all there with her, the man of her dreams back home . . . and the dress of her dreams hanging in the cupboard just metres away. She let out a happy sigh, and whispered a 'Thanks for everything, Eve' in the dark, before sleep swiftly caught up with her.

4

'I thought we were meant to be chilling out with cocktails to hand . . .' A slightly frazzled-looking Hannah, hard hat firmly planted on her head, was squeaking down to her fellow hens from the top of the rock face. The climbing harness was wedged up her bum and she was clinging on to the rope for dear life.

'No worries, there'll be plenty of time for that later,' called Eve from below, who'd already managed the descent and was loving the excitement of the adrenalin-buzzing activity.

Jill gave it a go next, pulling a wry smile and a courageous, 'Here goes', as she stepped out over the ledge, managing a fifteen-metre drop under the guidance of the abseiling instructor.

Then it was Rachel's turn. The male instructor rigged her up, with a *very* snug harness, showed her how to hold the rope and work the belay plate to make her way down safely. Now all she needed to do was to step off what was basically a rocky cliff edge. She took a deep breath. Life had presented her with enough metaphorical cliffhangers lately, without her choosing to tackle a literal one, but hey ho, she couldn't wriggle out of this challenge . . .

'Woo-hoo!' she called out as she felt herself dangle precariously, whilst she was actually thinking, *Shite, oooh, shite.* But step-by-wide-angled-step, and inch-by-inch, she made her way down, with a quick, heart-stopping downwards lurch when she let through too much rope, then into a calmer final descent. As Rachel reached the bottom, a big cheer went up from the girls, and with her heart still thumping she realised she had actually enjoyed it.

Once they'd all had a turn, they tried the same descent again. Rachel got the hang of it, one foot at a time, and once she'd mastered controlling the belay and prusik rope, she decided it was brilliant fun, and went back for another challenge on a slightly higher face, along with daredevil Kirsty. The others in the group were happy to watch from solid ground and cheer them on at this point.

All this activity was followed by a much-needed chill-out back at base in the lodge's Jacuzzi. Limbs were aching and muscles they hadn't used in years sore, but they all felt proud of themselves for having given it a go and getting themselves down successfully.

'Was a bit worried I wouldn't make it down that ravine. I felt my stomach churn as I took my first step over the side, I must say,' admitted Jill.

'But you still did it – well done you, Mum.'

'Face the fear and do it anyway! That's the way.' Hannah grinned.

'Well, I suppose it was better than a bungee jump or something. Thank heavens you hadn't organised that for us, Eve. Hah, at least this was one foot at a time. At one point I was so worried I'd let too much rope slip through. But once you got the hang of it . . .' Rachel was beaming.

'It wasn't half as bad as I'd feared,' added Hannah.

'It never is . . .' smiled Kirsty.

'Especially when you've got a safety harness on and your friends by your side,' chuckled Eve.

And that's exactly how it had felt this past couple of years, mused Rachel, looking across at her group of fabulous friends and her brave mum. It had been friends and family providing the safety net just when she needed it. 'You all did great,' Eve added, so pleased her idea had gone down well with everyone. She knew that Rachel wouldn't have wanted to prance about in a bride-to-be sash and sit drinking all weekend. But well, maybe just for a few hours . . .

'Well, I bloody loved it,' enthused Kirsty. 'I might even look for more classes back home. Can't wait to tell Josh and little Callum all about what Mummy's been up to. Beats changing nappies and mashing up baby food, any day.'

It was time to get themselves out of the warm bubbles and put their glad rags on, ready for their evening out in Oban. Well, there needed to be at least part of the hen weekend spent sitting in a lurid pink sash with a drink to hand!

First, they had to head to the train station to collect

Charlotte, who was hopping with excitement on the platform, with her overnight bag and a relieved grin. 'Thank heavens, I've made it. I've been thinking of you lot all here these past twenty-four hours. And those photos on Facebook of the lodge, a-maz-ing! But, I'm here now and I'm *so* ready for this.'

Rachel took her friend's bag from her and pulled her in for a hug. 'I'm *so* glad you're here, and thank you for taking on the train trek today. Now I've got all my besties here together, as well as my wonderful mum, of course. I'm so happy.'

There were hugs and hellos all round, and the group started strolling along the platform for the exit.

'Right then, off to the first pub,' announced Kirsty. 'I do believe Charlotte here has a bit of catching up to do.'

'I spotted one just along the road as we passed that looked all right,' said Rachel. 'It's not far from the harbour. Shall we walk from here and give it a try?'

'Sounds good to me,' replied Charlotte, with the others all in agreement.

A round of gin and tonics and a juice for Jill, who'd offered to drive them back, went down rather well in the old-fashioned, black-beamed Scottish pub, accompanied by lots of chatter and laughter. It was soon time to head on to the bistro, which they discovered in a cute spot on the seafront. The owner had reserved them the large front table with a great harbour view.

A supper of local scallops, chilli prawns, steak burgers and freshly made fish and chips followed. The desserts were a triumph – it had to be done, of course – with raspberry cranachan coming out the firm favourite, followed closely by a velvety chocolate mousse made with whisky and orange.

Proseccos were poured, and the chatter continued, as they finished their gorgeous meal. After thanking the staff and owners, and leaving a generous tip, they headed out into the cooling evening air. It had been a real treat, one which admittedly Rachel and Jill couldn't afford to do often, but this was a special weekend, after all.

'Okay ladies, one last pub stop, and then we'll head back to the lodge, yes?' suggested Kirsty.

'Are you okay with that, Mum?' Rachel checked, aware that Jill was driving.

'Of course, love. It's great seeing you all enjoying yourselves.'

And so it was that they ended up in The Lobster Pot, further along the seafront. They all crammed around a small table in a corner near the bustling bar, large glasses of wine in hand, and Eve dug something out of her handbag – six sparkly pink sashes that read, 'Team Bride', and one that said 'Bride-to-Be', along with a twinkly plastic tiara. And, as a grand finale, a pair of silver deely boppers.

Rachel looked aghast. 'You're kidding . . . I said no fuss, and absolutely *no* deely boppers!'

'Argh, come on Rach, you only get married once . . . well, hopefully,' Kirsty gave a cheeky grin.

'Let's do this thing; look, we're all in it together.' Eve

started passing around the sashes and Jill, who was totally sober, bless her, put hers straight on.

'It is your hen do, after all,' Charlotte cajoled.

'Ah, okay, this pub only, all right. And I'm only doing it to please you lot . . .'

Of course, nearing the bottom of her glass and realising she needed the bathroom, Rachel had totally forgotten she was wearing her sash, tiara and deely boppers as she tootled off to the toilet. She wondered why she was getting several stares and a wolf-whistle as she passed the blokes at the bar. On the way back, an old guy started singing, 'I'm getting married in the morning', at which there was a flash of a camera from Kirsty – oh damn, there'd be photographic evidence – and the hen do party collapsed into fits of giggles.

Rachel blushed pink and began tugging at her tiara, just as a tall, good-looking bloke stepped forward from the bar.

'Hey, haven't I seen you somewhere before?' He gave a cheeky grin and then gestured across to their table.

What a line, Rachel thought, rolling her eyes. 'I don't think s—' She was keen to make her getaway.

'No, really, I'm not one to forget a pretty face.' *Cheesy or what?* 'You and two of your friends there, you were at the service station near Glasgow.'

Oh blimey . . . She took in the sandy-blond hair, the broad chest. It was him. Coca-Cola T-shirt Man. He walked across with her back to their table. 'Good evening, ladies.'

'Hell-ooo.' 'Hi.' 'Hi, there' came a chorus of chirpy responses accompanied by broad smiles.

'It's T-shirt Man,' Rachel mouthed to Eve, over his shoulder.

'Nice to see you again.' He smiled directly at Eve.

'Yeah, apparently this, er, gentleman, remembers us from the service station. What are the chances, hey Eve?'

Eve's mouth dropped open. 'Gosh, yes. Hah.'

'So, you lot know each other?' quizzed Hannah.

'I wouldn't say that. We just happened to be getting out of our cars at the same time at the service station yesterday,' said Rachel.

'It's Ross, by the way.' He introduced himself to the group.

'Hi, Ross.'

'So, you girls were on your way to a hen do then? *Your* hen do, in fact.' His hand was now resting on Rachel's shoulder. It felt like a friendly gesture, nothing more.

'Yep.'

'One lucky guy.'

'He sure is,' said Eve, proud of her friend.

Soon a few of Ross's mates had joined the group and there was more chat and laughter. They were keen to know where the girls were from and what they all did. Ross, it turned out, did garden maintenance; mostly bigger jobs like lopping tree branches, cutting back shrubs, mowing large lawns, he explained.

'Yeah, I'd been to Glasgow that day to pick up a new ride-on.'

Several of the girls raised their eyebrows at that, with a giggle bursting forth from Eve.

'Lawn mower,' he added, shaking his head but grinning all the while.

It was all harmless fun and added to the jollity of the night. But after one more round of drinks, which the local lads insisted on buying, Rachel spotted Eve sidling up to Ross and batting her eyelashes, getting a little too up close and personal. Now that really wasn't like Eve at all. What was she up to? She was definitely starting to look a little the worse for wear, wobbling on her high-heeled shoes too.

'Time to go, Eve,' Rachel called out, moving in to steer her away from Mr T. The others were already popping on their jackets anyhow, deciding it was time to head back to the lodge.

'They were a nice bunch of lads, weren't they?' said Rachel.

The girls were crammed in the back of the Land Rover, chatting away on the slightly bumpy ride home along the winding lane to the cabin.

'Yeah, pretty cute too,' chipped in Kirsty.

'Hah, well, we'd only be looking. We're all married – or *nearly* married – ladies, after all,' added Charlotte.

'Hmmm, absolutely,' Eve said a little drowsily.

'Well, I only have eyes for Tom. Honestly, I couldn't even imagine wanting anyone else, ever.' Just thinking about him made Rachel feel all warm and fuzzy.

'Well, that's a good job, seeing as you're getting married on the fourth of July,' added Hannah.

Eve was unusually quiet, sitting a little slumped in the seat next to Rachel. 'You okay, hun?'

'Yeah,' Eve's voice was a whisper. 'Think I might need a bit of air.'

'You're not going to be sick, are you? Shall I shout on Mum to stop?'

'No, no, I'll be fine, honest. Just a bit woozy . . .'

'Anybody got a carrier bag as insurance?' added Kirsty wryly.

The hens got sleepier on the last mile back, the winding road and effects of the alcohol lulling them. Eve rested her head on Rachel's shoulder, and Rachel stroked her friend's hair gently.

Half an hour later, after a brief nightcap back at the lodge, Hannah and Kirsty had given in and headed to bed, followed soon afterwards by Charlotte and then Eve. Jill, who still remained sober, started clearing the glasses into the sink, and gathered up a handful of confetti from the floor. 'Oh . . .' She suddenly stopped in her tracks.

'What's up?

'Oh nothing . . . well,' she burst into a daft grin, 'I didn't realise they did willy-shaped confetti, I must say!'

'Hah, nor did I.' Rachel scooped some up from the table top, taking a closer look.

'Bloody hell, it is too. I'd better warn them not to bring *that* to church, the vicar would have a fit.'

They had a good old chuckle.

'Don't worry about the washing up now, Mum. We can do that in the morning.'

'Well, I am pretty shattered,' admitted Jill. 'It was a great night though.'

'Yeah, it was . . . and thanks again for driving.'

'No worries . . . and at least I won't have a thick head in the morning.'

'Night then, Mum.'

'Night, love.'

Rachel headed over and gave her mum a kiss on the cheek and a warm hug. 'I'm glad you're here with us.'

'Me too. Sleep tight, pet. Hope the bed bugs . . .'

'. . . don't bite,' they chanted together, with a shared smile. A saying from Rachel's childhood.

It was all dark in the room that Rachel and Eve were sharing. Rachel decided not to blast the light on, as Eve should be all tucked up in bed, but strangely things just didn't *feel* right as Rachel entered.

'Eve?'

'Ah . . . huh,' the answer didn't seem to be coming from the bed.

Rachel moved forward cautiously and fumbled for the bedside lamp. She clicked the switch. 'Oh, Eve . . . are you okay?' Her maid of honour was splayed out, still fully clothed, propped on the floor at the foot of the bed. 'What are you doing down there, hun?' Rachel started to sober up amazingly quickly.

'I . . . I don't know . . .' Eve looked about her,

seemingly as surprised as Rachel was to see herself at floor level.

'Okay then, hun. Let's get you up and into bed.' Rachel helped hoist her friend up onto the mattress and proceeded to help her off with her clothes, leaving her with bra and knickers on, then tucked her in under the duvet. She seemed extremely tipsy, which wasn't like Eve at all, as she could usually hold her drink better than Rachel.

'Right, I think I'll fetch us both a big glass of water. Help clear our heads a bit,' said Rachel, hoping to stave off the hangover from hell the next morning. 'Stay there then, hun.' To be fair, Eve didn't look as if she was going anywhere.

'Hmm,' was all her friend could utter, whilst clinging on to the duvet cover as if it were a life raft.

Rachel hoped Eve wasn't about to be sick. Thinking quickly, she moved the waste-paper bin across to Eve's side of the bed – better safe than sorry. She headed for the kitchen and was soon back with two large glasses of water, making her friend take a few big sips before glugging down her own. Soon in her PJs, Rachel slipped into bed, turned off the lamp and then whispered, 'Night, Eve.'

'Nigh . . . Rach . . .' There was a pause and then a whisper sounded in the darkness. 'Rach?'

'Yes, hun?'

'I can tell you anything, right? You . . . you can keep a secret?'

'Yeah, of course. Eve, I'm your best friend.' Rachel waited for her friend's voice again, holding her breath. Silence. Well, except for a little puffing, snoring sound.

Rachel sighed. She was sound asleep, bless her. But what 'secret' did Eve want to share? And, Rachel reflected again, she had behaved a little out of character that night. It was also unusual for Eve to have drunk so much. Still, Rachel mused, we could all have our moments and let our hair down just a little *too* much. Oh yes, Eve had looked after her more than a few times as a teenager, she remembered fondly.

But Rachel felt a bit unsettled. She vowed to keep an ear out through the night, and make sure her friend was all right.

5

EVE

A full-blown marching band was thumping away inside Eve's head the next morning.

Bloody hell, how had she let herself get so damned tipsy? Oh God, there was a vague memory lurking in her car-crash of a brain . . . of T-shirt Man. Oh yes . . . she might just have told him she'd been very impressed by his gorgeous bare chest. She gave a groan from beneath the duvet. She really didn't want to spoil the last full day of Rachel's hen do. Nope, she ought to try and get herself up and out of bed right now. But, trying to shift up from the pillow was proving extremely difficult, every movement producing a hammer blow inside her skull.

There was a knock on the door and, peeking through one squint eye, Eve saw Jill appearing with two large mugs of tea. 'Morning, girls.'

Oh, so Rachel was still there in bed too.

'Hi, Jill.' Eve could hardly recognise her own voice, which came out as a rasp, but at least she had managed to speak.

'Morning, Mum.' Rachel sounded slightly fresher.

'No rush, but I thought you might need these . . . and these . . .' She placed down a packet of paracetamol beside the two mugs.

'Thanks, Mum. How're you doing there, Eve?' Rachel asked sympathetically.

'Not sure yet . . .' answered Eve, struggling.

'You don't happen to have a full schedule of activities planned for today, do you hun? No bungee jumping or anything lined up?' Rachel said wryly.

'No . . .' *Thank the Lord.*

'That's good to know.' Rachel managed a chuckle.

'Definitely a day for us all to chill out then,' Jill chipped in.

'Absolutely.'

'Hmmm . . .' The power of speech was failing Eve.

'Right, well, you two just take your time.' Jill's voice was chirpy, far too chirpy. 'Me and Hannah are up, but we're more than happy out on the deck enjoying the sunshine and having a natter over a cuppa. The other two are still in the land of nod.'

Eve heard footsteps retreating, uttered a groan-like 'thanks', and then buried herself back under the duvet. She most definitely wasn't ready to face the day just yet. As she sank back into the pillows, something else was niggling at her too. Something besides her hangover. Her emotions had been pretty wobbly over the past few weeks . . . a certain worry keeping her awake at night. Normally, she'd share her concerns with her best friend, but it was a bit trickier than that. She went through a mental check list of all the reasons to keep schtum:

a) She really didn't want to air her silly worries now, and spoil what should be a fab hen party for them all.
b) She could hardly make any sense of it herself just yet.
c) Telling someone might make it all the more *real*. At the moment, she could just leave well alone, pretend nothing at all had happened, and just carry on with life as normal. Right?

The only trouble was that *it* wasn't leaving her alone, and it was starting to do her head in, as well as leaving her heart wallowing in a weird, splodgy puddle.

Eve let out a long, slow sigh. Just thinking about her dilemma made her head pound even more. She fumbled on the bedside table for the paracetamol packet, managed to push two of the pills out and glugged them down with a slurp of tea. Urgh, they tasted foul as they lodged in her throat.

Why did life have to be so bloody complicated?

A long, leisurely soak in the Jacuzzi soothed them all that afternoon – warm and bubbly, with good company and relaxed chatter. Bliss. It was certainly just what Eve needed.

When early evening swung around, Rachel and Hannah

nipped out to the town to buy some treats for an easy supper. As soon as they left, Eve ran into the middle of the living room and called the fellow hens over.

'Right, ladies, it's go time! Let's get transforming!' she shouted, rallying the troops as they started to turn the lodge into a *DIY SOS*-style hen-do decoration zone. Pearlised pink and silver balloons were blown up and hung from the ceiling, streamers were draped artistically, along with bunting that Eve had made especially for the wedding and brought with her from home. The 'Team Bride' sashes were back out, and the girls even set up a cardboard 'photo booth' picture frame you could stand behind with lots of fun props – spectacles, hats, feather boas, and more.

When Rachel and Hannah arrived back thirty minutes later, they were surprised by a blast of party poppers and hooters, their friends leaping out at them as they came through the cabin door.

'Well you lot have certainly perked up!' Rachel grinned, looking around her at the transformation. 'Aw, this is amazing, you guys.'

'Well, we couldn't let the last night pass without a bit of a bang,' exclaimed Charlotte.

Jill approached from the kitchen with a tray of freshly frosted, salted caramel cupcakes. 'I think it's time we popped open the prosecco again then, girls.'

Eve's tummy gave a gurgle of protest at the mere thought of alcohol. 'I'll pass on the prosecco just now, Jill,' she gulped. 'But I might well have to try one of those.'

They ate the cupcakes as dessert first, followed by a platter of local breads, cheeses, and pâtés. They sipped their prosecco, bar Eve who opted for fizzy water, and then settled down for a night of hen-do fun. A proper Girls' Night In.

The photo booth proved a great hit, and lots of silly, smiley photos were taken. Games were played, including an 'interesting' hen-do version of what might be known as 'Pin the Tail on the Donkey', which produced much hilarity, especially when a blindfolded and blushing Jill managed to place the 'tail' appendage slap-bang in the middle of the cartoon man's face.

It was getting late when Kirsty suggested a quick-fire game of 'Truth or Dare', along with an Irish cream nightcap. Kirsty nominated herself as question master a sneaky move, the others agreed, giggling. They'd have to think of a humdinger of a group question for her as a grand finale.

It came to Jill's turn.

'Truth or Dare?'

'Truth. Go on, I've nothing to hide.'

'Be careful of the question here, Kirst,' Rachel piped up. 'Remember it's my mother you're asking. There are certain things I really *don't* want to hear.'

'Okay, okay. So, Jill, how many different people have you kissed – romantically, that is?'

'Ooh, now then . . .' Jill held out her hand as she was thinking, counting off digits. 'Blimey, some of them will be way back. School stuff and first boyfriends.'

'Better be before Dad . . .'

Robert was counted in as number four – Eve spotted Rachel sighing slightly, bless her, as Jill mouthed her dad's name. And then Jill paused before counting out one more . . . oh, Dan? She must have kissed Dan. Eve didn't know too much about Jill's new romance, but she knew it had been a bit tough for Rachel to come to terms with.

'Five. Yes, five.'

Five in all her fifty-two years. She'd married young, Eve supposed. Times were different then.

'Thank you, Jill!'

'Next, Rachel. Bride-to-be. We need to know your first kiss – when, where *and* who with.'

'Really? Okay, so it was at school, in the summer, school field, I was fifteen . . .' She pinked up, remembering. 'It was pretty awful, a clash of teeth and metal braces, in fact.' Rachel had wondered what the fuss was all about. 'Hah, yes, his lips were a bit like a washing machine on full spin.'

The group were in fits of giggles now.

'And . . . it was with Matty Douglas,' came Rachel's confession.

'Hah, yes.' Eve smiled, having been privy to this 'major' news at the time.

'Ooh, really?' Hannah raised her eyebrows.

'Yes, of course,' Charlotte chipped in. Matty was still about in the village. He was a nice lad, had improved since the braces had come off. He now had a car-valeting business and was married with a kid.

'Eve's turn,' the girls called out, grinning. They were nearly all done now, bar Kirsty.

Eve felt a flash of concern. She hated this kind of game at the best of times, and now it made her feel a bit queasy . . . especially with everything that was going on in her life right now. 'Okay, okay.'

'So, Eve, *last* kiss, when, where and with whom?'

'You didn't give me the chance to say Truth or Dare,' Eve blurted out.

'Hmm . . . Eve Jones, you are reluctant to tell the truth . . . interesting . . .' Kirsty put on an interrogative tone, then took a big sip of her Irish cream.

'Okay, yes, it was Amelia when we said goodbye on Thursday morning.'

'Romantic kisses, we're talking,' added Kirsty.

Eve felt herself flush before quickly saying, 'Ben, of course.'

'Right then, we need a question for Kirsty now,' Rachel said, swiftly rolling the game on. Eve saw her friend glance across at her, seeming to sense her unease. 'Come on, ladies, group confab. It needs it be a good one,' Rachel continued.

The group whispered between themselves, until Charlotte came up with a great question. 'Have you ever had a crush on a teacher at high school? If so, which one and why?'

Between them, they pretty much knew all the high-school teachers, having been to the same school (except for Hannah, who'd moved to the village once she'd married), and it opened up a fun conversation with a few cringeworthy teachers' names thrown in the mix. Kirsty bypassed the obvious choice of Mr Adams the PE teacher, and plumped for Mr Stephens who'd taught Geography. 'Tall, not bad looking, and he made Geography seem pretty cool.'

'Fair enough,' commented Rachel. 'I can see how he might have some appeal.'

'Hah, you were too busy looking at Jake to be eyeing up the teachers,' said Charlotte.

'Yeah well, look where that led me . . .' Eve knew that Rachel didn't regret having her beautiful daughter for a minute, but her relationship with Maisy's dad, Jake, had been a bit of a disaster. 'Maybe I *should* have been harbouring secret crushes on the teachers at that point.'

With the game over, they relaxed back into the sofas. With Hannah putting some music to play on her iPhone, they chilled out and enjoyed the rest of their last night away. It was just before midnight when Eve found herself yawning. She felt shattered. It was time to crash out. 'Sorry to wimp out, but I'm going to have to get to my bed, folks . . .'

'Yeah, me too.' Kirsty caught the yawning bug.

'Sounds a good idea. We'll be driving back tomorrow and need clear heads,' added Jill sensibly.

'Back to reality,' said Hannah.

Indeed, back to reality, thought Eve with a heavy heart.

6

Before they all headed off to their beds, Rachel felt she wanted to say a few words. It had been such a wonderful few days with her besties beside her. 'Thanks so much, everyone, for making this long weekend so special. It's been a ball. I've loved it . . . and I've loved being with you lot.' She found herself feeling a bit emotional.

'Aww.'

'It's been fab. I haven't laughed so much in ages. I actually have sore ribs,' said Hannah.

'And hey, we've still got loads of fun to come, remember,' added Charlotte with a wide smile. 'There's a bloody beauty of a wedding day to celebrate in July.'

'Hah – yes!'

Thinking of Tom, and of her beautiful surprise wedding dress that was hidden in the wardrobe, of welcoming yet more friends to the celebrations, and having the rest of her family around her – including little Maisy, bless her, who was going to be a flower girl along with Amelia, and Granny Ruth, who wasn't quite up to a hen do (though Rachel would have bet she'd have given the abseiling a go!) – all filled her with joy. Not to mention the amazing food they were planning for the reception, and the celebratory bubbly.

Yes, the best was yet to come, of course it was.

A little while later, with everyone settling for bed, Eve wandered back into their bedroom from the bathroom, uttering a subdued, 'Night, Rach.'

Her friend didn't seem right at all. She'd been way too quiet today. Yes, she was nursing a hangover, but Rachel had seen that before. This was different; it was as though she was keeping something in. And . . . what was that with the Truth or Dare game? The others hadn't seemed to pick up on it, but that question about the kiss, she'd gone all weird and cagey. She and Eve were so close, Rachel had a feeling there was something deeper going on.

'Hey, you okay, Eve?' Rachel ventured, as she scrubbed her face with a cleansing wipe. 'It's just . . . you seemed a bit . . . off . . . today.'

'Yeah, no worries. I'm fine, Rach.'

But the tone of Eve's voice and the look on her face told Rachel that her friend wasn't fine at all.

'Eve, come on . . . it's me . . . tell me.'

'Everything's all right, Rach. I'm just being silly. It's your hen do, this is a celebration, you don't need to listen to me harping on.'

'Well, whatever it is, I can see it's troubling you. So, hun, I'd rather you harp on, than sit stewing on it. Is it to do with Amelia, Ben? Something with me?'

Eve let out a long slow sigh. 'Oh, Rach . . . I don't even know how to say it.'

'Well try, just blurt it out. It can't be that bad . . . and if it is, I'm here for you, whatever it is.' Rachel sat down on the bed beside Eve, the two of them slumped together against the headboard, taking them back to being teenagers.

'Umm . . .' Eve let out another sigh. 'It's just . . . there might be someone else.'

Rachel couldn't hide her shock. What on earth was her friend talking about? Someone else for Tom? What did she mean? There was a lump in her throat like a stone, and Rachel's heart felt as if it had fallen down a mine shaft.

Eve must have seen her face drop. 'No, it's not anything to do with you or Tom,' she blurted out to clarify. 'Me . . . it's me.'

'What do mean, Eve. Another man?'

Eve nodded sheepishly. 'Don't worry. I haven't done anything stupid; well not quite, not yet. There's been a near-kiss moment, that's all.'

Rachel was still trying to take this all in. Eve and Ben were such a lovely couple. So solid. And there was little Amelia. Rachel would never have imagined that anything like this might happen.

'What about Ben? Your family, Eve? What's happened?' Rachel was still pretty incredulous. Eve just wasn't the gallivanting sort.

'I can't get him out of my head,' Eve stated, looking

sad and torn. 'And I don't know if that means I don't love Ben any more . . . I don't know what to think.'

'Oh, Eve. Who is this guy . . . how?'

'He's someone I met through the craft events. He's an artist, really talented. He does the most amazing seascapes in oils.' There was a note of adoration in Eve's tone.

'Oh, Eve. Be careful, hun. Surely you can't know this guy very well. It'll just be some crush. And, what about Ben and Amelia and everything you have together? You're a family. A lovely family.' Rachel couldn't bear to think of the implications for their fabulous little unit. She loved them all dearly.

'I know, I know. I'm married to Ben . . . and we used to be so close. And it scares me too, and I don't know how I've got to feeling this way . . .' Her voice had dropped to a whisper as a big fat tear plopped down on her lap. 'But I do.'

Rachel held her friend's hand, concerned for her and her family. 'Maybe you and Ben have just got a bit stuck in a rut,' she said gently, but with a note of warning too. 'Maybe you need some time as a couple. I'll look after Amelia, if you want a night away or something . . .'

'Yeah, well, maybe we do take each other a bit for granted. We have had a bit of a wobble lately. But, this guy – Aiden – it's like we've got so much in common. He's creative, and he's enthusiastic about my crafts. For Ben, my business is all just a big mess taking up space in the dining room, and my time.'

Oh dear, Eve seemed to have it bad. 'Eve, it's got to be different living with someone day to day, I'm sure. Life's not always glamorous and romantic, is it?' In fact, Rachel had it all to find out. She hadn't even had a chance to move in with Tom yet, wanting to keep things simple for Maisy up until now. But she was realistic and knew it couldn't always be plain sailing. 'Don't do anything stupid, hun. Promise me.'

'I won't . . . I won't.' It was as though Eve was trying to convince herself. She went quiet for a few seconds. 'Rachel, you can't tell *anyone*. Not even Tom.'

'Of course, I won't.'

'It's just . . . if Ben found out, even this much, that might be it. I don't think it would ever be the same again between us.' She sounded so afraid.

'I promise. It's our secret. And you keep talking to me . . . and keep thinking of your family, Eve. Don't let yourself get swept up in something you might live to regret.'

'Ah-huh.' Eve's fingers were shaking inside Rachel's palm.

Rachel gave her friend a warm hug. 'Hey, petal, let's get to bed and get some sleep, hey. Things'll work out somehow.'

'Yeah . . .'

They both slid down under the covers.

'Night, Eve.'

'Night, Rach.'

Rachel held Eve's hand gently beneath the duvet as

she waited for her to drift off to sleep. Two friends lying side by side, one about to embark on her marriage journey, the other several years in and finding herself drifting on a turbulent tide.

Jill's Hen-Do Tiramisu

A lovely and easy *new* recipe for you to try!

Ingredients

2 eggs, separated (please be aware this recipe does contain raw egg)
4 tablespoons golden caster sugar
250g (9oz) mascarpone cheese
125ml (4½fl. oz) fresh strong coffee
4 tablespoons Marsala
125g (4½oz) sponge fingers/boudoir biscuits
1 tablespoon cocoa powder

Method

Top tip – make in advance and leave the flavours to develop.

Beat the egg yolks and sugar in a bowl until light and frothy. Fold in the mascarpone.

In a clean bowl, beat the egg whites until stiff and carefully fold into the cream-cheese mixture.

In another bowl, mix the coffee and Marsala together. Dip half the sponge fingers in this and lay them over the base of a large dish. Spoon over half the cream-cheese mixture, and dust with cocoa powder. Repeat this stage to make another layer. Smooth the surface gently and dust with more cocoa powder.

Chill for at least two hours before serving and preferably overnight.

Seriously scrumptious!

7

A warm welcome awaited Rachel and Jill at Primrose Farm. It lifted Rachel's soul as they came back into the gentle folds of the lush green valley; though she'd had a great time away with her friends, and had loved the rugged Scottish countryside and her lake view, here was where her heart lay.

They dropped Eve off first, Rachel getting out and helping her with her things, including the precious wedding dress that her friend was going to keep safe for her. Rachel gave her an extra big hug as she waved her into her cottage, and back into the arms of her husband and daughter. She still felt pretty stunned by last night's revelation, and wished them all a silent good luck.

Soon they were turning onto their farm track, and as they pulled up by the farmhouse, Rachel spotted a big homemade banner over the front door that read: 'Welcome home, Mummy and Grandma!' with bold sunny flowers in pink and yellow painted each side of the writing. A 'Maisy creation' for sure, with a bit of help from Granny Ruth. Though hopefully someone other than Granny had hoisted it into place, Rachel thought, not wanting to imagine Granny teetering up stepladders or suchlike at her grand age.

'Oh, look, how lovely.' Jill was grinning from the passenger seat.

Within seconds the front door opened and out bowled Maisy. No sooner was Rachel out of the truck than she was in her arms. 'I missed you *sooo* much, Mummy!'

'Missed you too, petal.' It was gorgeous to feel her daughter's solid weight in her arms, smell the shampoo-fresh blonde curls.

'So, have you been a good girl for everyone?'

'Yep . . .'

'Been good as gold,' confirmed Ruth, who had trundled out and was there beside them now too.

'I love the special banner,' said Grandma Jill, who was next in line to receive a huge Maisy hug.

'And we've made coming-home cupcakes,' beamed Maisy from Jill's arms. 'Chocolate ones.'

'Wow, you have been busy.'

'I'll head in and pop the kettle on then, my lovelies,' said Ruth, 'and we can hear all about your trip away.'

Daniel popped out of the Pudding Pantry – the wonderful tearoom venture that they had set up last summer in the converted barn – where he had been helping to serve with Jan today, the pair of them holding the fort whilst Jill and Rachel were away. Jill went across for a few words, and Rachel spied her mum giving him an affectionate kiss on the cheek. It still felt strange to watch, and her heart dipped slightly as she inevitably thought about her dad; yet she was starting to understand and accept her mum's new relationship.

Moss, their Border collie, gave a welcome bark from his kennel in the yard. Rachel quickly went around to greet him with Maisy at her heels.

'Hey, boy.' She opened the catch and he bounded out, skirting her legs as she leaned over to pat the soft fur on his black-and-white head. Moss's tail never stopped wagging as he happily herded them all back inside the farmhouse kitchen. Home.

There was someone else who Rachel couldn't wait to see too.

Fifteen minutes later, the sound of his truck pulling up in the yard made her heart sing even more. She dropped her mug of tea down on the kitchen table and dashed out to meet him.

'Tom!' She couldn't hide her excitement.

'Good time . . .?' Before he could get to the door, she was in his arms and smacking a big kiss on his grinning lips.

'I guess you missed me then, hey?' He pulled away, laughing.

It was only a few days, and she'd had a great time with her friends, but she *had* missed him. His broad smile, the feeling of his strong arms around her, the woody smell of his aftershave, the promise of slow nights making love . . . if she could get away this evening, that was.

As she finally touched her feet back on the ground, she took Tom by the hand and led him inside towards the family gathering.

'Hello, Tom.'

'Hi, all.'

'Hey Mummy, Tom helped me with my jigsaw yesterday, *and* he took me out to see Petie in his truck.'

'Thought I'd give Ruth a bit of a breather,' he smiled.

'Aw, thanks, that's so thoughtful of you.'

'And I went and helped Dan in the Pantry. We made cheese scones together . . . but they were triangle ones and not circles. He's not as good as you, Grandma . . .'

'Well, you have been busy,' replied Grandma Jill with a grin.

'Cupcake, Tom?' Ruth passed the plate across. 'Double chocolate sprinkles, courtesy of Maisy.' She gave a wry smile.

'Don't mind if I do.' He took one, and gave a thumbs-up to Maisy, who beamed with pride.

'So, everything's been fine with the farm?' Rachel asked, turning to Tom.

'Yeah, just one of your ewes got a bit tangled in a fence. I got her out okay, but she's got a deep nick on her foreleg. Treated it with the purple spray; looks like it'll heal okay.'

'Ah, there's always some trouble, hey?'

The usual farmyard niggles.

'You'll find her in the Top Field, still limping a bit this morning.'

'Well, thank you. It was great knowing Primrose Farm was in good hands.'

'You're welcome. And Maisy filled me in on lots of things while we were out and about. I've learnt all kinds of things while you were away.' His eyes were twinkling mischievously.

'Hah, I bet she did, little chatterbox.' Rachel squeezed her daughter's cheek affectionately.

Back in the fold of Primrose Farm: Moss stretched out by the Aga, his tail rhythmically giving a happy thump on the tiles, the Baking Bible set there high on the shelf above the well-used food mixer, and the glorious view of the valley beyond the square-paned window, green and lush. Sitting in the hub of the kitchen with her fiancé and her family, Rachel felt such warmth. There was a glow of happy love around that table. It felt good, and Rachel was so thankful. Her mind drifted to her best friend Eve, and the recent revelation that had rocked her. She sent a silent prayer that Eve was feeling that same warmth on her arrival home.

8

EVE

Eve walked up the path to her cottage with her suitcase and the precious dress carrier in tow, and saw Ben and Amelia waiting on the doorstep. Her daughter dashed out to greet her in a rush of miss-you hugs and chatter, telling her all about her weekend.

'Maisy was here and we had pizza and ice creams . . . and Haribo . . . *and* we stayed up till eleven o'clock!' her cute six-year-old voice raced on.

Argh, so that's what happened when she wasn't around. Eve raised an eyebrow sharply at Ben, just as Ben gave Amelia a cheeky *shush*, that's enough, kind of look. She couldn't really be cross, though – a late night once in a blue moon probably wasn't going to hurt. It was good to think that they'd been having fun together. She knew that Ben was a lovely dad to Amelia, it was nice for them to have some father–daughter bonding time. And, she had been away herself, having a brilliant time with the girls.

'Hey . . .' Ben was there at the doorway, helping to take her case before brushing her cheek with a kiss. 'Had a good time then?'

'Yeah, it was great.'

The three of them bundled in over the threshold, Eve finding a safe place to hang *the* dress, using the top ledge of the open lounge door. 'And Rachel so loved the dress, phew.'

'Well, that's good,' Ben replied, a little distractedly.

The number of hours Eve had spent on the dress had already caused some tension between her and Ben, that and trying to keep up with all her Etsy orders online. Her craft business was doing well, and she made soft toys, knits and home decorations to sell at the Pudding Pantry and at local craft fairs, but all this took time and sometimes stole into their evenings. The dress was yet more work, but she really wanted to make her best friend's wedding extra special. After hearing from Jill about the frock that Rachel had left behind, she couldn't get her friend's disappointment out of her mind, and she had been determined to play Fairy Godmother. Ben had huffed and puffed his way through many an evening of late as she sat stitching chiffon flowers onto the skirt, saying he couldn't see why Rachel couldn't just go and buy a wedding dress like most other people did.

'You load so much pressure on yourself already,' he'd commented. 'You don't have to take even more on.'

But Eve wanted Rachel's big day to be perfect for her bestie, and was almost as excited about Tom and Rachel's wedding as the happy couple were.

Ben was looking at her. 'So, what did you get up to? What was it like there? It sounded a great place.'

'Oh, yeah, we had a fab time,' Eve answered quickly, realising her husband was waiting for a response. 'Yep, the lodge was amazing, a proper log cabin, set right by a lake.'

'Oooh, it sounds pretty there, Mummy.' Amelia was standing beside them in the hallway.

'Yes, it was, really pretty. With woods to walk in and a lovely seaside town nearby.' Eve felt a little nostalgic about it already.

'That's good. Glad it all worked out for you all. And . . . you deserved a bit of a break.'

'We missed you, Mummy.'

'Yeah, we did,' Ben agreed, raising a warm smile, with a reassuring glimmer of his old self back. They'd seemed sadly distant of late. 'Right, great. So, what's for tea?'

Ah, back to normal then, thought Eve.

Echoes of Kirsty's domestic complaints rattled through Eve's mind, mocking her.

'Oh . . .' she hadn't even thought. Mealtimes and cooking were usually her domain, but after her long journey and busy weekend, she had kind of hoped that Ben might have come up with something for her arrival supper himself.

'Well, I have been cooking all weekend,' he began.

That wasn't strictly true, as she knew they'd been over to his parents for dinner last night, and she'd left that lasagne in the fridge. Warming up a frozen pizza and serving ice cream for the girls didn't exactly take all evening or make him *MasterChef* material. But she bit her tongue; she'd had her wonderful, if slightly emotional, weekend away after all.

'Right, well, I'll have a look in the freezer, there's bound to be something there,' Eve mumbled, wracking her brain. There might be some breaded fish, oven chips, peas? So, there she was, straight back to it. Reality hitting home already.

And there *they* were, slipping back into tired roles, family life. Everything back to normal . . . or so it seemed. Tea time. Popping Amelia in the bath for some splash-filled fun and more chatter. Bedtime routine: a book and a hug, and a tender kiss on her strawberry-soap-smelling cheek. An evening for two in front of the television. Comfortable, uninspiring. Time to turn in themselves.

Once they were in bed, Eve turned to her husband to snuggle up. She knew she needed to make more of an effort herself. Things weren't so bad at home; she just needed to try a bit harder, that was all. For all their sakes. They were a family.

She'd made her own wedding vows six years ago, till death do us part, and she had meant every word as she'd spoken them in the church that day. She and Ben could get back to how they used to be, surely. But as she leaned against him, brushing a hand over his chest, with fingertips that used to make his skin quiver under her touch, she realised his breathing had slowed. A snort of a snore emitted from his mouth.

She rolled away to the coolness of the other side of the bed, feeling the moisture of a tear brush her lashes, wondering how life – how *they* – had changed so much.

9

A shaft of warm sunlight fell on Rachel's face. She got up to open the curtains on a glorious gold-flecked morning. The sky an azure blue with mere puffs of candy-floss cloud. Summer was here at last.

After a breakfast of toast spread thickly with Ruth's bramble jelly, and having seen Maisy off on the school bus, Rachel headed across the sun-dappled farmyard to the Pudding Pantry, where she and Jill were back on duty. The May sunshine warmed the honeyed-stone walls, and danced off the white wooden tables where little posies of pink roses, plucked from their garden and mixed with sprigs of delicate white gypsophila, sat in mini milk bottles.

The coffee machine was gurgling. Elderly yet spritely Frank, one of their regulars, was seated at his favourite window table, overlooking the valley, with his newspaper propped up before him. 'Nice to see you back, ladies.' He gave them a smile.

'Nice to *be* back, Frank,' replied Rachel warmly, 'though we did have a lovely time, I must say.' Rachel was standing in the little kitchen area behind the counter, spooning creamy cheesecake mix on top of buttery biscuit crumbs for a summery lemon dessert. The zingy citrus smell was delightful.

'Fabulous, it was, Frank. We had our own wooden lodge right by a lake,' added Jill, as she lifted a batch of freshly baked scones out of the oven, ready to put out for cream teas – it most definitely was that time of the year. She'd already baked two halves of a Victoria sponge in the farmhouse Aga earlier this morning, ready to sandwich together with whipped cream and strawberries.

'Sounds delightful. Oh, and has Tom had his stag do yet, then?' enquired Frank. 'You young ones seem to do all sorts of exciting things these days. Mine was a few drinks down at The Black Bull with my pals. In fact,' he gave a chuckle, 'I remember ending up a little worse for wear, and my mother being extremely cross with me when I finally staggered home. I do believe I might have been a tad poorly in one of the front garden flower beds.'

'Hah, those were the days, Frank, hey,' chipped in Jill.

'Tom's had his stag already,' Rachel replied. 'He and his friends went down to Newcastle for a night out. They're big rugby fans so they tied it in with watching a match there at the Newcastle Falcons.'

'Ah, right. I bet they had a good time.'

'No doubt – though I didn't ask for too many details,' she laughed. 'So, do you think we should freshen up the menus, Mum?' added Rachel, changing tack. 'Make sure we add some new summery puds?'

'Oh yes, good idea, love. We'll need something for the gluten-free range too. Oh, and let's make a new selection for our mini pudding platters. What about a small rhubarb and vanilla pudding, with a slice of your lemon cheesecake and a bite-size strawberry meringue, and then something chocolatey, perhaps?'

'A mini brownie, maybe?'

Frank, who'd been listening in, called out, 'Yes, please. I'll be your taste-tester if you like.'

'Of course, you can be the first to try it out, Frank,' replied Jill with a grin.

A couple arrived, whose rugged footwear and practical clothing suggested they'd been out hiking. They asked for two coffees whilst browsing the glass counter with wide eyes as they discovered the delicious selection.

'How to choose?' The man raised his eyebrows.

'I know,' agreed the woman. 'Everything looks so delicious.'

'Well, you can always have a couple of things and share,' suggested Rachel.

'Or, they do a fabulous pudding platter,' chipped in Frank with a wink. 'Why just have one or two things when you can taste three or four,' he added naughtily. 'The new summer selection sounds divine.'

'Well, we'd better have one of those then,' the gentleman said in a lilting Yorkshire accent. 'Just the thing after a bracing walk in the hills.'

'Oh, it'll have been lovely up there this morning,' commented Rachel.

'It was indeed; the views were stunning,' his partner added, as they settled down at a nearby table.

As Jill went to serve the pudding platter a few minutes later, Rachel stopped her in her tracks. 'Wait, that looks amazing, Mum. Let me take a quick pic, and I'll pop it straight on to our Instagram and Facebook pages. The puddings look *sooo* pretty.'

'And delicious too,' Frank chipped in.

'Yes,' Rachel continued, 'seeing a picture of that summer selection might well help entice a few more customers in.'

Rachel liked to keep their social media pages updated, and with images like that going online, their followers' mouths would soon be watering.

A bustling half-hour followed, with several more customers turning up. Then they had space for a quick breather and a cup of tea for themselves.

'We need to have a proper think about the food for the wedding, Mum. It's less than seven weeks away now. We did say we'd make all the puddings ourselves . . . and we need to create some kind of savoury buffet for the afternoon reception, as well as the hog roast that Tom has got organised for the evening.'

Costs for the wedding had already been mounting. If they made the buffet themselves it would certainly save them some much-needed funds, but they were well aware it would be a lot of extra work. 'We'll need to decide exactly what we'll be baking,' Rachel continued, starting to spiral a little, 'or it'll creep up on us all too fast. And . . . there's so much else to think of too.' Rachel had to admit it was beginning to feel a bit overwhelming. They were still to finalise the flowers, table decorations, favours, some thank you gifts . . . the list went on. Thank goodness the dress at least was sorted. 'So, we'll need to be organised as far ahead as we can.'

'Puddings for a wedding . . . Hmm, I'll get my Queen of the Pudding Pantry thinking cap on.' With a broad smile, Jill raised the bespoke mug that Rachel had bought her last Christmas. 'Don't you worry, Rachel. It'll all work out wonderfully, I'm sure.'

Rachel hoped they'd manage to pull it all together in the end. But organising a wedding, her *own* wedding, on top of the farming chores and looking after Maisy seemed a big ask right now. She hated being the centre of attention at the best of times, and she now wondered if inviting what felt like the whole of the small town of Kirkton had been wise.

After a further busy spell over the lunch time, Tom appeared in his farming gear. 'Afternoon, ladies.'

'We missed you this morning,' said Jill. You could set your watch by Tom's bacon sandwich at elevenses.

Rachel had missed him last night too. Having been away all weekend, she'd stayed home with Maisy for the early evening, and then – just as she'd hoped to call round to Tom's after putting her little girl to bed – he'd ended up having to dash out to help a farming friend bring a cow and her calf down into their shed; the cow having got herself caught up in some broken wire and in a bit of a state. So, they hadn't had the evening together they'd hoped for.

'Ah, I know, I was kept away earlier with a delivery. But, I've managed to wangle a couple of free hours this afternoon. So, I was wondering if . . .' He raised his eyebrows enquiringly at Rachel. She shrugged her shoulders as she busied herself with the coffee machine. Much as she'd love to escape with Tom, she should really be helping her mum here at the Pantry.

'Jill, can I possibly steal your daughter for a few hours, do you think? We have important wedding plans to make.' He gave his warmest smile, the one that always made Rachel melt.

Jill wiped her hands on her apron. 'Oh, well, I don't see why not . . . it's bound to quieten off a bit now that lunch time's over. And it's after-school club for Maisy tonight, isn't it, Rachel? So, I'm sure I can manage here.'

'Are you sure, Mum?'

Jill nodded.

'Well, we could pick Maisy up on the way back, I suppose. That would work, wouldn't it, Tom?' Rachel was still feeling a little guilty at leaving her mum in the lurch.

'Of course. No problem.'

'Go on then, get yourself away, lass. Before I get a chance to change my mind.'

'Thank you, Mum.' Rachel whipped off her apron and leapt around the other side of the counter.

'Cheers, Jill, we owe you one,' Tom beamed.

Forty minutes later, strolling the golden sands of Low Newton Bay, with the ruins of Dunstanburgh Castle creating a dramatic backdrop on the far cliffs, and Tom holding her hand, Rachel felt a sense of happy calm. The smell of salt and sea filled the air. The sun glinted in silver bursts off the waves that rolled gently into the shore. They'd made their escape to the coast, and they finally had a little time to themselves.

'It's gorgeous here, isn't it?' Rachel took in the panoramic seascape.

'Yeah, don't know why we don't try and get down here more often.'

'Oh, I don't know. Work . . . the farms . . . Pudding Pantry to run.' She pulled at his arm playfully.

'Well yes, there is all that.'

'But yes, it's lovely just to take a bit of time out. I'm getting spoilt, what with a weekend away and now this . . . Heaven forbid I'll get used to it. Anyway, what are these wedding plans you needed to discuss so urgently?' Tom had been happy to let her, Jill, and maid of honour Eve, get on with most of the organising up until now. He'd been firmly in agreement that they should have a big celebration back at Primrose Farm after the church wedding in Kirkton but, as for the finer details, he was grateful for them to take the lead.

'Ah, well,' he looked a little sheepish, 'I have to confess it was just a ploy to get you away early.'

'Hah, so I've been brought here under false pretences,' she pulled a pretend-grumpy face. 'Sneaky.'

'Guilty as charged.' He grinned.

'But we probably *do* have loads of things to catch up on wedding-wise, you know. Like, did you finally sort your suit out and those you need to hire for the best man and ushers?'

'Of course. All done. I have found the perfect attire for us all, and we'll look very smart indeed.' He gave a wink.

'Those grey suits I pointed out online?'

He pursed his lips and gave a slow nod, looking a little sheepish.

She wasn't buying it, Tom definitely had something up his sleeve, but she couldn't work out what.

'Yeah, so no need to fret, I've got everything sorted for us men. We'll look great, don't you worry.'

They walked hand in hand, Rachel's fingers slotted through Tom's, as if it was where they belonged. Strolling further along the bay, away from the dog walkers, the picnickers and the children building sandcastles, they discovered a sand-filled dip in the dunes, hidden from view of the beach, where they decided to sit for a while and make the most of the sunny afternoon.

'Ah, bliss.' Rachel stretched out, the sand warm beneath her, feeling the tingle of the sun on her face.

They were soon lying side by side, holding hands,

looking up at the fluffy white clouds slowly scudding across the sky. It was nice just to stop and be still, to take a moment out of their hectic lives. And, it was so *very* nice to be lying here next to Tom.

'So, what do you see up there?' Tom asked, gazing up at the sky.

'Some clouds and blue sky.'

'Hah, practical as always. Look again, do you see that boat moving out of the cloud mass over there, and oh, the face of a wolf in that one? Two pointy ears and a sharp nose.'

'Yeah, I can just about make that out.'

He should have been playing this game with Maisy, Rachel mused. She had the imagination; she'd have spotted a full zoo and more by now. Rachel was just happy seeing a lovely blue sky, and having this gorgeous man by her side. She gave a contented sigh. Tom had slotted into her and Maisy's lives so well. She'd been anxious at first about bringing a new father figure into her daughter's life, but he had moved slowly and thoughtfully into that role. Tom didn't have any children from his previous marriage – his relationship with the infamous Caitlin had ended in a rather bitter divorce five years ago – but, despite never having had a child of his own, he seemed a natural.

She rolled towards him, quickly checking that there didn't seem to be anyone around in this part of the dunes. 'I do think I might just have to block your view, however.' She grinned cheekily as she climbed on board, until she was flat out over him, legs to legs, chest to chest, face to face. She smiled foxily as she dipped her chin, edging her mouth towards his, their lips meeting in a gorgeously sexy kiss. Her body tingling from top to toe, feeling so alive. Tom's arms tightened around her back, holding her closer still.

'Shame there are people about, just down there . . .' sighed Tom, as he drew away to take a breath.

'Hmm, but I'm sure they haven't banned kissing in public quite yet, and we are fully clothed.'

'I know. But . . . it's killing me. It's like revving up the engine and not being able to go anywhere.' He gave a frustrated grin.

Rachel laughed, then moved in for kiss number two – such glorious and heart-warming seconds, enjoying the feeling of his cheeky erection beneath her.

'Well, you'll just have to wait, Mr Watson.' She smiled, then nibbled his ear lobe ever so gently.

'Nope, no, no. That'll send me over the edge, you minx.'

Rachel leapt up from him, laughing, 'Okay then, last one down to the sea's a ninny.'

Tom scrambled after her.

She could feel the thud of his feet in the sand just behind her as she ran full pelt down the dune bank and away to the shore, pulling off her trainers in the final few metres before dashing right up to her knees in the chilly water.

Tom swept her up in his arms, about to dunk her into the waves.

'So, I'm a ninny, am I?'

'Yes!'

With one swift movement, he dipped her body until her head touched the cold sea froth.

'No, no, no!'

They were both laughing. He dipped her once more, enough to dampen her hair.

'No, stop, I'll end up all curls,' she giggled.

'I love your curls.' He dipped her again.

'Ooo-kay, no more. I surrender, I'll get brain freeze!'

The legs of Tom's jeans were soaked through; as he deposited Rachel back on the sands, they both looked down at his sodden legs, grinning.

'Do you think they'll still let us in the pub? I fancy a quick pint,' said Tom.

'Yeah, course. It is the beach, after all. We might manage to bag a seat outside anyhow.'

'Have you eaten?'

'Nah, I was too busy serving at lunch time,' answered Rachel. 'I'd forgotten. Hmm, I am feeling a bit peckish . . .'

'Right then, to the pub it is.'

They were soon perched on a wooden bench outside the Ship Inn, tucking in to fresh crab sandwiches and a bowl of homemade chips, all salt and vinegary – delicious. They chatted as they ate, Rachel sipping a glass of chilled white wine while Tom enjoyed a half-pint of the local ale, soaking up the atmosphere of a sunny afternoon by the sea.

All too soon, it was time to head back. Maisy's after-school gym club would be finishing in half an hour, and they'd have to be there in time to collect her. Back to mum mode, back to reality.

'Time to go . . .' Rachel admitted reluctantly.

'Yep, it is indeed. I've got a few things to finish up on the farm too.'

'It's been lovely, Tom. Thank you for whisking me away.'

'The pleasure's all mine,' answered Tom.

He gathered their glasses and took them back inside to the bar, whilst Rachel took a last look at the rippling blue of the sea. It had been a gorgeous afternoon.

Hmm, maybe she could call and see Tom later this evening, and pick up where they'd left off in the dunes . . .

Heading back inland in Tom's truck, Rachel gazed across at her fiancé. 'Won't it be great when we don't have to keep saying goodbye, when we can go home together, just *be* together . . .'

With their wedding in less than two months' time, it would be a wonderful reality. Going home with Tom and Maisy, back to Primrose Farm.

'Yeah,' his smile was warm, genuine, 'knowing that when I get back from a day out in the fields, or on the tractor, that you'll be there, you and Maisy, back at my farmhouse.'

At *my* farmhouse.

Oh . . . did he imagine she and Maisy would be moving in there with him?

Rachel had assumed he'd move in with them, there at Primrose Farm, and maybe put his farmhouse up for rent or something. Primrose was Maisy's home; it was all her little girl had ever known. Dammit, it was all Rachel had ever known. It was where she'd grown up with Dad, Mum. It was *home*. She felt a wrench in her heart just thinking about leaving.

'Ah . . . did you mean . . . you want us to move in with *you*?' She tried to keep the tremble from her voice, reasoning with herself that it was only a mile down the road.

'Well, yeah. I just thought . . . with your mum still living at the farm, you'd want to come over to mine, have some privacy. Our own space. Me, you and Maisy. I can do up the spare room for her, let her choose the colours and all that.'

Rachel was still trying to process this. Her mouth an 'o' of surprise. Why the hell hadn't they had this conversation before? She'd just assumed, very naively as it turned out, that they'd be staying put . . . but then apparently, so had he . . .

'Well, you can still carry on looking after Primrose easily from there, and the Pantry and everything's close by.'

'Oh, but it'd mean moving Maisy . . . it might be unsettling for her.'

'I'm sure she'd be fine, Rach, kids adapt. We needn't all be crammed under one roof, and it makes sense for Jill to stay put; it's her home and where she does the baking for the Pantry, after all.'

Rachel opened her mouth to speak but found herself tongue-tied. For Tom it was obviously a done deal. Straightforward, in fact. But, as Rachel looked out of the truck window at the country lanes whizzing by, she was reeling.

10

Rachel had tossed and turned all night, her frazzled mind trying to get to grips with the prospect of living at Tom's farm once they were married. Primrose Farm was everything to her, and as the only child she would naturally have taken the mantle as the next generation of working farmer. The farm was a place of stories passed down, of memories cherished. From Great-Grandad's Aberdeen Angus prize bull, Macbeth, winning at the Kirkton Country Show, to Great-Aunt Iris's oven-bottom muffins lurking unseen in the Aga for six weeks and turning into charcoal – she hadn't inherited the baking gene, bless her – to Dad making a swing for Rachel out of a tractor tyre on the old apple tree . . . She knew that memories stayed with you wherever you went, they settled in hearts not bricks and mortar, but sometimes when she sat around the kitchen table at Primrose with her mum, it was like the walls were speaking to her. She could almost hear the voices of the generations gone by. It was her legacy. She knew, practically, she could run the farm fine from next door, but the idea seemed all wrong. Rachel feared she had been burying her head in the sand by not talking through their future living arrangements properly with Tom. But it felt just too painful for her to even contemplate leaving.

She desperately needed a friendly ear, *and* she also wanted to catch up with Eve to find out how she was getting on at home. Eve's own dilemma and confession on their weekend away was still fresh in Rachel's mind, and she wanted to be there for her friend should she need it. Neither issue was a conversation they could have in earshot of anyone else, so Rachel was relieved to see only Eve's car in the driveway of her cottage when she rolled up on the quad.

She knocked on the white wooden door, and then opened it with a putting-a-brave-face-on-it, 'Hello.'

'Hi Rach, come on in. I'm in the dining room, covered in bunting.'

Rachel popped her head around the door to see a table loaded with pretty bolts of materials, the sewing machine on the go, and just-made flags of soft pinks, patterned whites, florals, and spotted sage greens, laid out ready to string together. 'Guess who these are for?' she beamed. 'I take it they are the right colours to match your bouquets and the tipi-tent flowers?'

'Oh my, Eve, they are just gorgeous. But haven't you got all your own orders to make up for your customers too?'

'Yep, it's okay, I've done some of them this morning, rose with the lark I did. But well, I just couldn't resist. And, I did promise you more of these, so I'd have to make them soon enough anyhow. And, I figured if I put a few pics of these finished ones on my Etsy page, it might create interest in my new wedding range too.'

The Craft Queen of Kirkton looked as though she was in her element.

'Good thinking.'

'Okay hun, well that's another strand finished, so can I get you a coffee?'

'I'd love one, thank you.'

They vacated to the kitchen where Rachel took up a stool whilst Eve popped the kettle on. 'So, how's life at the farm then?' Eve asked.

The farm that Rachel might soon have to leave.

Rachel couldn't help the sigh that escaped her lips.

'Is everything okay?' Eve was on it like a car bonnet. 'Do we need cake?'

'Definitely cake,' Rachel raised a small smile.

'No problem, there's a couple of spare slices of lemon drizzle left that I made for Ben's packed lunches this week. He'll never know.'

The cafetière was filled and the cake plated, a zing of lemon and sugar filling the galley kitchen. 'So . . .?'

'So, I've just found out . . . Tom wants us to live there. At his house. Me and Maisy . . . after the wedding.' Rachel looked down at her hands around the coffee mug.

'O-kay. And that's a problem, I take it . . . so, what do you want?'

'I just thought we'd all be at Primrose Farm, that he'd move in there with us.'

'And you haven't discussed this till now?' Eve sounded surprised.

'No . . . I suppose we both just imagined . . . Ah, shit, we were both thinking we'd stay. It's a farming thing . . . you stay on your farm. But how the hell do two married farmers both stay on their own farms?'

'Hmm, well one of you's going to have to compromise. I assume you actually want to live together, sleep together . . . be a couple.' Eve raised an eyebrow, ironically.

'Of course.'

'Hmm.'

'And there's Maisy to think of in all of this,' added Rachel. 'Surely, she'd be better off staying in her own home? It'll be a big change for her as it is, what with getting used to Tom being around all the time.'

'Yes, I can see that. But, what about for your mum . . .?'

'Well, that was Tom's point,' Rachel conceded.

'Might be a bit crowded at yours . . . and what about when you want to have mad passionate sex in the living room or something? I can see Tom's point . . .'

Great, now even Eve was siding with him.

'Well, when was the last time you and Ben had mad passionate sex in the living room?' Rachel couldn't stop her mounting frustration.

Eve's face dropped.

'Sorry hun, that was a bit tactless. I'd actually come to ask how you were doing too, you and Ben? Since you got back . . .' *Since the confession.*

'Ah, it's been okay, I suppose. What's weird is that nothing's really changed here. Me and Ben, we're just ticking along . . . same old, same old. It's me, Rach . . . it's me that's changed.'

Rachel sat listening, allowing Eve to open up, whilst studying her friend's face that suddenly looked so sad.

'Oh Rachel, I wish I could stop thinking about this guy, but I can't. There's no simple on–off switch with the way I'm feeling . . . and I don't know what it all means. Have I fallen out of love with Ben, Rach? Is that it?' Eve paused, taking a slow sip of coffee. 'I don't know what to think any more . . . and I just feel so damned sad . . . sad that it might really be over between us. Jeez, I'm all mixed up.'

'Give it time, you'll find a way back. I know Granny Ruth always says "marriages have to be worked at". I had the lecture when we got engaged.' Rachel raised a supportive smile.

'Maybe you're right,' Eve sighed. 'But is that it? Are me and Ben just going to shuffle along for the rest of our lives? We're more like friends than lovers just now.'

'Well, at least you're friends, honey. That's a real good place to come back from. You two have always been good together up till now.'

'Really? Maybe from the outside looking in, but I feel we've been drifting apart for ages. I just didn't see it happening. Too busy . . . with Amelia, with my craft business. How did it all change? And, why *don't* we have bloody rampant sex on the living-room floor anymore?'

'Probably 'cos it's covered in your craft materials . . .' Rachel tried to lighten the mood. 'Now you wouldn't want a pin cushion getting anywhere it shouldn't.'

Eve just shook her head, conceding a wry smile. 'Oh, Rach, what happened to the time when Ben and I couldn't keep our hands off each other?'

'Oh petal, relationships change, life changes, but you can still work this out, you and Ben,' Rachel reassured, though little alarm bells were ringing in her mind. Is this what happened . . . four, five, six years down the line? But no, up until Dad's hidden depression, up until the end in fact, her parents had had a good marriage. It didn't have to be that way. Rachel remembered so many happy times as she grew up. There was always a lot of love in that farmhouse.

She took Eve's hand in her own. 'It'll be okay, hun. We'll work this out. I'm here for you too. Just don't do anything stupid, hey? And try and keep some distance from this artist guy.'

'That's not so easy; there's a craft event we'll both be at in two weeks' time.'

'Ah, right . . . well just be polite, but that's it. Keep yourself to yourself.'

'Yeah, I suppose.' Eve didn't sound convinced.

Another of Granny Ruth's phrases filled Rachel's mind: 'Love and marriage, go together like a horse and carriage'. But unfortunately, it looked as though the wheel had fallen off this particular carriage for Ben and Eve right now. Rachel was determined to help them fix it.

11

As the end of the week rolled around, it spelled the revival of Pudding Club.

Rachel found herself looking forward to these bi-monthly meet-ups at the Pudding Pantry. Her idea last winter to drum up extra custom by creating a regular evening event in the barn tearoom was still going strong. There was now a group of around twelve or thirteen 'Clubbers', most of them regulars *and* friends by now.

They had a different theme each time, and tonight was 'Dreamy Ice Cream' – a special request from little Maisy who was always keen to get involved. They'd invited along Andrew, the owner of the local dairy that made its own ice cream, to give a talk, *and* here was the best part, a tasting session. He had mentioned there'd be a honeycomb ice cream, ginger, traditional vanilla and a choc-chip to sample. Rachel and Jill had also been busy making several puddings to pair with the delicious ice-cream flavours.

Maisy had been allowed to stay up late to attend, even though it was a school night – well, she couldn't miss her own theme night, could she now? She was excitedly helping Rachel set out the Pantry. Rachel and Jill had already moved two of the white wooden tables together to create a large space for the group to sit around.

'We'll need about fourteen chairs, I'd say,' Rachel called out.

Several members had already messaged to say they were coming, and often one or two extras turned up on the night.

'Okay, Mummy.' Chairs were scraped and bumped across the stone flags, but Rachel didn't have the heart to stop her little helper.

Rachel switched on the white fairy lights that were strung along the counter to give the barn that extra bit of sparkle, and refreshed the pretty posy milk jugs with fragrant sweet peas set at the centre of each table. The two girls then popped a spoon and fork, wrapped in a red-checked gingham napkin, at each place setting.

'It looks really pretty.' Maisy stood back with a smile, admiring their work.

Rachel's heart warmed watching her little girl.

'It does indeed. Just perfect for an ice-cream and pudding night.'

They clapped their hands together in a high five.

It wasn't long before Andrew from the dairy arrived with a cool box full of fabulous ice-cream booty.

'Hi Andrew, great to see you again. Thank you so much for coming along tonight.' Rachel shook hands warmly with him.

It was always nice to see a fellow farmer in the area;

their families had known each other for years now. And, they'd got to know each other even more last summer when Rachel was setting up supplies for the Pudding Pantry.

'No worries. You're most welcome.'

'Can I help bring anything in?' Rachel offered.

'There's another cool box in the back of the Jeep, if you don't mind.'

'Yummy, ice cream. Hello Andrew,' Maisy was beaming up at him.

'Hey there, little Maisy. And, how are you?'

'Good, thank you.'

Rachel was pleased to hear that she was minding her manners.

'Mummy says I can stay up late and eat ice cream!' She grinned.

'Well, that sounds a good plan for a Thursday night.' He smiled back at her.

Andrew was soon set up, with his samples at the ready, and some flyers to hand out about the dairy. Jill came back across from the farmhouse with a freshly baked sticky toffee pudding, warm from the oven. The evening was balmy, so the barn doors were open wide and welcoming. And, in no time at all, no doubt lured in by the gorgeous caramel smells and the thought of dreamy ice cream, the first Pudding Club attendees began to arrive.

First was Frank, in his summer attire of beige slacks and pale blue shirt, closely followed by Kirsty and

Hannah, who'd picked up new-to-the-village young mum, Alice, on their way. Hot on their heels were keen bakers, Pamela and Nigel, a middle-aged couple from the nearby town of Alnwick with two of their friends. Daniel arrived next, with a kiss on the cheek for Jill and a cheery hello to the group, followed by Christine and Eileen, keen members of the local Women's Institute, along with friend and Pantry helper Jan. Brenda from the local deli came rolling in just in time for the seven o'clock start. And, last but not least, Eve crashed in all in a fluster.

'Phew, sorry guys, I hadn't realised the time, I was flat out putting the finishing touches to a soft toy hedgehog family for an Etsy order! Can't wait for some delicious ice cream, though.'

Wow, it certainly was a full house tonight.

After teas and coffees were served, Andrew did a brief introduction to the group. 'Hello everyone! I'm so pleased that you'll be testing some of our wares this evening, and I'm very proud to announce that the dairy has just received a Gold award for "Northumberland Producer of the Year"!'

At that the group all whooped and gave a hearty round of applause.

The first tasting was Jill's sticky toffee pudding served with the dairy's honeycomb ice cream – what a delight! There were so many 'Umms' and 'Ahhs' and contented sighs, the room sounded as though it was filled with the buzz of happy bees. Next, they tried the dairy's Eton

Mess ice cream on its own. It really didn't need any additions – being the creamiest ice cream with meringue pieces and crushed strawberries.

'Delicious', 'Divine', 'Scrumptious', 'Summer in a dish', were just some of the comments.

Then there was Jill's rhubarb tart, paired with spiced ginger ice cream, followed by a melt-in-the mouth rich chocolate-chip ice cream to try.

'What could be better,' sighed Hannah, 'than eating ice creams and puddings galore in a pretty country barn, with a view like that?'

Indeed, the summer evening sun was casting a soft, golden glow over the verdant hills and valley around them. It was a moment to treasure. Friends, family, food and Primrose Farm. Rachel couldn't imagine wanting to be anywhere else, and a little grain of panic filled her once more at the thought of leaving, even if only to move in next door. She pushed the thought aside, realising that Andrew was now standing quietly at the head of the group, looking at her expectantly, with the ice-cream tasting coming to a close.

'Well, that was brilliant.' She stepped forward, assuming a bright tone, 'Thank you so much for coming along, Andrew, and for telling us more about the dairy, and of course letting us taste these delightful flavours. I'm sure we'll all be stocking up – there are cartons to buy, folks. And, I look forward to selling lots of your ice creams here at the Pantry in the future.' She started to clap, which resulted in a thankful round of applause and lots of praise from the gathering. With Andrew on his way a short while later, the group chatted amongst themselves and had a top-up brew from the big red polka-dot teapot.

'Now then, Rachel, how are all the wedding plans going?' asked Alice. 'And thank you so much for the invite; that was so kind of you.'

'Oh, you're welcome,' replied Rachel. 'We wanted everyone to come along from the Pudding Club as you're all friends now.'

'Aw, that's so lovely,' added Kirsty.

'I can't believe it's less than two months away,' said Charlotte.

'Well, I now have a gorgeous wedding dress.' She gave Eve a big grin.

'Ooh, any details?' 'Tell us more . . .'

'Nope, sorry. You'll have to wait and see on that one.' Rachel was determined to keep schtum.

'Oh, the suspense,' added Eileen, with a smile.

'So, the reception is here at the farm, then?'

'Yes, after the church ceremony. We have a tipi arranged in the field next to the farmhouse – a bit of an expense, but we really can't count on our good old Northumbrian weather, even if it will be summer. And, we can always use the Pantry space as well.' Rachel really was beginning to feel excited about it all, despite all the planning involved.

'Well, that sounds great.'

'And what about the food? Will there be puddings is the big question?' Pamela asked animatedly.

'Hah, of course!' Jill answered. 'In fact, we're planning a smorgasbord – is that the right word? – of puddings.'

'Ooh, naughty but nice. Brilliant!' chimed Brenda.

'Well, won't that be an awful lot of work for you both? Just before the wedding? Are you doing the baking all yourselves?' Eileen looked concerned.

'Well, that was the plan. The budget's not bottomless I'm afraid, and well . . . I think it will make it extra special having our own puddings,' explained Rachel.

'It might well be, but you'll be shattered, my lovelies,' piped up Christine.

'No, that won't do at all. Look, why don't you let us help make some of them at least?' Eileen looked around the table at her fellow attendees to rally some support.

'Yeah, we'd love to help.'

'We can share the load.'

'Maybe we could have a special Pudding Club night just before the wedding?' suggested Daniel. 'Where we can all help out? A Wedding Pudding Night, where everything we make goes towards the desserts for your big day? What do you reckon everyone?'

There were nods of agreement all round.

'Of course. It'll be fun too,' said Eve.

'Really? You'd do that for us?' Rachel was gob-smacked.

'You don't want to start your wedding day worn out now, do you? I think it's a great idea,' added Charlotte.

'So, who's in?' piped up Eileen.

Every single person around that table put their hand

up, even Frank who hardly knew how to bake. Rachel felt her heart swell, and a little tear filled her eye.

'Oh, bless you all,' said Jill, looking somewhat overcome.

Rachel was finding it hard to speak. She took a gulp of air and managed a breathy, 'Thank you.'

The Pudding Club really had risen to the occasion for them. This group had grown into something very special indeed over the past few months. There was friendship and support in abundance here. In fact, Rachel realised, the Pudding Club at Primrose Farm really did have all the perfect ingredients.

12

'We need to chat about your flowers, Rachel. I know I'm all booked in for you, but I do need some more detail on what you want bloom and colour-wise, so I can get them all ordered in and organised for you.' It was Wendy, the florist from the village, on the phone.

'Oh, yes.' Crikey, decisions, decisions. There was so much to think of and, well, Rachel felt much more at home with her hands-on farm work compared with the creative tasks involved in wedding planning. Right now, in fact, she was grappling with an errant sheep, trying to get it through the gate as she balanced the phone in the crook of her shoulder. They were rounding the herd of ewes and lambs up, moving them between fields. Farmhand Simon had a flicker of impatience across his brow, and sheepdog Moss was awaiting further commands; her phone call was clearly holding things up. She felt rather flustered.

Tom hadn't been much help on the floral front either, as he'd said he was happy to go with the flow on things like the flowers and decorations. 'Okay . . . right, well I had kind of thought pale pinks and whites . . .' She found herself floundering, looking about her at the nearby hedgerow for inspiration. Ah yes, the blue of a cornflower stood out at her. 'And yes, we've chosen bridesmaids' dresses in a sort of lilac-blue colour. Perhaps a country look to go with that – nothing too formal?' The rogue sheep head-butted her stomach. 'Urgh . . . to be honest, Wendy, I hoped you might have some ideas too . . .'

'Well, why don't you come down to the shop, and we can look at a few designs along the lines that I've done in the past, which we can tweak to your own taste? Oh, and bring in any ideas or images that you've seen too.'

'Okay . . .' She really was feeling out of her depth. 'Can I bring Eve along? She's the artistic one, after all.' Yes, she'd have far more idea. Hmm, there was method in choosing her as her maid of honour.

'Of course. So, when can you pop down?'

'I'll check with Eve, but perhaps tomorrow afternoon, say three o'clock, once the Pantry eases off a bit?'

'That's fine by me. Just let me know if it's going to be any different. See you then. Bye pet.'

'Bye, Wendy.'

Rachel sighed as she hung up. Blimey, all this planning was even more tiring than sheep wrestling. She looked out towards Tom's farmhouse, wondering what oh-so-glamorous task was occupying him right now. They hadn't spoken any more about where they were going to live after the wedding, and it was niggling her. Could she picture herself and little Maisy over there with him, day after day, away from Primrose? She hated all the uncertainty clouding the future.

She saw that Simon had already whizzed on through the gate on the quad, leaving her and Moss to round up this last ewe. 'Can we talk?' She popped Tom a quick text. As tempting as it was to bury her head in the sand, she knew she had to face things, talk it through. 'Ain't that right, Mrs Sheep? Nobody likes change. But come on, let's get you in the next field.'

Naturally, Eve was in her element with flower ideas and had gone all out that evening in her internet searches for 'country wedding flowers', 'boho-chic' florals, wedding posies and more. She had sketches, print-outs and images saved on her mobile phone – the works.

The next day the three of them gathered around the table in the back of the colourful and scent-laden 'Flower Basket' shop. Seeing both Eve's and Wendy's ideas laid out was brilliant. It made it so much easier for Rachel to sit and say, yes like that, *love* that, nope, no way, yes, gorgeous. Within a half-hour, and two cups of coffee and a slice of Victoria sponge later, they'd narrowed it down to some lovely natural-looking bouquets in soft pinks and whites with just a touch of blue, tied with a cornflower-blue satin ribbon to match the bridesmaids' dresses. There'd be wicker baskets filled with flowers for Maisy and Amelia, and – for the tables in the tipi back at the farm – large milk jugs would be filled with blooms, with some wildflowers too, and posy-filled jam jars for the church and the Pantry – Granny Ruth and the WI-ers would have plenty of empties between them for sure.

'Now then, Rachel, what about your hair?' asked Wendy. 'A lot of brides like something floral for their headwear . . . are you thinking of putting it up?'

'They do? Oh . . .' Her voice trailed. More decisions. 'Well, I had kind of thought of leaving it fairly natural.' In truth, she hadn't really thought much about it at all.

'And do you have a veil?'

'Nope, no veil. Just a bloomin' gorgeous dress, made by my lovely friend here.'

'Oh wow, really, Eve? You've made it yourself? You clever thing.'

'Thanks.' Eve gave a shy smile.

'Anyway, back to the hair?' Wendy was not the sort to be sidetracked.

Luckily Eve piped up: 'Ooh Rachel, what about delicate soft braids which join at the back, and then have the rest loose and wavy down to your shoulders?'

'Hmm, that could work, yeah.' Rachel could kind of picture that.

'Don't you remember we used to plait each other's hair as little girls?'

'Hah, yeah, of course.' Two little girls, sitting out in the meadow, chattering away, braiding each other's hair, Rachel remembered those days fondly. She and Eve went back so far.

'That sounds pretty,' said Wendy, taking up her florist's photo album. 'And look,' she leafed through some images, finding the picture she wanted. 'I was helping a local hairdresser; we worked some flowers through the bridesmaids' braids, and that looked gorgeous. Oh, and this one was for the bride, I made a flower wreath. If we kept it to the small pink rosebuds, a cornflower here and there to add contrast, and something white and delicate like gypsophila, that could work really well.'

'What about daisies? It used to be daisies when we were little . . .' Rachel reminisced. It was all coming back now; how they'd make daisy chains and pop them like wreaths on top of each other's heads, sometimes tucking a single one above their ear.

'Well, normal daisies would wilt very quickly, especially if it's a warm summer's day, but leave it with me, as there are certain florist types that will last longer. Hmm, I might be able to delicately wire the stalks, so they'll stay secure. Yes, that could work well, and I'll get the colours to all tie in with your bouquet.' Wendy was clearly getting into the flow of the idea now.

'I think that sounds absolutely lovely.' Rachel gave a wide grin, happy and relieved that it was all settled, just as Eve burst tunefully into, 'Daisy, Daisy, give me your answer do . . .'

The two girls dissolved into happy giggles.

'That look is just you, Rach, and definitely boho-chic. And, how perfect will it be with your dress?' she added with a beam.

It certainly did all look pretty, but Rachel couldn't help but be aware of her limited budget. Yet Wendy assured her these were sensible choices with costings in mind, and that she'd work out detailed prices for Rachel as soon as possible.

They left with grateful thanks, a hug from Wendy, and a sigh of relief from Rachel. It had gone blooming well. And it was yet another item for Rachel to check off the mammoth wedding planning list – phew.

'Oh, I can just picture the name settings for the tables now . . . handwritten on cute brown luggage labels with a dried pink rosebud stuck on to match your wedding flowers. What do you think, Rach?' Eve was on a creative high as they made their way back in the Land Rover along the country lanes.

Rachel thanked heavens that her best friend was full of artistic ideas. Goodness knows how her big day might turn out if she was left to her own devices. She might well have resorted to using black marker pens on cattle tags for her place names!

'So,' Eve gave a big grin from the passenger seat, 'the flowers are going to look stunning. I can already picture the tables in the tipi, set up with that gorgeous country look. Everything's coming together brilliantly, isn't it? Oh Rach, it's going to be such a fantastic day.'

'Yeah,' Rachel answered, a little flat. Of course, it was all great, but the small matter of *where exactly* they were going to live as a married couple was still weighing on her mind.

'Okay . . . what's up? You're about to marry Mr Absolutely Gorgeous and your face looks like a wet weekend. What's going on, Rach?'

Rachel concentrated on the road ahead for a few seconds. The text she'd sent to Tom earlier had so far gone unanswered. He might well have been busy out and about on the farm – it wasn't always easy to chat as she well knew – but his silence had left her feeling distinctly uneasy. 'Oh, Eve . . . if we can't even sort out where we are going to live, how are we going to get through the months and years ahead? All the decisions, the curveballs that life throws at you on the way?'

'Look, I know it's hard making the right decision about where to live, but you're no quitter, Rachel Swinton. That's not enough to pull the rug from under you . . . I've seen you two together, how bloody amazing you are together. You really are made for each other; it just took you both a while to realise it. You'll work it out, hun.'

'Yes, I suppose . . . I just haven't heard from him either. I want to talk but I'm getting a bit of radio silence.'

'Oh, don't worry, hun, he's probably just caught up. And would it really be so bad living there, at Tom's? It's not as though you'd be a million miles away, and it'd give you both some space. You can't really be canoodling in front of your mum.'

'No, I know,' Rachel managed a small smile. 'But hah, remember we do have Maisy in tow too. So, there won't be *that* much canoodling going on.'

'Tell me about it . . .' Eve gave an understanding groan.

'But you're right about Mum, there's no way I'd ever want to suggest she finds somewhere new to live. I'd feel like I was chucking her out. It's her home as much as mine. More so, as it's where she and dad have been since they were married . . .' She realised she needed to make this clear to Jill too, once she and Tom had had a proper heart-to-heart. It was time to sort all this out, for everyone's sake.

Maybe it was the thought of leaving all of those memories of Dad behind that was really holding her back – her childhood home, the tug of her heartstrings. Was she being stubborn, selfish? But after his death, she'd given a silent promise that she'd take the farm forward, keep it precious for them all. Could she still do that if she lived next door? So many thoughts were pulling her in contrary directions.

'It needn't be for ever, either,' added Eve sagely. 'Life can change. Look, if Tom's so keen on having you both there, why not try starting out at his and see how it goes? You'll be at Primrose every day to work, for the farm, the Pantry too. So, you'll still be there in essence.'

It was beginning to make sense, and it was good to have a new perspective on all this.

'Thanks, Eve. That's great advice.' Rachel smiled across at her friend as she pulled to a stop outside Eve's cottage. 'Time for a coffee, hun?'

'Much as I'd love to, I've a million jobs waiting for me on the farm. The most exciting prospect being checking the sheep's armpits and arses for fly-strike.' Oh, the glamorous life of a farmer.

'Ha! No worries, maybe another time soon.'

Rachel sensed a hint of disappointment in her friend's

tone. Damn, she hadn't had a chance to ask Eve how things were with her and Ben lately. Maybe Eve wanted more time to talk, just the two of them.

'You okay?' She looked across at Eve.

'Of course.' It came out in a tight cheery tone – a lie?

Maybe she could take ten more minutes . . . But, with that, Rachel's phone started buzzing. It was Simon, their farmhand. She'd better answer it. His voice came in an urgent tone. One of their cows, Morag, was sick with what appeared to be mastitis. With such conditions, things could get serious, and quickly. She had a young calf in tow too, and she was already reluctant to feed it.

'Sorry, hun. I'm going to have to go.' She took Eve's hand for a second. 'Morag's not well at all.'

Eve also knew the cows at Rachel's farm by name. 'It's fine, I understand. You get on.'

'We'll catch up real soon, I promise.' Rachel sensed there was a lot going on under the surface with Eve just now.

'Yeah, of course. Go. Go. You're needed elsewhere.'

The girls shared a quick hug and Eve hopped down out of the truck. Rachel quickly turned the Land Rover in the lane, her heart pulling as she saw her friend linger outside her cottage gate watching her go – her earlier joy in the flower shop now shaded by a look of sadness.

13

The days rolled on, never-ending tasks on the farm occupying Rachel and stopping her mind from drifting towards the dilemma with Tom. And thankfully Morag and her calf made a full recovery. The balmy early June weather broke with a stormy grey sky that turned into pelting summer rain. Typical, as they'd been hoping to start cutting the hay soon.

Rachel had heard from a customer at the Pantry that some of her errant sheep and their lambs had made a bid for freedom; they were now roadside and happily grazing the verges in the lane, apparently. So, she needed to go and herd them back, and check on the pasture's fencing a.s.a.p. Honestly, keeping the farm's borders and fence line intact felt like maintaining the Forth Rail Bridge: no sooner had you finished one repair than another turned up. Rachel dashed across to the farmhouse, popped a waterproof mac on, grabbed her wire-repair kit from the shed, and called Moss up to ride on the back ledge of the quad, ready to round up the escapees.

After securing the mischievous Petie – who was most likely the ringleader of the escape team – and his ovine pals back in their field, Rachel discovered the damaged area of fencing and set to work on a repair, crouching beneath a rather prickly row of hawthorns that made up part of the hedge line.

Just as she was concentrating on re-fixing some new wire, she heard a truck slow in the lane, just as another car approached. The vehicles paused. Strange, they didn't usually get much traffic on the lane at this time of day. Rachel looked up to see the dark grey of Tom's truck on her side of the lane. She was just about to stand up and call out to him when another voice sounded out.

'Hey!' It was Ben, calling to Tom from the other car.

'Hi, Ben.' Tom's toffee-warm tones; Rachel would recognise them anywhere. 'Where are you off to?'

'Just popping over to Brenda's Deli to get a few bits for lunch for the missus. All okay?'

'Yeah, so so.' Tom's voice sounded strangely flat.

'Hey, anything up, mate?' asked Ben.

Rachel remained crouched down in the verge. She could easily just spring up and say hello, but something kept her rooted to the spot.

'No, it's all okay, honest.'

'Come on mate, I can read you like a book. A problem shared is a problem halved and all that.'

'Ah, just women trouble . . . *ex* trouble, I mean. Honestly Ben, I don't know why I'm even *thinking* of getting married again.'

Rachel's breath caught in her throat. She didn't hear Ben's response, her heart plummeting like a stone in her chest, a horrid queasiness swirling in her gut. She stopped her work at the fence and slumped to the rain-sodden ground.

Tom . . . was he having second thoughts? Why was he suddenly questioning everything?

Oh, God.

Yes, she knew how much Tom's ex-wife, Caitlin, could wind him up. But she was in the past, wasn't she? And to think he was worried he was about to make another huge mistake . . . No wonder he hadn't answered Rachel's earlier text about them having 'a talk'. There were obviously other things on his mind.

Wet grass and mud dampened the seat of her jeans. Plops of rain spotted her face like tears. A part of her mind told her to calm down, to put it into context. Maybe he was just letting off steam. It was a throwaway comment. But it didn't *seem* throwaway, and it loitered uneasily in her mind.

Tom and Ben must have been talking more, but Rachel heard none of the next few seconds, as she was reeling from Tom's revelation. She felt panicked, finding it hard to breathe, like she was underwater. Eventually she caught Ben wrapping up the conversation.

'Well, see you later, mate.'

'You too, thanks for listening, eh?' said Tom. 'I'll see you about.'

She heard the clunk of a gear, the slight rev of Tom's truck engine, and the two vehicles started to move off down the lane.

Tom's words lingered ominously in Rachel's mind: '*Don't know why I'm even thinking of getting married again . . .*'

The storm clouds up above suddenly looked a whole lot darker.

14

'Mummy, can Daddy come and see me in my pretty bridesmaid's dress for your getting married day?' Later that day, Maisy was twirling around in her gorgeous cornflower blue, off-the-peg and in-the-sale, flower-girl frock.

It was one scenario that Rachel hadn't contemplated; having Jake, her wayward ex and Maisy's dad, there at her wedding to Tom. She certainly hadn't sent out an invitation to him.

'And Chelsea too. She'd love to see this. It's like a princess dress.' Maisy was still in motion, dancing on tippy-toes around the room.

Chelsea was Jake's latest girlfriend, though heaven knew if they were even still together – what with his track record, most likely not.

Jill and Eve gave Rachel an empathetic grimace: *awkward or what?* Charlotte, who was having her hemline pinned up, merely raised her eyebrows whilst they awaited Rachel's response.

The girls were having a trying-on session at the farmhouse, with Jill's close friend and hobby seamstress, Jan, taking final measurements and pinning here and there, so she could make some last-minute alterations to the bridesmaids' and flower girls' dresses. Eve had offered to do the sewing for these too, but Rachel had insisted someone else do this job at least. With all of Eve's work so far on Rachel's wedding dress, and the many beautiful craft creations she was making for the tables and the tipi, as well as her own business to run, Rachel was concerned that her friend might be at the point of burn-out.

'Umm . . . well, petal . . .' Rachel floundered. 'I'm not sure if he'd be able to come.'

'Why not?'

Rachel didn't want to go into the complications of adult relationships, and how having your ex at your wedding might be a little bit awkward. She tried to imagine having Caitlin there, no doubt cursing her from the pews, as Rachel made her way down the aisle. It really wouldn't be fair on Tom.

'So why don't you just ask him?' Maisy persisted. It all seemed so simple when you were six years old.

Rachel hated to disappoint Maisy, who was already looking confused. Oh crikey, would it be so awful if Jake turned up, even with Chelsea in tow? It'd be a busy day with so many other people there. It's not as though she or Tom would have to spend much time with them . . . and he was Maisy's dad after all.

All eyes were on Rachel now, Jan kneeling with a large pin poking from the side of her mouth, Maisy's eyes pleading. She felt her resolve floundering. Maisy saw so little of her father as it was, with him living hundreds of miles away. 'Well, I suppose we could ask him. But I can't make any promises that he'll be able to come.'

'Yay!' The beam on Maisy's face said it all. 'We can ring him tonight, and we can tell him all about my pretty dress, and the sparkly hair things . . . and the big tent and the lots of puddings.'

'Y-es.' Rachel was still trying to convince herself that she hadn't just made *the* most dreadful decision.

'Yippee.' Maisy grasped Amelia's hands and they did a little spin together, their lilac-blue skirts flying out in a whirl. The rest of the gathering couldn't help but smile, but if anyone looked at Rachel, they'd see that hers didn't quite reach her eyes.

'He said "yes".' The words reverberated around the kitchen.

Rachel hadn't long come off the phone call with Jake upstairs and was still rather incredulous.

'Oh crikey, right,' said Jill, floundering.

Unreliable, wayward, flippant Jake had only gone and said 'he'd love to come' to Maisy, backing it up with a, 'Yeah, I'll make it up there for your do' to Rachel as she took the mobile from her daughter at the end of the call. 'I was thinking of calling up to the farm soon and seeing Maisy again, anyhow,' he'd continued breezily.

'Bloody hell, Mum. That's so typical of Jake.' Rachel had popped down to fetch Maisy a glass of bedtime milk and found herself feeling all hot and bothered.

Jill was finishing drying the last of the supper dishes,

tea towel in hand. 'He might not make it yet . . .' They both knew her ex's tendency to let people down at the last minute.

'Well yes, but how am I going to explain his presence to Tom if he *does* go and turn up?'

Once she'd settled Maisy, Rachel resolved to call Tom and explain. But, would that just be stirring up more trouble between them? From what she'd heard in the lane earlier, Tom was already feeling wobbly about the wedding as it was. And Jake could still let Maisy down. Maybe there was no harm in keeping quiet for now, just holding this little secret close to her chest.

How would she feel if Tom asked Caitlin to the wedding, Rachel mused? Not that that was likely to happen in a month of Sundays, their relationship being much like World War III at the moment, with a huge post-divorce bomb about to erupt at any point.

Rachel lay wide awake in bed that night, tossing and turning for what felt like hours.

Tom's words in the lane were haunting her. Just as she tried to clear her mind and shake off the day, that scene in the lane reared its ugly head. Did he mean it? *Did Tom really want to bow out?*

What about those long, tender nights when they had lain together? The excitement at their engagement. Dancing with Maisy in the kitchen as they shared the news. Did it all suddenly mean nothing? Didn't he remember how they had held each other so tightly after that scary night of the snowstorm in the winter, how in spring they had shared midnight sticky toffee pudding in the lambing shed after saving that ewe and her new-born lamb, how life could be so beautiful? All those shared memories . . .

Somewhere out in the dark an owl hooted, a lonely sound, followed by the rustling of leaves blown on a blustery summer breeze on the old apple tree beneath her window. Rachel got up and wandered across to draw open the curtains, looking out over moonlit fields towards his farm. No lights were on there. Was Tom lying there thinking of her too? She hoped so.

The physical distance between them didn't help. If she could just reach across the bed to talk to him, maybe that would help, just like they would be able to do when they were a married couple – *if* that ever came to reality . . . What had happened to Tom to shake him so badly? Too many questions lay unanswered, taunting her tired mind.

Somehow, they had lost their way, and she needed to find a path back to him.

15

With all the recent stresses and strains, Rachel was in need of a wise and friendly ear and she knew just where to go.

They'd had a busy lunch session at the Pudding Pantry. Rachel and Jill were now a well-oiled team as they worked, Jill doing most of the prepping and plating up, Rachel serving and clearing. The white chocolate raspberry cheesecake Rachel had made that morning was proving particularly popular, along with Jill's lemon meringue pie. Business was growing steadily after the blips and bumps of starting out last year, and their name and good reputation was becoming known among the locals and tourists alike. Whilst life was looking stormy in one respect, at least the business was in fairly good health.

'Oh, I promised I'd pop some more eggs over to Granny's today,' Jill said to Rachel once all the customers were served. 'She called earlier; she's been doing some extra baking for the village coffee morning and has run out.'

'No worries, I'll go.' Rachel leapt at the chance. 'I feel like I haven't caught up with Granny for a while.'

'Okay then, love. I'm sure I'll manage fine here for a while.'

'It's after-school club for Maisy, so I'll collect her on the way back.' It was nearly three p.m., but with an hour in hand, that'd give Rachel time to 'bide a wee while' with Granny and have a much-needed chat.

'Of course. Send Ruth my love and tell her I'll pop in to see her in the next day or two.'

'Will do, see you soon, Mum.'

Granny Ruth's cottage was bright and cheery; adorned as it was with tall, pastel-shaded hollyhocks, pretty pink roses that arched around the front door, and old-fashioned snapdragons that sprang up in the borders and peeped out of the cracks in the low stone wall that bordered the lane.

Rachel parked up, feeling her heart lift a little already. Whatever problems you had in this world, Granny Ruth had the knack of putting them into perspective. She was also highly likely to have something tantalising and just-baked out of the oven.

Rachel knocked, and headed right on in, calling out, 'Hel-lo, it's just me, Rachel.'

The aroma from the kitchen didn't disappoint, and as Rachel poked her head around the door, she was welcomed by the sight and smell of warm, buttery baked scones.

'Oh, hello pet.' Ruth gave a smile as she rose a little stiffly, lifting the tray up to the kitchen side.

'Ooh, they look good, Granny,' Rachel said as she popped down the box of eggs.

'Thank you, pet. Aye, well, if you've got a few minutes to spare, lass, we can let them cool a little and then have one each with some jam and cream, what do you think? I've just made my first batch of strawberry jam this last week. I do like a blob of strawberry preserve on a scone, I must say.'

'With your own jam too, Granny? I think that sounds perfect.'

'Cream-tea time it is, then. Let's pop the kettle on, lass.'

Despite Granny Ruth busying herself around the kitchen, Rachel could see how stooped she had become over these past months, and her movements were strained. Also, she hadn't managed to totally get rid of the cough that had troubled her all winter. It seemed to flare up every now and again, and left her rather breathless at times. She watched her grandmother hold on to the side for a second or two to steady herself.

'Here, let me make the tea for us, Granny. You go on outside and have a seat on our favourite bench. It's lovely and warm out there.' Luckily the summer showers had dispersed today. 'I'll get sorted here and bring out a tray.'

Ruth looked at Rachel and nodded, accepting her granddaughter's offer.

'Aye, it has been a busy day so far. I've been down helping at the coffee morning for the old folks.'

Rachel couldn't help but grin; Granny said 'old folks' as though she certainly *wasn't* one of them, despite her eighty-one years.

The kettle soon came to the boil and Rachel set out a tray with china cups and saucers, a jug of cold milk and a pot of loose-leaf tea, just as Granny would have made it herself. She joined Ruth at the wooden bench, nestled at the back of the cottage, that overlooked the valley. Everything was so lush and green, vibrant in the early June sunshine. Rachel set the tray on the little wrought-iron table beside them.

'Gorgeous day, isn't it, lass? I'm so glad for my garden. So, how are you? Tell me all.' Granny's blue eyes crinkled into a warm smile.

'Oh fine. Busy, as you can imagine, with the farm, the Pantry, the wedding . . .' She edged cautiously to the root of her concerns. 'All go, really.'

'Yes, I bet. The wedding day is coming around so fast.'

'I know . . .' Rachel couldn't help the crease in her brow.

'So, pet. What's on your mind?' Ruth could read her like a book.

'Oh, I don't know. I'm just so busy trying to get everything organised. I just want it all to go right for everybody, you know . . .' She was still skirting away from her real fear; terrified that Tom was having second thoughts.

'Tell me about your wedding day, Granny?' Rachel

continued, suddenly wondering why she had never asked this before.

'Oh well, there's a question. I remember it like it was yesterday. My dress was just beautiful, I felt a million dollars, it was to-the-floor and a lovely satin. I had a long veil – they were all the fashion then, you see – and a bouquet of yellow and white roses. It was such a chilly April day, though, nothing like this nice June weather we're having now, and I was freezing standing outside the church having umpteen photos with Grandad Ken. Who,' she said with a poignant smile, as the memories flooded back, 'looked so dashing in his smart black suit and yellow tie.' She blushed a little and continued to tell Rachel how all the locals in the little Scottish border village came out to watch, and there was a big tea party back at the village hall. 'I'll have to fetch out the old photo album next time you pop by, Rachel.'

'That'd be lovely. So, what was your wedding cake like, Granny?' Rachel was enjoying losing herself in Granny's lovely memories.

'Oh, quite traditional, lass. Two tiers of white-iced fruit cake. No one thought of using sponge back then. Lasted longer, and was often the same recipe as our Christmas cake. Mother made mine, Great-Granny Tessa, aye, she was a good baker. Lovely and moist her fruit cake was. She'd been feeding it for weeks – splash of brandy and a nip of whisky, if I remember rightly. Decorated so pretty it was, with a beading of icing around each layer. Hah yes, and one of those little model bride and grooms on the top with fresh flowers, tiny yellow roses they were . . . I think there was enough to feed the whole village.'

'Sounds perfect.' On the contrary, Rachel's life felt far from perfect right now. 'Oh Granny, it's all a bit of a mess . . .' Her tone changed completely as her fears threatened to spill over. 'I'm so worried.'

'Oh lass, it's not unusual to feel a bit shaky just before your wedding day. It's a big thing, or at least it should be: a lifelong commitment. Although, I have to say, some of the young folk these days seem to think of it as a throwaway commodity . . .'

Rachel took a sip of her tea, as the thought dawned on her that Tom had already thrown away one marriage. Was he right to feel so wary about the next? Was she acting like some romantic fool, blinded to reality? Rachel sighed, trying to smother her fears. She loved Tom so very much, but was love enough? He'd made her feel better than she had in such a long time . . . experiencing emotions and sensations that she hadn't ever imagined she could. He made her feel complete. But to him was she just a spare part? *Arrrgh.* Those words she'd overheard in the lane had sent everything spiralling into uncertainty. She knew she should be trying harder to ask Tom directly, she should probably be banging on his farmhouse door, but that seemed too scary a prospect right now . . . what if it was true? She was frightened of what his response might be.

'Oh, Granny, there's so much going on . . . and I'm

worried about Tom. How he feels about me . . . about the wedding,' she finally blurted out.

'What's been happening, pet?' Granny's warm tones soothed.

'So, I was mending the fence by the road, yesterday . . . I was on the other side, out of sight, and I heard Tom pull up, he was talking to Ben. I know he's having a rough time with Caitlin as she's a real pain at the best of times, but . . . oh, it hurt so much to hear it, Granny . . .' Rachel paused.

Ruth looked on kindly and listened, waiting for Rachel to find the words.

'He said . . . he said that he couldn't believe he was even thinking of getting married again.' There, it was out.

'Oh, dear lassie, it sounds as though he was just feeling exasperated, that's all. That Caitlin woman . . . well, there's not many folk that I don't take to, but I never did warm to her when she was living here in the village. No, I didn't much like her, if I'll be honest. She was always one to pick fault in others, and never judged herself on the same terms. I remember her having a go at Brenda in the deli once, for not stocking her favourite olives. What a palaver over nothing. It was her tone, as though we were a load of country bumpkins out here.'

'Oh . . .' Rachel was still feeling at a loss. Caitlin didn't sound a very nice person. She hadn't really got to know her – or seen a lot of her – when she was married to Tom, being too busy with a young baby at the time.

'Of course Tom loves you, lassie. You can see it plain as day from the way he looks at you. And you're a good match, the pair of you. Don't let something like this unsettle the apple cart. And if you're fretting, why don't you just ask him about it? I'm sure he'd be upset if he thought he'd hurt you, by saying something like that in the heat of the moment.'

'I suppose.' Rachel took a bite of her cream scone, but it didn't taste half as good as it should have done – emotions stealing her appetite. 'There's something else too . . . All the wedding arrangements and everything, it's all bustling on around me, and that's kind of nice, but I can't help but feel sad too.'

'Oh, pet.' Ruth seemed to know what was coming.

'There'll always be someone missing, Granny.'

'Aye.' Ruth nodded her head in understanding. 'It's true. But life must go on, Rachel. Your dad wouldn't want to be spoiling your big day for you now, would he.'

'But . . . he should be there, walking me down the aisle, my arm linked through his. Giving me away. Making his father-of-the-bride speech.' Rachel's heart felt sore just thinking about his absence.

'Yes, he should. But that cannot be, pet. You need to keep remembering him, of course, and it might be difficult at times on that day especially, but you also need to make sure you have a damned good time and celebrate your wedding with your family and friends. That's what he'd want for you.' Ruth laid a gentle, stoical hand on Rachel's shoulder. 'We'll get by just fine, and we'll be sure to have a lovely day of it.'

Rachel gave a slow sigh, took a sip of fragrant tea, and looked out across the green curves of the valley. Although she knew that Granny was probably right, somehow, she just couldn't shake her feelings of unease over what the future held.

16

Arriving back at the farmhouse, after picking Maisy up from her after-school club, Rachel found Jill and Daniel looking rather cosy at the kitchen table. Argh, that was all she needed right now. Having talked about her dad with Granny Ruth just before, his absence felt especially raw. It wasn't that she didn't like Daniel – he was a nice enough guy – but seeing him sitting there, in Dad's place, his long legs stretched out, relaxed, it just felt all wrong to Rachel.

She spotted Mum pull her hand away from Daniel's across the table top.

'Really, Mum. You're acting like a pair of teenagers.' The words were out before Rachel knew it. She realised she was behaving like a surly teenager herself, and tried hard to stop the frown that was threatening to break out across her face, but today of all days she didn't need to have this new relationship rubbed in her face. She missed Dad so much. Wasn't Mum feeling that too? How was it so easy for her to move on?

'Rachel,' Jill warned, her grimace saying it all.

'Hi, Rachel, Maisy,' Daniel ventured, tactfully ignoring Rachel's spikiness, even though the air in the kitchen could have been cut with a knife.

'So, how was Granny?' Jill said, moving the conversation on and deciding to behave like the adult in the room.

'Oh, umm, she was in pretty good spirits. Though she's still got a bit of a cough hanging on.'

'Hmm, she's never been quite right since that bad spell last winter. We'll have to keep a careful eye on her.'

'Yeah, we will.'

'I'll watch her if you like, Grandma?' Maisy offered, bless her.

'Well that'd be good, Maisy. We'll all keep an eye out for Granny Ruth, shall we? Tea, love?' Jill turned to Rachel, hoping the offer of a cuppa would be an olive branch of sorts. 'The kettle's just boiled.'

'Umm, I've only just had one. I think I'll crack on and do my early evening checks on the animals before supper.' Rachel didn't feel quite like cosying up in the kitchen with Mum and Daniel right now. She knew she was feeling out of sorts, and some fresh air and a job to do was what she needed. A new focus for her thoughts. 'Maisy, do you want to come with me or stay with Grandma?'

'Hmm, are there any cupcakes, Grandma?'

'I think there might be. There were some chocolate ones left from the Pantry today.'

'I'll stay.'

'Cake trumps everything else, does it? That's my girl. Okay, I'll just get my wellies on and jump on the quad. I'll not be too long – if all's well out there, that is.'

'All right, love. See you later.'

'Bye, Daniel,' Rachel managed to say politely.

With the handlebars held tightly, the quad engine revving beneath her, and the fresh Northumberland wind in her hair, she began to feel a little better. Whatever her problems, this place, the hills, helped settle her. Big skies (today's was an ultramarine blue with just a few puffy wisps of cloud), undulating valleys, and pastures that morphed higher up into moorland. There was an amazing sense of space and freedom here. The valley rolled away below her now as she roared up the bank, pausing the vehicle at a rise to take in the view; those curves and folds of vibrant summer greens, dotted with her cattle and sheep. The hay fields near the farmhouse had grown long and were nearly ready to cut. She hoped the recent good weather would hold out for that.

She headed to the top fields where her flock were happily grazing. Rachel liked to do a check twice daily, early morning and evening. Mostly things were fine on the farm at this time of year, but there could be problems with minor injuries, lameness from issues with their hooves being a common ailment in her flock of ewes. And she liked to know that the water troughs out in the fields still had their supply flowing freely.

After trimming a sheep's hoof and cleaning it with her purple antibacterial spray, Rachel got back on the quad bike and drove slowly around the hillside to check on the rest of the flock. All seemed well thankfully, with the other ewes and lambs enjoying the sunshine and settled weather. Heading back down the bank, she caught sight of Tom's neighbouring farmhouse in the valley – her potential future home.

She'd been sheltering behind the cover of text messages the last day or so. Suddenly the urge to go and see him, to feel his arms around her, was overwhelming. She knew it was no good hiding from her fears, not when they were getting married in only four weeks' time. And actually, looking down at his solid stone-built farmhouse, maybe it wouldn't be so bad after all, just to move in, give it a try, see how she and Maisy settled? After all, that little cosy scenario with Dan and Mum had felt pretty awkward in the kitchen back at Primrose Farm. Maybe Jill needed a little space and privacy too.

Yes, Rachel resolved to go and see Tom. They could chat about all that, and maybe she might find the words to say how she'd felt overhearing him and Ben talk, get all that off her chest and give him a chance to explain. She felt lighter, more positive, as she took the track that crossed her farm and led to Tom's land. Arriving at his yard a few minutes later, she was relieved to see his grey truck parked up outside the house. She might even be able to broach the matter of Jake being at the wedding too. And then . . . well, they could reconnect in the loveliest, sexiest way she could think of.

She leapt off the quad, with a bounce in her step, rapped on the door that led into the kitchen, and waltzed in.

'Hey!' She gave a beam of a smile and saw Tom on the phone pacing the flagstone tiles.

He gave a nod of acknowledgement, and the tightest of smiles, then continued his conversation. The dip of a frown was etched into his forehead.

It might well be work, she reasoned, problems with suppliers or equipment maybe, which often led to all sorts of frustrations. Not to be deterred, Rachel went ahead and filled the kettle to get some coffee ready.

'Okay, well, keep me posted,' Rachel heard, even though Tom's voice was low. 'Thanks for your advice.' He pursed his lips together as he turned off the mobile.

'Hi . . . sorry about that.' He seemed distracted as he ran his hand through his longer-than-usual, chestnut-brown wavy hair.

'It's all right. Coffee?' Rachel gave him the chance to come down from the conversation. Maybe he'd open up about it in a minute or two. She spooned instant coffee into two mugs.

Tom stayed silent. He didn't look at all happy as he stared across the kitchen into some void.

'Everything all right?' Rachel ventured after a few more moments.

'Ah . . . been better.'

'Wanna talk about it?' She passed him a steaming mug.

'No, not really.' He sounded distant; wherever Tom was, it wasn't in this kitchen with Rachel.

'Oh . . . Tom,' Rachel wanted to hold him, kiss him,

bring him back to the present, but he seemed so damned bristly that she daren't. 'Is it to do with the farm?'

'Yes, it's to do with the bloody farm. If I have any sodding farm left at the end of it.'

'Caitlin?'

He visibly flinched. 'Who else . . .?'

Tom's bitter ex was obviously rearing her head again. Despite a generous divorce settlement, she'd been out to get more from the farm since Christmas, claiming that she'd been handed a raw deal in the split. Tom suspected she was just out of cash, flashing it around too freely on fancy holidays and expensive meals out.

'Oh,' sighed Rachel. Caitlin was never good news.

She risked walking over to him. He'd already placed his mug absently on the side, so she wrapped her arms around him as she looked him in the eye. 'I'm here for you, you know that. If I can help, tell me how, my love?' But he felt stiff within her embrace, and his eyes had a coolness that she'd not seen before.

'I've damn well given her enough already . . . more than enough. There's no point raking over it, Rach.' He sounded bitter, angry. It was no wonder he was frustrated, but it felt as though he was shutting Rachel out.

His earlier haunting words suddenly rang true, as he stood taut in her arms: '*I can't believe I'm even thinking of getting married.*'

'Tom, I wanted to ask . . .' She faltered.

'What is it?'

She tried to muster the courage to follow through and

ask him about that conversation on the lane with Ben, but the words failed her.

'It's OK, it's nothing.'

But she wouldn't let Caitlin win, no way. Rachel wasn't the same person; she was nothing like his ex. She was totally different – kinder than that, stronger than that. And . . . she loved Tom so much. It was hard seeing him hurting like this. Her arms reached around to stroke his back tenderly and she gazed up at him for a few seconds, hoping for some connection. He stayed close physically, but mentally he seemed distant. Maybe now was the ideal time to offer her olive branch and tell him she was prepared to move in there with Maisy, to give living there a go. That should cheer him, surely.

'Tom, I've been thinking. About where we will live, after the wedding. You're right, Primrose Farm will be crowded with Mum there . . . and with Daniel about at times. So, Maisy and I will be happy to come here and live with you.' She smiled, even though her words felt strange on her lips, the reality hitting home that she would finally be leaving her beloved farm.

'Hah, there might not even be a bloody farmhouse left by the time she's finished with me. She'll be after half of that too.'

'Tom . . .' Rachel swallowed hard, feeling hurt. She'd thought he'd be pleased that she'd come around to his way of thinking, that she wanted to be there with him, and would make that move with Maisy too, but he still seemed irked about friggin' Caitlin. Crikey, there was *no* point discussing where they were going to live now, not with him in this mood, and she didn't dare mention about Jake coming to the bloody wedding – that'd fire Tom right up again for sure. And the chance of some steamy making-up romance in the bedroom seemed to be absolutely nil.

'Well, I thought you might be a bit more pleased about us moving in. I'm trying here, Tom, but you've got to give me something back.' Rachel slammed half a cup of coffee down her throat, annoyingly scalding herself, and then turned on her heels and marched out, launching the words, 'Let me know when the bear with the sore head is out of its cave!' as she slammed the door.

17

'Good morning to you, Rachel. And how's our lovely bride-to-be today?' Frank doffed his tweed cap as he entered the Pudding Pantry.

'I'm fine thanks, Frank.' There was no point being down in the dumps – not in front of the customers anyhow. And Rachel hadn't even told her mum about yesterday evening's scenario at Tom's. Jill was having a baking morning over at the farmhouse to keep up the supplies, so Rachel was solo just now. She busied herself making Frank his coffee, just as he liked it, with warm milk and one heaped spoonful of sugar.

'Well, the weeks are surely skipping by. It won't be long at all until the big day,' Frank continued chirpily. 'I'm very much looking forward to it, I must say. I'll have to get my best suit out and dusted off.'

'Hmm, yeah.' Rachel swallowed a lump that had formed in her throat. After yesterday's antics, who knew what might happen? Her head had been spinning all night, trying to make some sense of it. Was Tom so fed up that he might really just jack it all in? Give up on their relationship because of the shitty first one he'd had?

'Can I tempt you with any of our baking this morning, Frank?' Rachel needed to focus on something else.

'Go on then, try me. What's on the specials today?'

'Well, we have some just-baked honey cake.' (Jill had been up early baking this morning.) 'There's also a ginger pudding, chocolate melt-in-the-middle puddings, some strawberry shortcake . . .' The local strawberries were in season, plump and juicy. 'Our usual selection of scones and teacakes. Oh, and there's an almond and raspberry flan.'

'Spoilt for choice as always . . . ooh, I think I'll go with the ginger pudding. That'll take me back. My mother used to make a delightful one, and I'm sure yours will be just as good.'

The cakes and bakes were always freshly made at Primrose Farm in the farmhouse kitchen Aga, and there was usually a 'special' or two on the menu at the Pudding Pantry, to make the most of seasonal ingredients and to keep the selection interesting. Jill loved trialling new puddings, often scrolling through the pages of the family's Baking Bible, or taking a look at Mary Berry's or Delia's recipes for inspiration. Rachel enjoyed baking too when she got the chance; it made a refreshing change from her farm work. Carrot cake and cheesecakes were her speciality, and she'd made the melt-in-the-middle puds.

She plated up a generous portion of ginger pudding, which smelt all tangy-sweet ginger as she spooned into it, serving it with a small jug of double cream on the side. 'There you go, Frank. Enjoy.' She delivered it to the gentleman's favourite spot by the window overlooking the valley, where he was sitting looking very comfy with the local broadsheet set out before him.

'Thank you, lass. I'm sure I will. It looks delicious.'

Shortly afterwards, two young mums from the village appeared with pushchairs and hungry toddlers in tow, shortly followed by Denise and Christine from the local WI group, who were also regulars at the Pudding Club.

'Morning,' said Denise. 'And how are all the wedding plans going, pet? It's what . . . only three-and-a-half weeks to go?'

Not another wedding well-wisher. 'Yes, not long at all,' Rachel chirped out a reply, in the hope of sounding cheery, though her heart felt as if it was currently lurking somewhere down near her shoes.

Their wedding was evidently the hot topic of conversation in the village right now. Rachel suppressed a groan, smiled sweetly, and held back the urge to give up and lie down behind the glass-fronted pudding counter or hide behind the coffee machine.

'And how's your lovely fiancé? Haven't seen him about for a while,' added Christine.

'Oh fine. All good. Just perfect,' Rachel lied. Would he turn up for his bacon roll elevenses today, she wondered? And more to the point, *would he actually even make it to the church at this rate? A wedding without a groom, now that would be interesting.* Her heart felt as though it was sinking.

'So, ladies, what can I get for you?' She needed to move on from all this wedding chitchat.

Rachel felt relieved when they ordered, enabling her to tootle off, make their teas, and escape from the verbal firing line for a little while at least. It wasn't their fault, the villagers were just getting excited about the wedding event to come, which was evidently a highlight on the Kirkton calendar. How were they to know things were rocky between the two of them just now?

Jill arrived with a freshly baked Victoria sponge, sandwiched together with cream and fruit. 'Ooh, that looks good, Mum,' commented Rachel, as the smell of sponge and sweet strawberries wafted by.

'Thanks, love.'

With all the wedding chatter still clamouring in her ears, and Jill back on hand to take the Pantry helm, Rachel saw her chance of escape, even if it was only for a half-hour or so. 'Is it okay if I nip out for a short while? Everybody's served and happy just now. It's just I've noticed the milk's running a bit low and I – er – need to pick up some fresh fruit for Maisy's packed lunches.'

'Yes, that'll be fine, love.'

'Anything else we need at all?'

'Hmm, I'm nearly out of baking powder, so perhaps a tub of that.'

'No problem. I won't be long.'

Rachel's idea of getting a little space to clear her head backfired in the queue at the village stores.

'Oh, hello Rachel. Not long now until you tie the knot. I'm so looking forward to it . . . even bought a new hat,' said Susan Davenport, one of her mum's acquaintances, who had crept up behind her. Blimey, they were even sneaking up on her in the shop.

And then at the till: 'Hi Rach, how are the wedding plans going? I bet you're all excited now!'

'Thrilled,' she answered on autopilot, passing over her bag of apples, satsumas and a large carton of milk, and feeling distinctly cornered.

She needed a place to go, somewhere quiet, somewhere nearby, just to gather her thoughts. But where? And then it dawned on her . . . At the same time, she spotted the bucket of fresh flowers placed beside the till. A bunch of cheerful yellow roses called out to her. 'I'll take these, too.'

Yellow roses, yes, how fitting. The very same colour that Granny Ruth had chosen for her wedding day.

'Thank you.' And off she set on her way.

Dappled sunlight and shade, the soothing twitter of bird-song, the smell of recently mowed grass. Rachel made her way through the churchyard, knowing just where she was headed.

She found the marble headstone and brushed a hand gently along the top of it. It felt cool beneath her touch. 'Hello, Dad.'

Of course, he wasn't really here, not any more. If anything, the essence of him was there on the farm still, up high in the hills, lingering in the yard, and in the valley. The places he loved so much . . . But occasionally she was drawn to come here too; it was always calm, a place to chat unhindered. She tidied the grave, pulling out some tufts of grass that had rooted amongst the granite stones. Then she took the roses from their wrapper and laid them there; immediately they gave the sombre space a splash of colour.

'Just me,' she continued softly, 'Feeling a bit cheesed off really, Dad . . . if you must know.' And her thoughts took over: Tom, Eve, Mum and Daniel . . . oh, that seemed a bit weird thinking of the two of them here. She uttered a silent, 'Sorry, Dad.' But she had to face up to all that was happening of late, and for Mum and the others it sometimes felt as though life was moving on, Dad left in the past.

'Miss you.' She traced her fingers once more along the cool grey marble, and then sat herself down on the grass beside him. 'To the moon and back . . .' Bedtime stories of Nutbrown Hare filled her mind . . . her dad sitting beside her on her duvet back home. She found herself fighting back tears, and then she realised she didn't have to. It was just her and Dad, and a brown and red robin perched on the stone wall a few metres away. The tears began to flow, and then finally to slow again.

It's all right, our lass . . . Dad's voice, strong in her mind. *It's all right to move on, to let yourself be happy.*

'And Tom? What a mess that is right now . . .'

He'll come around. But you two need to keep talking.

Like you didn't, she thought, ironically. Her dad had never opened up about his depression, those heavy burdens, and it had killed him. Rachel would never forget that, nor the day that they found him. Her poor, poor dad.

Exactly, lass . . . Like I didn't . . . and look where that got me.

Rachel's gaze drifted across to the old stone church. Gosh, they'd be here for the wedding in just a few weeks, with Rachel walking down the church aisle. Well, they had better be . . . She needed to make sure she and Tom worked through this horrid glitch. It was true, hiding from your problems never made them any better.

The earth beneath her legs and bottom felt solid, grounding. She was alive, and she too needed to find a way to move forward. She felt the warmth of the sun on her face, through her clothes, the mossy grass soft and pleasant beneath her, and she closed her eyes for a few mellow seconds. The birdsong of a blackbird trilling nearby, leaves rustling in a gentle breeze. Life was still sweet, even if it did keep throwing up these damned curveballs at her. She just needed to find her way through them.

'Love you, Dad.'

I love you too, sweetheart.

It was time to head back to Primrose Farm.

18

EVE

Eve was sitting at her sewing machine at her dining-room table. Heaped before her was a mini mountain of craft items: scraps of material, felt, buttons, cotton thread in all colours.

She was currently working on some more bunting to decorate the tipi for Rachel's wedding – they'd need plenty to cover the large space. Eve had chosen pretty offcuts of materials in vintage spots, stripes and florals to complement the wedding colour scheme. She was now stitching the gorgeous flags onto a thin white band, ready for hanging. Despite her own troubles, she couldn't help but smile; she was so looking forward to being maid of honour for her best friend. It was going to be such a special day.

There was also a big craft fair coming up very soon, at which Eve had booked herself a stall. It was to be held at a village hall at a popular spot on the coast, and last year she'd done well there. She needed to make lots more of her felt soft toys, some extra knits – cute little children's jumpers and cardigans. The pressure was on and she needed to make sure she had plenty of stock ready.

There were other pressures on her too. She had heard that a certain someone else was going to be exhibiting there too . . . and though she kept trying to put him to the back of her mind, or out of it altogether, that was proving nigh on impossible. In fact, her stomach was a tangle of nerves and – she had to admit – also bubbling with excitement at the thought of seeing him again.

They had exchanged a few short chatty texts over the past couple of weeks, mentioning that they were booked into this craft event. Aiden had said he was looking forward to seeing her again, which made her heart give a little leap when she read it, and she noted the one little 'x' that came after that. It was all fairly innocent, she told herself, just friends with a shared interest in arts and crafts. She'd even left the texts on her phone. But why the hell did it feel so much more than that? Why was she getting all churned up about it, if it was just friends? And why did his face, his striking blue eyes, and handsomely scruffy dark-blond hair keep appearing in her mind? Just thinking about him now left a tremble in her fingertips, and her sewing went skewwhiff, with the next bunting flag sewn on wonkily, dammit. She paused, took a slow breath, and looked up and out of the window for a while at the drifting summer clouds in the sky.

Aiden was a local artist who painted seascapes, mostly in oils. Bold, dramatic and moody paintings that captured the stormy north coast seas. She glanced at the picture that she had recently hung on the wall across from her work station; Aiden's painting. It captured, uniquely, the arc of the waves, the sea spray. It was as if she was there watching the waves crash to shore. She'd bought it at the last craft fair they had both attended. A small treat for herself. She hadn't told Ben how much it had cost, or anything about the artist behind the image. She felt a flash of guilt. This man had certainly put a storm in Eve's heart, and she wondered where all these crazy new feelings were taking her.

Bloody hell, she needed to get a grip. She spotted the family photo of the three of them there on the mantlepiece, down at the beach a year or two ago, a happy, sunny picture of better days. She was a married woman. Her relationship with Ben was okay, really. It was fine, mostly calm, but it was just so *predictable* – boring, even. Ben watching football on a Saturday after work, followed by a takeaway for two in front of the telly. And then, to top it all, whilst she had been hoovering the other day, she'd found a heap of his toenail clippings on the floor by his side of the bed . . . *really*. How was *that* the most exciting thing that had happened in their bedroom of late?

Their marriage was a safe haven, no doubt. But why did it feel almost *too* safe; as if they were going through the motions most of the time. Crikey, they hadn't even kissed in months, not a proper passionate kiss. And sex, well it had become infrequent and, to be honest, pretty uninspiring. Her mind drifted then; how might it feel to make love with Aiden? She felt a mix of yearning and guilt swirl in her stomach just letting her imagination stray like that.

She slammed the thought down. What was she even thinking? She was married to Ben, for goodness' sake. She had a gorgeous little girl to think of – their Amelia. She wasn't the sort of woman to have a fling, to hurt them all, not on some selfish whim. But the guilt sat tinged with curiosity, the 'what ifs', the 'grass might be greeners'. Perhaps it was laced with a yearning for a different kind of life.

Okay, okay . . . stop these stupid, crazy notions. She had work to do, bunting to finish. Felt toys to make. This dithering was helping no one. She only had an hour and a half left before Amelia was due to be dropped off from the school bus. She put the strand of slightly wonky bunting to one side and started to cut out the felt pattern for her Mr Fox, who was to wear a smart tweed waistcoat, and another for Sammy Squirrel with his red spotted bow tie.

A message pinged onto her phone. She pulled it across from its position on the table top, wondering if it might be Aiden:

Hi Eve. Everything okay with you? It was Rachel, of course it was.

Yeah, not bad. How about you? She remembered Rachel had been wrestling with the 'where to live post-wedding' scenario the last time they had talked.

Okay.

Even by text the word sounded flat.

And Tom?

A pause and then: *Things are a bit difficult, to be honest. He's a right Mr Grumpy just now.*

Oh, sorry hun. Do you want to call round? x

Can't just now. Heading back to work at the Pantry. x

Okay, I'll catch you soon then. Why don't you pop round when you get a few mins later on?

Thanks. Might do that. x

Eve went back to her crafting with a sigh. She wasn't the only one with troubles on her mind, by the sounds of it. She hoped her friend was all right. And suddenly she felt awful, for there she had been mooching on about some other guy, when all this was going on with Rachel and Tom. The two of them shouldn't be arguing, no, they should be all excited about their upcoming wedding, and feeling well and truly loved-up right now, with just over three weeks to go. Poor Rachel; she'd sounded worried. It wasn't like her to send a message like that – she was no drama queen. Eve well knew that her friend would rather keep things to herself most of the time.

She put down the material for the small waistcoat. She'd go and see Rachel right now, find out what was wrong and cheer her up. Maybe she could go and see Tom herself, too, and help iron things out between them. She took their friendship and her maid-of-honour role seriously, and it was time to spring into action. She packed away her materials and popped the cover over her trusted Singer sewing machine that her mother had passed on to her. She'd come back later and crack on again, maybe work late into the evening if needs be to get some more of the toys done, but right now her friend needed her, and some things were more important.

She hopped into her little hatchback car, wondering if anything further might have happened to make Rachel feel down. It was probably just a misunderstanding or some pre-wedding tension building up – but really, those two were *so* made for each other.

Stepping into the Pudding Pantry, Eve smiled supportively across at Rachel who was serving behind the counter. A smile that said: 'I'm here for you.' She stood to one side for a few moments, allowing a couple to finish ordering.

'Hey, what are you doing here? I thought today was a full-on craft-making day?'

'It is . . . well, it was. Thought I'd come and say "Hi", take a quick break and see how you are?' Eve tried to keep her tone light, realising it would be hard for Rachel to share details of her private life whilst at work.

'Ah, well, I'm okay. And, it's been pretty busy here. All go.' Rachel was on fake-cheery autopilot, and Eve suddenly felt a bit daft having turned up to save the day, when Rachel clearly wouldn't be able to talk about what had been going on right now.

'Umm, well, I'll have a coffee please. Actually, can you make that a cappuccino,' Eve said, adding quietly,

'And if you manage to get a couple of minutes free, come across.'

'Okay.' Rachel managed a brief, keep-your-chin-up smile.

Eve headed for the table that was tucked away in the far corner; a place where it might be safe for the friends to talk for a minute or two, should chance allow it. 'I'll just be over here,' she said breezily. She sat for a few moments, taking in the cosy ambience of the Pantry. With the fine weather, the barn door was flung open welcomingly. Sunlight shafted in, making the stone walls glow a warm, buttery shade of cream. Customers were chatting away whilst sipping their drinks, with ice creams and brownies, strawberry scones and an array of delightful puddings before them. Heavenly scents of cake, cocoa, butterscotch, rich coffee and fragrant tea filled the air.

Rachel bustled around for a while, and then just as Eve was nearing the bottom inch of coffee, she saw her friend wander over, her tea towel slung over her shoulder.

'Are you okay, hun?' Eve uttered in hushed tones. 'After that text, I've been a bit worried about you.'

Rachel looked around her and then took up a seat. 'Oh Eve,' she whispered, 'I'm feeling a bit calmer now, honest. I went to see Dad at the churchyard and, well, aired some things. But . . . I'm just so worried that Tom might be thinking of calling the whole thing off.'

'What? The wedding?' Eve's mouth dropped open.

'Yeah.' Rachel looked gutted.

'You're kidding. You two are like . . . well, cheese and biscuits. Ant and Dec. Crumble and custard. You're *made* to be together.'

'Yeah, well, try telling that to Tom right now, will you.'

With that, an old lady a couple of tables across coughed, catching Rachel's eye, then asking sweetly if she could have a refill of coffee.

'Yes, of course, no problem. I'll bring one across straight away.' Rachel got up, duty calling again. 'Maybe we can catch up later, yeah?'

Eve's head was still spinning with the news, and she went back to sipping the last of her cappuccino, trying to maintain a semblance of normality.

The two friends were so busy pretending to the tearoom clients that everything was fine, that neither of them had spotted Tom walking in through the door. He was heading for the counter. Rachel had her back to him, busying herself at the coffee machine. Jill was at the till, blissfully unaware of any of the previous day's dramas. Rachel hadn't yet broached the latest living arrangements with her, wanting it all to be settled with Tom first.

'Hello Tom, love. What can I get for you?' greeted Jill.

Eve looked up, startled, and saw Rachel freeze instantly.

'Ah, I'm actually here to see Rachel.' He sounded rather awkward.

Rachel turned and Eve could see her face was a shade paler than usual. 'It's really busy here just now, Tom. I'm in the middle of serving,' Rachel said brusquely.

'It's all right. I can wait.' He moved to stand near the open doorway, looking out.

Rachel stomped about pouring coffee into a cup, her eyes fixed firmly downwards, intent on the task in hand. She headed off down the barn towards the elderly customer, without glancing further at him.

Tom stepped gently into her path as she walked back. 'Look, I just came to say sorry . . . I shouldn't have spoken to you like that.'

'No, you shouldn't have.' Tom's words had cut deep, and Rachel looked so down. 'Look, Tom, this really isn't the time or the place.' Several customers were already looking up, curious as to the developments near the counter.

'Yes, I know this isn't ideal . . . but it couldn't wait.'

They stood silently for a second or two. 'Look, I'll come back later, when you're finished here. We need to talk, Rach.'

Eve stood up and found herself swiftly heading for the counter, ready for action. 'It's okay Rachel, I'll help out here for a while; looks like you two might need a bit of time.'

Rachel seemed to falter. 'Umm.'

'Go on,' Eve encouraged, thinking that if Tom was here apologising, then they could surely sort out their differences, whatever had gone on before.

'Okay.' Rachel took a slow breath, as if bracing herself.

Eve watched as the pair of them walked out of the barn and across to the farmhouse. She hoped to goodness they'd be able to put things right. Having her own relationship crumbling was bad enough, but she wouldn't stand by and see these two getting in a mess too.

19

'So . . .' Rachel stood in the middle of the farmhouse kitchen with her hands on her hips, bracing herself for what Tom was about to say.

'Okay, I spoke out of turn yesterday. I didn't mean it to come out like that . . .' Tom looked sheepish.

Rachel took a deep breath. She needed to know what was really going on with her fiancé, however hard it might be to take. 'If you're having doubts, then you need to be honest with me, Tom. Right here, right now. No more messing about. We've been friends for so long. The least we can be is honest with each other.' She felt sick as she waited for his response. Were all her dreams, her hopes, her new belief in romance after the past traumas with Jake – this new romance that was solid and truthful and passionate – about to be shattered once more?

'I know. That's why I'm here, Rach.' His voice was warm yet seemed to be tinged with sadness. Was he trying to let her down gently? *Oh, God.*

She grabbed the kettle from the hob, needing something to do, and began to fill it at the sink. Tom walked to stand behind her and, slowly, with his hands on her shoulders, turned her to face him.

'Rachel, it's so hard for me to let my real feelings show after all I've been through with Caitlin. It's been so hard to trust again . . . to love again.' He paused.

Rachel felt a tear crowd her eye, and gulped back a knot in her throat.

'Look, I didn't want you to find out before the wedding . . . I thought I could keep it to myself, to save us both the stress. I thought that'd be best.'

There was a stark silence as the two of them held each other's gaze, Rachel wondering where on earth this was going.

'What?' Rachel asked firmly, yet dreading his words to come.

'Caitlin has pursued the claim against me, the farm. There's a case coming up . . . soon. Very soon.'

'Oh Tom, why didn't you tell me all this . . .?' Although this was dreadful, Rachel also felt a jolt of relief. If this was it, the crux of the problem, there was hope for them. Yet, there still might be more to this . . .

'When's the case?'

'On the first of July.'

'The *first?*'

'I'm afraid so, yep.' Tom's brow furrowed.

What bloody shit timing. 'But, that's three days before our wedding!' Rachel suddenly had a sinking feeling that it was timed to perfection as far as Caitlin was concerned, as if she'd planned to stir up as much mischief as she could.

'Umm, yes . . . Caitlin always did have a knack of

choosing the worst possible timings for things,' Tom answered drily.

'Could you postpone the hearing? Contest it?' Rachel quizzed.

'I did think about that. But it will still be hanging over me . . . and I've been advised that the only way to contest it is to be there in court and tell them my side of the story. I'm sorry, Rach, but I just want it done and dusted, even if it is just before the wedding. Then maybe I can get on and finally relax, and we can enjoy our big day like we should.'

He was talking as if their wedding was still on. Rachel felt a rush of relief. Oh, thank heavens. But . . . would all this with Caitlin serve to remind him just how disastrous some marriages could be? His words from the lane were still taunting her.

'And you've been keeping all this to yourself?' Rachel tried not to spiral, focusing on the problem right in front of them for now.

'I didn't want to mention it, not in the lead-up to our wedding. You should be having fun, enjoying all the last-minute plans. But Christ, it's been feeling like a huge weight . . .'

'No bloody wonder you've been like a bear with a sore head.'

'Yeah, sorry. I guess I wasn't so good at keeping the emotions under wraps.'

'Tom Watson, if we are getting married, it's all about supporting each other, being there for each other.' She took a step closer towards him. He really needed to let her in if they were going to be Team Watson going forward.

He gave a cautious nod, and then took her into his arms. It felt good to chat, to feel like they were reconnecting. After a few precious moments, Rachel remembered that Mum and Eve were manning the fort at the Pantry. 'Tom, I'd really better get back over to the barn to help out. It's busy . . . and I know Eve had an awful lot on her plate today.'

'Yeah, that's okay.' He sounded a little disappointed, but not quite as despondent as before. 'Shall we catch up this evening? Maybe you could come over and I can cook?'

'Now *that* sounds perfect.' Rachel smiled broadly. 'Ah sorry,' she said distractedly as her phone started vibrating in her jeans pocket. 'I'd better just get this . . .' Rachel stepped back, fishing the phone from her pocket.

'No worries.' Tom lingered for a while, seeming reluctant to leave.

Rachel looked down at her phone. Glancing at the screen she saw the Caller ID; it wasn't Jill, oh no . . . it was Jake, Maisy's mostly missing father. Oh, good lord, talk about timing. She was tempted to let it ring out, but he was Maisy's dad, after all.

'Jake?'

She saw Tom frown out of the corner of her eye.

'Hey babe, how's it going?'

Babe? Really. It had been many a year since she'd been his babe, and even back then she'd hated the pet name.

'You okay?' he continued.

'Umm, yes, fine.' Try to be polite, Rachel, she told herself, for Maisy's sake.

'And how's my gorgeous little girl?'

'Yes, she's fine too. At school, right now.'

Tom stood watching. Rachel pulled a face, and mouthed, 'Sorry.' She wished Jake would get to the bloody point.

'Well, I thought I'd come up and see Maisy.'

'Right, okay . . .' But he was coming up for the wedding in three weeks' time anyway. Shite, she hadn't yet mentioned that to Tom either. All this was such a mess. 'So, when were you thinking of coming?'

'Uh, well, today.'

'*Today?*' Was she hearing right? Jake lived two hundred miles away.

'Yep, thought I'd take a trip up. See my little princess, you know.'

Rachel *didn't* know. What had happened to arranging things in advance? Letting them know first? Asking if it might be convenient just three weeks before her wedding? *Grrrrr.*

She saw Tom turn on his heels and head for the door. She held the phone away and called to him. 'I'll see you later, yeah?'

But Tom didn't turn around. Damn it. Jake sure knew how to spoil a moment.

'So, where are you?' she resumed, wondering what on earth was going on with her ex now.

'Here.'

'What do you mean, here?' She felt a little surge of panic.

'I'm in the village . . . in Kirkton. I've driven up this morning and checked into a B & B for a couple of nights. Needed a bit of a break, to be honest.'

She *really* didn't want to know what was happening in *his* life at the moment; there was enough going on in her own.

So, Jake, her irresponsible, wayward, commitment-phobe ex was here, and would no doubt be appearing on her doorstep very soon. Oh Jeez, that was the last thing she needed right now.

Just as she and Tom took one step forward, life pulled them another three steps back.

20

Jake's little grey van revved up the farm track, pulling to a stop outside the Pantry. Rachel gave a sigh, clearing the plates and cups from the table she was tidying with a bit too much gusto. A teacup went clattering to the floor. It was almost three thirty and she'd be going to collect Maisy from the school bus at any minute. Damn it, Jake would probably have to come too. This would be some surprise for Maisy – she hadn't even had a chance to warn her little girl yet.

'Hey.' Jake strolled into the tearooms with a big smile, slicking back his blond hair with his fingertips. His vivid blue eyes were still striking. But Rachel was immune to his boyish charms; she knew they were coupled with some very juvenile behaviour.

'Hello, Jake,' she said a little coolly.

'Hi, Rach, Jill. Good to see you.'

'Hello there, Jake.' Jill managed an awkward smile.

'So, where's my princess?'

'Ah, not quite back from school yet. I was about to walk down and fetch her from the minibus. I suppose you could come too.'

'Brilliant. I'll surprise her. She'll love that, won't she.'

Rachel hoped so, though she feared it might also prove a bit of a shock. Seeing a father who was mostly missing, out of the blue, could also be a bit overwhelming when you were only six years old.

'I'll head on down then, Mum. If that's okay?'

'Yes, get yourselves away. You won't want to be late.'

Rachel hung her spotted pinafore on the kitchen hook. 'Okay, let's go. It's just a short walk down to the farm entrance,' Rachel explained.

They fell into step alongside each other.

'So come on Jake, spill,' she hissed. 'What the hell are you doing here?' Rachel wanted to get this over with before Maisy joined them. With Jake there was always an ulterior motive, and she needed to know what it was this time.

'Coming to see Maisy, like I said.' He sounded affronted.

'And . . .? It's just so out of the blue, and you'll have to be back for the wedding in just a few weeks. That's if you're not crying wolf and backing out on Maisy.' Though she didn't particularly want him there herself, she knew her daughter would be mightily disappointed if he didn't make it for her starring flower-girl moment.

'I just needed a bit of time out, and seeing Maisy seemed a good way to spend it.' He did sound strangely genuine. In fact, he was almost deflated, not his usual full-of-bravado self at all.

'Oh, so, how have you been keeping then?' she asked.

'Ah, just great.' But it came out a little flat.

'And Chelsea? How is she?' On their last visit to the

farm back in the autumn, the pair of them had been all loved-up. But there had been no mention of her yet.

'Well, that's a bit tricky just now.'

Well, that was no surprise. Jake wasn't good at long-term relationships. 'You two still together?'

'Guess so. We've just had a couple of barneys . . . and that kid, Kelvin . . . man, he's been doing my head in.' Kelvin was Chelsea's nine-year-old son from a previous relationship.

'She hasn't chucked you out, has she?' The jigsaw seemed to be piecing together.

'Nah, nothing like that. Just needed a bit of time out . . . you know, sort my head space. Had a couple of days off, thought it'd be an ideal chance to come and catch up with my princess. Enjoy some quality dad–daughter time, you know.'

'Right.' Rachel could smell a commitment-phobe rat a mile off.

With that, came the phut-phut of the minibus up the winding lane, just as she and Jake reached the farm's entrance gate where the school bus dropped off. Eve was already standing there waiting for Amelia and gave Rachel a wide-eyed stare as if to say, 'What the hell is going on now?'

'Jake decided to have a trip up and visit Maisy,' Rachel explained, as calmly as she could.

'O-kay. Hi, Jake.' They knew each other from school days, Eve being in the year above the two of them. And Eve knew Jake from Rachel's many tears, from the tales of first kisses, the excitement of Rachel falling in love, and then being let down over and over . . . and being left pregnant at only eighteen. Eve had been there for her friend through it all.

The bus pulled up, with Amelia down the steps first, followed by Maisy – cardigan and dress askew – who jumped off the bus with her usual bounce, then ground to a startled halt.

'Daddy's come up to see you, for a surprise visit.' Rachel tried to bring her little girl up to speed.

Suddenly, Maisy was leaping forward and in her daddy's arms. It was touching to see, but also – for Rachel – tinged with a bitterness that he wasn't there more often for her. That he'd never really been there for either of them, in fact.

'So, have you missed your old dad, then?'

'Yes-s.' Maisy's voice was brimming with excitement.

'Now then, what shall we do? Your choice. I've got this evening and all tomorrow with you.'

'Hmm,' Maisy was thinking, a little overwhelmed by this unexpected arrival.

Tomorrow was Saturday, so Maisy and her dad could in fact spend all day together. Rachel wanted to be pleased for her little girl, but her overriding feeling was of apprehension.

'Well, you have a think on it, sweetheart, and then let me know.' Jake was trying to be accommodating at least.

Eve glanced over Jake's shoulder and mouthed 'Good luck' to Rachel, followed by a 'call me' hand gesture.

Rachel, Jake and Maisy were soon walking back up the farm track. Maisy, stuck like glue to her father's side, had the biggest beam on her face, with one hand in her daddy's and the other in her mummy's. For a minute or two, as they strolled, they looked like a happy family, but Rachel knew all too well that it was just a charade.

'So, you're up for the weekend then, Jake?' asked Jill, making polite conversation in the farm's kitchen, once she'd finished at the Pantry.

'Yeah, got a few days off. Been a tad quieter with the building company that I've been doing a bit of work for lately, so I thought I'd get up and visit this little sweetheart.'

'Where's your friend Chelsea, Daddy?'

Jake gave a small cough, 'Oh . . . well, Chelsea's real busy just now, so she couldn't make it up this time.'

'Ah, I see,' Jill responded.

She and Rachel remembered well his visit with his latest girlfriend, the petite, glamorous and white-trainered Chelsea, a few months back. The chickens had terrified her, the natural farmyard smells disgusted her, so the farm really hadn't been her ideal place to visit.

Maisy looked up at her dad with affection. She had ensured he was seated next to her at the kitchen table, where she was playing with her Jessie and Woody *Toy Story* characters, and her wooden farm. It had been handmade for her by Grandad Robert, soon after she'd been born, for her 'to grow into', and she certainly had. It was one of her all-time favourite toys. Jake was trying his best to actively join in, taking Woody off hopping away across the table to go and feed the cattle at one point (as directed by Maisy), whilst Jessie helped a sheep in labour. Rachel couldn't help but smile at that.

'Can Chelsea come next time, Daddy, to the wedding? To see me in my bridesmaid's dress? I like Chelsea,' Maisy piped up.

'Ah, well maybe. We'll have to see,' he replied, keeping his answer purposely vague.

Rachel was pleased at least that he wasn't making more promises he might not be able to keep.

'You can all come if you like. I'd like to see Kelvin too,' Maisy was persistent.

Rachel groaned inwardly. Not more unwanted guests.

Jake went quiet for a few seconds, rubbing a hand through his sandy-blond hair.

'You are coming, Daddy, aren't you? You did say so.' Maisy had folded her arms, a sure sign she was getting tense.

'Yes, yes . . . I'll be there, of course. When is it again?' He turned to Rachel.

'Three weeks tomorrow. The fourth,' she responded coolly, thinking the leopard hadn't changed his spots at all, had he.

'Ah yes, no probs, I'll be back for the big day, no worries, princess. And we'll just have to see about Chelsea, and uh, Kelvin, okay?'

'O-kay,' Maisy conceded.

'Would you like to join us for supper, Jake?' offered Jill politely, as she bustled about by the Aga. 'I've got a cottage pie to go in the oven and plenty of fresh veg. It'll easily do for four. I'm sure Maisy would like you to stay.'

Rachel gave an inner sigh, but conceded that Jill was doing the right thing. Although the relationship was somewhat strained between Jill, Rachel and Jake, Primrose Farm was always welcoming to visitors. Maisy's grandmother and mother also understood how important having some kind of an ongoing relationship with her father was for Maisy, too. They had to support that, even if that relationship was frustratingly infrequent and inadequate on his part. And, if he did stay for supper with them, then at least they could keep an eye on how things were going, see how Maisy was coping with it all, and field any awkward moments or questions. You never knew what Maisy might come out with!

Dinner was soon ready and they chatted amicably enough around the kitchen table, with Maisy filling in any gaps with her incessant chatter, trying to remember all the things she'd been doing at school and at home since her daddy had last visited seven months ago.

Supper was delicious, with tasty minced beef topped with cheesy mashed potatoes, accompanied by sweet young carrots, fresh from the vegetable patch, and spring greens. Mum was offering out little pots of lemon posset with raspberries on the side, when Rachel thought that she'd better send Tom a quick message, letting him know she'd be there around eight p.m., a little later than intended, but it couldn't be helped. After their heart-to-heart today, she had said she'd go across this evening, and she was really looking forward to seeing him. With Jake being about tomorrow now too, she absolutely wanted to be home for Maisy in the morning, so unfortunately there'd be no sexy sleepover there tonight. Oh well, they could wait in anticipation for that one. And soon, *very* soon, they'd be waking up every day together; how amazing would that be?

Rachel excused herself from the table, before they started their puds, and in the privacy of the hallway quickly sent the text. A message soon pinged back:

Okay, thanks for letting me know. I'll put the supper on hold for a little while. X

Rachel froze. *Supper?* Oh, no! With all the kerfuffle surrounding Jake's arrival, she'd totally forgotten that Tom had said he'd cook for her. Her stomach was pleasantly full with Jill's cottage pie. But she couldn't let him down, especially as it sounded as if he was making a real effort, and with things still so delicate between them . . . Okay, she'd miss out on pudding here and go and eat whatever Tom had prepared, that was it. It would be fine, if a bit stomach-busting. He'd never realise and she'd ask Mum to keep schtum.

She replied: *Just getting Maisy bathed and to bed. See you soon. Look forward to it! xx*

She came back to the dinner table with a forced smile as she spotted the dessert set at her place. 'Ah, that looks great Mum, but I might just give pudding a miss tonight.'

'You sure? That's not like you, Rachel. You usually love your sweet things.'

'Yeah, feel a bit full, and I do need to get across to Tom's soon. So, I'll head on up and start running Maisy's bath. And you, little miss, can pop on up as soon as you're finished.'

'Okay, Mummy.'

She hoped that Jake would take the hint and make himself scarce soon after his pudding too.

'Can Daddy do my bedtime story tonight, Mummy? I'd really like that.'

'Ah . . .' Rachel floundered for a second or two.

'Great, I can stay to do that for Maisy, no problem,' Jake chipped in cheerily, adding, 'Then you can get yourself all brushed up and ready to meet the hunk that is Tom.' There was a hint of sarcasm in his tone, or was it a touch of jealousy? That was weird, Rachel mused, as it had been years since they were last together. And he had been involved with several women since then.

'Oh, and I know where I want to go tomorrow, Daddy,' added Maisy, who'd obviously been pondering his earlier question. 'To the beach.'

'Well, that sounds great. The beach it is then, Mais.' He turned to Rachel, 'Is that okay with you, Rach?'

'Yes, it sounds a nice idea.'

'Do you want to come along?' he added, looking at Rachel with a sparkle in his eye.

'Ah, no, it's okay. I've got my shift to do at the Pantry.' Rachel couldn't imagine having a day out with Jake. They'd been distant for so long, and he'd hurt her badly, giving up on her and Maisy when the reality of becoming a parent had hit home. He hadn't even hung around for the birth, never mind for anything else. But here they were, six years on, and he was trying to be a part of Maisy's life again.

'Oh Mummy, but that would be so much fun . . . with you *and* Daddy there. Pretty please.'

'I do have work to do, Maisy.'

'Remember, Jan's in tomorrow to help out,' Jill chipped in. 'We could probably manage, you know.'

Blimey, they were ganging up on her now. She supposed she did need to get across to Warkton-by-the-Sea soon anyway, to collect the wedding-favour chocolates – and, she suddenly remembered that Eve had her craft fair event there tomorrow too; it'd be lovely to go and say hello and support her. So, perhaps she could tie that in, spend an hour or two doing her own thing, and then meet the two of them for fish and chips at the harbour. A happy compromise.

'Okay, okay . . .' and she told them her plan, which met with a squeal of delight from Maisy.

'Right then, let's go and get this bath run for you, Miss Maisy.'

After bubbles, splashing and bath-time fun for Maisy, during which time Jake helped Jill to wash up (miracle of miracles), her little girl was eager to get dressed in her pyjamas, and leapt into her bed, shouting out as loudly as she could, 'I'm ready for my story, Daddy!' She seemed so excited, bless her.

Jake's footsteps made their way up the stairs, and Rachel poked her head out of Maisy's room. She left them to it for ten minutes, hearing his lilting tones telling the tale, and Maisy with her many questions as the story unfolded. Rachel got herself freshened up for Tom's, with a slick of pale pink lipstick and some mascara. She sent another text to say she shouldn't be long now. Oh my, she was still feeling full. She hoped to goodness he hadn't made a big dinner.

She gave Maisy a goodnight kiss and tucked her in.

'I'm so looking forward to the beach tomorrow, Mummy.'

'Yeah, it should be good. Night, petal.'

'Night, Mummy. Night, Daddy.' And she smiled sleepily, as though she'd been longing to say those words together for a long, long time, before nestling down into her pillows.

'She's a good kid,' Jake said as they closed her bedroom door.

'Yeah, she is.' Rachel felt a little glow of pride.

When they reached the kitchen, Jake thanked them both for a lovely evening and then excused himself, saying it was time he headed back to his B & B. 'Well,' he confessed, 'perhaps via a quick pint at the Black Bull.' He gave a wink.

Rachel went to see him out at the doorstep. It was ten

to eight by then and she was aware of the time ticking away.

'Night, Jake.'

'See ya, Rach.' He faced her with a grin. 'We'll have a good day tomorrow.'

And suddenly it reminded her of years gone by, when they were both so young. Jake with his killer smile, always a bit of a charmer, a jack-the-lad. But hey, she well knew where that had got her. And though she would never for the world wish that she hadn't had Maisy, she also knew how hard life had been as a young single parent, even with her mum and dad's support. He might be trying harder this time with Maisy, but Jake still had a million miles to go.

21

EVE

Eve felt a frisson of anticipation as she slicked some red gloss over her lips.

She had perhaps neglected herself somewhat of late, she realised, as she looked at the shinier person staring back at her from the bedroom mirror – throwing on a pair of black leggings and some kind of Breton or floral top as a matter of course each morning (sometimes even the very same top as the day before). Other than a quick brush of her curly brown hair, which often had a life of its own, and a morning swipe of mascara, her make-up routine was pretty nonexistent. Except for the last two craft fair events, she confessed to herself, where rather a lot of personal care and attention had come into play.

She slipped a dress on – a vintage-style tea dress, with a delicate red rose pattern. A dress she usually kept for going out . . . but she and Ben hadn't been out for such a long time, the frock had hung neglected in the wardrobe.

Yes, it was about time she made the effort for her

husband. It was no wonder she felt rather invisible to him at home, she was somewhat invisible even to herself. The cook, the cleaner, the carer, the mum . . . where had the glamorous, carefree young Eve gone?

A sudden memory flashed up, of her and Ben dancing in the kitchen. Oh my, it'd be several years ago now, Amelia just a baby tucked up in her cot upstairs. And a song, *their* song – Ed Sheeran's 'Thinking Out Loud' – coming on to the radio. They were halfway down a bottle of wine, and he'd taken her hand and they'd swayed gently together. A spontaneous joyful moment to treasure. Could they ever get those moments back? Make new ones?

She hoped this evening would be one step in the right direction. She glanced at her wristwatch; five twenty. Ben should be home in about fifteen minutes. He usually got away by five thirty, when the garage closed, and it was only a short drive home.

She suddenly felt excited. They could turn things around. She still thought the world of Ben really, but they had become more like buddies – admittedly slightly grumpy buddies of late – than lovers.

She ventured down the stairs. Supper was already warming in the oven. Lasagne, one of his favourites.

'Oh, Mummy, you look nice.' Amelia, who was playing with her dolls in the living room, looked up and gave her a big smile.

'Aw, thank you so much, sweetie.' It was lovely for Amelia to notice but, gosh, did she really look so different to usual? She supposed that confirmed how much she'd let things slip.

Eve headed for the kitchen, thinking that they might eat al fresco in the garden for a change. The wind was low and it was still warm out there as she stood on the back step gauging the weather. Yes, they might even have a glass of wine as a treat and just chill together outside looking over the valley, after Amelia went to bed. She'd picked up a bottle of rosé and a couple of beers at the Co-op shop this afternoon, and had pointedly tidied all her craft-making stuff away for the night.

The sound of an engine slowing to a halt brought her back to the here and now.

'Daddy's here!' called Amelia excitedly, and Eve's heart did a little flip. She couldn't remember the last time that had happened for Ben.

'Hi, Daddy.' Amelia was there at the front door in a rush. Eve lingered behind her in the hallway, feeling strangely shy.

'Hi, guys.' He picked up Amelia for a hug, and moved to file past Eve, brushing the briefest of kisses on her perfumed cheek. 'Ah, what a day. Never stopped, I'm knackered. We had a breakdown in on top of the services we already had booked. Then, just at the last moment, some old guy rolled in with a puncture; well, we couldn't let him down, but really, at five to five on a Friday . . .'

He strode past Eve and headed to the kitchen to fill a glass of water.

'Hey Ben, I've made—'

'Just gonna shower,' he cut in, draining his glass.

'Oh okay,' she whispered, lingering a little awkwardly by the entrance to the kitchen.

He didn't seem to have noticed her dress, her lipstick, her hair . . . but maybe he was still in his after-work autopilot mode. Eve decided to give him the benefit of the doubt. Perhaps after his shower as she passed him his cold beer . . . then he'd really *see* her.

'I thought we might eat out in the garden,' she ventured, as he popped his empty glass down on the side, ready to head upstairs to the bathroom. 'We could have some nice chilled time, just you and me . . .'

'Ah, right. Better be quick though.'

'Oh . . . why?'

Ben was opposite her now. She suddenly felt horribly self-conscious in her get-up, the lipstick and jewellery. Had he not noticed any change?

'It's darts tonight. The Black Bull team are one short. I said I'd fill in. You don't mind, do you?'

'Oh . . .'

'I'll be heading off soon after my shower.'

And that was it. Her heart plummeted faster than a stone. All her anticipation and excitement landed in a heap around her kitten-heeled ankles.

22

Rachel rapped on the side door to Tom's kitchen and walked on in. Tom was there at the stove, looking slightly harassed yet very handsome, in dark jeans and a navy shirt worn open at the neck.

'Sorry I'm late. It's just been one of those days,' she explained, as she walked across to greet him.

He was stirring a creamy-looking sauce. 'It's okay, you're here now and that's all that matters.'

Aw, that was sweet of him. 'Yeah, it's been a bit of a crazy afternoon, what with Jake arriving out of the blue and–' she almost let the cat out of the bag and said 'staying for tea' – 'and everything.'

'Oh, right, yeah, of course.'

Rachel moved in to kiss him on the cheek. He turned towards her, holding the wooden spoon in the air, smelling rather deliciously of aftershave and cooking aromas. 'So, are you hungry?' he grinned.

'Yep! Can't wait to tuck in.' Rachel put on her cheeriest voice.

'Great, as I've gone all out and cooked three courses. I know I've been a bit of a grump and I want to make it up to you.'

'Brilliant.' *Oh my God.*

'So, pour yourself a glass of wine, relax and take a seat. There's a bottle of red already open on the island unit – I used some in the mushroom starter I've made.'

A glass of wine was probably just what she needed right now, but definitely not a full three-course dinner. She sat and sipped the mellow red, chatting away, whilst Tom got the starter plates ready with rocket and toasted ciabatta, then spooned over some garlicky mushrooms (very impressive).

'Okay, we'll go and eat in the dining room. I've got it all set up ready.' He looked pleased with himself.

'Ooh, sounds very nice.' Rachel felt suddenly anxious.

They hadn't ever eaten in the dining room. Usually, if Tom cooked, it was a more casual affair at the kitchen island. When Rachel walked into the room, she realised just how much effort Tom had put into this meal. There was a white tablecloth set out on the table, with soft lighting and tealights glowing in two pretty glass holders. He'd even put some flowers in a vase; white roses that she recognised from his garden. And, there was another bottle of wine, a white, in a cooler. She'd have to ditch the Land Rover at this rate and come back and fetch it in the morning.

'It looks gorgeous in here. Like a restaurant. Thank you.'

'You're welcome. I just wanted to make tonight special for you.' He placed her starter before her. 'Mushrooms à la Tom. I kind of made it up.'

'Well, they look delicious.' Rachel made a start, digging her fork in. 'Thanks for going to all this effort.' The mushrooms were so tasty they went down well, luckily.

The conversation was light and easy for a while. They chatted about the farms, then Maisy, with Rachel briefly mentioning Jake's arrival, without going into too much detail.

'So, have you heard any more about the court hearing? Or thought about how you are going to approach it?' She wanted Tom to know he could talk about what was going on with Caitlin and that he had her full support.

'Well, I've had advice from my solicitor, and obviously we are going to contest. He's got all the details on the original claim, as I'm using the same law firm. We can show how much was paid and how that came to be decided in the first place. But . . . if Caitlin's claim's agreed, then I will have to sell off some land, it's the only thing for it. And if it doesn't sell quickly, then I'll have to get a loan.'

'That sucks, Tom . . . it's not as though she even helped work on the farm or added to its income in any way. It's been years now, too.'

'I know . . . but I need to be prepared for the worst. And even if it does go my way, the solicitor's fees in themselves will be pretty stiff.'

'It just seems all wrong.'

'Yeah, I can really do without all the hassle and the financial implications right now. But it is what it is, and I'm just going to have to face it.'

'I can come down with you on the day, Tom. Go to the court in Newcastle with you,' Rachel offered, willing to share some of the load, to try and support him however she could.

'No need. Honestly, thanks, but I'd rather just deal with this on my own. There's no point dragging you into it all. And, the hearing is due the week before our wedding . . . you should be out with Eve and your mates drinking prosecco and getting ready for the celebrations.'

'I wouldn't mind going if you needed me, or if you just wanted someone to have a strong coffee with afterwards.' She placed her hand over his. She wanted to get back to that feeling of being a team.

'Thanks, but I've got this.'

'Okay.' He seemed determined to sit this one out alone.

'On the glorious subject of our exes, how is good old Jake?'

'All right. Turns up like a bad penny, doesn't he?' she added wryly. 'At least he seems keen to spend some time with Maisy, which is nice for her. He even stayed and read her bedtime story.'

Tom raised an eyebrow at that, it being suddenly apparent that Jake had been at Primrose Farm for quite some time today. 'Well,' he conceded, 'I suppose it's good he's finally making the effort.'

'Yeah, that's what I thought. And Maisy was thrilled to see him. You should have seen her face when she got off the school bus and realised who it was.'

'Yes, I bet. Let's hope he doesn't let her down again though.' Tom's tone was cautious, protective.

'Yeah, it's always hit and miss with Jake, isn't it? But hey, he's here now and she seems happy enough. These mushrooms are delightful by the way.' Rachel was keen to move off subject. 'I think I need the "recipe à la Tom".' She smiled.

'It may well be a guarded secret . . . or more that I can't quite remember what I threw into the sauce!'

They laughed. Despite her misgivings, Rachel was beginning to feel a sense of her future. It could be good cooking here together, eating together. Having Maisy here at the farmhouse too – maybe they'd start to feel like a real family at last.

A third of the way through the creamy chicken pasta dish that Tom had cooked for the main course, Rachel found herself struggling. It seemed like a never-ending pile of tagliatelle, and the sauce was so rich.

'Just nipping to the loo,' she excused herself, and sat there on the throne for a couple of minutes, trying to let the food go down a bit. It felt as though it was still jammed somewhere up in her oesophagus, that her stomach was so full it had nowhere to go! She realised she couldn't be too long or it'd seem odd, so she flushed, washed her hands, and headed back to the dining room, smiling.

She managed two more mouthfuls before she began to feel awfully sick.

'Are you feeling all right, Rach?' Tom was staring across the table at her.

She must have gone a bit green.

'Yeah . . .' she floundered. Oh crikey, there was no point carrying on the lie, or pretending she was ill. Wasn't their relationship meant to be based on honesty from now on? There was no way she could stomach another mouthful. 'I'm so sorry, Tom, I should have told you earlier . . . but you'd gone to so much trouble. And it was my fault forgetting . . .'

'Forgetting what?'

'That you were cooking tonight. I've already eaten back at home. I got caught up with Jake arriving so suddenly . . . and then Mum offered him tea and Maisy wanted him to stay . . .' It was sounding all wrong, she knew.

'You had tea with Jake? Wow. He's really got his feet under the table already, hasn't he?' He sounded truly irked. 'I thought you couldn't stand the guy, Rachel?'

'I can't. Not personally. He's been a right twat over the years. But it's not just about me, is it . . . whether I like him or not, he's still Maisy's dad. And he's come up to see her, to spend time with her, and I need to support that.'

'But you don't need to sit having cosy suppers with him . . . not least when you were meant to be bloody well here.' The colour had risen in Tom's face. 'I . . . I . . . Jeez, Rachel, I've gone all out here, I don't know what to say.'

'I just forgot . . . I made a mistake. It was difficult with him turning up unexpectedly like that.'

'Yeah, and you forgot about me. The man you're marrying in a few weeks' time.' He paused, looking gutted. 'Bloody hell, Rach. I wanted tonight to be special. A great lead-up to our wedding. To say sorry, for being a grump lately about all this court case stuff, and to show you how good it can be here, how I want to look after you . . . you and Maisy. I know you're worried about leaving Primrose Farm, about bringing Maisy here too . . .' He sat looking stunned. 'It's just disappointing, that's all.'

'It *is* special, Tom. It's been lovely, and all the thought you've put into it, I really appreciate it. I'm sorry, Tom, don't be mad . . .'

'I even made a sticky toffee pudding for you. It took me back to sharing it with you in the lambing shed that day. I think that's where it all started, where things changed for us . . .' He sounded nostalgic.

'Oh, Tom . . .' Rachel remembered the moment well.

'Look, maybe I can come back tomorrow and we can share some sticky toffee. How does that sound?' Rachel was desperate to put things right between them, she hated all this rockiness, it wasn't like them.

Tom managed a small smile, which made Rachel's heart leap. Thank heavens.

'What about lunchtime, then?' Tom prompted, catching on with the idea. 'Can you sneak off work for a half-hour perhaps?'

Ah . . . this was getting trickier. 'Oh . . . I've promised to take Maisy across to the beach . . . And we were going to tie in picking up the wedding favours at the chocolate shop. One less job to do before the big day.'

'So, maybe I could come along too? The sticky toffee can wait till later.' He arched an eyebrow suggestively.

'Ah . . .' She was digging herself in deeper now.

'Hang on, isn't Jake still about tomorrow? Where does he figure in all this then? Won't he want to see Maisy?'

'Yes, he does. Look, he's coming along too,' she admitted. No more hiding the truth. 'Maisy wanted us both to go.'

'Oh, so it'll be sticky toffee with me, and what . . . 99 flake ice creams on the seafront with "Jakey", will it?'

'It's not like that, Tom. Don't be daft. There's nothing at all between me and Jake but our little girl. Maisy has a hard enough time as it is, not having her dad around for most of the year. She just wanted one day – well, a few hours even – with both her mum and dad together.'

'Well, don't spoil your plans for me.' Tom stood up to clear the plates, scooping up Rachel's half-finished dish with a frown.

Mabel, the terrier, who'd been sat under the table, gave a little whimper; the tension was obviously palpable.

Rachel felt as though her world had gone topsy-turvy. Doing the right thing by Maisy felt like the wrong thing by Tom. But Maisy was, and always would be, her priority. Tom had to realise that, however much they loved each other.

'Do you want me to go?' Rachel asked in hushed tones, not really wanting to, but feeling the meal and the evening were pretty much ruined now. She was overwhelmed by so many emotions right then; she could feel the sting in her eyes. She hadn't meant to hurt Tom tonight. She hadn't meant to forget about him cooking for her . . . she could see why he'd been annoyed, of course, but this was about Maisy and her relationship with her dad too. Her mixed-up single family needed her fiancé's support right now, and she wasn't sure if they had it.

23

EVE

It was past midnight. Eve sat in the old, comfy armchair in her dining room, sewing a black-and-white felt waistcoat for a toy puffin. Once Ben had left for the pub darts and she'd settled Amelia to bed, she'd got her arts and crafts back out again. She'd needed something to keep her occupied and ease her frazzled mind after all that palaver, though she still felt extremely disgruntled. Her favourite Ed Sheeran album was playing on low, and she was trying to keep quiet, so as not to disturb Ben and Amelia who were sleeping upstairs. Mind you, from the low drone of Ben's snoring reaching her from the bedroom above, it was highly unlikely, even with the volume up, that would happen. Yes, he'd come home, still oblivious to her dress and make-up, smelling of stale beer and saying that he was shattered and would have to 'leave her to it'. So much for their romantic night; what a fool she felt.

It was the night before the Coastal Craft Fair in the village hall at Warkton-by-the-Sea and, seeing as her evening plans had been scuppered, she might as well ensure she had plenty of stock for her stall. It wasn't as though Ben's job as a mechanic brought in enough money to keep the family going. Eve's income was important too; it helped with the bills and meant they could have the odd trip out or treat occasionally. And, Amelia seemed to be having a growth spurt right now, meaning new clothes and shoes were a must. This craft fair tomorrow should help boost the family funds.

Ben seemed to see her work as 'just a hobby' most of the time. Okay, so it might never turn into a booming business venture, but she was making a steady income, it fitted in with family life (generally) – the recent late nights had been the exception rather than the rule – and she was starting to get established, building her reputation for quality handmade crafts in the local area. Her husband didn't seem to 'get' that, muttering just a few days ago that she ought to think about getting herself a 'real' job. She hated that he didn't get it; this was her passion, but it was a viable job too, wasn't it? What she really wanted to do was to try and make a business out of doing what she loved. She had a talent and it would be a shame to waste that; she'd had some lovely comments and reviews on her Etsy sales page, and the customers at the craft events were always mightily impressed.

Was Ben right? Should people like her – a normal country girl – dare to chase their dreams? Her confidence had dipped these past few years, but she needed to try at least. And what she really wanted was her husband to support her in that, to have a partner who cared enough to cherish *her* dreams too.

Oh well, if she had a successful day tomorrow, then maybe Ben might be a bit more understanding, realise why she'd had to stay up so late and appreciate all the effort she'd put in. Miracles might happen.

And . . . there was that familiar churn in her stomach. She took a look at her phone, just to see if there might be another message. But no, nothing today from Aiden. They'd be at the same event, in the same hall, just metres away from each other . . . for several hours. They'd surely get a chance to chat, catch up a bit. She was excited to see his new paintings – she loved his dramatic seascapes. He had such a talent. She looked once again at the picture hanging on her wall, *his* picture. She began to feel a little bit giddy, with that twist of anticipation in her gut. Had he been thinking of her lately, too? She remembered all too well the moment as they said goodbye in a near-empty hall at the last event. He'd held her gaze for a second or two too long, and then dipped his face towards her ever so slightly, as though about to kiss her, as his arm brushed her shoulder . . . Or so she had thought at the time, but maybe her imagination was in overdrive. Was there a spark there for him too? Best not to know . . .

But, if they could chat, just as friends, talk creatively, maybe inspire each other . . . could that be enough? It'd have to be. Because the thought of *never* seeing him again made her feel sick inside. Just friends it was, then. She could manage that . . . for all their sakes.

Putting the final touches to her work, she finished off stitching two little pockets onto the waistcoat, and fitted the item on the cute puffin toy. He looked good, ideal for a coastal craft stall. She then gave a slow sigh, followed by a yawn. Time for bed herself. Time to head up those slightly creaky cottage stairs, to her husband. Her eyes were tired and her fingers stiff from all the fine needle-work.

She got to the bedroom door and looked at Ben sleeping soundly in the gloom, his chest rising and falling. She tried to imagine peeling off her clothes, kneeling on the bed and shaking him awake, planting a kiss on his lips. The thought quickly evaporated into the night as she turned off the landing light with a sigh.

Something Borrowed

Lavender Shortbread

Inspired by Eve's Nanna, and the lavender that grows in Eve's cottage garden

Ingredients

100g (3½oz) unsalted butter
2 tsp fresh, unsprayed, finely chopped lavender flowers (or use 1½ tsp ready-made culinary lavender)
50g (1¾oz) caster sugar
150g (5¼oz) plain flour (sifted)

Method

Line a large baking tray with baking paper.

Beat the softened butter with the caster sugar, then stir the lavender into this mixture. Sift the flour into the mix and bring together with a wooden spoon until it resembles breadcrumbs. Using floured hands, work the mixture together, and knead until smooth.

Chill the dough in a fridge for 15 minutes.

Preheat oven to 170°C/Fan 150°C/Gas mark 3. Roll the dough out to 5mm (¼in) thickness. Cut out the biscuits with a circle or heart-shaped cutter. Place onto the baking tray and sprinkle with a little extra caster sugar.

Bake for 15 to 20 minutes until pale golden-brown. Set aside to cool completely.

Fragrant and delightful, perfect with a cup of Earl Grey tea. Or, why not sandwich them together with fresh strawberries and whipped cream for a divinely different strawberry shortcake.

24

Walking down the hill from the little car park at Warkton, the view to the sea was stunning. Rachel wished she could get to the coast more. The harbour nestled at the bottom of a street, lined by characterful old stone cottages, with the open sea out beyond, today calmly glinting with silvers and golds, reflecting the azure blues and puffy clouds of this gorgeous summer day. 'Flaming June' was actually true for once, and the warm sun lit up the sea and sky with a little summer magic.

Maisy, eagle-eyed as ever, spotted the ice-cream van parked down by the harbour. 'Daddy, can I have an ice cream, please?'

Jake gave a quick glance at Rachel, who had to smile at her daughter's wily ways and gave a small nod.

'Yeah, I think that sounds a great idea, Mais. We can take it down to the beach and go for a walk, and maybe make a sandcastle – that's if we can find somewhere to buy a bucket and spade.'

'I think there's a little shop just down there,' Maisy added sweetly. She'd remembered from the last time they came here, a whole year ago now.

'Well, that's us sorted then.'

They were now approaching 'The Chocolate Shop by the Sea', the chocolate business run by another local, Emma. They'd met and kept in touch since the Christmas Craft Fair at Claverham Castle. Rachel and Tom had ordered mini boxes of chocolates as wedding favours for their guests, one for each place setting.

'Right, well this is me,' she said. 'I'll let you two have some time together. So, shall I meet you back at the harbour in say an hour?' She glanced at her watch. 'Then it might well be time for fish and chips.'

'Yay!' cheered Maisy, who was already enjoying her day, and looking forward to all the delights to come.

'Sounds good to me,' added Jake.

Rachel waved them off, and couldn't help but stand and watch as the two of them made their way down to the harbour and the ice-cream van, Maisy placing her hand trustfully in his, the pair of them soon swinging their arms in tandem. It was nice to see her little girl happy.

Okay, time to step away and let them have a bit of father–daughter time, she told herself. She opened the wooden door to the chocolate shop and the rich cocoa aromas hit her straight away. Emma was there serving a customer from a tray of gorgeous-smelling coffee and moist-looking brownies. She looked up, recognising Rachel immediately. 'Hi, Rachel, won't be a minute.'

'There's no rush.' Rachel well knew what it was like to constantly multitask, running a small business with limited staff. She occupied herself by checking out all the mouth-watering delights at the counter. Oh yes, she could get a gift for Mum and Granny Ruth today, as a thank you for all their support in the build-up to the wedding. Oh, and something special for Eve too, for her wonderful, mind-bogglingly beautiful wedding dress, and her fabulous friendship.

Emma soon appeared at her side. 'So, how's it all going? Not long till the big day now. I bet you can't wait.'

'No, I know. It's all pretty much organised, but it just seems a bit surreal still.' She tried to hide any fears she was having on the fiancé front.

'Hah, yes, I remember that feeling well. Me and Max, my other half, we got married in September last year. It was a wonderful day. I was really nervous on the run-up to it, though. It wasn't a big do or anything, but I just wanted it to be right, you know.'

Rachel nodded, understanding that all too well. 'Yes, that's exactly how I feel.'

'We held it at the hotel at the top of the road, with just a few friends and family. We were lucky with the weather and it was just a gorgeous day. Goes by in a flash, mind, so try and fix it in your mind as it happens, and get people to take lots of photos and some videos too.'

'Yes, we've got a photographer organised. A friend in the village who does some amateur work. I've seen his stuff and he's good.' Geoff, from the Kirkton photography club, had offered to help out for a small fee.

'Well, best of luck with everything. So, I take it you're

here to collect your favours. They're all made up and ready. I've done a mixed-duo selection as you asked, so there's a mix of white, plain and dark chocolates with Irish cream, brandy, whisky, raspberry gin and Alnwick rum.'

'Oh goodness, they sound delicious. Hah, I'm going to have to keep myself away from them or they'll all be gone before the big day.'

'I have given you a couple of spares, just in case.' Emma gave a wink. 'They're all ready and boxed up out in the back kitchen for you.'

'Great, and I'd like to buy a few gifts while I'm here too.' Rachel chose her mum a bag of chocolate caramels and Granny some rose and violet creams, all packaged in pretty gift bags. For Eve, she chose a mixed box of truffles, tied with a gold satin ribbon.

A minute or two later Emma led her to the back kitchen where, she explained, all the crafting took place. It was like a cocoa-inspired Aladdin's cave, with chocolates of all shapes, sizes and colours setting on the side, and some just-baked brownies were cooling alongside some golden-baked chocolate croissants.

'So, here we are.' Emma lifted the lid on a cardboard box and there they were: 150 ivory mini boxes of chocolates all tied with a tiny satin bow in the exact same shade of pale purple-blue as the bridesmaids' dresses.

'Wow.' They were so pretty, Rachel felt lost for words. And the significance hit her: this was really it, in a few weeks' time, guests would be arriving at Kirkton Church, the tipi would be up and in place at Primrose Farm complete with decorations and flowers, and these favours set out by each place, ready to be enjoyed and savoured. And, ta-dah, she would be Mrs Watson. It was crazy, lovely, exciting, a bit scary . . . Could it really all come off? Life had thrown her so many lemons, she was almost always waiting for the 'but' . . . And, with her and Tom's scuppered dinner party yesterday, well . . . it could be a bloody big 'but'.

'They look just wonderful, thank you.'

They shared a brief hug; the chocolates were stunning, and Emma felt like a friend. And, from the very reasonable price the chocolatier quoted her at the till, she was certain she'd given her a discount on the original quote.

'Right well, do you have a car nearby?' Emma asked. 'I can help you carry them out.'

'Actually, I'm staying in the village a bit longer yet. My daughter's here and we're going to check out the craft fair that's on today, so can I pop back and collect them a bit later, maybe in an hour or so?'

'Absolutely, no problem.'

'In fact, I might stop here for a quick coffee first. She's with her dad, my ex,' Rachel explained. 'I need to give them a bit of time together, he doesn't get up to see her often. I said I'd meet them at twelve.'

'Yeah, no worries, the courtyard out the back is lovely, if you like being outside.'

'Sounds perfect.' Rachel really was an outside kind of girl.

'So, what kind of coffee?'

'Oh, an Americano with hot milk please, and . . . I might just have to have some of that just-baked brownie I spotted in the kitchen.' Rachel grinned. 'Who needs a pre-wedding diet, right?'

'I'd say that's the perfect accompaniment. Well, I'd better crack on. There might be more customers waiting. I'll bring it out to you in a short while, so go ahead and take a seat.'

Rachel enjoyed twenty minutes of peace, watching a blackbird perched happily on the wall, whilst eating gooey-rich chocolate brownie washed down with the best of coffees. It was so nice to be on the other side of the counter for once, to be the guest not the server. She hoped her customers felt like this, made welcome with gorgeous treats and a peaceful place to sit and chill or chat.

It was soon time to meet up with the others. Rachel went to settle up for the coffee but Emma wouldn't hear of it. 'On the house, for the bride-to-be. I'll catch you again when you pick up the chocolates. But you make sure to have the best of days at your wedding. Enjoy every moment of your special day.'

Rachel felt wrapped in a warm chocolatey hug at that point. She headed out of the cosy little shop with a big smile.

Glancing down the street, she could see that the two of them weren't back at the harbour yet, so Rachel went to see if they were still on the beach. Maisy loved the sea and sand; Jake might be having trouble dragging her away. And yes, as she came out of the track through the dunes, there they were finishing off a big sandcastle that had four turrets with walls between each – a real work of art.

'I'm just going to fetch shells to decorate the castle bits, Mummy,' Maisy chattered away, before heading off with her new plastic bucket for her booty, scouring for the prettiest shells and any pieces of colourful sea glass.

Rachel sat down on the sand beside Jake, both of them watching their daughter for a few moments.

'She's enjoying herself,' Rachel commented.

'Yeah.' Jake grinned.

'So, how's life? Are you doing okay?' Rachel asked, softening. She felt she might as well make some conversation, and Jake hadn't been too forthcoming about his personal life at all yesterday.

'Not bad, yeah . . .' He paused, as though wondering whether to keep up the bravado. 'Actually, I've had a couple of big barneys with Chelsea lately. It's been a bit tricky.' He looked glum.

So, Rachel's theory was right then.

'It's just so hard with a kid in tow all the time . . .' he moaned.

'Hah, yeah.' Rachel saw the irony in that line. 'Tell me about it.'

'Right, yeah, so I guess that isn't news to you . . .' He suddenly seemed a bit sheepish.

'Look Jake, life's not always easy, but sometimes the hard stuff's worth working through. And, somehow, it's getting through all the crappy stuff that makes it all worthwhile.' She looked out across the sea, thinking of all the pain and hurt since her dad had died. Thinking of all the times she'd struggled as a young mum, but also all the joy that Maisy had brought to her life. 'Maybe you should try and give this Kelvin kid a chance, and Chelsea . . . it must be strange for him having a new man in his mum's life.' Rachel was thinking of how Tom had come into Maisy's life in a big way recently, and how her fiancé was always so kind and patient with her. 'Parenting isn't easy,' she continued, 'but it can be so rewarding.' She looked down the beach to see her, *their*, little Maisy, who was heading back with her bucket in one hand, clutching a big purple mussel shell in the other to show them both.

'Oh, yes, that's a beauty of a shell, Maisy,' she called out.

'It is, isn't it,' Maisy beamed.

Before she reached them, Jake looked across at Rachel. 'You've done a great job with Maisy, Rach. Anyone can see that.' He nodded, looking thoughtful.

'Thank you.'

And Maisy was back finishing her castle, with Jake helping to put the last few 'gems' on top of each turret.

Rachel realised that this was the first open and honest conversation that she and Jake had had in years. However tricky he was finding it with Chelsea and young Kelvin, it had certainly given him a little more patience with Maisy and improved his parenting skills. Perhaps the smart-alec and wanderlusting lad was finally beginning to grow up.

25

Fish and chips in cardboard trays with lashings of salt and vinegar. Those little crispy bits of batter, crunchy then melting on the tongue, the soft white fish beneath, eaten with little wooden forks. The taste of summer at the seaside.

The three of them were sitting on the inner harbour wall. Rachel was amazed that she was actually enjoying her trip out with Jake, and seeing Maisy's smiling face right now made it all the more worthwhile. Perhaps she was able to move on, forgive Jake his wayward past, and have a future that meant Maisy could be happy and loved by both parents. She wasn't holding out too much hope that he'd be around very regularly in this future, but perhaps it could work okay for the three of them.

'Right then, would you like to go and see Auntie Eve at the craft fair? It's just in the village hall here,' she added for Jake's benefit.

'Okay, yeah, no worries.'

'Yes! Is Amelia there too?' Maisy asked.

'I'm not sure, petal. I think she was staying with her daddy today, as Eve is busy with all her crafts for sale.'

The hall was bustling, with tourists and locals browsing

the various displays. There were so many talented stall-holders selling a range of toys, woodwork, candles, photography and art. Rachel clocked the stand at the end with the big seascapes on canvas, and wondered if that was 'the guy'. As they neared, she saw a sign that read 'Aiden Cole – freelance artist. The coast is my canvas.' Ah yes, that must be him.

Behind his stand were several paintings, and a tall blond chap was talking to some prospective buyers about the quality of light and the fantastic skies here in Northumberland. Rachel had to admit that he was quite handsome, though a little too arty-farty looking for her taste. He was sporting a dashing neckerchief in blues and greys, a pale blue linen shirt, beige shorts, and there were Crocs on his feet. It was a look that was a million miles away from Eve's husband, Ben, in his practical navy work overalls or off-duty jeans and T-shirt. The artist's paintings looked rather stormy and moody, and she couldn't help but wonder if, despite his charming smile with his customers, his temperament might reflect that.

Looking around the hall, she spotted her friend's stall in the opposite direction and zigzagged her way across the venue, holding Maisy's hand and dodging several slow-moving browsers, and a couple of spaniels on leads.

'Hey, Eve! How's it going?' She finally reached her best friend.

'Hi Rach, thanks so much for dropping in. Good so far. I've sold quite a bit already, mostly my toys – they're proving popular with the families on holiday. And some cards, and the wooden coasters: the "Prosecco time!" and "Gin O'Clock" seem to be doing especially well. There are lots of people coming through, which is great.'

'Brilliant, and are you doing okay?' Rachel didn't want to mention Aiden out loud, but she knew it couldn't be easy for Eve.

'Yep, all fine.' But she sounded distracted, glancing across at Aiden at that point.

Rachel saw her friend's cheeks flush.

Maisy and Jake had wandered along to the next stall by now, where Maisy was holding up a charm bracelet and chattering away.

'Oh Eve, for goodness' sake be careful,' Rachel whispered. 'Just keep your distance and don't get wrapped up in something you'll regret.'

'I'm fine. I've got this.' Eve's tone was full of bravado.

It wasn't the place to take the conversation further, but Rachel couldn't shift her sense of unease. 'Anyhow, what about you?' Eve continued. 'How's today been with Dodgy Daddy?'

'Hah, yes, all right actually.'

'Been behaving himself, has he?'

'Yeah, surprisingly.'

'That's good. Maisy looks happy anyhow.'

They both looked up at Jake and Maisy, who were wandering back over to them holding hands.

'Well best of luck, hun.' And Rachel meant in more ways than sales. 'We'll take a little look about and then

I need to go and pick up my wedding chocolates, and get this little one home.'

'Oh yes, you were collecting your favours, weren't you. I bet Emma's done a smashing job.'

'She really has. They looked gorgeous when I called in earlier.'

'Ooh, exciting times, Rach.' Eve smiled warmly.

Exciting and *worrying*, Rachel mused. She hadn't had the chance to share all the latest woes in her complicated pre-wedding life with her best friend.

'Aw, look, Mummy, these are so sweet.' Maisy was holding up a felt finger puppet sheep. 'I could pretend it was Petie and he could play with the Christmas mouse and hedgehog ones I have at home.'

The tag read £4.50, which was reasonable, but after buying the extra chocolates and insisting on paying half for the fish and chips, Rachel's funds were all out for today.

'Go on then, I'll get it,' Jake offered, peering over Maisy's shoulder. 'Are you sure that one's your favourite?'

'Yes, he's called Petie, and I love him already.'

'Ah, you spoil her,' Rachel said, but with a smile.

'And why not, we don't get to spend much time together, do we, princess?' He ruffled her blonde hair. 'It'll be a little something to remember today by. You don't want a puffin or a seal one, do you? For the seaside?'

'Nope.'

'All righty.' Jake took a five-pound note out of his pocket and paid.

Maisy was already popping the sheep on her finger and baaing. Luckily her antics were drawing a few other children to the stall, who tried on some of the other puppets, wiggling fingers and giggling, and two more sales swiftly followed.

'Hah, I need you to stay a bit longer, Maisy,' Eve grinned. 'You're a sales magnet.'

Rachel had a feeling she should stay on too, as chaperone, whisking Eve swiftly away at the end of the event. But it was time to move on and get back to the farm.

She gave her friend a farewell hug, whispering 'best of luck'. After a quick whizz around the stalls, they were soon heading for the exit; Rachel turning at the last to see artist Aiden making a beeline for Eve's stand. Oh crikey. But, she told herself, Eve was a big girl now. And she *usually* had a sensible head on her shoulders. It just seemed to have been turned of late.

With the wedding chocolates collected and safely stowed in the back of the Land Rover, the three of them were soon weaving their way home along country lanes. Maisy was snoozing, with her head tucked against Jake's side, his arm around her. Despite her concerns for Eve, it had been a good day.

Yet, as they edged closer to Kirkton, the three of them singing along to George Ezra's 'Shotgun' at the tops of their voices, Rachel saw a familiar truck coming around the bend. *Tom.*

Rachel paused to wind the window down to say hello,

but her fiancé had a face on him like thunder. The three of them singing in unison and playing happy families wasn't exactly a welcome sight, she supposed.

'All right? Had a good day?' Tom was trying his best to be polite.

'Yeah, great mate,' Jake cut in, leaning across to the open window.

Tom gave him a look that said he was anything *but* his mate.

'Good, thanks,' replied Rachel calmly, trying to hold it together. 'It was . . . nice at the beach. And lovely to see Eve at the craft fair.'

'Well . . . see you later then,' Tom said to Rachel, as he put the truck back into gear. He couldn't get out of there quickly enough.

'Okay. See you later.' Why did life and relationships have to be so damned complicated?

26

EVE

The hall was beginning to empty out and Eve felt a sense of foreboding. She and Aiden would soon get the chance to snatch a few moments of conversation before packing up and heading home. He had come across to say 'hi' earlier in the day, which she had to admit had set her all a-flutter. But other than offering to fetch her a cup of coffee mid-afternoon, they'd both been busy since . . . and that had probably been a good thing.

Thankfully, her cash box had several notes in. She'd counted over £100 in takings by lunch time, and this afternoon had seen a lot more people coming through. Of course, she'd have to take all her costs into account – materials, fuel to get here and the hire of the stall, not to mention her time – but she was pretty certain the day had been a success. If she could clear a couple of hundred pounds to add to the family funds, then that would be brilliant . . . *and* it might just help cheer Ben up a bit.

Eve glanced up to see Aiden staring at her from the far end of the room. Their eyes locked for a few seconds, before a warm smile lit his face. Oh my, she felt a bit jelly-legged.

How could a mere smile do that to your insides?

'You okay?' he mouthed.

'Yeah, you?'

'I am now,' he grinned. 'Catch you in a mo.'

Melting, toffee-warm feelings oozed over her. Eve had to compose herself as a late straggler paused and looked at one of her toys; a gentlemanly-looking hare in a tweed waistcoat.

'It's all hand-sewn,' she confirmed. 'I make them myself.'

'He's gorgeous. My granddaughter will love him, I'm sure, and it's her birthday soon. I'll take it, thank you.'

'That's great.' Eve packaged up the toy, popping a business card in the brown paper bag too – a tip from savvy Rachel – and passed the purchase over with a smile. 'Many thanks, and I hope your granddaughter enjoys him.'

The woman paid, adding, 'I'm sure she will.'

Another satisfied customer, and that felt good.

After popping the notes in her cash box, Eve looked up to see Aiden standing right beside her stall with his movie-star grin. Actually, this close, there was something about him that reminded her of the actor Tom Hiddleston . . . and that made it *so* hard to concentrate when she tried to say 'Hello'.

'Had a good day? It looks like you've been busy.' His voice was warm and velvety.

'Yeah, I have been. Haven't had a chance to count the takings yet, but it's been busier here than most of the events I've done lately. What about you?' She looked up into his deep blue eyes.

'Well, I sold one painting, a couple of prints, and I have taken a commission for another. So, it's definitely been worthwhile. To be fair, with my originals priced at around £500, I don't expect to get much casual trade at this type of event. It's more about getting my name out there, and letting people know about the gallery.'

'Yes, of course.'

'Talking of which . . . I'm about to open a new exhibition for the summer. I've just finished a new collection, using lighter tones and brush strokes – summer seas and skies, summer storms.'

'Sounds amazing.'

'It opens officially next Saturday, but I've a preview night coming up at the gallery, Friday evening, for a few special guests and friends. Would you like to come?'

A giddy mix of excitement and foreboding hit Eve all at once.

'You can let me know what you think about the exhibition . . . cast your artistic eye over the displays and see if you think I've got the positioning right?' Aiden continued. 'So it can be spot-on for the opening day.'

'Ahmm . . .' Another evening away. How could she justify that to Ben? And, should she even be *thinking* about meeting up with Aiden with the way she was feeling?

'There'll be drinks and nibbles. Some other artists and gallery owners you could meet with . . .'

The contacts might be handy, she told herself. And it wasn't as though it would be just the two of them there, or anything.

'It sounds wonderful, Aiden. I'll just have to check it's all right babysitting-wise . . . that Ben' – it seemed weird saying her husband's name right now – 'hasn't got any plans that night.' But actually, yes, mentioning his name was a good thing. A reminder to Aiden that she had a *husband*. Oh, bloody hell, her emotions were so mixed right now, was she just being daft and over-hyping this whole thing? He might not even fancy her at all.

'It'd mean a lot if you could come.'

Oh my, that look. Well, maybe he did, just a little. 'Thank you. I'll try my best. I'll message you as soon as I know. What kind of time would it be?'

'Say six thirty to start. You can stay as long or as little as you like then. It's on until around nine thirty.'

'Well, I might be able to manage an hour or so.' Eve smiled.

'Great. Right, well, time to get packed up and get my paintings crated and back to the gallery.'

'Yeah . . . me too.'

'Can I give you a hand with anything?'

'Oh, I'm sure I can manage, but thanks,' she spluttered.

'Okay. Your work is stunning, by the way. Really well crafted. I love all the detail on the animals . . . you've given them all such character too,' he enthused, picking up Mr Fox.

'Aw, that's lovely to hear. But it's nothing compared to what you do.'

'No, I mean it. Don't put yourself down, you're really talented. Creativity comes in all forms, not just painting.'

And that meant so much to Eve. Someone who was artistic himself recognising her talent. It was a shame that Ben couldn't see beyond the pounds and pence, and 'wasted time'.

'Thank you, Aiden.' Eve felt a weird pang inside as she watched Aiden turn to walk away. He was a kindred spirit; he understood what it felt like to create something. There was a palpable connection between them, and he seemed a really special person. And right then, it felt bloody awful that she'd never be able to touch him, hold him, find out all about him. *Oh hell*, she was falling for him good and proper.

Should she even go to this opening night? She felt a bit wobbly just watching him walk across the hall. But it was just a viewing of his new paintings, after all, so why did it feel like so much more than that?

27

'Bye then my princess,' Jake said to Maisy the next morning, gathering her up in a big hug. 'And I'll be seeing you very soon for the wedding, yeah? I can't wait to see you in your special bridesmaid dress.'

'Bye, Daddy,' said Maisy, squeezing him back.

Jake caught Rachel's eye for a moment over their daughter's shoulder. It was a look full of feeling and nostalgia. And as he stepped forward, Rachel was hit with the strange thought that he was about to kiss her. Whether it was to be on the cheek or lips, she didn't risk finding out, recoiling with a quick step backwards and politely rubbing his arm instead. After all, one good day out with Maisy didn't mend all those broken bridges, or give him licence to get up close and personal. She had seen enough over the years to know that she wanted no romantic involvement with that lad ever again.

'Ah, okay, well it's been great . . . this weekend. See you both soon.' He sounded a little awkward, no doubt realising his error.

'Bye, Daddy.' Maisy moved in for another hug, wrapping herself tightly around his legs.

He leaned back down. 'Bye, sweetheart . . . and be a good girl for your mummy, yeah?'

'I will.'

They watched and waved as his van headed away down the farm track. Rachel was sad to see Maisy's face drop, as the vehicle got smaller and smaller. But at least their little girl had had a lovely time. And, amazingly, Jake did seem to be bucking up his act.

'He'll be back again soon, Mais,' Rachel soothed; she was pretty sure he'd keep his promise to be there for the wedding. 'Come on, let's go and find Grandma and help set up the Pudding Pantry for the day.' Diversionary tactics were needed.

Later that afternoon, with Maisy still at the Pantry happily helping Grandma to decorate cupcakes, and the tearooms a little quieter, Rachel took the opportunity to head over to Tom's to finally catch up with him after their recent disasters. They'd texted briefly last night, but the emotions behind the everyday chitchat were difficult to gauge. Hopefully a little time apart might have helped to put things back in perspective. After all, life was too short for them to be cross with each other about the little things. Their relationship was worth so much more than that. Yes, she resolved, as she parked up outside Tom's house, what they really needed to do was to mend their own rather rickety bridge in time for their wedding day.

'Hi, I'm here for my sticky toffee!' She popped her head around Tom's kitchen door, ready to make her apologies for their lost weekend. But Tom was seated at the kitchen table with his head in his hands, looking totally worn down, a pile of documents spread out in front of him.

'What's all this on the table?' What had happened now? she wondered. Couldn't they catch a break? The carton of honey ice cream that she'd brought along to add to the pudding was now melting in her hands.

'It's the paperwork from the local land agent,' Tom said glumly. *Oh god*, thought Rachel, *information on how to sell.*

'Oh,' was all she could muster at first. She took the seat next to him, feeling a heaviness in her heart. 'Are you all right?' she said softly. 'Is it really coming to that?'

Tom nodded slowly and then sighed. 'I'm trying to get a step ahead and be prepared for the worst, should it happen. But yes, it might well come to selling.'

'Oh Tom, I'm so sorry.'

He looked up, with the weight of the world on his broad shoulders. 'I had to break the news to my parents today. I've been holding back until now. But they need to know what's going on, if they see the "land for sale" signs going up . . . well. And, you know what the village is like for spreading news. Bad news always travels fast.'

Rachel rested a hand on his shoulder. She knew all too well from their own recent troubles what the thought of losing it all – your land, your inheritance, your livelihood – felt like.

'Dad was gutted, as you can well imagine, though he was trying his best to hide it,' Tom continued. 'He's worked all his life for this place, and his father and grandfather before him.' A brief smile then warmed his face. 'Still can't keep away, though he's meant to be retired. Always popping in to see if he can lend a hand . . . Oh, Rach, I've let them all down. Trust me to choose such a bloody toxic relationship . . .'

Rachel could tell how much he was hurting. It seemed so bloody unfair. It also made her skin prickle. After all this drama with Caitlin, was he really able to love again, to trust again?

'Oh, Tom,' her voice was a whisper; so afraid the whole thing might fall down around them like a house of cards. She placed her hand over his, to show support, give hope; but he felt so very tense.

'Anyway,' he looked up, 'enough of that. How are things with you? How's it been with Maisy and her dad?' The effort it took to ask about Jake was plain on his face.

'Yeah, it went all right, actually. Maisy enjoyed her day on the beach.'

'Well, that's good.'

'Yeah, I think Jake's trying really hard . . . he seems to have changed this time. It's like he finally wants to be there, be a proper dad for Maisy.'

Tom looked at her with a frown, 'You've changed your tune, Rach. What happened to "the unreliable little twat"?'

'Well, we all deserve a second chance, don't we? The opportunity to put things right.'

'Yeah, but it seems like he's had a whole load of second chances, Rach.'

'Tom, he's Maisy's dad. And, whether you like it or not, he's going to be around and a part of her future.' Somehow, they'd have to work this out – her, Tom, Maisy *and* Jake, when he made his visits.

'That's not really a given, is it, the way he flits off on a whim. Christ, we didn't choose our exes well, did we?' He sounded exasperated.

Rachel had hoped to smooth things over by coming around, but they still seemed miles apart. Tom was in a black mood, and some of it was justified, but she needed him to click out of it soon.

'No, we didn't,' she admitted. 'Look, I know everything's a bit tough right now, but we can get through it. And . . . bloody hell, Tom,' she couldn't help her frustrations spilling over, 'could you just try and be a bit more positive about the future? We're getting married in less than three weeks' time and I want us to enjoy it, to celebrate with our family and friends, Jake included.'

'What?' Tom looked gobsmacked. 'You've gone and invited Jake to our wedding?'

Oh god, she'd let it slip. The cat was well and truly out of the bag now.

'Look, Maisy invited him, I couldn't very well say no. It's not the end of the world, Tom. Maisy wanted him there.'

'But *I* don't. How would you feel if Caitlin was coming to the wedding?'

'That's different and you know it. I'm sorry I didn't tell you sooner, but it's all arranged with Jake now. I'm not going to let Maisy down.' Rachel was undeterred. 'I want her to be looking forward to our wedding day, Tom, and if that means Jake coming, so be it.'

'Jeez.'

'Look, I came around to try and make things better between us,' Rachel let out an exasperated sigh. Whatever she said or did lately, it seemed to keep spiralling them back down into conflict. 'And I know you're having a tough time with all this, with Caitlin and the farm, but can you at least try to look at things from my perspective? It's hard for me too, and you're so damned grumpy about everything lately.'

'Sorry for speaking some home truths. Look, I just don't trust the guy, that's all. There's only one person that Jake cares about, and that's Jake.' His tone softened, 'Look, I . . . I just don't want to see you or Maisy getting hurt again.'

She recognised some truth in that. Perhaps Tom was only trying to look out for the two of them.

Tom sighed once more, 'Look, I really need to get on with this paperwork, Rach. I've a lot to think about right now.'

Did he mean *them*? *Their* relationship, *their* wedding, as well as all the practical stuff?

She swallowed a lump in her throat. 'Okay, I'll see you soon, though. Yeah?'

'Yeah, of course,' he answered, although his tone was flat.

As Rachel closed the farmhouse door behind her, she found herself shedding a tear. It was less than three weeks until their wedding day, so why was she feeling so sad and lonely?

28

Rachel posted a lovely image of Jill's latest baking masterpiece on both Instagram and the Pantry's Facebook page – a delicious-looking lemon meringue pie with a piled-high soft meringue top. 'When life gives you lemons . . . bake a pie', she typed. She liked to put up pictures of their puddings on social media to provide a little online cheer and hopefully tempt customers in.

'Another delicious-looking pud there, Mum. That'll please the online crowd no end. Right, I'm going to pop into town to pick up a few essentials, I'll be back before long.'

'OK, thanks love, I'll hold the fort here.'

In all honesty, Rachel needed a moment to clear her head. First, she headed to the post office and got in the queue to send off a parcel of ginger pudding. It was for someone who'd called at the Pantry on their holidays, sampled their culinary delights, and wondered if they did a postal service. Rachel was delighted and jumped at the chance to help.

She was four back in the queue, tapping her foot, when she couldn't help but overhear the conversation at the counter.

'By the way,' the well-to-do lady at the front asked, 'can you recommend anywhere local for a bite of lunch?'

'Oh, well.' It was Susan on the counter today. 'There's the Cheviot Café here on the high street, and if you'd like somewhere cosy which does lovely food nearby, there's the Pudding Pantry out at Primrose Farm, just outside the village.'

Ah, bless her for recommending them.

'Oh . . . funny you should say that, I did a bit of research just this morning,' the woman countered, 'and I saw some poor reviews on that Pantry place . . .'

Rachel felt herself flush with embarrassment, luckily hidden from view by the tall chap in front of her. How? They generally had such lovely comments and good reviews.

'Well, I've been there myself and had some wonderful food,' Susan replied. 'The soup and sandwiches are very nice, and all the cakes and puddings are homemade.'

'Well, perhaps it's changed lately,' said the lady, before bustling out of the post office. She evidently wasn't keen on giving them the benefit of the doubt.

When it was Rachel's turn, Susan looked up with a start, 'Oh, hi Rach,' she blushed. 'Sorry, I didn't see you there in the queue. Did you hear that?' she added in hushed tones.

'Yeah, but don't worry, it's not your fault. I wonder what these online reviews are, though? I've never spotted anything like that.'

'No, might just be one Minnie Moaner. Can't be helped sometimes.'

'No, maybe not. You can't always please everyone, I suppose.' But Rachel was desperate to find out what had been said. It could be affecting their trade already.

Rachel sorted the parcel delivery and made her way out to the street. Perhaps there was time for a quick diversion, to check out the competition . . . She walked towards the Cheviot Café and couldn't help but hear the teenage waitress chatting away with a local middle-aged lady by the doorway.

'Oh, and did you see those awful comments on Facebook? About the Pudding Pantry? Think we might be getting more customers coming back here now,' the young waitress said with a wink.

Rachel's ears pricked up. She was fiercely protective of her business and their reputation; they worked so bloody hard. She stepped up to the café's threshold: 'I'd mind your tongue if I were you, Grace.' Blimey, bad news certainly did travel fast in this town.

'Oh, sorry, Rachel. It's just what I saw on Facebook,' the young girl floundered, blushing pink.

Rachel just shook her head, then stepped away and carried on walking towards the truck. Hopefully the girl might think twice about gossiping in the future but, in the meantime, Rachel needed to find out for herself what was going on.

*

Sitting in the truck a few minutes later, Rachel dug out her mobile phone and clicked onto Facebook, her fingers trembling.

There were several 'likes' on the lemon meringue image, and a couple of positive comments. And then she read one comment which made her stop, her hands frozen above the phone: 'The food might look great, but the staff are not friendly in the least. Had a very frosty reception, and a lukewarm coffee. Wouldn't recommend.'

Oh, it was awful to think someone had had a bad experience with them. Rachel didn't remember anyone saying the coffee hadn't been warm enough, or they'd have certainly given them a fresh cup straight away. She'd have to ask Mum if she'd spoken with anyone over the last few days.

Next, she took a look at Instagram. There were comments below the lemon meringue pie image of 'Looks scrumptious!' and 'Lemonlicious', which made Rachel smile, and then another of 'I'm coming right away. Save me a slice.' A further comment read, 'Been to your Pudding Pantry last month and it was a delight. Looking forward to visiting again soon'. She sent a little 'thank you' reply, saying that they looked forward to welcoming them back. Aw, this was heart-warming, and the best kind of publicity when customers had a lovely time and shared their experiences.

And then came the worst kind of publicity in another comment: 'Never to return! Food very average. Stodgy scone. Poor staff, no acknowledgement or friendliness, almost verging on rudeness.'

Reading it made Rachel go cold. Rachel was ready to champion Jill's melt-in-the-mouth scones, though it was just possible someone hadn't enjoyed theirs, but they *always* made a point of welcoming every guest with a smile and a hello, often a quick chat too. Even in the busiest of times, if someone came in, they would at the very least acknowledge them. Rachel knew that you couldn't be perfect all the time and that expectations might be different for different customers. One person had commented a few weeks ago that they had been put off by the dreadful farmyard smells in the yard – well, the Pantry *was* on a farm, after all. But this latest comment seemed different – malicious, almost . . .

Next she turned to TripAdvisor. Rachel opened the page whilst holding her breath. And yes, below a couple of lovely four- and five-star reviews, there was a one-star, their very first. She read on with a feeling of dread. All their hard work, their achievements so far, felt as if they were being obliterated: 'Absolutely shocking! Awful all round. The woman serving was rude and uninterested. Sticky toffee pudding vile – dry, tasteless and like a brick. Overpriced. One of the worst tearooms I have ever been in. Never to return. WOULD NOT RECOMMEND.'

Underneath that were some additional comments in reply, saying, 'Thanks for the heads-up.' And, 'Sounds like another café that doesn't live up to the hype.'

Rachel sat at the steering wheel feeling gutted. Had

someone really felt they had had such a bad time? And why had nobody drawn it to their attention on the day? Her head was spinning.

With trembling fingers, she rang Eve. She needed a second opinion. An outsider's view. Maybe she was just taking it too much to heart with it being their business – the venture they'd put all their savings and soul into. 'Hi . . . Eve, can you do me a quick favour? Take a look at our Pudding Pantry Instagram and TripAdvisor reviews, can you? And ring me back, hun.'

'Ah, okay. Why?'

'Just see what you think.' She didn't want to influence her friend either way.

Within a minute her mobile was ringing.

'Oh, my God. That's awful, Rach. That's trolling, that is.'

'Do you think it's real? That those customers have had such bad experiences? But we haven't had any complaints made in the Pantry at all.'

'Well, maybe one person had a rare off experience, or it could just be one of those professional moaners,' Eve conceded, 'though I can't see you or Jill being rude to *anyone*. Might there have been a stodgy scone lurking in the batch? Who knows!'

'Hey, you, don't be so cheeky! But yeah, I could cope with one poor comment coming in in the last couple of days, but suddenly these three or four together on Facebook and Instagram, and then that TripAdvisor one was particularly dreadful . . .'

'I know, and Jill's sticky toffee is *famous* around here.'

'Oh Eve. What if people believe this? It'll put them off coming. After all the hard work we've put in this last year, setting the Pantry up, getting our name established.' She went quiet for a moment or two, with Eve sighing in support down the line. 'Maybe I can delete the bad comments off our Facebook page? I suppose I could look into that, but who's seen them already? I can't take anything off TripAdvisor, though, that's out of my control.'

'You could maybe report it?'

'Maybe . . . But how do they know it wasn't justified? Like, no wonder I'm saying we're great, 'cos I run the place.'

'Well, why don't you see if anything else goes on tomorrow, and I'll help you look into what we can do to counter it in the meanwhile? See if we can block the comments or something.'

'Okay . . . Thank you, my friend.'

'No worries, I'll defend Jill's sticky toffee till the death!'

It was on her mind all night. Rachel found herself restless and unsettled, trying to think who might possibly be behind it. Could there be another Pudding Pantry somewhere and they were mistakenly getting their reviews?

She felt very much like joining Tom in his bear cave. By three a.m., she was up and standing in the kitchen, hugging a mug of tea by the light of a half-moon. She looked out over her moon-bathed fields, mellow in their night-time grey filter. It was so peaceful, a beautiful, calm summer's night – in contrast to her troubled mind. Opening the porch door as quietly as she could, she stepped outside, her feet bare. It was cool but not cold. It grounded her in fact. She gazed across her land, and then back to the barn across the yard, the Pudding Pantry. She loved this place, her farm, and the fabulous tearooms they had created. No one should be able to say these awful things, not if they weren't true. Whatever happened next, she vowed to do her utmost to stand up for the Pudding Pantry, and all that it meant to them.

29

Sure enough, the next day, there were yet more negative comments spilling in, some on TripAdvisor, some on their Instagram page, one on Facebook. This time Rachel checked out the profiles of those who were posting. They were all different. Some with pictures of pets, or places in the North of England. But, suspiciously, none had a face in the profile picture and nearly all of them had been created within the last week or so. Very curious.

She read: 'Looked like the place has never seen a mop or cloth', and, 'Staff rude, never bothered to say hello', 'Unfriendly and uninspiring'. And again: 'I would not recommend.'

There was an air of ingenuity about them all. In fact, an air of maliciousness.

Rachel took a deep breath. There was no way she was going to take this lying down. Let battle commence.

She answered the comments one by one, saying that they took huge pride and care in the quality and friendliness of their tearooms, and pointing out that these matters should have been drawn to their attention at the time so they could have been discussed and rectified straight away. She also started compiling a log of comments, profiles and timings of these negative responses. Then, if needs be, she was ready to report them.

In the whole of their last year of trading there had been just one 'two-star' review on TripAdvisor. And there had been six 'one-stars' in the past three days – something was definitely up.

Despite the fact she was putting on a brave face and mentally preparing a way forward, there was no denying that Rachel felt troubled and saddened by what was happening. She had heard this morning from Frank that his elderly neighbour Irene, one of the Pantry's regulars, had cancelled her morning coffee trip with a friend, as her daughter had passed on her concerns about the cleanliness of the place after reading one of the reviews. Frank, bless him, had told Irene it was 'all a load of old tosh' and 'nonsense'. But Rachel was undeniably worried about the trickle-down effect of the comments. She prayed it wasn't about to get worse.

Life on the farm had to go on, however, and the next day Rachel made her usual early morning rounds, checking on her cattle and sheep grazing out in the fields. Thankfully, all seemed well on that front, and the country views and fresh air lifted her spirits a little. Mum had nipped out to Kirkton to see Brenda and to pick up a few items at the deli, and Rachel had a spare hour before she was due to open the Pantry. She decided that a little baking therapy was what was needed. Unsure of what to make, she took down the Baking Bible from its shelf in the kitchen and, intending to leaf through it, she found it had fallen open at one of Jill's handwritten recipes: blueberry and lemon muffins. A perfect pick-me-up. Something they could sell at the Pantry *and* enjoy on their coffee break themselves. Maisy would also be delighted to find a zingy, fruity muffin ready for her when she got back from school.

Rachel rummaged through the kitchen cupboards for the ingredients, finding flour, sugar, fresh eggs collected from the farm, creamy butter in the fridge. Luckily, they had a punnet of blueberries in, as they were one of Maisy's favourites. Pinafore on, her bright red spotty one, radio playing in the background, and she was ready to cook. As she weighed out all the ingredients, sieving the flour and listening to the reassuring hum of the mixer, it all felt therapeutic. The muffin tins were lined with polka-dot paper cases, and the oven of the Aga awaited. Spooning the pale-cream mixture into each case, whilst humming along to some country music on the radio, took her mind off her troubles, for a short while at least. The warm, sugar-sweet aroma of baking – with a hint of berry and citrus – soon began to fill the kitchen.

Baking might not make all your problems go away, but it sure seemed like therapy to Rachel just now.

30

It was the following evening, and Rachel was about to hold the last Pudding Club session before the wedding, although there would also be the special bonus club night on the eve of the festivities, when all the members would be pitching in from home to make the catering spread extra-special. Cake stands had already been offered to ensure that every table at the reception had its own very pretty feast.

Rachel was taking the helm solo tonight, as Jill was staying home to look after Maisy; the little girl still seemed tired after a busy few days at school and all the emotions of Jake's recent visit, and she needed to get a good night's sleep to be up and perky for her lessons the next day. Granny Ruth was feeling poorly, her cough back with a vengeance, bless her. So Rachel told her to stay in and have an early night, hoping to goodness she'd be feeling better by the wedding day.

Rachel needed to visit Ruth soon. She had a special request to make of her. Perhaps she'd pop over tomorrow and check on how her granny was; take her some fresh eggs and some homemade soup from the Pantry. That might perk her up a bit.

With all that had been going on recently, Rachel hadn't had time to plan particularly well for tonight's meet-up. So yesterday, after baking the lemon and blueberry muffins when she had been feeling low, she had typed up that recipe to hand out at this evening's meeting. She thought they could have a chat about 'baking as therapy'. What were everyone's go-to bakes when they felt a bit down or needed to take their mind off things? She hoped it would prove to be an interesting theme. It would certainly be a conversation starter, anyhow.

A quarter of an hour before the start time, Rachel was all set up in the Pantry with cups and saucers at the ready and the lemon and blueberry muffins stacked temptingly, centre-stage, at the club's table for the evening. The members soon started arriving, taking up their seats with friendly 'hellos' and easy chatter.

As the guests filtered in, Rachel overheard young mum Alice whispering to Hannah, 'Have you seen their Instagram page this week? It's been dreadful.'

'Yes, I know, I feel so sorry for Rachel and Jill.'

So, word was out. Rachel felt her cheeks burning. Bad news really did travel fast in this village. It wasn't surprising, really; everyone seemed to be on social media these days – even Granny Ruth, rumour had it!

By seven o'clock, there were eleven Pudding Clubbers at the table: Charlotte, Eve, Jan and Brenda, Denise and Christine, Alice and Hannah, as well as Pamela and Nigel, and stalwart, Frank. Daniel had already sent in his apologies as he was filling in for holidays at the care home and had taken on an extra shift, and Kirsty's little boy Callum had a sore tummy, so she was staying home just in case. Rachel took a deep breath, and thought she might as well make a start.

'Hi, everyone. Hope you are all doing great.'

'Yum, these look good, Rach. Are we having a muffin night or something?' asked Brenda.

'Not quite . . .' Rachel suddenly wondered if her theme might seem a bit dour.

Before she could mention her 'baking as therapy' idea, Denise burst in with, 'Ooh, before we get started, I must ask: how are the wedding preparations going? Not long to go now, lass. The village is getting rather excited about it, I must say. So lovely to have a happy event to look forward to.'

'We can't wait,' added Charlotte – who was seated next to Eve – with a beaming smile.

'What is it now, just over two weeks?' asked Pamela.

'It is indeed,' Rachel managed a smile. There was a buzz of anticipation in the air. The wedding was so near, but there seemed to be so many hiccups along the way, and she hadn't been able to let herself relax and enjoy the build-up to it at all – especially with the latest social media problems.

'Ooh, can you remind us of the colour schemes for the flowers and dresses again? I want to make sure my mini cupcakes work well with it all. Can't have any garish icing clashes,' quizzed Christine.

'Yes, now don't forget, Rachel, that we are all more

than happy to contribute to the wedding catering, so don't you and Jill put too much pressure on yourselves. It's all in hand. We'll make sure there's plenty for a real feast,' added Denise, with Jan and Brenda nodding vigorously in agreement.

'Absolutely,' continued Christine. 'All of us here have been planning our bakes, and Daniel's on board too. We will be sure to have a wonderful array of goodies on offer. We're bringing our cake stands to help out, too, so every table at the reception will have its own "Tower of Treats".' She grinned.

'Aw thank you, guys.' Rachel felt warmed by their support, and by the offers of help so freely given.

'Well, the colours in the flowers are white, soft pinks and a touch of cornflower blue,' advised Eve. 'So, anything along those lines would be lovely, thank you.'

'Oh yes, I've heard all about the flowers from Wendy,' added Brenda. 'They sound absolutely beautiful.'

'Perfect,' said Christine, 'and some of the other WI members will be helping out too. I've even got a certain Vanessa offering to bake some mini cheese scones.'

'Oh my, beware,' jested Charlotte, 'they might be laced with curry powder or something out of spite.'

'Hah, I doubt it, actually, seeing as I've invited her,' explained Rachel, 'so, I'm sure she'll make sure they are her best ever, as she'll be there to listen in to all the comments.'

'Wow, that was kind in the circumstances,' remarked Jan. There had been several 'moments' between Rachel and village gossip Vanessa in the past, the most notable being Rachel's carrot cake beating hers in a cake competition at the country show, which had really put her nose out of joint.

'Ah well, most of the village have been invited. It seemed a bit mean to exclude her, and well . . . let bygones be bygones, that's what I say.'

'As long as she doesn't want to come back to the Pudding Club too soon!' Frank chuckled. 'What a nightmare she was.'

'Hah, yes. Oh, the wedding is going to be so amazing,' gushed Alice. 'Thank you so much for inviting me and Simon, I'm so looking forward to it. I've got a babysitter lined up and everything.'

They were all excited for her and rallying to help; that in itself lifted Rachel's spirits. She hoped to goodness that Tom bucked up soon . . . she really, really hoped there would actually be a wedding for them all to go to.

'Right then, back to today's Pudding Club. My theme this week is "baking as therapy". You know the kind of thing, so, we're talking your turn-to bakes if you're feeling a little low.'

'O-kay.'

'Right . . .'

They were waiting to hear more so she thought she may as well explain. 'Well, despite all the excitement of the wedding, I have to admit I've had a bit of a tricky week.' It felt okay to be open with this supportive bunch.

'Oh, pet,' Jan was the first to speak.

'Aw, hun, you should have told me,' Charlotte added.

'So, you might have heard about the recent negative reviews. I have to say there have been some downright nasty comments on the Pantry's Facebook and Instagram pages,' Rachel added.

'Yes, we had, lass,' said Nigel, on behalf of them all, 'and I'm sorry to hear it.'

There were nods, and utterings of, 'Such a shame', 'So sorry', 'Oh no, I hadn't heard.'

'It's okay, it'll all work out somehow, I'm sure.' Rachel tried to sound upbeat, but her words were followed by a sigh. She decided not to share the private problems between herself and Tom. That was something for the two of them to sort out.

'But that's so unfair,' cried Pamela.

'And just not right.' Christine frowned. 'The Pantry always puts its customers first, it's real service with a smile.'

Checking with Rachel that it would be OK, Nigel took his phone out and started reading out some of the comments from TripAdvisor. The audience looked shocked.

'Unfriendly staff . . . lack of ambience . . . What a load of shite!' Brenda was indignant.

'It's a lot of utter tosh,' added Frank, looking upset and annoyed. 'If I could get my hands on the little blighters . . . well, it shouldn't be allowed.'

'Well then,' Denise cried out, 'if someone can put downright nasty and untruthful comments on, then surely we can put on some very lovely truthful ones.'

'Of course we can,' rallied Eve.

'The Pudding Pantry is brilliant and has such a lovely cosy, atmosphere. I've made some real friends here,' said Alice, who'd only recently moved to the village.

'Well, as soon as I get home, I'm going to put on a five-star review,' added Hannah.

'That's so mean, calling the staff rude, and going on about "the unfriendly younger woman".' (There had been another vitriolic comment this afternoon.) 'What horrible timing with your wedding being so soon too. *Oh* . . . do you think there might be some kind of link?' Charlotte ventured.

Her words hung in the air, and then they dropped like a bad penny. *Perhaps there was.*

'Some miserable, bitchy old bag of an ex . . . I wonder . . .' Eve joined in. 'It seems a big coincidence that it's all started just before you're about to marry gorgeous Tom, right?'

'Do you think . . .?' Rachel was finding it hard to fathom that someone could be that calculating and nasty. Yet, there was this court case now coming up with Caitlin . . . who knew?

'Seems plausible,' added Denise. 'Never did warm to the woman, I must say. I remember that Caitlin well.'

'But I suppose we'd better not cast aspersions, when we really don't have any proof . . .' Jan was erring on the side of caution. 'Not that I liked the girl much either, to be fair.'

'No, you're right, Jan,' said Rachel. 'Enough of the speculation, so let's move on with tonight's "baking ourselves better", shall we? And to start, I'm going to pop the kettle on, make us a big pot of tea and pass around those blueberry and lemon muffins.'

'Now that sounds a grand idea,' said Frank with a warm smile. 'They've been making my mouth water ever since I arrived.'

Bless him. Rachel wondered how well he had been faring at home in the kitchen since his wife died. He had always put on a brave face and said he was managing fine, mentioning that he made sandwiches for himself, but he always enjoyed the home baking here at the Pantry, eating heartily; perhaps he hadn't had an awful lot for supper. Maybe she should pack him off home with extra snacks or a dish of soup now and again. Rachel made a mental note for the future.

'Oh my, these are wonderful. I love the fruity berries and then you get that zesty zing,' commented Hannah after taking a big bite.

'The sponge is delightful, very moist,' added Jan.

'Definitely a hug in a paper case,' Alice grinned.

'And perfect with a cuppa.' Rachel passed the hot drinks around. She took her seat again, 'So, folks, spill, what are your favourite bakes when you're feeling a bit blue?'

'Well, I do enjoy a spot of baking if I'm feeling a bit off,' admitted Brenda. 'I think it's having to concentrate on the ingredients and the process, the weighing out, mixing. And then, it's like alchemy what happens in the oven, and next . . . hey presto, you have, hopefully, a gorgeous cake. And it can cheer other people up too, something to share, so it's not just for yourself.'

'Brownies are my go-to,' confessed Eve. 'It has to be something chocolatey and they are just the *most* comforting thing ever.'

'I'm with you on that,' agreed Hannah.

Denise sighed. 'Do you remember our old Labrador, Barney?' she said fondly. 'The day we had to have him put down, we all went home and made a big chicken pie, in his honour. Chicken was always his favourite. His defining moment was stealing the leftover half-chicken from the kitchen counter top while we were eating our roast dinner one day, the monkey!'

'Aw, bless him.'

'Mine would be crumble with plenty of custard,' said Christine. 'Great to eat *and* to make. It's simple to do and I just love the feel of the mix on my fingertips, you know, when you rub in the flour and butter – definitely therapeutic. Way back, I remember my mum used to make it for me when I was revising for my A levels to keep me going.'

'Mum's sticky toffee pudding has to be one of mine,' added Rachel, remembering poignantly that special night with Tom, sharing sticky toffee pudding with him in the early hours of the morning, in the lambing shed.

'True, that stuff is amazing. Heaven in a dish, that is.' Frank gave a grin.

'Rice pudding, made with really good double cream

and then baked oh-so-slowly. The smell and then the taste . . .' chipped in Nigel. 'Reminds me of home.'

'Oh, I really am in pudding heaven. Thank goodness we have these muffins to munch on,' said Charlotte.

'They are delish. Love the lemony tang.'

'Yeah, I add the grated zest as well as the juice of a lemon. The recipe's there typed up for you all to take home too.'

'Brilliant, I'll be making these with little Amelia very soon.'

The chatter continued over tea and cake, and Rachel watched her Pudding Club family. And it wasn't the muffin that was cheering her up, though that did help, it was her fabulous and supportive friends from the Pudding Club. This baking-loving group were just the best tonic for those blue days. They were going to support her in the battle against the troll online – could it be Caitlin? – and they were going to play a huge part in making a gorgeous feast for the wedding. They had hearts of gold, the lot of them.

Something Blue

Blueberry and Lemon Muffins

A perfect pick-me-up for those feeling-blue days

Ingredients

220g (7½oz) plain flour
1 tsp baking powder
Pinch salt
125g (4½oz) unsalted butter, softened
220g (7½oz) caster sugar
2 eggs (at room temperature)
Juice and zest of 2 medium lemons
4 tbsp milk
150g (5oz) blueberries
Makes 12 medium muffins or cupcakes

Method

Preheat oven to 170°C/Fan 150°C/Gas mark 3. Line a 12-hole muffin tin with cupcake or muffin cases.

In a large mixing bowl, slowly whisk together the flour, baking powder and salt, and set aside.

Cream together the butter and sugar until fluffy. Add the eggs, one by one, slowly mixing. Add the lemon juice and zest, and mix until well combined. Add the dry ingredients in three stages, with a little of the milk at each turn. Mix thoroughly.

Finally, gently fold in the blueberries with a wooden spoon until evenly dispersed.

Spoon the mixture into the paper cases (two-thirds full) and bake in a preheated oven for 25–30 minutes until golden brown. The tops should spring back when lightly touched, and test that a skewer inserted in the centre comes out clean.

Ah, baking therapy!

31

EVE

'Oh hi, Rach, what's up?' said Eve. The sight of her friend's face popping up on her mobile always cheered her.

It was Friday, late afternoon, the day of Aiden's art exhibition launch. Eve's stomach was already feeling churned up. She moved out into the hallway away from Ben, fearing that her voice might tremble and give her away.

'I'm okay . . . I was just wondering whether you were going to go to the exhibition tonight? Have you thought any more about it?'

'Ah, yeah, I thought I would.' She was trying her best to sound casual.

'Are you sure that's wise, Eve?' Her friend's tone was caring, rather than judgemental.

'Umm, well, he's just a friend, after all.' She was speaking in hushed tones and had wandered into the dining room now. 'It's for the launch of his new collection, at the gallery. There'll be loads of other people there . . .' Her voice dipped to a whisper as she checked the hallway and ducked back out of earshot.

'I suppose . . . but just be careful, and look out for yourself, okay?'

'I will. Hey, and thanks.'

'Well, you know where I am if you need me. Or, if you need an excuse for a quick getaway, I can call you . . . get you picked up. We can have a CODE X or something . . . like in the movies. You can text me from the toilet and I'll make the emergency call, you know, like Amelia's been throwing up or something, and you need to get back immediately.'

'Hah, okay. But I'm sure I can manage an hour or so at an art gallery without incident. I'm not sixteen you know.' (Okay, so yes, she did feel a bit like a giddy teenager with a crush right now; it was weird how those feelings didn't change with time. They could still feel as intense and chaotic at twenty-seven, like your heart was on spin-cycle. But she was a mature adult with a child . . . and a *husband*, and she had it all under control.)

'Okay, fair enough.'

She *could* do this thing. Go and see an exhibition, appreciate a fellow art lover and creative's work, make some constructive comments, and then come on home. Easy.

But she couldn't help the frisson of excitement she was feeling at the thought of seeing Aiden again. And then there was the haircut that she'd finally got around to having done this week, and the new top she'd bought online. But she'd needed those things anyhow. It was nothing to do with Aiden, she told herself.

'Right, well, I'd better go.' She was wandering back through to the kitchen. 'Ben's home now,' a warning that the conversation needed to play safe from here on, 'and we need to grab a quick bite of tea before I head off out. You all okay?' She deftly switched the conversation. 'Oh, any more news on the trolling situation? I put a fab review on TripAdvisor for you today, by the way.'

'I saw that, and thank you. And, so many of the Pudding Clubbers have been adding great reviews and comments too. You're all stars. The Pantry's overall rating has come right back up again.'

'Well, that'll show Caitlin.'

'*If* it is her . . .' Rachel was still trying to keep an open mind. 'A big "if". I did mention it to Tom when I called him last night, though. He seemed concerned, but I tried not to make too big a deal of it either. He's got enough on his plate right now, what with the hearing next week and all. We'll get through that and then – hopefully – we can finally relax a bit and enjoy the run-up to the big day.'

'Was he still being a grump?'

'Yeah, a bit, I suppose. But I've decided that positivity is the only way forward; I'm going to be supportive and try and cheer him up a bit. In fact, I think I'll take him a picnic lunch tomorrow whilst he's out cutting the hay. It's always a full-on job.'

'That sounds a good idea. Look, I'd better go, hun.' She was aware that time was ticking away.

'Okay. Take care, Eve.' The words were said with warmth and a hint of caution.

'Will do.'

'Everything okay?' Ben asked as she walked back into the kitchen.

'Yeah, fine.' The lie burning on her lips. Things hadn't been fine at home for a while now. 'It was just Rachel,' she explained.

'Ah, right.' His look was distant. Eve felt so sad. They were so out of tune nowadays it was hard to tell what he might be thinking any more.

Eve's heart was hammering as she tried to find a parking space. This time of day, there should be a space to pull into by the village green. Bamburgh Castle dominated the skyline at the lower end of the street, perched on ancient rocks between the cricket pitch and a dramatic sweep of blond-sand beach that was buffeted by the North Sea. The small high street was lined with cottages, a few small shops, a tearoom and an ice-cream parlour. And here at the top end of the village was Aiden's gallery, nestled beside a seafood restaurant.

A car pulled out just ahead and Eve reversed into the space. So, she had made it and in good time; glancing at her dashboard clock she saw she had five minutes to spare. Checking her look in the rear-view mirror, she gave herself a nervous smile as she took a slow breath. She then smoothed on some pale-peach lipstick, and gave her long dark curly hair a flick through with her fingertips. Well, this was it. Time to go and see Aiden.

Outside the gallery, she stopped to look at a picture of the beach at Warkton. The sea in the painting was turbulent, and echoed the rolling wave of emotion that was building inside her. Why was she so damned nervous? Take a breath. Focus. Just good friends. That was all they were. She reached out; the door gave a little old-fashioned bell ring as it opened.

She was evidently the first to arrive. A tray of empty champagne flutes stood ready, and some crisps and nibbles were set out, untouched, on a coffee table in the centre of the room.

'Hi.' Aiden came out from a doorway at the rear of the gallery, looking very dashing in beige chinos and a crisp white linen shirt.

'Hey.' She felt suddenly shy. She pointedly looked up and around the walls, trying to avoid his gaze. 'Can I take a look about?'

'Of course. It's not a huge collection, by any means. As you can see, the gallery is basically two rooms of the cottage opened up. Have you been in before?'

'No, no I haven't, sorry.'

'Well, I haven't been here that long really.'

'Life's just busy . . .' Eve trailed apologetically.

There was an amazingly powerful seascape hanging on the wall opposite her. The waves crashing over each other, in arcs and rolls of pinks and greys and whites, even notes of yellow, not a shade of blue in sight, and yet it looked just right. Whoever said the sea was blue anyhow? The painting captured the power of the surf, its energy. She could almost hear it crash and roll in with a boom.

She was brought back to the present with the explosive pop of a cork.

'May as well celebrate my first night.' Aiden appeared with a bottle of Moët & Chandon to hand and a broad grin. He passed her a glass of champagne.

'Oh, I'll just have a half. I've got the car,' she explained.

He kept the full glass for himself and poured another smaller one.

'Cheers.' They clinked flutes.

'Cheers, and I hope it goes so well for you, Aiden. You are such an amazing artist.' She scanned the artwork once more. 'And I love the old stone walls behind the paintings; they add character, timelessness. A cottage that's been here for centuries. Like your paintings are timeless – the sea, the tides, the ebb and flow.' It was hard to describe it all in words, how his paintings made her feel, but she was giving it her best creative shot. She took a large sip of fizz. It bubbled and melted fragrantly on her tongue.

'Thank you.' He gave a warm smile.

'Your other guests?' she asked.

'Oh, they'll be here soon enough.'

It seemed a little strange that no one else had arrived as yet. He had definitely said six thirty to her. Perhaps they were all being fashionably late; maybe that was the arty way to do things, she mused.

Her eye was then drawn to a trio of paintings. She

shifted a few steps across the room to take a better look. She recognised the setting; it was Low Newton, a beach not far away, southwards along the coast. Together, the paintings worked as a panorama, and yet singly they were stunningly beautiful too. It was a night scene, almost haunting, mesmerising, with the waves catching silver trails of moonlight as they rolled to the shore, the moon itself half hidden by clouds and that iridescent glow that the artist had captured so well, the ruins of Dunstanburgh Castle brooding on the darkened cliffs.

'You look beautiful when you're concentrating like that.' Aiden was suddenly behind her. His breath warm near her shoulder.

'Oh.' She didn't know what else to say.

Oh my, oh my. Just friends. Just friends. But no one had called her beautiful in a long, long time. He sounded so earnest too.

She then felt Aiden's arms pass around her waist and clasp together somewhere near her bellybutton, drawing her close. She held her breath. It felt almost surreal . . . yet very real. Then she turned, ever so slowly, aware of him close. So close, in fact, that she could feel the firm contours of his body beneath his shirt. Aware that she was finally feeling what it was like to be in his arms.

Their faces were just inches apart, eyes fixed; his, a liquid blue with flecks of grey. And then his lips met hers, as his hands drew her in tighter still. His lips were warm, moist, moving with a pressure that was new and fast, and exciting, yes, but—

'Stop . . . I can't do this. I didn't come here for this.'

The burn of his lips was still imprinted upon hers, her face reddening with shame. She had a husband, a child. What the hell was she thinking? 'I have to go . . .' She gathered her handbag. Stumbled, as she dashed for the door. 'Good luck with the exhibition. With everything . . .'

And she left the gallery in a fog of reluctant desire and confusion. Yet, what she had done was all too clear in her mind. What had she even been thinking, agreeing to go there, when there was that obvious frisson between them? She shouldn't be here kissing some other guy; she should be at home trying to put things right between her and Ben. Yes, she knew that this had been building; she would be lying to herself if she pretended that she hadn't liked – even *craved* – the attention from Aiden. But the kiss had brought the reality crashing in with cold, hard clarity.

She crossed the street and slumped down in the driver's seat of her car, gazing ahead blankly whilst she gathered herself. She had done it, she had just kissed another man, and yes, it had felt exciting, and sort of passionate . . . but it was so, so wrong.

And . . . she couldn't ever now change what she'd done. She suddenly felt quite sick.

And, oh hell, imagine if someone had seen? Thank God – in some senses – she and Aiden had been alone, that it was just her at the exhibition. She glanced across the street to the gallery. Thankfully, the village looked pretty quiet this evening. A couple, most likely tourists, were wandering about further down the street; someone was going into the Castle pub, and there was a bloke heading for the beach with a spaniel. No one was staring at her. Life appeared to be carrying on as normal, although Eve's felt as if it had flipped on its head.

Brenda from the Kirkton Deli had closed up a little early and, deciding to make the most of this lovely balmy evening, had taken her seven-year-old grandson, Luke, down to the coast for a walk on the sands and a short game of beach cricket. She had fielded and he'd batted. After ten minutes of dashing about like that, she was blooming shattered and had worked up a very unladylike sweat; he was getting to be a good strong shot now that he was growing up.

'Right, that's it. You've worn your grandma out, pet. Let's go and see if the ice-cream shop is still open. I think it opens later through the summer.'

They were in luck. Luke chose a choc-dipped cone with a scoop of raspberry ripple, and Brenda went for a vanilla with chocolate sauce. Delicious. They meandered slowly back to their car which was parked further up the little main street, near to the village green. They were in no rush as they were licking and munching their ice creams as they went.

'Good, isn't it?'

'Lush,' answered Luke. 'Thanks, Grandma. And thanks for trying to play cricket with me.'

She had to laugh at the 'trying'.

Oh, look, there was a new exhibition in the Coastal Gallery. A painting in the window caught her eye . . . and then something else too. Unusually, but rather sweetly, a couple were having a smooch inside the gallery. Aw, how romantic.

Brenda paused. There was something very familiar about the girl's gorgeously wavy dark hair . . . Oh gosh, it hit Brenda like a steam train. It was Eve. Married-to-Ben *Eve*. Brenda did a double take, pausing outside on the pavement for a second. Surely, it was just someone who *looked like* Eve. But the young woman from their village was quite distinctive and Brenda could have sworn on it. She looked closer. The girl pulled away . . . oh yes, it had to be Eve. And the man who she was with was certainly not her husband. *Oh* . . . Brenda didn't know quite what to think, and moved on swiftly. Her grandson was oblivious to the scenario inside the window, munching away on the chocolatey biscuit of his cone.

'Let's head back then, Luke.' Brenda tried her best not to sound flustered. 'Your mum'll be expecting you for your tea.'

32

Earlier that afternoon, Rachel had been up in the attic, raking through a box of old photographs. She wanted to take some special memories and mementoes along with her to Tom's farmhouse. A couple of extra photos of Dad and Mum would be a lovely boost for her and Maisy to have around them there.

There was one photo in particular that she was searching for. It captured her as a kid, sitting on her dad's shoulders with the fields and farmyard behind them. She used to love it when Dad used to sweep her up high in the air and then prop her there, hands to hands, as she leaned against the back of his head, jiggling about the farmyard or taking a trek to check on the sheep or cattle together. She'd felt on top of the world then, invincible. She would have been about six in that photo: Maisy's age.

She sifted through the images: pics of their caravan holidays in Yorkshire, one of Granny Ruth and Grandad Ken looking oh-so-young, Mum all dressed smartly for her silver wedding anniversary celebrations, and then oh . . . one of Mum and Dad together, sitting on a hay bale in sunnier times. Right, that one was definitely going with her. She picked up a few of her as a baby – hah, what on earth was she wearing? It looked like some kind of Victorian smocked milkmaid outfit. Oh, and then there was the golden ticket, the photo of her riding high on her dad's strong shoulders, looking out across Primrose Farm.

She held the picture in front of her, and her eyes misted. She held it further away, not wanting her impending tears to spoil the image. 'Oh, Dad.' She'd go and buy a new frame in the village to keep it safe and special, and pop it somewhere where she'd see it every day at Tom's.

She was just packing away the other photos when there was a call from the bottom of the attic ladder.

'You okay up there? Ready for a cuppa, love?' shouted Jill.

'Yeah, I'll be down in a minute.'

'Did you find what you wanted?'

'Yes, and more. I'll bring the photos down with me. Some lovely memories there.'

'Oh, that's nice, I love a trip down memory lane.'

Rachel had yet to break the news to her mum that she and Maisy would be moving in with Tom, away from Primrose. Deep down she knew her mum would respect any decision that she made, but it still wasn't something she was desperate to discuss, though she knew she'd have to. She braced herself and hugged the precious photos to her chest, before making her way back down the ladder.

*

Ten minutes later, with the nostalgic photos spread out before them on the kitchen table, and a mug of coffee and squares of flapjack to hand, Rachel took a slow breath.

'Mum, there's something I need to tell you.'

'Yes, pet?' Jill looked up, her eyes filled with warmth.

Rachel took a second; she hoped her mum wouldn't be too disappointed.

'Tom and I have decided . . . well, me and Maisy are going to move in and live there after the wedding . . . with Tom.' There, she'd ripped off the Band-Aid.

Jill nodded, looking down at her hands. 'Yes, of course that makes sense, love. Whatever you decide. And you'll be over here every day just the same, I know that.' If she was feeling disappointed, she was doing her best to hide it, bless her.

'We'll only be around the corner,' Rachel said, her voice quaking. She hated to think of her mum feeling lonely.

Jill reached out and took her daughter's hand. 'I know. I know.'

'We'll not be able to keep Maisy away either,' Rachel managed a smile. 'And I *have* to come back for my Sunday roast and your sticky toffee pudding. Or . . . maybe I can cook you and granny a roast dinner over there and have you all round – that'd be good too.'

'Yes, and Maisy can have sleepovers here whenever she wants to. We'll all be seeing plenty of each other, there's no doubt of that,' Jill said with a sniff.

'Absolutely. And hey Mum, maybe this will give you and Daniel a chance to have a bit more time together, more space.' She paused with a gulp. 'He's not so bad, you know. He really cares about you; he might just be a keeper.'

Jill squeezed her daughter's hand. 'Thank you, love, that means a lot.'

They smiled at each other, both floating on memories of the past, and looking forward to the future.

Phew, Rachel was relieved to have that off her chest. And her mum was right, she'd be back here all the time. It was her home; it was too special to leave behind for good.

Breaking the news to Maisy later that afternoon, however, didn't go quite as smoothly.

Walking up the farm track together after the school minibus drop-off, Rachel started to explain. 'Maisy, you know when Mummy and Tom get married . . .'

'Yes,' she said excitedly, 'that's when I get to wear my pretty dress.'

'Yep, so, well after that . . .' Rachel wondered quite how to put this. 'Well, married people, like Eve and Ben, they live together in the same house.'

Maisy nodded, seeming to take it in. So far so good.

'Well, we're going to live with Tom, in his house. So, after the wedding day, we'll be staying there. You'll have your own bedroom there and everything.'

Maisy slowed her steps, 'But what about my room

here . . . and what about Grandma? Is she coming too?' Maisy was trying hard to process all this.

'No, petal. Grandma will stay here at Primrose Farm.'

Maisy's lip began to quiver. 'But I want to stay here with Grandma.' She stood rooted on the spot, her arms flapping wildly.

The sheep the other side of the fence bobbed their heads up at the noise, and a pair of sparrows darted out of the hedgerow.

'Oh sweetie, you can still come and see Grandma every day. But you have to live with me and Tom. How can I look after you otherwise? Read you your bedtime story, tuck you in? And, you can choose a new duvet set for your new bedroom – we can have a look online tonight if you like . . . and Tom's going to paint the walls whatever colour you want.'

Maisy stayed silent.

'It'll be good there,' Rachel coaxed, 'I promise.'

They took a few steps forward, and then Maisy stopped again, her arms folded. 'Don't want to go,' was her parting shot.

Rachel knew not to push the conversation any further right now. Sometimes you needed a little time to get your head around things. Change was hard enough to deal with at twenty-six, never mind six.

33

EVE

Eve tried to clear her head on the journey home from the exhibition. The feeling of guilt prickled over her skin like a rash. She also felt as if she'd been slightly duped. Had Aiden asked her to go early, before the main event, so they would have some time alone? Or, was she just trying to distract from her own guilt with excuses? She had known full well what she was doing, after all. She had allowed him to hold her . . . enjoyed that moment in his arms . . . the kiss.

But this was serious, she wasn't free to do any of that. This could really hurt her family. Could destroy her relationship with Ben. She felt sickened by her actions.

No one could ever know. She'd go home . . . act as normally as she could. And try so hard to put things right with Ben. Confessing would be no good, would it? If he knew the truth, he might not be able to forgive or forget. She had to think of Amelia in all of this too. Why, oh why had she put them all in jeopardy? If she could turn back the clock . . . could have made some excuse to Aiden and just stayed at home. But what was done, was done. And, maybe in time, when things had moved on, it wouldn't have the power to hurt them anymore.

It was just a stupid crush. She saw it for what it was now . . . laid bare in a barrel of guilt. Just a silly crush. And Aiden, yes, he was attractive and creative, but he really didn't seem the type to want to be tied down with a woman with a six-year-old in tow. He was a free spirit, an artist. She'd let herself get drawn in, be flattered. Stupid, stupid, stupid.

Life wasn't all glamour and passion. Love wasn't all kisses and romance. You had to work at relationships, and yes, you could get stuck in a rut, but did she still love Ben? Yes, a voice in her heart spoke out. Even with his *Game of Thrones* addiction, three sugars in his coffee, and dirty socks strewn across the bedroom floor. Hah, and no wonder they were bloody stuck in a rut. She couldn't think of when they'd had any real alone time since they'd had Amelia. And yes she'd tried, and failed, to rekindle things the other night. But they'd just have to try harder – she'd have to show Ben that they were worth fighting for.

The drive passed in a tumble of thoughts, and promises to herself that she'd do better from now on. She passed the entrance to Rachel's farm – whoa, what would her friend think if she knew? – and carried on up the lane to arrive outside their cottage, where Ben would most likely be sitting in the lounge watching TV, totally oblivious to her misdemeanours.

She felt a gut-churn of fear as she undid her seat belt and gazed at her cottage, her home. *Take a deep breath. Steel yourself. Try and behave like normal.* Ben could *never* find out.

Walking up the path. Opening the door. Amelia would be upstairs in bed asleep by now, for sure. So, she dropped down her handbag in the hall and gathered herself, before opening the sitting-room door and popping her head around.

'Hi, Ben. I'm home.'

Yes, there was Ben lounging on the sofa with a packet of crisps to hand and an episode of *Game of Thrones* going on in full noisy battle. He paused it and turned to her with a small smile. 'Hiya . . . go okay? You're a bit earlier than I thought you'd be.'

'Ah, yeah. It was fine . . . Some great paintings.' She felt her cheeks burn. Hoped Ben didn't notice.

'So, did you get to meet any good contacts? For your own crafts?'

'Oh . . . well, the people there just seemed a bit more highbrow, like owners of proper art galleries.' The white lie spilled out.

'Ah, right okay. Well, this episode is brilliant. You wanna watch it with me or catch up later?' He didn't seem keen to chat about her evening further, and that suited Eve just fine.

'Yeah, I'll come and watch. Just let me get a cuppa. Can I get you anything?'

'Nah, I'm fine, thanks.'

Eve felt like a bloody stiff drink, never mind a cup of tea. But raiding the drinks cupboard for a large gin and tonic was not the answer.

'Amelia been fine?'

'Yeah, sound. We've been playing Connect 4. Can't believe she beat me twice, too. I wasn't even trying to lose.' He was grinning.

He'd always been a good dad, Eve realised, even if the two of them had drifted in the wrong direction of late. Her mind drifted back to the day Amelia was born, all pink and scrawny with her battle cry of a hello to the world. Whilst Eve had lain on the hospital bed being stitched up, she had looked across at Ben gently holding their brand-new little girl and he'd smiled at Eve with tears in his eyes, saying how proud he was of both of them. Oh . . . family life suddenly seemed so precious.

'Well, I won't be a minute.' Eve needed a moment to gather herself.

She stepped out into the welcome coolness of the hallway. She then clicked on the kettle in the galley kitchen, and couldn't resist making her way upstairs to look in on her daughter. She opened the doorway just a fraction and peeped in. She looked so small and innocent, sleeping soundly there. Tears crowded Eve's eyes as she gazed down. *Stupid idiot, Eve.* She brushed away the teardrops with the back of her hand and then went and stood in the bathroom for a few seconds, catching her reflection in the mirror, before splashing her eyes with cold water. Who was this woman?

She went back downstairs, trying to avoid the creaky steps, so as not to disturb Amelia. She took her mug through, taking a slow, steadying breath at the threshold to the lounge, and went to sit with her husband . . . the husband she had just betrayed.

34

The sweet smell of freshly cut hay wafted across the fields towards the yard of Primrose Farm. Rachel had heard the hum of the tractor from the Pantry, signalling that Tom was now at work on her meadows, having cut his own yesterday.

'Is it okay if I bob out to see Tom and take him a bite of lunch?' Rachel asked Jill. It was past one thirty now and had got slightly quieter at the Pantry.

'Of course, all the tables are served here just now. Get yourself away.'

'I'll take a few things for him, and for Mark, too.' Tom's farmhand, Mark, would often help out on Tom's farm at the busier times of year. So, Rachel made up a picnic lunch of ham sandwiches, with ham fresh from the local butcher, some buttered cheese scones, two chocolate cupcakes and a mini sticky toffee pudding, especially for Tom.

'I'll be back shortly. You know what it's like at hay-making time. No one wants to stop for long. You have to crack on while it stays dry.'

Getting on to her quad, with her goodies secured in a small box, Rachel felt a familiar surge of excitement breaking through. She was reminded of this time last year, when Tom had offered to help her to mow her hay for the first time, and she'd done a picnic delivery. Back then, she'd wanted to thank him for his kindness and support, and a tasty lunch taken to him in the field had seemed a good idea. There had been a real connection between them that day, the realisation hitting that their friendship promised so much more. And a year on, here they were, about to be married.

She headed for the hum of the tractor. The saying 'make hay while the sun shines' was very true, and today was a scorcher. As she whizzed off, the breeze on the quad was wonderfully refreshing on such a warm day. Arms bare, shorts on, her farmer's suntan apparent – with marked T-shirt-and-shorts lines. Ah, she'd *so* have to remember to get a spray tan done before the wedding – to match up the tops of her arms for her dress, and the tops of her legs and tummy for her new fancy lace lingerie!

Tom was cutting the headland – the outer area of the field – of the second field now. And by the sounds of it, Mark was 'tedding' – aerating the cut hay – in the first field. So, Primrose Farm's two hay fields were well on the way. Tomorrow, she'd help with the rowing and baling, so fingers crossed that it stayed dry. It was always a good feeling getting the hay in, and knowing you had a good store of food for your animals over the winter. It looked as though it was going to be a decent yield this season too, which they'd need if there was another hard winter ahead.

But, for now, the sun was blasting, the bees were buzzing, and her fiancé was pulling to a halt. He looked surprised as he opened the door of his tractor cab and climbed out.

Rachel approached with a little trepidation. The sunshine had carried her over to the fields in good spirits, but she was suddenly all too aware of the storm clouds that had followed her and Tom around the last couple of weeks.

'Lunch?' she asked tentatively.

'That sounds great, thanks.' He strolled across.

Rachel started unloading the goods a little nervously. 'There's plenty here for Mark too, so give him a shout.'

'Yeah, will do, I'll phone him in a sec . . . Thank you for doing this, I really appreciate it. And hey, Rach, it's good to see you.'

'You too.' She smiled, her agitation starting to evaporate.

'Hey, have you realised where we are?' His tone was soft.

'On my farm . . .'

'But where exactly?'

It was lovely to hear the hint of warmth in his voice. Rachel pulled a face, still unsure of what he was getting at.

'Look, I've just been cutting the grass for our wedding venue.'

'Oh, yes. We're in just the spot.'

This was *the field*, nearest to the farmyard and the Pudding Pantry, where the tipi was going to be put up for the reception. The whole place would be transformed, with all the beautiful flowers they'd chosen, Eve's crafts and bunting decorations, and their Towers of Pudding, and the absolutely gorgeous wedding cake that they had ordered – a three-tiered sponge and buttercream affair with the prettiest floral garnish. It was going to look stunningly 'boho chic', in a countryside 'fairy-tale palace' as Maisy was calling it. Rachel didn't have the heart to correct her that it was just a tent.

It was wonderful to see that Tom was finally getting that buzz of anticipation too. But Rachel understood what a hard time he'd been having. It was only a week until the court hearing.

She didn't want to spoil the moment but she wanted to remind him she was there for him too. 'How are you feeling about Wednesday?'

'Kind of resigned to getting it over with. I just want to know what's going to happen now, and to move on. My solicitor's doing all he can and there's a couple of new developments he's looking into, but all I can do is tell the truth and do my best . . . then it's over to the judge.'

'I can still come down to Newcastle with you if you'd like?'

'No, honestly, this is between me and Caitlin. I'll be fine.'

'Okay.'

'And Rach . . .' Tom looked at her in earnest, before stroking the back of her hand gently. 'Look, I'm really sorry if I've been a bit irritable these past few weeks. I-I've just found all this with the farm and Caitlin really tough.'

'It's okay. I understand, Tom. I'd have been furious and stressed-out too if it was my farm under threat. And . . . I'm sorry too, for perhaps not being as understanding as I might have been, and for not letting you know earlier about Jake coming to the wedding.'

'Hey, no worries. We'll work it all out somehow.'

'Yeah, we will.' Rachel smiled, feeling like a weight had been lifted.

They began tucking into the tasty food.

'Suppose I'd better give young Mark a shout.' He took his mobile out of his pocket.

'Hah, yeah, before it all goes.'

Tom looked as if he hadn't eaten in a week, the way it was being piled in . . . hmm, maybe he *hadn't* had much of a square meal lately. He did look a bit thinner than normal. Perhaps it was all the recent stress. Oh well, she'd soon be there, living at the house with him; she could keep a better eye and look after him.

Though it would still be strange to be moving out of Primrose Farm, which would *always* have the most special place in her heart, it was beginning to feel as if things would work out. Maisy had even started to come around to the idea of the move over the past couple of days. She had chosen a new unicorn bed-linen set for her brand-new bedroom at Tom's. He'd also promised that she could choose whatever shade of paint she wanted for her bedroom walls. Rachel had raised her eyebrows at that – knowing Maisy, it might well end up all the colours of the rainbow.

They were sitting on an uncut section of grass verge, close by the hedgerow, where bees buzzed in and out of the ox-eye daisies and buttercups swayed gently in the breeze. A butterfly fluttered past and then settled on a wild-flower head, a delicate blue cornflower. Rachel felt its significance, being her choice for her bouquet and bridal head garland. A smile spread over her lips. Summer, hazy sunshine, the glow of heat on your skin – being outside on the farm with nature doing its thing all around them was so calming.

'Mark's on his way,' Tom started, as they heard the tractor in the other field pull to a stop. 'But . . . just before he gets here, there's one thing I really need to do.'

Tom pulled Rachel towards him, tenderly pressing his lips against hers. Making every little nerve in her body flicker to life. How did his kiss manage to do that to her every time? It was like lighting the touch paper of her senses. She responded warmly, passionately.

Evidently, they'd been kissing longer than anticipated, as they heard Mark's gruff shout from the gateway. 'Enough, you two – get a room, will you! I know you're getting married soon, but really,' he jested.

'Sorry.' Rachel couldn't help but grin.

'Well then, where's the bait? That's all I'm here for.' He strolled towards them, swigging from a can of fizzy drink.

As Rachel handed him a selection of the food, his eyes lit up. 'Great stuff. Cheers, Rach. I'll take it back to the cab. Don't want to get in the way of you two lovebirds here. No point being a spare wheel.' His eyes smiled as he spoke, shaking his head at them as he left.

'Hah, I'll not be long, Mark. Back to it in five, yeah,' Tom called after him. They needed to crack on while the weather stayed fine.

'Yeah, no worries, mate.'

'I'd better get back to help Mum in the Pantry, too. If there've been any new customers in, she'll be run off her feet. Maybe catch you later?'

'That would be great, but I've got a meeting with my accountant late afternoon, and then I'll probably need to go over details of the paperwork a bit more, get it in my head.'

Perhaps he was organising his finances before this court case. It was there looming over them, even in the sunshine-filled meadow. 'No worries, you do what you need to. I'll catch you soon. Better love you and leave you, then.'

They managed another brief, but still all-over tingly kiss.

As Rachel mounted the quad, and despite the imminent court case, she felt happier than she had in a while. It felt as if they were a team again. She gave Tom a wave and was warmed through by his smile back. Their future was bright. They'd get through this legal battle, whatever the result, and then . . . well, they would have the party of their lives with their friends and families, celebrating their wedding and their love, in a gorgeously decorated tipi on a beautiful grassy hill at Primrose Farm. *This* hill. Yes, life felt good.

Back at the Pantry, she and Jill put in a manic hour, serving a table of eight hikers who had arrived for a late lunch, and there were orders for afternoon teas, pudding platters and more coming in. Rachel never minded a busy spell, though her feet might say otherwise: it was a sure sign that their business was growing well. Whilst there had been a dip after the initial spate of bad reviews, the response from her Pudding Clubbers and support from the local community had helped to rally things, and the negative comments hadn't seemed to have put too many people off, thank god.

After three p.m., it began to calm a little, and the conversation behind the counter turned to the last-minute wedding details. Jill was chattering away: Had Rachel remembered to order the 'thank you' gifts for the bridesmaids? And, what about the table plan? Did they have final guest numbers yet?

So many people had said 'yes', it seemed as if the whole village – as well as a host of distant relatives – were coming. There were going to be well over a hundred and fifty people attending the reception. Gulp. Whilst they were trying to do this on a budget, it was hard in such a small community to miss out friends and long-held acquaintances, and this celebration was also a way of thanking them all for their help and support in the three years since the death of Rachel's father. She really hoped Tom didn't get hit by a huge pay-out to Caitlin. They'd have kept their wedding plans much smaller if they'd known all of that was going to crop up.

'Oh,' Jill was on a roll now. 'And have you re-contacted the cake lady, to confirm the order and delivery?'

'No, not yet. One for my to-do list.'

Despite their love of baking, they had decided to splash out and buy the wedding cake. With having so much to do themselves towards the buffet and the now-named 'Towers of Treats', as well as all the other tasks on the day itself, they had decided not to take on creating the wedding cake. So, Rachel and Jill had chosen a beautiful, three-tiered 'naked'-style sponge cake with a delicate scraping of ivory buttercream around the sides. There were oh-so-pretty floral garnishes on all three layers to complement the wedding flowers. In the photos they'd seen, it looked stunningly simple. They'd had a tasting session several weeks back when they'd first visited the cake designer, and the vanilla sponge was delicious too. Rachel and Tom's cake was to be baked and delivered to them the day before the wedding, so it would be super fresh.

'Oh, and I'm going to call and see Granny this afternoon, too. Once we've closed up here.' Rachel still had something most important to ask her.

'Oh, can you take her some more eggs then, love? She phoned this morning – she's been baking again and run out. Wasn't feeling quite well enough to make the walk into town. I was going to pop in myself, but if you're going, I might use the time to pop and get a birthday card I need to post, and pick up a few bits and bobs in the Co-op.'

'Of course.'

Maisy was going for tea at Eve's tonight to have a play date with Amelia after school, so that would all work out. Rachel suddenly remembered her latest conversation with Eve; when Rachel had asked how the exhibition night had gone, Eve had been quite cagey in answering. They'd texted in between times, in their own coded-style messages, Rachel wanting her buddy to know she was there for her if needed, but Eve was keeping something close to her chest. Hmm, when they were next on their own, she'd prise some more details from her friend.

'Cooee, Jill,' Brenda popped her head out from the door of the deli. 'I'm glad I've spotted you.'

It was later that afternoon and Jill was in town. She backtracked along the pavement to catch up with her friend.

'How's it going, Brenda? Lovely day, isn't it?'

'Aye, it is. So, how's everything going with the wedding planning then?'

'Yes, all fine. Keeping us busy. *Very* busy, in fact!' Jill smiled.

'So, it's all going to plan? That's good. Well, I'll be baking along with the Pudding Club, but if there's anything else I can help with, let me know.'

'Yes, I will. Oh, it's so near now, I'm really looking forward to it. Rachel is going to look a real picture in that beautiful dress. Did you know that Eve made it? Her best friend?'

At the mention of Eve, Brenda looked distinctly uncomfortable. 'Yes . . .' Her voice trailed off and she went a bit pale.

'Brenda, are you all right?'

'Yes, yes,' she squeaked, looking down at her shoes.

'You don't seem okay, what's the matter?'

'Ah, yes . . . well . . . oh crikey, I don't know if I should say anything really . . . It's just been eating me up a bit, you see.'

Jill was suddenly all ears; she hoped to goodness this wasn't bad news. 'Well, you can't start saying things like that and not tell me what's on your mind, Brenda. Come on, spill.'

'Oh, I'm not sure I should really. It'll all blow over. Ah, it'll be something and nothing.' Brenda was trying hard to backtrack. She might be a bit gossipy, but the last thing she wanted to do was stir up trouble.

'Come on, Brenda, it can't be that bad. I'm your friend, you can tell me. A problem shared is a problem halved and all that!'

'Oh blimey – well, as long as it stays between us two.' Brenda was still reluctant to spill. 'It's just, well, I saw Eve . . . with another man. They were . . . kissing.'

'What? I can't believe it, not Eve. Are . . . are you sure?' Jill was incredulous.

'Yes, I have to say I did a double take myself. Stopped a while to check if it really was Eve. I was over in Bamburgh with young Luke and I just happened to look in at that new gallery place. And there they were.' Brenda paused, seeing Jim the taxi driver pull up across the way and then nip into the post office. 'Oh, Jill, Ben'll be devastated if he learns of this. I'm sure it must have just been a mistake. I wonder if Rachel could maybe have a word with Eve, with them being close . . . find out what's going on. Make her see sense.'

'Yes, perhaps.' Jill was still struggling to get to grips with the news.

'Or, heaven forbid, if there's a bust-up around the time of the wedding, at least it won't be quite such a shock if you and Rachel are in the know. I'm sorry to put this on you, Jill.'

'I see.' Jill was still processing it. It seemed so unlike family-minded Eve.

'I've not spoken a word of it to anyone else,' Brenda assured. 'It's their marriage at the end of the day, but well, it seems so out of character. She's a good girl at heart, is Eve. Hopefully, I've read it all wrong. But it looked like much more than a friendly kiss on the cheek.'

'Well, thanks for letting me know, Brenda. I'll think about it and maybe have a word with Rachel.' Jill really wasn't sure whether it should be before the wedding, though. There was already so much on her daughter's plate right now. After a further chat about the up-and-coming wedding, and family life in general, the two women said their goodbyes, and Jill bustled off up the quiet street to do her chores, her head swimming with the revelation.

What they hadn't been aware of, however, was that in a car parked just two spaces from where they were standing talking, was a certain Vanessa Palmer-Pilkington – gossipmonger extraordinaire. Her window had been wound down, with it being such a warm day, and she had been waiting for her husband to come back from the newsagent's. Juicy snippets of the conversation had drifted on the breeze to her raised and ready ear: 'Have a word . . . with Rachel'; 'a bust-up at the time of the wedding' and 'another man'. Two and two were put together to make a mighty one hundred and it wouldn't be long before village tongues would begin to wag.

35

'Hi, Granny, it's Rachel.'

Rachel stepped through the cottage hallway, which was decorated with jugs of pastel-coloured sweet peas.

'Ah, come on in, lass. I'm just here in the sitting room . . . catching up with *Escape to the Country*.'

Rachel popped her head around the door.

'Hello, pet.' Granny was looking rather pale beneath her smile. Her illness last winter had really taken its toll. Despite her age, it was unusual to see her sitting down at this time of the afternoon. 'Yes, they're in the Cotswolds today, pretty enough place, but not a patch on what we have up here.'

Rachel went to stand beside her. 'No, I don't suppose it is.'

'It's a hidden gem we have up here in the Scottish borders.' She gave a wink of her wise old blue eyes, 'and let's keep it that way, hey lass. Anyway, you won't get me moving again. I'll be coming out of this wee cottage feet first, I tell you.'

'Oh Granny, don't talk like that.'

'Well, I'm not going to live for ever, hinnie.' Ruth was down to earth as always.

'Yes, but we've got a wedding to look forward to and happier times. And . . . on that note, I'll go and put the kettle on, as there's something I want to ask you.'

'Sounds important.'

'It is,' answered Rachel with a knowing smile, not giving anything away. 'I've brought you those eggs that you asked for, by the way, and there's a summer pudding that Mum's made.'

'Oh, that's grand. Yes, I've been busy baking again this week. Made a load of buns and a sponge cake for the stall at the coffee morning for the toddler group.' It made Granny happy to bake for others, and to help the community in her own small but lovely way.

With that, Rachel set off for the kitchen. She hoped Granny would be pleased when she came out with her question. It might not be easy for either of them, but it was the only thing that felt right . . .

With the tea pot set up on a tray, and cups and saucers set out the old-fashioned way, Granny pottered through to the kitchen to help Rachel dig out the cakes. There was a Madeira cake and some rock buns. She sliced the cake and set out two gorgeous yellow squares on a plate; their Primrose Farm free-range eggs were always wonderfully good for baking and gave such a golden colour.

Settled back in the living room, with Rachel seated on the slightly worn, but very comfy sofa, and Ruth in her high-backed armchair, Rachel let out a deep breath. 'So, Granny, I've been thinking . . . and . . . I know who

I'd love to walk me down the aisle at my wedding. So, I thought I'd come and run it past you.'

'Okay, lass . . .' Granny looked up.

'You.' Rachel beamed.

'Me? Are you sure . . .? Well, we won't be going very fast!'

Rachel laughed. 'That's fine. We'll be in no rush . . . everybody will be gawping at my dress then, for sure.'

'Oh, yes, I haven't seen it yet. Eve's made it, hasn't she? I bet it's beautiful.'

'It really is. I'm not really a dress person, as you know, happier in my jeans and wellies, but . . . wow.'

'Oh, I can't wait to see you in it.'

'So, will you do it? Look, I know it's going to be hard for us . . .' She paused, catching her breath, 'as dad can't be there himself . . . but it just feels kind of right. You're his mother, and *my* best support. But if you think it'll be too emotional, too difficult . . .' She didn't want to make Ruth feel obliged to do anything she wasn't comfortable with.

'Oh, lass, I'd love to do it. That's if you don't mind some old bid being there by your side?'

'I can't think of anyone better. It might end up being a bit teary, mind.' She was welling up just thinking about it already. It was definitely going to be an emotional day.

'Aye, well . . . that's only natural, in the circumstances. Of course, if that's what you want, I'll be there beside you, lass . . .'

'. . . every step of the way,' Rachel took up, trying to stop herself getting too choked up.

'Yes, every doddery step.' Granny gave a warm smile. 'Ah, bless you pet . . . there'll be tears and laughter on the day, for sure. But we'll be certain to have a grand old time. Robert would want that and he'd be so proud of you.'

Rachel found that any words were stuck in her throat then, so she just nodded. For all the hurt and grief, she felt happy too. The Swinton ladies were taking life forward – without their gorgeous dad, husband, son – one doddery yet forceful step at a time.

Rachel headed home via Eve's to collect Maisy from her tea-time play date with Amelia. She was looking forward to catching up with her best friend, who'd been rather elusive these past few days.

'Hi-i.' After rapping on the door, she stepped into her friend's house.

'Hi, there.' Eve came out into the hallway to greet her, looking slightly flushed.

'All okay?'

'Yeah, the girls have been great. They're out playing in the garden. They've made a den.'

The friends walked out through the back door of the cottage.

'Mum-my,' Maisy dashed over. 'We had fish fingers and peas and chips, and ice cream with strawberries. Yummy. I ate all mine up.'

'Sounds great.'

'And look, come see our house.' She laced her fingers through Rachel's, tugging at her to follow her. A den had been created from a tented sheet draped over the wooden picnic table. Eve had pinned some bunting up inside for them, adorning the underside of the table, and there were dolls, animal toys, a mini tractor and some flowers, now wilting, evidently picked from Eve's garden borders. Rachel raised her eyebrows, hoping the girls hadn't just taken it upon themselves to raid the flowerbeds.

'It's okay,' Eve chuckled, spotting her concern, 'I said they could pick a few flowers.'

'It's a wedding,' announced Maisy with delight.

'And this is the tent like you're going to have,' added Amelia animatedly.

'Ah, yes, now I see . . . a tipi.'

'Told you it was a ti-pi.' Maisy crossed her arms huffily, as though the girls had had a difference of opinion earlier.

'Well, it is a kind of tent too, Maisy.' Rachel didn't want any falling outs.

'We can't wait to be your bridesmaids, Auntie Rachel. We've been practising,' said Amelia.

'They've been traipsing up and down the garden with nighties on over their school uniforms,' Eve grinned.

'Aw, bless them.' They were on real countdown now, with only ten days to go.

'Do you want a coffee or anything, Rach?' Despite asking, Eve looked slightly uneasy, as though fearful of having too much time to talk.

'Yes, just a quick one, if that's okay? That'd be great.' Rachel had already had her fill of tea at Granny's house, but she felt as if it might finally give them a chance to have a heart-to-heart.

'Okay, cool. Umm, Ben'll be home any time soon, too.'

Was that a warning not to get too personal? For Rachel not to probe?

'Tea or coffee then, hun?' Eve raised a smile.

'A coffee would be great.'

'Yeah, I'll just make it, and then let's go sit in the sunshine with the girls, shall we?'

'Sounds good.'

Rachel followed Eve to her galley kitchen, hoping a moment in private might just be the spur Eve needed, but the conversation stuck closely with the wedding. Eve chattering on a little nervously: Did Rachel want another dress fitting at the weekend, for any final tweaks?, How was she feeling?, How were things now with Tom?

Rachel answered, telling her friend how relieved she was that she and Tom were so much more at ease with each other again; it was as though a black cloud had been lifted.

'And you and Ben?' Rachel asked, seeing her opening.

'Ah, we're fine. All good here.' Eve didn't meet Rachel's eye, and carried on spooning coffee granules into the mugs. 'Oh . . . I've made some shortbreads,' she said, swiftly changing tack. 'I've experimented with adding a little fresh lavender to them. It was a tip I remembered from my nanna. You can be my taste tester, if you like.'

'Sure.' Rachel could spot a diversionary tactic a mile off, but the biscuits did look delightful.

They were soon sitting out in the garden, listening to their daughters' chatter, sipping coffee and eating the delicately fragrant lavender shortbreads, whilst taking in the glorious green-field view across the valley, clouds billowing like pillows above them.

'These are delicious, Eve. Who'd have thought?' Rachel was definitely going to borrow that recipe from Eve for the Pantry.

'Thanks. Well, let's hope you get a gorgeous sunny day like this, Rach. Not long to go now, hun . . .'

'Yeah.' Rachel felt a giddy swirl of excitement, swished with a twist of anxiety that all would go well, that there'd be no last-minute hitches with the catering, flowers, the weather, Jake being there, the list could go on . . . But all of that could be sorted, she reassured herself. The most important thing in all this was the love and commitment between her and Tom.

The conversation stayed safe thereafter. Rachel knew not to push, but just hoped her friend really was okay. Eve didn't seem herself, and Rachel was sure she was holding something back.

Twenty minutes later, with coffee cups drained, and no more than wedding plans and breezy everyday conversation between them, Rachel was getting up to go when Ben arrived home.

'Hiya, Rach.' He appeared on the back step in his garage overalls with a smile.

'Hi Ben, you okay? Good day at work?' Rachel asked.

'Yeah, fine. I'll just go take a shower, get out of these oily clothes.' He dipped his head back through the door again, just as Amelia called out 'Daddy!' from their make-shift play-tent.

'Hey, sweetheart, I'll come and see you in a minute. I'm all sweaty just now,' he shouted back.

'O-kay.'

Rachel noted that Ben and Eve merely said the briefest of 'hellos' to each other; there was a definite coolness between them.

Over their years of friendship, she and Eve had shared all their ups and downs, their crushes, hurts, their hopes and dreams. Whatever it was, Eve wasn't yet ready to open up. But, whenever she did, Rachel would be there for her.

36

They lay in bed, Tom caressing her naked shoulder with gentle fingertips. Soon, they'd be able to do this every night, every morning . . . bliss.

Rachel was very much in need of some Tom tonic, and this was just the thing. She'd been unsettled seeing the distance between Eve and Ben, and then back at home, opening her laptop to do some admin for the farm, she'd found a new flurry of negative comments on their social media pages. Once Maisy was tucked up in bed, Rachel had rushed over to the farm next door and, this time, Tom had been more than happy to oblige.

'So, I've finally chosen someone special to walk me down the aisle . . .' Rachel spoke softly, happily. She loved this pillow-talk time.

'Oh, and who might that be?'

'Granny Ruth, I think she'll be just perfect.'

'Ah yes, I bet she'll love doing it too. Might be a bit emotional for you both, mind.'

'Yeah, it will. But whoever walks me down there, I know that moment will be hard as well as happy, knowing that it should be Dad there with me.'

'Hey, but remember I'll be there ready and waiting at the altar to make you both smile.' From the sound of his voice, she knew he was grinning even without looking up.

The excitement was building for the wedding. They shared a slow kiss which sent butterflies spinning through Rachel's stomach. It still seemed almost too good to be true.

'So, big day on Wednesday,' Rachel spoke cautiously, not wanting the magic between them to vanish, but knowing they had to face what lay ahead in the days before the wedding.

'Yeah . . .'

Rachel felt a sense of foreboding about the court case, along with the belief that it was something they could ultimately get past, a hurdle they would face and surmount together.

'At least we'll know.' Tom's face was close to hers, his breath warm on her cheek.

'Yeah.'

'And . . . if I have to sell some bloody land and that's the end of it, then so be it.'

'Whatever happens, Tom, we can make things work for us, with the two farms, we can join forces. We'll do whatever it takes.'

'I know. We will. I love you, Rachel.' The words were heartfelt.

'I love you, too.'

There was a pause, while they lay in each other's arms,

thinking, breathing, feeling that closeness. She nestled there, savouring the feel of his body next to hers, the warm-toast and aftershave smell of his skin.

'I need to get back soon, sorry. Better be back home for Maisy, for the morning routine.' It was already nearly one a.m. She often felt like a farmyard Cinderella, dashing back home on a quad instead of a carriage. She'd already missed the midnight hour.

'Yeah, I know.'

'Can't wait till I'm here every day.' Rachel tenderly stroked his bare chest.

'Me too . . . and you're definitely okay with that now?'

'Yes, it'll feel a bit strange at first to be leaving Primrose, if I'm being totally honest, but you know, now I've had time to get used to the idea, I think it'll work out really well for me and Maisy. It's time . . . time to leave some of those haunting memories behind . . . and it'll give Mum some space. And, hey, I'll be back over there just about every day, working the farm and at the Pantry. I'll not exactly be a million miles away.'

'We'll make it work fine, my love. More than fine . . .'

And the kiss that followed was filled with love and hope and all their dreams for their future.

Reluctantly, a few minutes later, she stole from under the covers, dressing by the cool moonlight of a Northumberland summer's night.

'Good luck, Tom. I'll be rooting for you every step of

the way.' She gave Tom a tender kiss on his forehead, and then made her way downstairs, past Mabel, who raised one eyelid and then settled back to snooze in her dog basket in the kitchen. Rachel set off with a sigh on her pumpkin quad.

37

The next morning, Rachel headed out to pick up some baler twine and washing powder at the agricultural merchant's, and decided to stop by the supermarket on the way back as they could do with some more flour and sugar. Old Mrs Jackson was standing in the sunshine on her terraced cottage doorstep on the high street. Rachel gave her a little friendly wave as she stepped out from the Land Rover, but the often-dour woman just tutted and shook her head at her. What was that all about?

Then, in the Co-op, three middle-aged ladies were chatting away, heads bowed close together. Yet as soon as Rachel walked in, the talking ceased abruptly and they looked up, rather flushed. She did get a 'hello' in the baking aisle from one of her regulars at the Pantry, thankfully, but even that greeting seemed a little subdued. Was she just being paranoid? No, this wasn't like the villagers; something was up, and Rachel was sure as hell going to find out what. If anyone knew what was going on, it'd be Sarah the shop supervisor, and she was currently serving behind the till.

With no one behind her in the queue, Rachel handed over her goods and seized her chance. 'Hi, Sarah.'

'Hey, Rachel. You okay?' At least Sarah was smiling at

her. They'd known each other for years, with Sarah having been in the year above her at school.

'I think so . . . Maybe I'm just being silly, but everyone's acting really strangely with me today. What's going on? I feel like I've grown two heads or something this morning here in town. I'm definitely being talked about . . . and not in a nice way.'

Sarah blushed and busied herself with packing the shopping.

'Come on, Sarah, you obviously know something.'

'Now Rach, don't think that *I* believe it – sure it's just the rumour mill in overdrive – but there is a story doing the rounds. I've said it'll be a load of nonsense. But you know what this place can be like when there's a bit of gossip going about. Everyone leaps on it.'

'And . . .?' Rachel felt her cheeks burn.

'I think it started with Vanessa.'

'Well, there's no surprise.'

'She heard something on good authority, apparently, and told Susan Davenport, who told Melanie at the Cheviot Café, who told Rog at the post office, who—'

'What did she say? What is it?'

'Well. I'm sorry Rach – and again don't think I'm buying into it – but Vanessa heard you'd been spotted kissing someone . . .'

Well, Rachel mused, there had been that rather gorgeous moment in the hay field recently, but when had public kissing been banned between a future man and wife? What was wrong with everyone?

'And it wasn't Tom,' Sarah clarified.

Oh.

'Well, who the hell was it? The bloody invisible man?'

'Again, according to rumour, it was Jake.'

'You what? *Jake?* Are you sure about that?'

'Well obviously *I* don't believe it, but that's what's being said . . . I suppose with him being around a few weeks ago . . .'

'Well, that's bloody ridiculous.' There were two people behind her in the queue now, in fact two of the little group who'd been gossiping as she came in, but she didn't mind ranting out loud, she might as well set a few records straight. 'You can put paid to that rumour. Bloody hell, you couldn't pay me to kiss Jake. He's only been about to see Maisy, his daughter. So, you can all stop your gassing right now. Thank you, Sarah.' Rachel picked up her shopping, and marched out of the store, head held high.

The rumour wagon was well and truly trundling away down in Kirkton, and what a load of tosh it was. But Rachel was suddenly hit with a scary thought out on the street. *What if Tom had heard any of this? How would he be feeling?*

What Vanessa had started with a simple, 'Oh, you'll never guess what I heard on the high street yesterday . . .' had rolled on to become the talk of the town.

Should she text him, warn him? But would that just stir up the hornets' nest even more? No, she wouldn't even give it airtime. It was a load of crap, and surely

Tom would never believe it even if he did hear anything. Tom had enough on his plate right now, what with the impending court case.

Even so, it left a queasy feeling in her stomach. Jake was always bad news as far as Tom was concerned – even if the latest was very much *fake* news.

It was six thirty p.m., and Tom had just come out of a long and stressful meeting with his accountant. He decided to stop for a quick pint at the Black Bull on his way home to let off a bit of steam.

The landlord, Mick, served him a frothy-headed pint of real ale that was delightfully cool and refreshing. Ah, bliss. But all too soon, Dennis Jones, who was already a few pints down the line, sidled up next to him.

'All right, mate,' he slapped him on the back.

'Hey Dennis, all good thanks.' He'd rather have had a quiet pint, but hey, that was always unlikely with the characters in the Bull.

'Here drowning your sorrows, are you? Heard the news, sorry about that mate.'

'What news?'

The barflies' heads lifted in unison, and Mick seemed to hold his breath.

'About your missus, Rachel. Not the kind of thing you want to be hearing about just before your wedding day . . .'

'What are you on about?' Tom stood up tall beside him.

Mick was wiping a glass rather furiously with a tea towel. The air in the pub felt static.

'Well, they say first love never dies and all that . . .' Dennis droned on, with a slight slur. 'Yeah, your Rachel has been spotted having a sneaky kiss – down at the seaside – with old flame Jake, as rumour has it.'

'That's enough, Dennis,' Mick intervened.

'It's all right Mick,' Tom cut in. 'Looks like Jonesy's just had a few too many jars this evening.'

Tom was irked, but he didn't actually believe the story, no way. He was more annoyed about this stupid tosspot spreading ridiculous gossip.

Tom downed the rest of his pint, needing to get out of there – the company was no longer appealing and the beer tasted sour.

'Sorry, Tom.' One of his farming mates stood up from his bar stool in support. But as Tom walked away, he couldn't be sure if his friend was apologising for daft Dennis, or if he was sorry about the rumours . . .

There was no way it could be true. Just no way, Rachel couldn't stand Jake.

But . . . as he got into his truck, the tiniest seed of doubt was trying to lodge itself in his mind. He'd already been hurt and let down by one woman; could it all be happening again? And Rachel and Jake had definitely been getting on better during his last visit. They'd been playing happy families, getting closer . . .

No, he knew Rachel. He trusted her. After these precious months, and the wonderful evening they had spent together only last night, there was no way he could doubt her. He wouldn't believe the village gossip; heaven knows it had caused enough troubles for them both in the past. Things got twisted and retold on the Kirkton grapevine, bearing no resemblance to the grain of truth. There was no way he was going to listen to a scumbag like Jonesy.

He swatted the rumours away like flies. So why did they keep buzzing around his head?

38

Rachel stepped into her wedding dress. Each time she tried it on, she felt transformed. Eve had made such a beautiful job of it, and she'd now finished all the appliqué flowers which fell gently like a floral waterfall from her waist to the floor on the ivory tulle skirt. After a few busy days on the farm and a flurry of one-week-to-go wedding preparations, it was the final dress fitting.

'Eve . . . this is so stunning. It's beautiful. You must have spent hours.'

Rachel looked in the full-length mirror. It just didn't look like her . . . more like some fairy-tale princess from a storybook or film.

'Just a few . . .' Her best friend smiled, as though she'd been more than happy to do it.

'Sorry if I've given you even more work to do, hun.'

'It's okay. I've needed to keep busy . . .' Eve's fingertips trembled ever so slightly as she held the material. She checked the fit on the shoulders and tweaked the waistline, popping a couple of pins in here and there. 'I think you've lost a little bit of weight these past few weeks,' she muttered, through a spare pin that she held between her teeth.

'Well, I haven't been trying. It's probably all the dashing around I've been doing.' And all the recent stresses and strains, pondered Rachel, remembering the latest developments in town.

'Been pretty much all go, hasn't it, for both of us?'

'Yeah, you can say that again. Oh, and yesterday was pretty weird.' Rachel decided to see what Eve thought of the latest village tittle-tattle. 'I was out and about in the village and guess what's doing the rounds . . .?'

Eve looked up with a flash of fear in her eyes.

'Yeah, there's only some crappy rumour going around about me kissing Jake. I mean, that's nuts. How do these things even start? Haven't they got anything better to do than make up nonsense like that?'

'That's so crazy . . .' Eve seemed distracted and managed to prick herself on the finger. A tiny drop of blood smeared on to the ivory dress. 'Oh shit, hold fire. I'll get a damp cloth on that . . . and I'll find a plaster for me.' She went dashing out to the bathroom.

They had been upstairs in Eve's bedroom. The house was quiet, Ben was out at a darts match and Amelia in bed asleep.

When Eve came back in, she was ghastly pale. 'Sorry, I didn't mean to spoil your dress. I'm so sorry . . .' Her eyes had misted. She dipped her head and quickly kneeled down to clean the stain.

There was something wrong. Not just the marked dress. Eve had been out of sorts for days now. Finally, this was Rachel's chance, 'Eve, are you okay, hun?'

Eve nodded, though her eyes began to fill with tears, which she tried to blink away.

'Oh honey, you're *so* not okay,' Rachel placed a gentle hand on her friend's shoulder. 'I know you. I can see how tense you've been. You've been like a coiled spring since you went to that exhibition . . .'

Eve looked like a rabbit caught in headlights. 'What do you mean?' she started defensively . . . and then she crumbled. Big, splodgy tears began to fall. 'Oh shit, I'm getting your dress wet . . . and there might even be snot on the shoulder.' Eve sniffed.

They couldn't help but laugh.

'Come on, hun,' Rachel soothed. 'Let's get this gorgeous dress off, before there's snot and tears all over it, and then you can tell me what's happened. All right?'

Eve looked wary.

'It's me, Eve . . . Tell me, it'll be in confidence.'

Her friend nodded, took a slow breath. Then, as Rachel was pulling her jeans and T-shirt back on, it all spilled out. 'Oh God, I didn't mean for it to happen. And I know you warned me . . . We kissed. Me and Aiden. That night at the exhibition.'

'Oh, Eve . . .' Rachel paused to allow her friend to carry on.

'It was just the once. And . . . I'd just got swept up in some daft romantic notion. But as soon as I'd done it, I felt dreadful . . . and I knew I should never have let it get that far.'

Rachel placed a caring hand on her friend's shoulder.

'But these rumours . . . do you think they might be about me? And they've got all mixed up on the grape-vine?'

'I doubt it, Eve. It'll just be coincidence. Your name hasn't been mentioned in anything I've heard at all. And could anyone have seen you?'

'I don't think so; it was just me and Aiden at the gallery. Oh Rachel, please . . . you can't say *anything*, to anyone. Especially now we've seen how vicious the rumour mill can be. You have to promise me.' Eve glanced up, looking so scared.

'Of course not.'

'I-I'm sick with worry. Have been ever since. What if Ben finds out? I don't think he'd ever forgive me. And I couldn't bear that. I know it's my own stupid fault . . . but I'd never do anything like it ever again. And there's Amelia . . . our family.' The big snotty tears were back in full force.

'It's all right, Eve, I promise I won't tell a soul.' Rachel gave her friend the biggest, heartfelt hug, stroking her back like an injured child, and soothing her with, 'It's okay, Eve. It'll all be all right,' until the sobbing ceased. 'Come on, petal. I'll go make us a cup of tea. We've got plenty of time before Ben's due back. I don't need to rush off.' She passed her friend a tissue from a box that was on Eve's dressing table.

They went downstairs together. A bond like blood between them. The truth now told.

Time to blow your nose, dry your eyes, put the mask

back up. Time to try your best to carry on with life and love and marriage and messy relationships.

All too soon, with only a few days until the wedding, it was the day of the court hearing, Wednesday 1 July. Rachel was at home at Primrose Farm and the hours – crikey, even the minutes, were dragging. Tom hadn't called as yet, but she didn't want to pester him, understanding that he might well have to have his phone switched off in the courtroom.

Rachel threw herself into some stress baking, making a batch of bread rolls and some scones for the Pantry. She had the radio on loudly in the farmhouse kitchen, and was kneading the dough like there was no tomorrow, pounding it as if it was a Caitlin punchbag. Her fist was a little sore, but she did feel slightly better by the time the warm, yeasty smells of fresh baking were floating from the Aga.

A short while later, Rachel was walking across the yard towards the barn with the tray of freshly baked cheese scones, the aromas making her tummy rumble, when she spotted a familiar grey van heading up the track. Surely not . . .

And yes, as it slowed to a halt, there *he* was, stepping out with a grin on his face.

'What the hell are you doing here?'

'Lovely to see you too . . .' answered Jake ironically.

'But . . . you're three days early. You do know the

wedding's not until Saturday.' She felt herself getting flustered. All she needed was her ex hanging about in the run-up to her wedding day. Especially given all the vicious rumours that were circulating . . . Oh god.

'Yeah, yeah, don't get your knickers in a twist. I've got a job up this way. Thought it'd work out nicely. I can settle a bit early and see Maisy.'

Nicely for *him*, perhaps. The court case was on today; she was hanging by a thread waiting for a call from Tom. She was just about holding it together . . . and now this. The wanderer returns, as usual without notice.

'Maisy's at school,' she said bluntly.

'Yeah, I guessed that. Thought it'd be a nice surprise if I was here for when she gets home.'

'Okay, so why don't you come back at – let's say – four o'clock?' Rachel was curt. She needed to go and help Mum in the Pudding Pantry anyway, and there was a list of people yet to call and chase up about all the final wedding arrangements.

'Thought I'd grab a coffee here first, stop by and say hello. My B & B won't let me in until after three, anyhow. My job doesn't start until tomorrow, so I've got the rest of the day free.'

Oh, boy. Bully for bloody you. 'Okay. Well, Maisy has a few things on after school this week.' Rachel wasn't exactly sure what at this point, other than craft club tomorrow, but she didn't want him to think he could stroll in unannounced and monopolise their time.

'No worries. I'm sure I can work around that. I'll bob on in, grab a latte, and you can fill me in.'

Grrr, how did her ex always seem to manage to throw a spanner in the works, turning up at just the wrong time? Here he was now, waltzing his way into the Pudding Pantry.

'Oh, hello Jake.' Jill looked up from the counter where she was spooning out a dish of summer pudding for a customer. 'This is a bit of a surprise.' She managed to be polite, whilst raising her eyebrows at Rachel.

'Yep, got some work lined up this way for the next week or so. Ties in great with popping by for the wedding and all that.'

'Right . . .' Jill nodded.

'So, there's no Chelsea or Kelvin coming with you to the wedding then?' Rachel probed. They'd not come back on the RSVP, once Maisy had twisted her arm to send an invite, other than Jake saying he'd be there for 'deffo'. With Maisy getting on well with Chelsea on their last visit and super keen for them to come along, Rachel had bitten the bullet and asked them all. They'd need to all be able to co-operate for Maisy's sake going forwards, so it seemed the right thing to do.

'Nah, they've got stuff on back home.'

'Okay.'

Who knew whether they were still an item even, but Rachel didn't want to know any more about Jake's messy private life than she had to. 'Oh well, that's a shame, Maisy was looking forward to seeing them.'

'Yeah, well . . .' he let it drift. 'I'm here.'

Oh, and didn't she know it. Rachel sighed. It was definitely going to be one of those days, and little did she know how much . . .

39

Later that afternoon, Rachel pulled up haphazardly in the yard near the farmhouse. She was coming back from fixing the water trough in the cattle field, which she'd noticed had sprung a leak. She still hadn't heard from Tom about the result of the hearing, and the suspense was killing her. Did no news mean good news? After the stress of these last few weeks, she really bloody hoped so.

She scrambled down from the quad and nearly lost her footing. Eurgh, she could hardly see; her left eye was stinging after a fly had gone right into it at speed on her drive back. Jeez, was it sore! She prayed she wouldn't have to wear some kind of eye patch for her wedding day – she was going more for country chic than pirate princess.

'Hey, Rach.'

Everything was a little blurry but it sounded like Jake approaching – so he was back hanging around then.

'Hi . . . can't really see . . . Bloody fly,' Rachel explained as she rubbed her eye.

'Ah, hold fire. Let me take a look.'

With her eye half-closed, Rachel was standing still

beside the quad. Jake approached, gently touching her face to open her streaming eye.

'Oi, get off you!' Rachel leaped back in surprise.

'Hey, I'm only trying to help. Come on, hold still.'

'Okay fine, go on,' she sighed.

'Okay, I can see the little bugger. Just blink a few times, and it might just move into the corner, where I'll be able to dab it out with a fingertip or a tissue or something.'

'Just go steady, I don't want to be blinded for my wedding day or end up with a massive bloodshot eye or something.'

'Well, if you don't let me get on with it, you might well do . . . it looks pretty bloodshot already.'

'Okay, okay.' She stood stock still as Jake leaned in closer.

Tom turned into the farm entrance; he couldn't wait to tell Rachel the good news. He hadn't let her know yet as he thought he'd do it in person, rather than on the phone. Finally, they could move on, and he could now allow himself to relax and look forward to their wedding day. He found himself grinning at the steering wheel. But as he drove up the track towards the Pantry barn, he spotted Rachel standing by her quad in the middle of the yard with what looked like . . . Jake. What the hell?

Jake had his back to him . . . but it was obvious that he was too damned close to Tom's fiancée. Tom slowed the vehicle, he was halfway up the track now, and refocused. He went cold. Their faces were just inches apart. *Oh no.* Jeez, Rachel, no, *no*. He couldn't believe it at first.

But it was there for him to see as plain as day. Not only were all those rumours likely to be true, but it looked as if Jake was back for another goddamned kiss.

Tom's heart hit the deck. His stomach lurched and he felt physically ill. He didn't want to see any more, his head crashing against the steering wheel.

He just couldn't believe it. Just a few nights ago she had been in his arms, telling him she loved him. *Did he even know her?* Could *his* Rachel, his fiancée, be so damned cool and calculating, so capable of deceit? He took one last glance. The two of them were still up close and personal. This was no normal conversation. No chat about Maisy . . . and what the hell was the guy even doing here? It was a bit bloody early to be arriving for the wedding. The sham of a bloody wedding . . .

He slammed the truck into reverse, and rolled back down the track, turning with a wheelspin at the farm gate. Devastation. Anger. Disbelief. Emotions slammed into him. He punched at the steering wheel, and then he drove, he didn't know where . . . just kept driving. Out of Primrose Farm, out of the valley, away from the rumours-turned-truths . . . to somewhere he could just crash and burn.

Sitting at the farmhouse table, having just doused her eye at the sink with some sterile eye drops, a stream of troubled thoughts rushed through Rachel's mind. Jake had headed off a while ago, to check in at the B & B he'd booked in Kirkton, saying he'd be back at four to see

Maisy. The old grandfather clock that stood in the corner was still ticking away; why-oh-why had she heard nothing from Tom as yet? She'd hoped he might try to contact her on a break during the hearing. She couldn't help but be concerned for him with his farm, his livelihood, at stake. She caved in and called his mobile. It went straight to answerphone.

'Hi, only me. Hope everything's going okay? Keep me posted when you get a chance. Good luck . . . Love you.'

She told herself not to worry, that he'd just be busy, and she took herself back over the yard to help Jill at the Pantry. At least the customers would help to keep her mind off things.

Five o'clock and tea time rolled up, with Jake now back and staying for a bite of supper with Maisy and the family. There was still no sign of Tom and no answer to her messages. Rachel was getting really anxious by now. This wasn't like Tom. Maybe things had gone badly in court, and he'd taken himself off to get his head around things, or to speak to the land agent to organise the sale of some of his farm? Surely, he should be on his way home by now . . . but why hadn't he thought to call her?

Whatever it was, she'd get to the bottom of it. She found she had no appetite, excused herself from the table, and told her mum that she was nipping over to Tom's farm. If he was there, they could have a good chat, face whatever had happened and deal with this thing together.

*

Rachel felt her heart plummet on finding Tom's farmhouse was all locked up. No one home. No sign or noise from Mabel. Strange. Rachel then remembered that Tom was going to leave the dog with his parents for the day in case he ended up being a long time. Should she call them? Might he be there? She didn't want to alarm them unnecessarily. But if there was something wrong, maybe they would know. Surely, they'd call her straight away if there was anything . . . Dark thoughts began to crowd her mind.

Sod it. She couldn't just sit and wait this out. She got back on her quad, looked out over the valley and, after trying Tom's mobile once more to no avail, she called his parents' house.

It was Geoff, Tom's father, who answered. 'Hello, Rachel. Good news, isn't it?'

'It is? I wouldn't know, Geoff. Look, sorry for calling, but I haven't heard from Tom at all and there's no sight of him at the farm . . .' She was flummoxed for a moment. 'Have *you* seen Tom, then?'

'Yes, he was here – when was it now? – about three hours ago. Yes, came to fetch the dog and told us the wonderful news that the case has been dropped. Yes, something about some social media scam and his solicitor having a bit of a word off the record. Seems to have done the trick. Caitlin has dropped the claim entirely. Our farm is safe. What a bloody relief.'

'Oh . . . So, he's been home . . . back to Kirkton?' Rachel clarified, trying to take it all in. *Yes, it really must have been Caitlin behind the trolling.* She wondered why on earth Tom hadn't come to share this good news with her.

'Yes. Is everything all right, Rachel love?' Geoff's tone became concerned.

'Ah, yes, of course. No problem, I'm sure we'll catch up with each other very soon. He must have had a lot on this afternoon.' At least it sounded as if he was fine and all was well, and the case was dropped . . . well, that was a relief.

'We're both so looking forward to the big day here,' Tom's father continued jollily. 'Weather forecast is looking good. And just let us know if there's anything at all we can do to help for it – with the setting up and all that. We're more than happy to get stuck in. I know Helen's on board with the baking team with the WI.'

'Oh, thank you both, and yes I will do . . . it'll be lovely.' She tried to sound upbeat, when all the while her heart and mind were racing.

What the hell was going on? Tom Watson had been back to Kirkton but was now AWOL. Might he have headed off, needing some time to think? Maybe the reality of Caitlin trying to claim against him, the acrimonious nature of his first marriage had hit him hard today, even though the case had been dropped at the last. Was he afraid he was going to be making the same mistake?

Hours passed in unseen and unanswered texts, another two trips to his farmhouse with still no one home, and a sickening churn in her stomach. The beep of her phone roused her; it was almost eleven p.m. by now, and Rachel was trying unsuccessfully to sleep. She snatched up her mobile from beside the bed and saw the screen. The message was from Tom. *Thank God.*

'I wanted to let you know I'm okay. But don't try to see me. I need time to think. I think we might be over.'

Rachel's heart went into free fall. What was he saying? What was happening?

She quickly texted back: 'Tom what are you talking about? I heard about the court case – it's good news, isn't it?'

She paused, frozen, completely baffled. She was desperate to reach out to him, to stop this – whatever *this* was – from spiralling further. There was no immediate response. 'But I can come to you. Whatever it is, we're in this together, remember?' she pressed.

The reply chilled her already aching heart: 'I don't think so, Rach.'

And then, silence.

40

Tom turned up at the Pantry at ten thirty the next morning, unshaven and looking as though he hadn't slept a wink. Rachel well knew that feeling, having only snatched a few hours herself.

She glanced up and caught those gorgeous green eyes, tinged with sadness. She really didn't understand what was going on; the result of the court case should have meant he'd be walking on air. But he very clearly wasn't. She shook her head: whatever it was, she could help him put it right. He was here now, that was the main thing.

'Tom . . .' She moved out from behind the counter, ready to take him in her arms . . . to do anything to ease his pain. But, as soon as she placed a hand on him, he flinched.

'I need to know the truth, Rachel.'

She was still at a loss as to what was going on, but this seemed like a conversation to have in private. 'Mum, we're just going across to the house.'

'No problem, love.' Jill was ready to take over the reins, and finished the order for Frank, who was peering nosily over the top of his newspaper.

They walked across the yard to the farmhouse. Rachel's hand was itching to hold Tom's, but he was keeping his pace at a distance. Last night's text message was haunting her: *I think we might be over*. But they could still face this together. If only she knew what *this* was.

In the sun-filled private space of the kitchen, Rachel got to it. 'Okay, Tom, what's going on?' Her voice was filled with love and concern.

'I think you know *what*, Rachel.'

'I honestly don't, you're going to have to fill me in.'

Yet Rachel had an inkling now. What if her worst fears were confirmed? What if he'd got wind of the false rumours flying around the village?

'Is it true? You and Jake?' He looked dejected, betrayed. 'If there's still something there between the two of you, then that's it . . . I can't marry you, Rachel.'

'Look Tom, if you've been hearing some crazy rumour going about the village, then please don't buy into it. You know me better than that, and you know what the gossip in this place can be like.'

He sighed. 'Of course, when I heard the tittle-tattle, I dismissed it as a load of shite. I trusted you, Rach. But . . . I also know what I saw with my own eyes. How could you betray me like that?' His voice was as hard as stone.

'I-I don't understand Tom . . .'

He looked at her, filled with hurt and anger. 'I saw you, I – I saw you both . . . kissing. When I arrived back here yesterday.'

'What? What are you talking about, that's—'

'Don't lie, Rachel,' he said, rubbing his hands over his eyes.

'I'm not! I swear, why would I . . . and look, these rumours we're all hearing, they're nothing to do with me and Jake . . .' she floundered. But, how could she tell him what was really going on? 'It's just . . .' *Shit*, if she told him the real truth behind those rumours, she could wreck Eve's marriage, blow apart her friend's gorgeous family. *She'd promised.*

'There are no "justs" in any of this, Rachel.'

'I know, and look, I don't know what you saw, but . . .' And then it came to her: the fly in her eye, Jake getting close as he tried to prise it out . . . Could Tom have seen that?

'This is all a complete misunderstanding. Jake was just helping me yesterday, I had something in my eye. Was that what you saw? Honestly, it was completely innocent, though I suppose it might have looked like something else. You know what a nightmare Jake is, how badly he's let me down. You know how much I love you . . . I would never, *ever*, go there . . .'

She knew the fly argument sounded thin, and was beginning to see how incriminating it might have looked. But at least Tom was finally looking her in the eye. If she wanted him to believe her, though, she had to come clean about the root of the rumours: Eve. She couldn't do it. She didn't know what else to say without betraying her best friend. So, she stood there in silence, trying to see a way out of this.

Tom shook his head so very sadly, then turned and walked away.

'Tom . . . I . . . don't go . . .' Her words trailed after him, but he didn't stop.

She stood frozen. Rachel felt as if her heart was being torn in two: between loyalty to her beautiful friend and the trust and love of her fiancé.

Unaware of any of the dramas that had been unfolding, Ben asked Tom if he fancied a pint after work that evening. He had best-man duties to talk through with him, after all. The Black Bull was pretty low down on the list of places Tom wanted to visit right now after his run-in with Dennis the Menace, and everything that had gone on since, but after the night and day Tom had just put in, a cold drink of beer with a mate in his local did actually sound like a good tonic. After all, Tom resolved, he had nothing to hide. He wasn't one to shy away from this mess, *and* if he fancied a pint in his local, why the hell not? It might help take his mind off things for a couple of hours, if nothing else.

Tom walked in at seven o'clock as agreed, finding that Ben wasn't there yet. And look who was standing at the bar: Jake. Of course, the last person he wanted to see right now. Barfly eyes scanned from Tom to Jake, evidently aware of the rumours that had been going around, and there was an audible hush as Tom stepped up to the counter – as far away from his rival as he could – and ordered a pint of real ale. The landlord, Mick, poured and passed it over the bar a little awkwardly. 'All right, Tom?'

'Yep.' Amazing how one small word could hold a storm inside it.

Mick sensed that perhaps this wasn't quite the time to mention the up-and-coming wedding. Let a man have his beer in peace, that was one of his lifelong mottos, born from experience. Especially when the customer in question had a face on him like thunder.

Tom stood bristling at the end of the bar. He took a sip of the cold beer. A couple of pints, that'd be all he'd stay for. A quick chat with Ben and then he'd be away home.

Unfortunately, Jake had other plans, sauntering his way across. He even had the cheek to smile at him. 'Hey, Tom. All right, mate?'

'I'm *not* your mate.'

'Okay, pal. What's up?'

His tone was too damned flippant for Tom's liking.

'What's up? What's *up* is how you've been loitering around the farm, pestering Rachel, getting way too *close* to my fiancée. Making a nuisance of yourself . . .'

Jake didn't much like his accusatory tone or the bullish look on his face. 'Don't know what you're talking about, mate. I've only been there to visit my daughter. I have rights, you know.'

'You've been doing a sight more than that, you slimy little toerag.' Tom's fist was primed now, but he wasn't the sort to get physical.

'Dunno what you're talking about.'

'You and Rachel . . .'

'Well, I haven't been *there* for a few years now . . . but boy she was a good 'un.' Jake's tone was lechy after a few pints on an empty stomach.

With that, the prickling in Tom's fist took over. Just looking at Jake's smug face was enough to tip him over . . .

Ben walked into the Bull to see Tom land a punch right on Jake's face. Ouch.

And Jake struck back, landing a fist on Tom's cheekbone. Ooh.

'Right lads, enough.' Mick swiftly broke up the fight. 'Not in my bar, you don't! Take it outside if you have to.'

Ben moved in to hustle Tom to one side, holding his friend back before he did something he really regretted. 'Woah Tom, take it easy now, let's calm down yeah?' Both Jake and Tom were ushered out of the door and onto the street. Tom stood breathing heavily, rubbing his knuckles. Jesus, he couldn't remember the last time he'd thrown a punch. But he didn't feel elated, far from it. Jake was standing beside him, rubbing his cheek. 'What the hell was that all about?' he muttered. 'Can't a man enjoy a quiet pint? You should be getting excited for your wedding, mate, not starting fights. Bloody hell.'

Jake was clearly in denial, like the lying cheat he was, Tom mused. Yet Jake, he could understand . . . Rachel, however, he had thought he knew her better than that.

He had thought she *was* better than that. His own cheek began throbbing. But a mere punch in the face was nothing compared to the pain he felt inside. Tom found he no longer had the heart to fight . . . suddenly he didn't have the heart for anything anymore.

41

Rachel did what she always did in times of trouble and got on with life and stuck into her work.

The farm animals still needed her care; they didn't know that her heart was breaking. The Pantry needed her puddings, and what energy she could muster to serve, and . . . *if* she could work all this out with Tom, there was still a wedding to prepare for. The tipi was being put up in the field beside the farmhouse right now – she could hear the hammering across the valley – and she, Mum and Daniel were set to move chairs and tables across there as soon as the Pantry closed for business.

She'd tried to speak with Tom again last night, a call that went unanswered. She had no option but to leave a voicemail, pleading with him to believe her.

After a blast of fresh air out on the quad with Moss – ears flapping – at her side, she headed back down the valley to Primrose Farm, catching sight of Tom's farm there beside hers. They were meant to be together. It had to work out, it just *had* to. But she knew Tom needed a bit of space right now. This was all such a mess. And the wedding was a mere day away, or – at least – it was supposed to be. Right now, she really didn't know if he was going to turn up or not.

That wasn't the end of her worries. As she walked into the Pantry fifteen minutes later, ready to help Jill serve the morning customers, trying to put on her best sunny smile with a heart that was shredded, Jill approached with a worried look on her face. 'Oh, Rachel, there's been a problem.'

Oh God, had Tom gone and called it off for good? Rachel felt a bit wobbly and had to hold onto the nearest chair.

Whatever it was she had to face it full on. 'What is it, Mum?'

'There's been an accident on the A1 . . .' Jill started.

Rachel's mind flashed, where was Maisy? Safely at school . . . Not Tom, please not Tom . . . driving off with a head full of hurt and false scenarios.

Her throat was in such a knot, she couldn't speak. Her knees wobbled.

'It's Jenn, the cake lady. She's had an accident on the way here.'

'Oh no, is she all right?'

'I think so, just a minor scrape, she was able to call me. She's going to pop to the doctors' to get checked out, might be a bit of whiplash. Her car's a bit of a mess, I think.'

'Oh, bless her, how awful.'

'But it's the cake, darling . . . Someone's gone into the back of her estate, and well . . . it's trashed.'

'Oh, right. Blimey.' Her wedding cake, crushed. Just a metaphor for the times, right? But there were more important things in life right now. 'Poor Jenn. She'll be devastated.' At least Jenn seemed to be okay.

'She said she'll not charge us for it,' Jill continued. 'But the thing is, she hasn't got time to make another . . . and, to be honest, I don't think she should pressure herself to even try. She did sound rather shaken up.'

'No, of course, she mustn't. I'll text her and see how she is, say we'll be fine. It's not the end of the world.'

'I must say you're taking it awfully well, love.'

Frank had been sipping his morning coffee and listening in. 'Oh ladies, I'm sorry to hear that,' he chipped in. 'I wish I could bake. I'd be going home and making you something right now. But I really don't think you'd be impressed with my meagre efforts.'

'No worries, Frank, we'll manage. Look, why don't we create something simple out of cupcakes . . . maybe set them out on a three-tiered cake stand? They'd be easy enough to whip up in a hurry.' Rachel was being resourceful.

'Good thinking,' Jill was on the case, 'I was going to be making some vanilla cupcakes with a pretty edible rosebud on top for the reception anyhow, so why don't I make a few extra and keep them back for that.'

'That sounds a great idea, Mum . . . and maybe Wendy will add a few floral strands to the cake stand for effect.'

They gave each other a high five.

Rachel could cope with a missing wedding cake, but what she couldn't cope with was a missing groom.

She tried calling Tom's mobile again, sending love and hope down the airwaves. Still no answer.

As she went to put her phone away, a message pinged in. *Oh* . . . her fingertips fumbled as she rushed to check it. But it wasn't Tom. It was just a notification for a private message on the Pudding Pantry Facebook page. But Rachel's eyes widened in shock as she started to read.

'Rachel, where do I begin . . . I'm so sorry. What started as a small, impulsive comment online, which I have to admit came out of jealousy, just got all out of hand. It wasn't easy for me thinking of Tom getting married again, I've been in quite a dark place. It's no excuse, I know that. And well, I realise now how damaging those nasty comments I made on the Pantry pages could be. I'm not proud of what I've done, and I wanted to come clean. You deserve the truth. Please accept my sincere apologies, which I know might seem too little too late. But I hope, in time, you can think about starting to forgive me. It's now time for us all to move on and I do wish you and Tom all the best – I really do. Sincerely, Caitlin.'

Oh my god. Rachel felt a bit winded, she stood clutching her phone to her chest. It really *was* Caitlin. She had strongly suspected she was behind it all, but it was another thing to be faced with the reality.

Phew, she had to admit it felt a relief to have that issue

resolved. And it felt like the threat of Caitlin was fading into the distance. It couldn't have been easy for her to write that, Rachel acknowledged. That took courage, at least. She resolved to reply when she'd had a chance to absorb it all. For now, though, she had a wedding to get back on track.

Just like old times, Rachel and Eve, bride-to-be and maid of honour, were sitting on the bed in Rachel's bedroom later that day. It was the eve of the wedding.

They'd had a frenetic couple of hours with all hands on deck at the newly set-up tipi, with electric cables being rolled out, and men from the village-hall committee up on a cherry picker stringing up lights. Extra tables and chairs, borrowed from the hall, were now all in place along with the Pantry's furniture, leaving the tearoom area free and about to be turned into a standing area for a fabulous drinks reception. For which Granny Ruth had insisted she make the perfect 'naughty nibbles', to accompany the lemon gin fizz welcome cocktails. It was all coming together perfectly on the outside, but on the inside Rachel's heart was still in tatters. All this help, and community effort, would it all be for nothing? After helping out, Ben had taken Amelia back home and Jill was now downstairs with Maisy, baking extra 'wedding cake' cupcakes. The girls had a token glass of prosecco each, and chocolates to hand, and were meant to be chilling out and pampering themselves with manicures and pedicures, ready for the big day tomorrow.

But there was far too much going on for either of them to feel in any way relaxed.

Rachel had to do something, and now. Her relationship with Tom was far too precious to wreck. She hadn't disclosed the truth about 'the kiss' to protect Eve, but look where that had got her. She took her friend's hand. 'Eve, look, I have something to ask you.'

'Of course, what is it chick?'

'It's time . . . you have to tell Ben the truth. About you and Aiden.'

'Oh my God. Why, what's happened, Rach?'

'It's Tom . . . He's seen me and Jake together and got the wrong impression. Honestly, it was nothing, you know exactly how I feel about Jake,' Rachel explained to her friend, 'but there was a fly in my eye, and he was getting it out.' She shook her head at the absurdity of the misunderstanding. 'Anyhow, Tom's taken it all the wrong way, and with these rumours flying about the village about two people sharing a kiss; well, he's jumped to completely the wrong conclusion and thinks that it was Jake and me. Oh Eve, I think he might call the wedding off. I've been trying to call him, but he's so angry, he's just ignoring me.'

'Nooo, that can't happen, no way! Oh Rach, I'm so sorry that you've been dragged into all of this. Somehow someone knows about what I did and it's all got mixed up in the village Chinese whispers.' Eve stood up, shaking but resolute. 'I'll go and see Tom, Rach. I'll tell him the truth.'

'What about Ben?'

'I'll come clean to him too, I promise . . . but please, let me ask Tom to let me do that in my own time. Soon . . . Oh God, Rachel.' Eve's hand was trembling, the girls were holding on to each other tight. 'What if Ben can't forgive me? What if it's all over between us? I've been so stupid . . .'

'Eve, you're upset. Sit tight. Let me go and talk to Tom. If I need you to explain any further, then maybe you can chat to him on the phone. Stay here for now. And Eve, thank you.' She sighed, gripping her friend's hand. 'You know I'm only telling Tom the truth because I absolutely have to. I'd never want to betray your trust.'

'Of course, I understand. Go find him, Rachel. Do what you have to, my lovely. I'm so, so sorry. It's all my fault. I've been selfish. I-I've bloody well ruined your wedding.'

'Not yet, you haven't.' Rachel managed a small, hopeful smile. 'Look, I'll be back soon, hopefully. Try and get some rest, or go and see Ben, whatever you feel you need to do.'

'I need to think about how I'm going to tell him. Maybe, if I wait until after the wedding. So, I don't spoil your day any more than I have already.'

'Okay, we can chat some more when I get back . . . I love you, Eve.'

'Love you too, Rach. Good luck. You don't deserve all this hassle right now. I'm so sorry, hun.' Eve gave her a big hug.

Rachel got up to go, pausing at the door of her

bedroom. 'And Eve . . . making a mistake, doing one bad thing, that doesn't make you a bad person.'

Eve gave a loud, snotty blub. 'Thanks, Rach.'

'Is everything okay, love?' Jill was in the kitchen putting some finishing touches to her rosebud-topped cupcakes.

Rachel hadn't told her mum all the ins and outs of the past two days – she was still hoping by hook or by crook that Tom would turn up at the church.

'I think so, or at least it will be. It's a bit complicated . . .' Rachel had to hold her nerve. She'd love to be able to tell her mum everything, ask for her advice, but with Eve's marriage – and her own – still on a tightrope, she needed to try and sort this out herself.

'Is Eve still upstairs?' Jill gave a small frown, her maternal instincts tuning in to the drama. 'Can I help with anything?'

'Ah yes, Eve's fine.' (White lie – she was in a heap on the bed upstairs.) 'She's up in my room, doing her nails. I've just remembered something for tomorrow and I just want to check it's all okay.' (The groom!) 'So, can you just keep an eye on Maisy for me?'

'Of course, love. There's nothing else I can help with . . . ?' Jill left an opening, wondering if this could well be about Eve, in light of what Brenda had told her earlier in the week.

'No, it's all fine. I shouldn't be too long.' The fewer people who knew about this the better, at least until it was all sorted. She intended to be back at home soon, to spend the rest of the evening with Maisy, Eve and Jill, and to sleep in her own room for her wedding evening, as tradition dictated . . . *Oh*, she realised, it would also be her last night at Primrose Farm. Rachel felt a pang, knowing tonight would feel so strange, but she didn't have time to dwell on that right now.

'All right then, love. Go and do what you have to, and if you need me at all . . . just ask.'

'Thank you.'

A look passed between them. Without having to say it, they both knew something momentous was in the offing.

Rachel was up high on the hill, looking over the valley. The landscape rolled in dusky velvety-green folds, the sun dipping down over the Cheviots, the sky softening to a peachy-blue. It looked as if the weather would be settled for tomorrow.

Rachel had got on the quad, needing some air, and a little space and time to think. She had to do this. Had to tell Tom everything, put this dreadful misunderstanding right that might wreck their wedding day, that might wreck *them*. Would Tom even believe her now? And where the hell had he been again these past twenty-four hours? Please, please let him be all right, and not have done anything stupid. Memories of finding her father that fateful day slammed into her mind . . . and a dreadful fear seeped through her soul. But not every hurt ended like that, she calmed herself. Tom probably just needed time to think.

This rock, cool and solid beneath her, was where she'd sit with her dad on many an evening after checking the sheep together out on the quad, with Moss lying at their feet. Dad would magic a Twix chocolate bar from his pocket and they'd have one stick each, chatting about school and what Dad had been doing on the farm that day, with the sweet melt of chocolate and toffee on their tongues, and a promise not to tell Mum that they'd been eating sweets before supper.

'Dad . . . where are you?' She spoke the words aloud, softly, 'Wish you could be here with us all tomorrow. Eve's made me a gorgeous dress,' she started chatting to the breeze. 'Hah, you didn't think you'd ever see me in a dress; always used to moan about me living in jeans . . . well, I will be now.'

Could he hear her, somehow? Might he be there tomorrow at her wedding in some way, be able to see her walking down the aisle in that beautiful gown? She threw a huge, heartfelt wish to the sky. But maybe her words were just floating to the sheep, drifting over the rye grass, the rocks and stones . . . Who knew?

I need to find Tom. To speak with him.

She stood up, jolted by a feeling so strong. No more wasting time or holding off. Their love was too precious. She hoped to God that Tom would be back home again by now.

'Go, lass.' It was her dad's voice, clear in her mind. And as she looked down over the valley once more, she saw there was a light on at Tom's farmhouse.

She raced to the quad, leapt on. The wind in her hair and hope in her heart.

She was relieved to see the grey truck parked up outside the farmhouse. She rushed into the kitchen, not bothering to knock. 'Tom. Tom!'

And there he was. All ruffled dark hair, pale blue shirt, forearms bare. Thank heavens. He was sat at the kitchen island and looked up at her . . . with such sadness behind those green eyes that she loved so much. A small glass of whisky was propped beside him. She was almost afraid to go to him. Yet, all she really wanted was to throw her arms around him.

'What do you want, Rach?' His tone was flat, broken.

'It's not what you think . . . and I-I'm sorry I didn't tell you the whole story before . . . I was trying not to hurt Eve and Ben . . .' The words spilled out.

'I don't want more excuses . . . I can't go back to a relationship that isn't honest, Rach. I thought what we had was better than that.'

'It is. Tom . . . it is,' she paused, trying to grasp the words to find her way back to him. 'Where were you last night, the night before? I've been worried sick.'

'Needed to think. Wondering if I can go ahead with all this . . .'

'Oh, Tom.' He flinched as she touched his shoulder.

She had hurt him so much by holding back on the truth. 'I'm so sorry . . . but that kiss, all those rumours, it was never me and Jake, honestly. I swore to Eve I wouldn't say anything, but it's gone too far, and I can't lose you. I can't lose *us*. I love you so much, Tom, and I can't bear that I've hurt you in all this.'

He looked up, his expression unreadable.

'Tom, listen, please . . . the rumours, that kiss they've all been talking about. It was Eve. Some stupid, crazy moment with an artist friend. Just one kiss. Someone must have seen them. She begged me not to tell anyone; she's afraid she might lose Ben over it.' Rachel sat down on the stool beside him. 'But once I knew I might lose *you*, I knew I had to say. It's the truth, Tom.'

'Eve . . .?' He looked up, his brow creased.

'Yes, Eve. I've left her in a right state back at ours. She's going to have to 'fess up. She knows it's all her own fault, and she's devastated.'

'So, you and Jake . . .?'

'Nothing, absolutely nothing at all going on there. Of course not.'

'But I saw you, Rach, outside the Pantry.'

'I promise, it's like I said it was, I had something in my eye and Jake was just helping me out.' It was like the gods were against her, such bloody awful timing. 'Look it's still bloodshot, it's been sore ever since. And why the hell would I want to kiss Jake? I'm not that bloody stupid. Give me *some* credit, Tom.'

A shadow of a smile appeared on his face. 'A fly. Honestly?'

'Yeah, I swear on Maisy's life.'

'Wow. And Eve . . .' It was as though he wanted to believe it all and yet hardly dared.

'Yes, Eve. Hand on heart. She'll tell you herself.' She placed a palm across her chest, every fibre in her body praying that he would believe her. What else could she do?

He sat looking dazed, as if he'd been hit with a sledge-hammer.

There was only one thing for it. She dropped to one knee onto the flagstone floor beside him. 'Tom Watson, will you marry me?'

There was a second or two of silence.

'Will you marry me, *tomorrow*?' she repeated, with every nerve in her body on edge, waiting.

Trust me. Love me. Her eyes spoke to his.

'Bloody hell, Rach. It's all true, isn't it? Jeez . . .' He ran a hand through his hair, took a breath. 'I will . . . of course, I bloody well will.'

And the smile that spread across his face was that of pure joy.

'Yeeeesss!!' Rachel punched the air, bouncing up off her stool, with Mabel barking at her feet animatedly. Tom then leapt up himself, bundled the two of them up into his strong arms and whirled them around.

42

Rachel arrived back at Primrose Farm half an hour later to find Eve sitting at the kitchen table, settled beside Jill. She had red-rimmed eyes and was nursing a mug of hot chocolate, whilst sporting her 'Maid of Honour' dressing gown.

'You okay?' Rachel asked.

'Yeah, not bad.' Her friend gave a sniff.

'We've had a bit of a heart-to-heart,' explained Jill.

'Oh.'

'Did you find Tom? Are you two okay?' Eve asked hurriedly, desperate to find out if things were all right for her friend.

'Yes,' Rachel couldn't help the beam that spread across her face. 'We're all fine. We have a groom, and there's a wedding day to look forward to.'

'*Yesss!* Ah, thank heavens. I could never have forgiven myself if I'd spoilt everything for you two, as well . . . It's okay, your mum knows all about it.'

Jill nodded, ready for the story to unfold further. Time to sit down around the table, for them to share their hurt, guilt, fears, and then to prop each other up with friendship and love.

'Hot chocolate for you too, pet?' Jill asked Rachel.

'Umm, actually, is there any of that prosecco left?' Tonight, they were meant to be doing their pedicures and manicures with a glass of bubbly and happy chatter. 'I don't know about you lot but, after all the emotions of today, I could do with a little bit of fizz.'

Jill found a bottle in the fridge and fetched three glasses. 'I'm sure a little tipple won't hurt. But go steady girls, it's a big day tomorrow.'

'Don't want to peak too soon.' Eve raised a smile. 'And, yes, we should be celebrating now, not sitting here all sad and blue.'

Jill popped the cork and poured them all some prosecco. 'Eve, it didn't come as a surprise what you've just told me,' she admitted. 'I'd kept it secret up till now, but I do know who saw you. The thing is, I *really* don't believe she was the one who started all these rumours.'

Eve and Rachel were all ears.

'It was Brenda,' Jill continued, 'and I know for a fact that she wouldn't have wanted to hurt you or your family. She told me that she happened to be walking past the gallery that day. She saw you and the artist. But as for who's spread the gossip since, I honestly don't know. She told me in private, and I've not shared it with a single soul until now.'

'Oh, I see. Well, however it got out, it doesn't really matter any more. It was my own stupid fault.'

'We can all make mistakes, love.' Jill reached across to

touch the back of Eve's hand affectionately. Eve felt like a second daughter to her after all these years. 'I'm sure you and Ben will find a way through all this, pet.'

'I hope so, Jill, with all my heart. But hey, let's not be maudlin, I'll just have to face the music afterwards. We have a wedding to prepare for! Rachel, I need to do your nails for you, hun. I've brought my box of tricks, so you can choose which shade of varnish you want. Actually no, scrap that idea . . . let your maid of honour choose. I know your weird and wonderful tastes at times. And, I know the colour palette for the wedding flowers and decorations off by heart. I'll find you the perfect match for the pretty pinks in your bouquet.'

'Sounds good to me.'

'And Jill, we'll do yours next.'

Eve went upstairs to grab her vanity bag.

'The poor lass seems devastated. We'll help her get through this, love, won't we?' Jill shook her head, concerned.

'Of course.'

'And you, you're all fine? Sounds as if you and Tom have had some last-minute dramas too. And I'm sorry if I could have prevented all that. I'd heard about Eve from Brenda but I didn't realise the whole thing had spiralled so badly out of control. Seems like I'm the last to know, eh? Perhaps because I've had my head down getting all the baking done for the wedding.'

'Don't worry, Mum. But let me fill you in, I wasn't even sure if there was going to be a wedding a couple of hours ago. Tom had got it into his head that the rumours were about me . . . and Jake.'

'You what?' Jill pulled a shocked face.

'Yes, I know, it's laughable really. But I've explained it all to him and, luckily, we're fine now.' She couldn't help but smile. 'Better than fine, in fact. Oh Mum, I can't wait until tomorrow. It's going to be just brilliant. Getting married to Tom. But . . .' She paused, 'It's still going to be hard too. Tonight, this is it: my last night here on the farm. It feels so strange.'

'I'm sure it does. But this is a gorgeous new start for you, Tom and Maisy. Life has a way of working out.'

'But Mum . . . I'm worried you'll be lonely here on your own,' Rachel confessed.

'Now don't you be fretting about me in all this. I'll be fine, love.' Jill was happy to put on a brave face. 'You just be sure to keep popping by. We'll be working together all the time anyhow, and Maisy can stay for sleepovers whenever she likes. And hey, I'm looking forward to you spoiling me over at Tom's place too.'

'Of course. Oh . . . I so wish Dad could be there tomorrow.'

'I know pet, I know.' Jill gave a heartfelt nod. 'We'll be fine though. Dad wouldn't want to be spoiling your big day.'

'No.'

They both had misty eyes at this point.

'Oh, I've just had a thought. I wonder . . . yes, there's something Tom might like to have . . . for the wedding.

Hold fire . . . I'll just go and find them.' And with that, Jill was up and out of her seat and dashing off up the stairs.

Rachel took a sip of the prosecco and sighed as a happy-sad feeling tugged inside.

Rachel listened to some rummaging sounds and drawers being pulled in and out, before hearing footsteps on the stairs once more.

'Found them.' Jill gave a proud beam, bearing a small, navy-blue box in her palm. 'You might remember them.'

Rachel opened the box to reveal a pair of tractor cufflinks made of silver.

'Oh, yes . . . they were Dad's!' Rachel remembered pulling up his shirt cuffs to play with them, sitting there on his knee. The years suddenly melted away.

'Yes, I bought them as a gift for your dad on our tenth wedding anniversary. He loved them, brought them out on special occasions. He'd have definitely been wearing them tomorrow . . .' Her voice trailed off. 'Well then . . .'

'Oh, Mum.'

'Anyway, I wondered if Tom might like them. What do you think?'

'I think that'd be absolutely wonderful. I'm sure he'll say yes if he knows they were Dad's.'

'Umm, it's a bit late to go over now, but I'll pop around first thing and see what he thinks.'

The wedding service at the church in Kirkton wasn't until twelve noon, so they had a few hours to get organised in the morning.

'I'll send him a message, let him know about them,' said Rachel.

'Good thinking.'

'That's so lovely, Mum . . . are you sure, though, about giving them away?'

'Absolutely; they're only getting dusty in the drawer there. About time they were worn again. And yes . . . I'd like it if Tom kept them. He's a part of our family now.'

With that, Eve came down carrying her make-up box. 'Thought I'd left that pink one at home for a minute. I must have taken it out ready, found it on the side in your room, Rach.' She looked up. 'Ah, are you two okay? Thought it was just me with the misty red eyes?'

'Yes, we're fine. Just found something of Dad's,' Rachel explained.

Jill opened the box once more.

'Aw, bless. Yes, I remember seeing those.'

Rachel explained Jill's idea.

'Aw, that sounds lovely. It's going to be such a beautiful day, Rachel. I know it'll have its emotional moments. We all miss your dad, bless him, he was such a character, but we'll make it the best day we can. You and your mum, Maisy and Tom, you all deserve it to be special.'

'Thank you.'

'Okay, nails. You need to look the part, Rach, a glamorous, gorgeous bride, not like you've just walked out of the cowshed. So, let's soak your hands first and get some lotion on them, then you're going to be buffed and polished.'

'Yes, ma'am,' Rachel laughed.

'And Jill, you're next. The mother of the bride needs lots of attention too.'

'Well, in that case, I'll get topping up the prosecco before I can't touch anything.'

'Sounds a plan. What happened to Mrs Sensible there a minute ago?'

'Well, I'm sure two glasses each won't send us into hangover mode. I've enjoyed that first one, I must say. May as well finish the bottle.'

They raised their glasses with a 'Cheers!'

Suddenly, there was a feeling of fizz and anticipation all around them.

43

The morning light crept in, warm and golden, through the gap in Rachel's curtains. She opened one eye, guessing it was early. Oh, someone else was in her bed . . . she focused, to find Eve slumbering there beside her . . .

Eve – her maid of honour.

It was today! Her wedding day!

Ah yes, it was coming back now; after all the emotions of yesterday, they'd both piled into Rachel's double bed, slightly tiddly on prosecco, memories, and a nightcap of Baileys on ice with a couple of Jill's rose-petal wedding cupcakes for good measure. The girls had decided they needed to taste-test them ready for the reception. They passed with mouth-wateringly, meltingly sweet flying colours.

Rachel was only just coming to when the bedroom door blasted open and a very excited six-year-old came bouncing onto the bed.

'Mummy . . . Auntie Eve . . . it's today!' She tumbled onto them in a rush of pyjama-clad limbs, sunny smiles and blonde curls.

Rachel bundled Maisy into her arms. 'I know, petal.'

Eve was a little slower on the uptake, it still being far too early. 'Ahh, hi Maisy . . . what time is it?'

Rachel glanced at her watch. 'Six thirty.' She was used to being up with the lark with all her farmyard chores. Farmhand Simon had offered to do this morning's jobs, thank goodness.

'Oooh,' Eve moaned softly, 'I think I need a huge cup of tea.'

'Come on Mais, let's go get the kettle on. We've a big day ahead.'

'Yay. And my pretty dress is all ready. Grandma has it in her room. Can I go see it?'

'Ah, let's just give Grandma a few more minutes, yet. It's still pretty early.'

'O-kay. Can we have pancakes for breakfast like you promised? Chocolate ones.'

'Ah-hah. With strawberries on the side?'

'Yum.'

'But . . . we need to wait just a little while longer.'

Rachel wondered then what Tom was doing . . . fast asleep still, probably. Or going over his speech, polishing his best shoes . . .? Maybe he'd be out checking his livestock on his quad, like on any normal day. He had ages until the service, after all, and no hair or make-up to do. A thought struck her: tomorrow, she'd be there with him at his house, waking up with him, and all the days after that. And she found that, yes, that was a very good thought indeed.

'Will there be lots of people at the church? And at the big party after?' Maisy was racing on with a gazillion questions.

'Yep. Well over a hundred.'

'Wow. And lots of cake?'

'Absolutely tons of cake.'

Hmm, except for the trashed wedding cake, that was. But hey ho, they'd make a pretty impressive stack of Jill's cupcakes on a cake stand, and once they'd added a few of the wedding flowers, it would look fine. The most important thing, after all the twists and turns of the past couple of weeks, was that she would be getting married to Tom. Today they were about to start a wonderful journey as man and wife, with gorgeous Maisy by their side.

'Good,' declared Maisy.

Rachel started to sing 'I Gotta Feeling' as they skipped out of the bedroom holding hands, whilst Eve buried herself back under the covers for just a while longer.

Rachel arrived in the kitchen to find an array of mini muffins and pretty cupcakes on display. Aw, Jill had stayed up baking even more last night, bless her. After a pick-me-up cup of tea, with Jill's and Eve's cuppas delivered bedside as a thank you, there was a Maisy-style special breakfast of homemade pancakes stacked with strawberries and chocolate sauce.

And then, Primrose Farm turned into a swarm of frenetic activity. The flowers arrived with Wendy, who began to turn the tipi and Pantry into a floral wonderland; cakes, pastries and scones were delivered en masse by the Pudding Clubbers and the fabulous WI-ers, a team who'd also agreed to dash back from the church service and get it all plated ready for the afternoon tea wedding reception.

Farmhands Simon and Mark were now setting out bales of hay as outdoor seating areas, and Mick, the landlord from the Black Bull, was positioning table stands that were cleverly converted from wooden kegs of beer. Jake was even giving a hand setting out large feed buckets, ready to add ice so that the bottled beers for later could be chilled. Tom had texted Rachel to say he'd apologised to Jake, so at least they were on steadier ground. She just hoped there'd be no more fisticuffs once the beer keg was running.

Eve and Charlotte were up ladders, festooning the tipi with Eve's handmade bunting, while Hannah and Kirsty were setting out white tablecloths, vintage teacups and saucers and tea plates – some from the Pantry and some borrowed from the WI – along with Emma's mini boxes of chocolate favours. With the bridesmaids and her friends sporting shorts and T-shirts with a pair of wellingtons, it looked as though they'd turned up at some fabulous countryside festival.

It really was a community affair, and as Rachel went out with a tray of teas, coffees and choc-chip cookies to keep the workers going, she stood for a second or two taking it all in. Ooh, she had a bit of a moment then, watching the villagers, her friends, rallying like an army of ants. She knew full well that her dad would have been out there among them, proud and practical, helping to get everything set up for his daughter's big day. He was going to be sorely missed.

The grass was still dewy beneath her wellingtons, but the sun was warm as it rose higher into an azure sky, with the odd puff of cotton-wool cloud. It looked to be a lovely day, though the forecast said there was a chance of showers this afternoon. But hey ho, they could cope with that: a little rain never hurt anyone. With Tom now back firmly by her side, and her family and friends all round, nothing was going to spoil their big day.

Maisy dashed up, happy among the hubbub. 'It looks like magic, Mummy, like a unicorn palace tent.'

'Hah, yes, sweetheart. Well then, let's give out these drinks and biscuits, and we'll see if anyone needs a hand.'

Drinks delivered, Maisy took Rachel's hand and tugged her across to the far side of the tipi. 'Look, have you seen the pretty flowers, Mummy? Me and 'Melia have got special baskets to hold. Come on . . . I'll show you.'

Florist Wendy was high up a ladder, twisting ivy and delicate white gypsophila around the wooden support posts of the tipi. In a shaded area of the tent nearby, in large cardboard boxes, lay the wedding bouquets and two little baskets. Maisy gingerly took up one of the baskets, holding it in front of her. Rachel picked up her own bouquet; it was beautiful, a gorgeous circular posy with all the colours she had asked for. It looked like a countryside summer, circled with a pale cornflower-blue satin bow and a thin twist of hessian twine, and it smelt delicately divine.

'Yours is pretty too, Mummy,' Maisy shouted out. 'When's Amelia coming? I want to show her hers.'

'Not quite yet.' Rachel checked the time, almost ten a.m. With the wedding service at twelve noon at Kirkton Church, just a five-minute drive away, the two girls were going to get ready much nearer to the wedding time when there would be less chance of spoiling their dresses. Ben was due at ten thirty with Amelia, and Rachel well knew that Eve would be feeling a little nervous about her husband's arrival. Eve was holding it together well this morning, though, bless her.

'Wendy, these are just beautiful, thank you,' Rachel called out, still clutching her bouquet.

'Oh, I'm so glad you like them, pet. They do look pretty. I loved making them up this morning.' Wendy smiled down from her perch. 'And I'm sure they'll go wonderfully with your dress that I've heard so much about.'

It was all coming together beautifully, and Rachel felt a mounting sense of excitement. After the wedding vows were made in church, what a party they were going to have!

With the tipi and the field next to the farmhouse mid-transformation, it was time for Rachel to go and get a bit of prepping and pampering herself. Eve was to do her hair, and Hannah her make-up. It was all happening 'in-house' to help with the budget, but she trusted her friends to do a great job. They knew that she wanted a natural look, and they'd had a practice run with prosecco just over a week ago – she'd been delighted with the results.

'Rachel, time to get out of the shorts and T, hun!' Eve called across, stepping down from her bunting and fairy-lights mission. 'We need to turn you into a wedding belle. Much as he loves you, I don't think Tom will want you turning up to the church like that.'

'He might not mind, knowing Tom. But, o-kay.'

Maisy came skipping up. 'Mummy, when *is* Amelia here? We need to put our pretty dresses on, too.'

'Not long now, petal.'

After a last check on all the arrangements, Rachel, Eve, Charlotte and Maisy were ready to head back across to the farmhouse. Just as they set off, Ben rolled up, walking across the field towards them, holding hands with a beaming Amelia.

'Hey, this all looks fantastic.' He glanced around the reception venue. 'And I've got one very excited little lady to deliver to you.'

'Hi, Ben. Hi, Amelia,' Rachel greeted them.

'Hi . . . you two.' Eve smiled at her family, fragile emotions coming to the surface.

Rachel saw her friend take a breath, her body tense. Little Amelia was there beside her, giggling with Maisy. Now was certainly not the time to take this forward.

And Rachel knew Eve too well; she'd not put her own desire to get things off her chest above Rachel's happy day.

'Wow, all your bunting and the table things you've made look great, by the way,' Ben noted, taking in the decorations. He looked at Eve. 'You've worked so hard on this. I can see how it's all come together now.' His tone was conciliatory, after having questioned and moaned about all the late nights, the hours spent by his wife on getting the details right for her best friend's wedding.

'Thanks,' Eve whispered.

Rachel looked from Eve to Ben to Amelia – this wonderful little family *had* to stay together. She prayed they'd make it through this emotional storm that was about to blast its way into their world. And, she also silently vowed that she'd be there for them all, whatever it took.

'Thanks for bringing Amelia over, Ben. So, are you ready for your big day, sweetie?' asked Rachel.

'Yes.' Amelia had the biggest grin on her face.

''Melia, come and see our flower baskets. They're so pretty. And . . . there's going to be cupcakes and big cakes, and puddings, and lemon fizzy drinks. And we get to dance, and stay up *sooo* late.' Maisy was full of the day to come.

Ben made to leave, 'I'll be off then. Unless there's anything you need a hand with.'

'I think we're pretty well organised here, thanks. So,

we'll all catch up at the church soon.' Rachel couldn't hide the beam that spread across her face.

'We will indeed,' confirmed Ben, the best man raring to go.

'How's Tom, have you seen him yet today?' Rachel couldn't resist asking.

'He's good, Rach. Real good. I just called there to check on the rings and everything. And on that note, I'll take Moss along with me now, shall I?'

'Of course, yes. He's just in his kennel. Mum'll give you a lead. Oh, and his bow-tie. Can you please put that on him?'

'Hah, no worries.' Ben gave a lovely grin.

Eve smiled too, but there was such a sad, scared look behind her eyes.

Ben seemed pretty cheerful, so Tom had obviously kept schtum on Eve's behalf – not that Rachel had doubted that. It was up to Eve and Ben to take this forward between them, when the time was right.

'Come on then, my lovely bridesmaids, let's get this party started. Race you to the farmhouse!' Rachel set off with a gaggle of 'hens' in wellingtons behind her, plus some real chickens joining in the fun at the farmyard.

Upstairs, Rachel's bedroom had been transformed into a bridal boudoir. They had their satin 'Bride-to-Be' and 'Bridesmaids' dressing gowns on, and a small glass of fizz to hand, and Rachel's favourite country music by The Shires was playing in the background. The makeovers had begun! Rachel sat on a stool whilst Eve brushed, curled and then weaved her hair. Two thin plaits were made from her long fridge, which were gathered to join at the back of her head, where loose dark-brown waves fell gorgeously in a boho style.

'That's so pretty, Mummy. Can I have mine like that, Auntie Eve?'

'I think that's a brilliant idea. Amelia, would you like yours done like that, too?'

Her daughter gave a big grin and a nod, and Eve moved on to do the two little girls' hair, whilst Hannah, who'd offered to help, set herself away with the bridal make-up. Charlotte was piling her hair into a soft up-do. The bridesmaids' dresses in their cornflower-blue shade hung expectantly on the wardrobe door, and Rachel's handmade bridal gown was next door in Jill's room for safekeeping, kept to one side for its very own magic moment.

'Coo-ey?' It was Wendy calling from the stairs.

'In here, come on in,' answered Rachel.

'I've just come with the flowers for your hair, girls.'

'Oh yes, of course.' Rachel had ordered a delicate floral garland designed to match her bouquet colours. Eve was to set it in place once her dress was on.

The girls had two mini garlands to echo Rachel's, and the others had a pretty burst of gypsophila with a single cornflower and a pale pink rose, to pop in their hair.

'These are gorgeous. Thank you so much, Wendy.'

'And I've brought your bouquets and baskets through

to the kitchen for you, all ready to collect when your transport to the church turns up. Everything's finished in the tipi, and I've popped some flowers as a little extra outside the Pudding Pantry doors to welcome your guests. Just a little something from me.'

'Oh, thank you so much, Wendy. That sounds wonderful. And you are coming along too? We've got a place set for you. You're not just here to work, you know.'

'Absolutely, wouldn't miss it for the world, pet.'

'Oh, well after all that hard work, come and have a glass of prosecco with us.' Charlotte raised the half-empty bottle and found a spare flute.

'Just a small one then. I'm yet to drive to and from the church.'

The bedroom door opened after a brief knock, to reveal Granny Ruth looking very smart in a plum-coloured jacket and skirt, followed closely by Jill, who was bearing a tray of tea and mini meringues with fresh cream and raspberries on top.

'Hello, lasses. Oh, it looks all go in here,' Granny beamed.

'And I've got a few treats here that Granny has made. It's a long while until the reception, and I think your tummies might need a bit of lining,' added Jill with a smile, as she popped the tray down on the side.

'Thank you, Granny. They look divine.' Rachel's eyes lit up.

'And,' Jill continued, 'your Granny's also been up half the night, by the looks of it, and made a hundred and fifty bite-sized lemon meringue pies and more of these raspberry meringues to go with your reception drinks at the Pantry.'

'Oh, Granny. You're very naughty, you should be resting. But thank you.' Rachel went over to give her a hug.

'I wanted to do my bit to help out, that's all, pet.'

'Love the outfit, Mrs Swinton. Gorgeous colour on you.' Eve was smiling across at Ruth.

'Thank you, Eve. Jill and I had a wee shopping expedition down to John Lewis in Newcastle. She persuaded me to splash out on something new.'

'Well, it's just perfect, Granny,' added Rachel proudly.

'Right then, time's rolling on,' said Jill, checking her watch. 'I'll catch up with you girls in a minute. I need to be getting my glad rags on too. Ruth, do you want a cup of tea down in the kitchen while I get ready, or are you happy here?'

'Well, if the young 'uns don't mind, I'd like to sit here and be part of all the preparations . . . and I might have a wee taste of that bubbly I've just spotted there, Rachel.' She gave a wink.

Hair and make-up done, prosecco sipped, Rachel sat back and took everything in for a few minutes. There seemed to be a whole heap of love, excitement and anticipation in that room. The bridesmaids were now putting on their satin dresses, and Maisy and Amelia were waltzing about having been popped into theirs.

Then, it was time for Rachel to get into her own dress. She went across the landing to Jill's room where it hung, knocked softly and walked in to see her mum ready in her frock, a lovely shift dress in soft pink florals with a short pale pink jacket.

'Oh, Mum, you look wonderful.' She'd seen her outfit on once before, as Jill had had a try-on after the shopping day out. But today, it looked even more special. Dad's photo was looking over at them from its place on the dressing table. Rachel gazed from that back to her mum, and they shared a poignant look.

'Now don't start me off already, love,' Jill smiled with misted eyes.

'I've come to fetch my dress. It's nearly time, Mum.'

'Yes, my love.' She took both her daughter's hands in hers.

'Shall I put it on in here? Then go and show the girls?'

'Yes, why not.'

Jill helped her into the beautiful gown. The care and attention to detail with which Eve had crafted it was stunning – it had a sleeveless bodice that fell from the shoulders to form a soft V at Rachel's bosom, and was tight into the waist, where it buttoned down the back. Below that, it fell into the most magical long tulle skirt, with appliquéd ivory flowers that Eve had sewn on from the waist down to the hem, scattered prettily like fragile blooms in the wind.

'Oh, well that's done it,' Jill sniffed, looking at her daughter with pride. 'Thank heavens for waterproof mascara, that's all I can say. Here, let me help with the buttons at the back.' Jill carefully fastened them. 'Oh love, you look beautiful. Tom is going to be bowled over.'

Rachel stepped before the full-length mirror. Wow, it didn't even look like her! Who was this imposter? Some girl from a fairy tale . . . but, she didn't believe in fairy tales, she reminded herself – well, not since she was six. You had to make your own way in life, and you didn't need a prince to make it work out. *But* . . . if you found that someone to love and respect you, someone who could hold you at night. If you loved them too, and wanted to help make their world a better place; if you were willing to work together through the ups and downs that life could throw at you, then that was as good a reason as any she could think of for getting married.

Jill tweaked the folds of the dress and then the waves in her daughter's hair. 'Perfect.'

'Oh, and there's my flower hair garland to put on top yet. It's in my room.'

'Well then, let's go and see the others and put the final touches in place.' They made to leave the room but Jill caught her by the hand. 'Rachel . . .' They both stopped, realising this might be the last private moment they'd have before the wedding service. 'You have the most wonderful day. Savour every precious moment . . . Oh, it'll fly by, and you'll both be so busy, so don't forget to go and find Tom every now and again, just for a few minutes, and make your own special memories.'

'I will. Thanks, Mum.'

'Dad would be so very proud of you, my love.'

Rachel took a huge breath and smiled, which was soon followed by a happy, emotional sniff. 'So glad Hannah used the waterproof mascara on me too,' she quipped.

With the finishing touches complete, garlands in place and bouquets to hand, it was time for the bridesmaids to go. Tom's father had offered to drive them down to the church in two trips, as he had the smartest car among them: a lovely Mercedes saloon. He came into the farmhouse to wish Rachel well, saying that he was looking forward very much to welcoming her into their family. Aw, that gave her a lovely, fuzzy feeling. Off went Charlotte and Eve with happy smiles and waves. 'Woo-hoo, see you at the church, hun!'

It felt weird a short while later, waving off the second contingent – Mum, Maisy and Amelia. All waving madly in the back seat, with the big ivory bow on the car bonnet flapping in the breeze as they set off down the farm track.

So, this was it . . . nearly time.

Tom should be there at the church by now. All the guests milling in, the pews filling up, and even more friends and acquaintances from the village who couldn't fit in the church waiting outside – as was the local custom – to wave at the bride and gasp, gawp, and comment on her dress. Rachel had no doubt that they would love Eve's creation. She felt so very special in it, and it meant all the more that it had been made lovingly by her best friend.

'Are you all right then, Rachel, lass?' Granny Ruth brought her back from her reverie.

'Yes. A bit nervous maybe, more about tripping up or not saying my words right. I'm not nervous about Tom or us getting married. It just feels so right.'

'Good, that's how it should be, pet. And, he's a fine young man, Rachel. I have no doubt you two will be happy together.'

'Thank you, Granny.'

'Oh, well this takes me right back to my wedding day . . . Yes, the village was pretty much out in force. Everyone loved a wedding – a chance for a feast and a good old knees-up afterwards.'

'Well, some things don't change,' smiled Rachel.

With that, there was the sound of clip-clopping up the farm track. Rachel's heart raced a little, realising that this was really it, her turn to go to the church.

There was a knock at the door and it was a local farming friend, David, one of her dad's close pals. He popped his head around the door with a grin. 'Well then, young lady, your carriage awaits.'

Rachel stood up. Granny gave her granddaughter's hair and gown some last tweaks, though Rachel had no idea why, as the transport that awaited them would surely leave them both to the whim of the elements.

'Well, this is really it. Any last words of wedding advice then, Granny?'

'Now then, I'd say be a team, work together, and don't take each other for granted. And don't expect it all to be easy.'

'Okay then, here we go.' Rachel beamed, whilst feeling a butterfly-queasy stomach.

Granny took her hand; they shared a smile filled with love and understanding. The last to leave. Rachel took a look around her; this would be the last day she lived here at Primrose Farm, and a wave of emotion swept over her. *Oh my*, she needed to get a grip. But then, she reminded herself, it was also going to be the first day of the rest of her life . . . as a married woman to caring, hard-working and handsome Tom. Her next step felt lighter.

Flash, a bay-and-white stocky – and ironically slow – pony, stood patiently outside, his dark-wood carriage decorated with white ribbons and pink and white roses. It looked very much as if Wendy had been working on more than she'd admitted or charged for, bless her. David's gorgeous pony and trap, which his grandchildren adored, was often brought out to help at summer fêtes and such like, and here it was today all ready to take Rachel and Ruth to the church.

As Rachel reached the carriage, she bustled up her sweeping skirt, anxious to keep it perfect, and she took David's hand to step up.

'Hah, I feel a bit like the Queen,' said Granny Ruth, who was now giving her best royal wave as she settled down beside her. 'Just practising . . .'

Rachel shook her head, grinning at her characterful grandmother.

'Oh, David,' Rachel called out, 'you couldn't do me a favour and grab my wellies from the porch, could you? I have an idea what Tom was planning for the journey back, and I really don't think white satin slingbacks will cut the mustard.'

'Of course, and Rachel, you look a real treat. I bet your dad'll be looking down right now with a right big grin on his face.'

'Thank you, David,' Rachel managed to reply with a lump in her throat.

Rachel and Ruth squeezed each other's hands tight.

David popped the wellingtons into the carriage, climbed onto his seat and took up the reins. 'Ready?'

'Ready.' And Rachel felt so very sure that she was.

44

The lane to Kirkton Church was lined with onlookers and well-wishers, and Ruth had managed to implement her royal wave several times, with Rachel beaming and waving too. A fashionably three minutes late, but not enough to give the groom any palpitations, the carriage drew up outside the church gate.

There was a flurry of activity as the bridesmaids and Jill gathered with excited chatter, Maisy and Amelia skipping up with their flower baskets swinging wildly. There were lots of 'Oohs' and 'Aahs' from the gathering, and 'Doesn't she look lovely' ringing out. A cheer went up as the bride-to-be stepped down from the carriage, and she spent a moment thanking David and giving Flash a gentle thank-you rub on his soft cheek.

Eve helped arrange Rachel's dress and tweaked her hair. And then a hush descended as the bridesmaids lined up behind Rachel, even the little ones going quiet – a sense that something momentous was about to happen.

As Rachel stepped through the narrow wooden churchyard gate, with Ruth by her side, her eyes were drawn to a grassy, shady area at the far end of the grounds where her dad's headstone lay. 'Love you, Dad,' she whispered, sending up a silent heartfelt message.

Life and death and love, centred here in this sacred place, next to the ancient stone walls she was about to step within. Where the journey of life and family were marked. A place of celebration and commiseration, of love and of loss. But today was about celebration, and her relationship with Tom, and she couldn't wait to see him – waiting for her. She hoped upon hope that he was there.

At the big wooden church door, she took a moment to pause and smile at Granny, who gave her a firm reassuring nod and a proud smile back. Chords of music struck up on the church's old and slightly cranky organ. The slow walk began, Ruth's stick echoing on the stone flags. Rachel's heart was so full as she stepped into that aisle. And there was Tom . . .

He was dressed in a smart black jacket, crisp white shirt, bow tie and . . . a black-and-white checked kilt. Ooh, he'd kept that a secret. Rachel felt her grin widen. She'd never seen Tom in a kilt before – it kind of suited him, she had to admit.

There was a sea of smiling faces from the pews at each side of the aisle, and as she took slow steps, Rachel could feel their gaze on her, but the only face she concentrated on was that of her fiancé. He had a gorgeous kind of awed look, a look of love warming his broad smile. And she knew that she would remember it for the rest of her life.

As she reached the altar, coming to stand beside the man she couldn't wait to marry, Tom whispered, 'You look so beautiful. Thanks for stopping by.'

Her smile answered all of his hopes and dreams.

The service began with the female vicar welcoming them all and saying some heartfelt words. The congregation sang, Charlotte read out a heart-warming poem that Tom and Rachel had chosen, and then it was time to make their vows, promising to love and cherish each other, for better or worse, in sickness and in health. And then came the moment for the rings to be exchanged. The vicar asked for the ring bearer to come forward. At that point, Rachel turned to look down the aisle and beamed as she saw her dad's faithful dog there ready as planned with Simon. 'Here Moss!'

Sporting a smart bow-tie collar with a sprig of pink rose and gypsophila tucked into it, Moss came bounding down the aisle, stopping to lie down beside the couple. A roll of mirth spread through the audience. Under Moss's collar was attached a velvet ring box, where two very precious rings were nestled together. Ben, as best man, stepped forward to detach it, and passed the first ring to Tom.

'I give you this ring as a sign of our marriage. With my body I honour you, all that I am I give to you . . .' Tom's voice was loud and clear and filled the church with its honesty. His hand was trembling a little, and Rachel stilled it with her smile as he placed the ring on her finger. As his jacket arm lifted, she saw the silver tractor cufflink in place and her heart skipped a beautiful beat.

Rachel then made her own vows, carefully positioning the platinum band on Tom's left hand. And then there was the gorgeous moment of joy and relief when the vicar pronounced them 'man and wife', with Tom and Rachel holding hands. And, at the words, 'You may now kiss the bride', a joyful whoop went up from the bridesmaids.

'Come here then, you,' Tom grinned. They shared a tender kiss before their friends and family, finding themselves a little overwhelmed, happy tears in their eyes. Moss, who'd stayed at Rachel's side throughout, gave a bark. It was time to sign the register, followed by a final prayer, and the couple then made their way down the aisle, holding hands and grinning broadly, with the church bells ringing out.

Rose-petal confetti like scented snowflakes was thrown over the two of them by the gathering outside, catching in eyelashes and scattering over Rachel's hair and gown. Photographs, giggling, chatter; appraisals on the dress and the service; a dash for cars. And a massive green tractor pulled up outside the church gate, with balloons, ribbons, and – for good measure – a few noisy tin cans trailing from it on strings. In the back window of the cab there was a handwritten sign that read 'Just Married'. Mark stepped down from it, dressed in his smart suit; he'd dashed round to fetch it, having parked it out of sight before the service.

'Well, I knew you were only after my tractor, really,' Tom said wryly.

'Absolutely.' Rachel laughed out loud.

Rachel's wellies were there ready by the church door, and she made a quick switch, Eve taking her fancy wedding shoes from her. Tom hauled her up in his arms as she giggled away, her dress splaying out in gorgeous tulle folds, and carried her to their wedding car – country-style. With a kiss on the lips and a beep of the horn, Tom and Rachel, Mr and Mrs Watson, set off for their wedding reception.

45

Arriving back at Primrose Farm in the wedding tractor, the newlywed couple found the Pantry barn doors open wide, with bunting flying gaily above them and two large metal milk urns filled with beautiful countryside flowers set each side of the entrance. Jan, Eileen and Christine from the WI were in position with beaming smiles and 'Congratulations', ready to serve drinks. Fairy lights had been strung up over the counter, and trays of lemon gin fizz cocktails and zingy lemon sodas were set out to welcome the guests. Platters of mini lemon meringue pies and bitesize raspberry meringues were passed around – perfect pudding canapés.

Cars arrived, guests spilled out, and Maisy and Amelia, along with Jill and Ruth, had a wonderful lift back on the pony and trap. Still wearing wellies that were peeking out under her wedding dress, Rachel greeted the wedding guests at the doors to the Pudding Pantry, with Tom right beside her.

'Congratulations, guys!' Eve came up with a big hug for Rachel, as Ben shook Tom's hand, 'Well done, mate.'

'You okay?' Rachel whispered in Eve's ear, as Ben stepped aside to help himself to a drink.

'Yeah, don't worry, hun.' Rachel could see her friend was putting a brave face on it. Eve swiftly moved the conversation on. 'Oh, and so many people have made such lovely comments about the dress. I feel right proud to have made it.'

'And so you should; it's just stunning.' Jill, who was now helping to pass around the nibbles, beamed at her.

So many people arrived, with smiles and gifts, all looking forward to the celebrations to come. With the beautiful ceremony now over, Rachel felt ready to let her hair down a little and go with the flow. She sipped the fragrant gin cocktail, and clinked her glass in a brief private moment with Tom.

'Cheers, my love.'

'Cheers, Mrs Watson.'

Across at the tipi, final touches were being put in place by a team of fabulous helpers and wedding attendees – with Rachel blissfully unaware. After the drinks reception, the guests made their way across the farmyard and into the grassy field where the tipi was set up, leaving Rachel and Tom for a few quiet moments.

Tom took Rachel's hands in his, standing within the old stone walls of the Pudding Pantry, those most special tearooms, which she and Jill had created in the barn from the seed of a dream. And now another dream had come to life.

'Are you all right?' he asked.

'Yes, better than all right. I feel amazing, I'm so happy, Tom. We did it!'

'Yeah, we did it. No going back now.'

'Don't want to.'

'Me neither. Never . . .' And he pulled her close into the most tender kiss, their foreheads resting gently together, and their arms wrapped around each other. And even when they had to pull away, neither had lost that feeling of finding each other, of coming home.

'I suppose we'd better get back and join the party. There might be just a few people waiting for us,' said Tom.

'Hah, yes, and I bet they're starving too.'

They made their way across the field holding hands, with the sun on their faces, and a breeze rippling through Rachel's hair. Strolling across the grass in a wedding gown, kilt, and wellies, should have felt slightly weird, but it felt just right.

As they entered the tipi, everyone at the gathering was standing up by their tables, with Ben calling out, 'Can we welcome Mr and Mrs Watson!' The crowd cheered and clapped, and gave a few raucous hoots. The couple's smiles suddenly widened. There was no official master of ceremonies, this being a very rustic, homemade wedding, but Ben was doing a grand job; he had a loud voice as he was used to shouting across the noise of banging at the garage where he worked.

Rachel and Tom wove their way towards the top table, created from the village-hall trestles and covered with white linen tablecloths, floral decorations, and lanterns with ivory candles inside. Then Rachel spotted the table beside that, where the wedding cake stood . . . yet, there shouldn't be a wedding cake . . . The wedding cake had been trashed just yesterday in a pile-up on the A1. But there it was, a three-tiered 'naked' sponge, very like the one she had ordered, with barely-there buttercream smeared in a white haze around the sides. *Oh my* . . .

She moved closer to take a proper look. On the top was pale green icing made to look like a field, which was drizzled very carefully down the top tier, with a tractor made of icing, two gorgeous little figures sitting on straw bales – hah yes, her and Tom – and even Petie the lamb stood looking on, and Moss was there in icing in a bow tie. Amazing.

'Oh, wow! Tom, come over and see this! Who's made this? How?' Rachel marvelled.

'Oh, well,' Jan moved in beside her, with a big smile on her face, 'we ladies at the WI can soon get into gear when needs must. It was a real team effort.'

'Wow,' Rachel repeated, gobsmacked.

'Yes, I made the top layer of sponge, Mary Stevens did the middle tier, that's a lemon sponge, and Christine the lower tier, that one's vanilla. The tractor was made by Eileen, and Sue Smith made the dog and sheep. Alice from your Pudding Club created the figures – aren't they great?'

'Hah, yes, look Tom, you're even in your red boiler suit.'

'Brilliant.' Tom grinned.

Rachel couldn't help but break into a smile. 'That's just wonderful.' She mouthed a big 'Thank you' across the gathering, trying to spot all the master bakers involved. It really was the icing on the literal cake.

Waiters and waitresses, dressed smartly in black with white aprons, then appeared ready to hand out the Towers of Treats, along with neatly cut triangle sandwiches, and large pots of tea. The vintage cups, saucers and tea plates had already been set out. But . . . Rachel was confused, she and Jill hadn't hired any waiting staff. The bridesmaids and some friends from the WI were going to help serve, or so Rachel had thought. It was then she recognised that the 'staff' were several of the teenagers from the village.

'Yes, it's our kids. Something to keep them out of mischief on a Saturday!' Eileen and Christine called across. 'They've been volunteered.'

Christine's lad, Ethan, then served a plate of scones to the top table, muttering, 'Feels like community service this,' right in front of Tom, but then he looked up at Rachel, cracked a broad smile and gave the newlyweds a wink.

The food was incredible: cakes and scones, tarts and treats, sandwiches, sausage rolls, and so much more. The fantastic Pudding Clubbers, the WI, and all the villagers had come together to create the best afternoon tea ever.

*

It was soon time for the speeches. Ben did a great job as best man, with touches of humour throughout, ending with a nice quip about how he could vouch for married life, sending Eve a bright shade of pink. And then it was Tom's turn. The tent hushed as he stood up and looked proudly at his new wife.

'Rachel, you look so beautiful today. Seeing you walk down that aisle; well, you took my breath away. And Eve, that dress, wow. I don't know how many hours you must have put in to create all that detail, but it's absolutely stunning.'

Eve gave a heartfelt smile.

'Rachel, thank you for showing me how to love again.' He took a breath. 'And, thank you for saying yes. And I knew if I took you on, then I had to take *all* of you Swinton ladies on – Maisy, Jill, Ruth . . . and if you know these ladies, then you know that's no mean feat.' A ripple of laughter washed over the room. 'I know how hard these last few years have been for you all. So, all I have to add is that, in all honesty, I will do everything in my power to love, respect and protect you all, always.'

Aw, Tom. Rachel took his hand, her eyes a little misty.

Jill had her hanky out and Ruth was looking on proudly, whilst Tom's parents were nodding in support. The whole tipi had an emotional hush over it.

Rachel then stood, feeling slightly nervous with all eyes now trained on her, but she had planned to say a few words. 'Thank you, Tom . . . hubbie.' She tried out the new word with a smile. 'Well then,' she continued, 'someone special is very noticeably missing from this table. Someone we all miss dearly every day. So, in my father's absence, I want to say a few brief words.' She paused, gathering herself for a second. 'I know how much my dad thought of you, Tom, before we even got together as a couple, so I know he would have given his full blessing to this marriage. Just before we left the house for the church this morning, I asked Granny what she thought made a good marriage, and if she had any tips. She told me we had to be a team, and to never take each other for granted.' Rachel looked at Tom and then up at the faces in the audience who were nodding and smiling. 'So, I promise to try my best to do that . . . and if ever we lose our way, I promise I'll do everything to find you again.'

Rachel caught Eve's eye by chance, who was nodding earnestly too. There wasn't a dry eye in the house by this point.

'Today has been so special already,' Rachel continued. 'Thank you all for coming, and supporting us, and for the gifts, for all the amazing food you've made . . . and *that* cake. But I know also that this, however special, is just one day. So Tom Watson, I am *so* looking forward to all the other days and the journey we'll take in life together. There's no one else I'd rather share it with.' They held each other's gaze for a second. 'Well then, all I have to add is . . . cheers folks and let's party!'

'Cheers!'

'Woo-hoo!'

There were claps and whoops, and glasses clinked. And the celebrations got into full and fabulous swing.

'Sorry, can I just borrow my wife for a few minutes?'

Tom caught up with Rachel whilst the hog roast was being set up, finding her chatting away with some distant relatives she hadn't seen in a while. After being introduced and a few minutes of chitchat, Tom saw the chance for them to make their escape.

'Of course. Catch you on the dance floor later, Rachel.' Uncle Arthur was renowned, weirdly enough, for his Eighties-style robot dancing, witnessed at many a family wedding and party.

'Okay. I'll keep you to that,' she chuckled.

'And where's Maisy?' Tom said to Rachel. 'We need her with us too.'

'What's all this about?' Her curiosity was piqued now.

'Oh, you'll find out soon enough. It's a wedding gift.'

'But Tom . . . I thought we weren't getting each other anything.' There had been so many other expenses, they'd agreed.

'True, and having you by my side is all I need. But well, I just couldn't resist . . .'

They found Maisy chattering away with the girl who was serving at the ice-cream parlour. Yes, Andrew from the dairy had turned up at the reception with his mobile ice-cream stand, how marvellous, as a little extra treat for everyone. How cool was that!

'Come on, Maisy, there's something I'd like you to see.'

They walked the ten minutes across the fields down to Tom's farm. Going over the events of the day so far, and chatting about how wonderful it had been. Maisy, now hoisted up onto Tom's shoulders, sat with chocolate-smudged cheeks and a big grin.

'Okay, nearly here now,' Tom announced.

The girls looked at each other, neither having a clue what was going on. They went past Tom's house, on through the yard, and arrived at the gate of the adjacent field.

'Come on, then,' Tom called, dropping Maisy down to her feet, as he then picked up a bucket of what looked like sheep feed.

And there appeared two beautiful woolly heads, one tall, one small, both with big brown eyes and the cutest thick eyelashes.

'You've got alpacas?'

'Well, actually they're yours. One for you, one for Maisy.'

'Oh, Tom . . .'

'I thought it might help Maisy to settle in,' he said for Rachel's benefit, 'And of course you'll have to help look after them, Mais. The big one is called Roberta, and Maisy, you can help choose a name for the young one, her daughter.'

'Oh, I need to think what's good . . . Oh, hello you . . . and you.' Maisy was rubbing their heads and patting their woolly shoulders. The beautiful creatures were so gentle and affectionate.

'They have a role on the farm too; they're really good at keeping foxes away,' he explained. 'Apparently, the foxes don't like the smell. And, they get on well with the sheep too.'

'Yay! Do you think Petie can be their friend, Tom? Can he come and see them?' Maisy was bouncing up and down.

'Yeah, I don't see why not. Maybe we can bring him over tomorrow. We can see how they all get on, and if he likes it, he can move into this field too.'

'Like me . . . moving in. Oh Mummy, I love them already. We must go and tell 'Melia and Auntie Eve, and Granny and Grandma.'

'Yes,' Rachel was beaming too. What a wonderful gift, she thought, and what a thoughtful way for Tom to help Maisy feel excited about moving into her new home. 'We really ought to be getting back to our wedding party soon, though. They'll be wondering what's happened to us.'

'Hmm, I bet there're some theories flying about already.' Tom gave a sexy wink.

46

EVE

It was wonderful to see Tom and Rachel so happy. But inside the tent of laughter, music and joy, there was one heart full of sorrow; heavy with the awful news that she would need to break, tomorrow. Let today be Rachel and Tom's, and then . . . tomorrow. It might be that Ben would never find out – Eve was sure that she could trust Rachel and Tom. But, in her heart of hearts, Eve knew that telling the truth was the only way forward. Ben had to know.

Eve had been dancing with Amelia and Maisy, holding hands and swirling in a loop to the happy beat of 'Cotton-Eyed Joe'. She saw that Ben was at the makeshift bar, chatting to some local pals. Eve suddenly felt the need to get outside and get some fresh air.

'See you in a minute, girls. Just nipping to the loo.' There were indeed two Portaloos set up for the event at the field edge.

The little ones giggled at that, and then carried on with their jigs and twirls, and as the next song started up Grandma Jill came on the dance floor to join them. They were full of cake and marshmallows, ice cream and lemonade, and they thought today was the best party *ever*.

It was just past eight o'clock now, still warm, but the early evening light had a fading quality.

Eve felt her adrenalin from the day start to fade too. How she wished she could just enjoy the celebrations, be happy and carefree, like she had been only a couple of months ago. Oh, God. What had she done? And why the hell had she done it?

But . . . there was no changing it, and she needed to face up to her actions, however crazy and misguided they were.

A voice she knew so well came from behind her. 'Eve, are you all right?'

'Ah . . .'

She turned to find her husband there, a look of concern etched across his brow.

'There's something wrong, isn't there?' he prompted.

'Oh, Ben . . .' Eve was so bloody afraid.

'You've not been yourself these past few weeks, Eve. What is it?' His tone was so caring, loving, and yet Eve knew she was about to shatter his trust in her, his world.

'Walk with me.'

They needed some space, away from the wedding capers, the joyful shrieks and hoots coming from the tipi . . . away from listening ears.

Ben took Eve's hand in his as they walked on up the

grassy hill, and that gesture felt as though it might break her heart further. She paused, and saw that the moon had begun to rise in the sky, even though it hadn't darkened yet.

'Ben, I'm so sorry . . .' She gulped. 'I've done something terrible . . . and I wish I hadn't. I know it's going to hurt you, and I'm so, so sorry.'

His face paled and his hand loosened on hers, but it was still there . . . for now.

She looked across the rolling countryside, the landscape of her home, *their* home, and took a deep breath.

'Just tell me, Eve.'

The truth.

'I started to fall for someone. It was crazy and stupid . . . and I got caught up in it all. We kissed. Just one kiss.'

'God, Eve. No . . . You've been kissing some other guy?'

The look in his eyes made something fracture inside her. She felt his grip release from her hand. The evening air now felt cool and lonely around her fingers.

Ben turned away, as though struggling to take it in. The silence was painful, but Eve didn't know what else to say.

He turned back sharply. 'How long? What's been going on, Eve? Are you seeing this guy or something? Who is it?' The questions barrelled out clumsily. The questions he had every right to ask.

'An artist friend . . . it's not a relationship. We've never been out as such . . . It was just a moment, one stupid, crazy moment.'

'That bloody artist . . . the exhibition. You've been acting weird ever since that night. Jeez, Eve. What the hell.'

'I'm sorry.'

'Do you love him, have you fallen in love with him?'

'No . . . *no*, never.' *Just some stupid crush.* She could see it for what it was now. The tears were falling thick and fast, hot with shame . . . and fear, that he might not be able to forgive her. 'I love you, Ben. Please forgive me. I just . . . look, things have been quite strained between us of late, and sometimes . . . well, it feels like we're miles apart, and yes, I feel like you take me for granted. All the effort I put into the crafting, running around to keep things ticking over at home.'

'Are you really trying to make excuses?'

'No! Of course not, I feel terrible. I'm just trying to explain how we got here. Look, I can see we've lost touch. I've been trying, honest to God I have . . . I even dressed up in that flowery dress you always loved the other night. I'd planned us a nice supper and everything . . . but you never even bloody noticed. You went swanning off to the darts . . .'

Ben had the decency to pale a little, but his lips were still set in a firm hard line.

'I know there's no excuse for what I did,' Eve continued. 'But things can change for us, Ben. We, *both* of us, have to try harder. And I'll never ever do anything like it again. I don't want to lose you. And . . . there's Amelia in all this . . .' her voice wavered.

'You should have thought of that a bit earlier.' His tone was as sharp as glass. 'I need some time to think, Eve.' He marched away further up the bank.

A peal of laughter broke from the tipi, and the band started up a new song. Should she go back? Would the others have noticed the two of them were missing? She was sure Amelia would be fine with Jill and Ruth and Maisy for now.

'Ben . . .' She ran after him. 'It's you I love, Ben. It's you I need. *Us.* We need to get back to how we were. Need to make some time for each other. Not be trodden down by work and life and *stuff* . . . We've just lost our way . . .' She was struggling to put it all into words, but she had to try. 'I'm asking you to forgive me.' She wiped her eyes with the back of her hands.

'It's a lot to take in, Eve. Just leave it, okay.' It was a warning shot to give him some space, and she had to respect that.

'All right.'

Ben headed back down the hill towards the tipi. She stayed a while longer, feeling a chill on her skin, watching the light begin to fade, letting her tears fall and then dry. After a while, she thought she'd better get back to the party herself – she was the maid of honour, after all. She'd walk down, put on her best smile, and pretend it was Happy Ever After.

47

'And now can we have the bride and groom on the dance floor for their first dance.' Jim, Kirkton's taxi driver and amateur DJ, was on his microphone making himself heard across the tipi.

Tom and Rachel were ushered to the centre of the makeshift dance floor, both looking a little shy at being the centre of attention once more. Tom was whispering in Rachel's ear, and whatever it was made her grin. Their chosen track started up, and the chords of 'From the Ground Up', a gorgeously romantic country song by Dan and Shay, rang out. The lyrical music calmed the gathering, voices hushed, soft fairy lights were glowing above the couple. The music and the magic took over and they swayed gently together, sharing a tender smile. Lost to the moment and to each other.

Towards the end of the track, Maisy and Amelia ran onto the floor, giggling and sprinkling the couple with yet more rose-petal confetti and silver strands. The little girls were soon joining hands with Tom and Rachel and dancing along with them. Rachel then beckoned for others to join in too, as the song changed to 'You Had Me from Hello' by Kenny Chesney, another of her all-time favourites. Charlotte and Sam, and several other couples made their way onto the dance floor. Granny Ruth was guided across by one of Tom's groomsmen, who looked very dashing in his waistcoat, white shirt and Northumbrian tartan kilt – and the room began to sway in time with them. Granny had a huge smile on her face.

'Thank you, young man,' she beamed. 'And I must say, there's something very fetching about a sporran!', which caused the young man to blush furiously. Rachel overheard and burst out laughing – Granny must have had one too many proseccos and gin fizzes today!

Daniel and Jill appeared and began to do a slow waltz together. Rachel spotted them, felt a moment of pain that it wasn't Dad dancing with Mum any more. But it was lovely to see Jill so happy; she deserved that and more. And love didn't have to end, just like grief didn't have to last for ever, either. She saw that their growing relationship was a real positive in her mum's life. Today had had its moments of sorrow amongst the joy too; they'd never ever forget Dad, but with so much love and support around them, the Swinton ladies knew they could be happy again.

Rachel leaned into Tom and gave him a gentle kiss. He smiled so proudly, honestly, lovingly; her heart felt full to the brim.

Looking over his shoulder a few seconds later, Rachel spotted Eve standing on her own at the side of the dance floor. Rachel scanned the tipi to see Ben at the bar with a cool, hurt look on his face. *Oh . . .*

She caught Eve's eye, and mouthed, 'Have you told him?'

Eve looked so sad and lonely, as she nodded a 'yes'.

'You Had Me from Hello' was still playing. Rachel was just about to whisper discreetly to warn Tom and make her way across to her friend, when she saw Ben look up, stare at Eve for a few heart-stopping moments, and then . . . he walked across to her. He took his wife's hand, who gazed up at him with such relief, yet the pain and shame was still clear for Rachel to see. He nodded a silent, 'Shall we dance?' They stepped onto the floor, and began their slow, tentative sway. Both fearful, confused, hurting, lost in limbo . . . yet still together. Rachel could see Eve's tears wetting her husband's shoulder, making his shirt damp. Spotting her mummy and daddy, Amelia came running up to them. Eve swiftly wiped her cheeks, and the three of them were soon dancing, holding hands in a circle; Eve's precious family.

Rachel sent out a silent prayer that everything would work out for them.

It was warm in the tipi an hour later, with so many people dancing. Rachel took a moment to step outside, where strands of lights were twinkling and storm lanterns were glinting on the outside 'barrel' tables, where couples and friends sat chatting. She walked a few steps away from the tent, feeling the cool night air on her bare arms, and looked up at the emerging stars. If Dad was out there somewhere, somehow, he'd be so glad she'd had the day she'd wished for.

She wandered a little further into the field, away from the hustle and bustle of the party. 'Love you, Dad,' she whispered into the night air. And she knew his spirit and his guidance would stay with her for life. Love didn't die.

'Hey . . .' Tom was there beside her, his arm coming around her, warm and tender. 'What an incredible day it's been.'

'The best,' answered Rachel.

Suddenly there was a burst of giggles, and sparks and light began flaming gently as hands lifted in a circle around them.

'Congratulations!' Eve called out, with Ben standing beside her.

'Happy Wedding Day, Mummy.' Maisy was grinning.

Oh yes, sparklers – she'd promised Maisy and Amelia the special fireworks they'd had at their Bonfire Night party last year.

'Wheeeeee,' shouted Amelia.

'Happy Tom and Rachel Day!' beamed Charlotte.

'Best wishes to you both,' called Frank.

'All the very best,' said Granny Ruth with a wink, still going strong.

'Lots and lots of love and happiness,' said Jill and Daniel.

And the stars and the dancing sparklers, bursting with light, seemed like hope and love and everything they could wish for, all rolled into one.

Happy Ever Afters!

Recipes to celebrate with . . .

Ruth's Raspberry Meringue Bites

Ingredients

2 free-range egg whites
125g (4½oz) caster sugar
237ml (½ pint) double cream
Few drops vanilla essence
Additional caster sugar
Fresh raspberries
1 large piping bag
Large baking tray
Makes approx. 25 mini meringue nests

Method

Meringues are best made with slightly older eggs; if they are too fresh they don't volumise very well, and they must always be at room temperature, never straight from the fridge.

Place the egg whites in a large bowl and whisk with an electric whisk on half-speed until the whites are volumised and foamy (there should be no clear white liquid left in the bottom of the bowl), then whisk at full speed until they are white and cloud-like.

Start adding the sugar a tablespoon at a time, while still whisking on full speed. Allow each spoon to be fully incorporated before adding the next, and continue like this until you have added three-quarters of the sugar. Reduce the whisk down to half-speed and add the remaining sugar a tablespoon at a time. The mixture should look very thick and glossy.

Place in a large piping bag with a small star nozzle and pipe onto a tray lined with baking paper. Pipe out a small circle 4cm (1½in.) in diameter, then continue to pipe around the edge leaving a small hole in the centre. Repeat until mixture used.

Bake in a cool oven, 120°C/Fan 100°C/Gas mark 1/2 for 1½–2 hours until they are fully dried and lift off the paper easily. Leave to cool.

Add a few drops of vanilla essence and a teaspoon or so of caster sugar to the cream and whip to soft peaks, then when ready to serve, fill the centre of the meringue with a teaspoon of cream and top with a fresh raspberry.

Delightful bite-sized treats. Enjoy!

Lemon Gin Fizz

Ingredients

Ice, cubed or crushed
30ml (1 fl. oz) measure of dry gin
30ml (1 fl. oz) freshly squeezed lemon juice
60ml (2 fl. oz) soda water
Lemon slices to serve
A sprig of mint or rosemary for the garnish
Makes 1 glass

Method

Fill a glass to two-thirds with ice; pour over the gin, lemon juice and soda. Add a slice or two of lemon, and stir gently. Garnish with a sprig of mint or rosemary. Sip and enjoy.

Perfect for summer evenings.

Cheers!

A LETTER FROM CAROLINE

Thank you so much for choosing to read *Summer at Rachel's Pudding Pantry*. I hope you've enjoyed spending time with the fabulous Swinton family at Primrose Farm. Hopefully you've been curled up with this novel with some scrumptious pudding to hand!

If you have enjoyed this book, please don't hesitate to get in touch or leave a review. I always love hearing my readers' reactions, and a comment or review also makes a real difference in helping new readers to discover my books for the first time. You'd make an author very happy. ☺

You are welcome to pop along to my Facebook, Instagram and Twitter pages. Please share your news, views, recipe tips, and drop by to read all about my favourite bakes and the inspirations behind my writing. It's lovely to make new friends, so keep in touch.

Thanks again, take care, and see you soon!

Caroline x

Facebook: /CarolineRobertsAuthor
Instagram: @carolinerobertsauthor
Twitter: @_caroroberts

ACKNOWLEDGEMENTS

So many people help to support an author and their writing. Here are my heartfelt thanks:

Family. I want to remember a very special lady, my mother-in-law Tessa, who sadly died over twenty years ago. I can picture her making fairy cakes with my daughter, who was then a toddler perched on a stool beside her granny, licking the leftover mixture from a spoon. Memories that make me think of Jill and Maisy in the book. Tessa would have loved to have been able to see her grandchildren grow up into the wonderful young adults they have become. She was a wonderful, kind woman who made me feel very welcome in her family.

My children, Amie and Harry, and their partners, Toby and Rowan. My little grandson Alfie and my husband Richard – thank you for everything. And a big hello and thank you to my sister, brothers, Mum and Dad, and to all the wider family too.

Friends. Thank you to my writing community friends: the fabulous book bloggers, and the wonderful Romantic Novelists' Association who are celebrating their 60th Anniversary this year. I also consider my talented editor, Charlotte Brabbin, and all the team at HarperCollins and

One More Chapter as friends, having worked closely with them over the past five years. Thank you for giving me the opportunity to become a published author – a dream I had long cherished and worked towards. Hannah Ferguson, my lovely agent and the team at Hardman & Swainson – a big thank you.

Farming friends, Helen and Johnny Renner and Jane and Duncan Ord, who helped advise on farming life in Northumberland, kindly answering my many questions to inform the Pudding Pantry books – your support is much appreciated. Thanks also to Susan Green, the inspiration behind the Pudding Pantry idea, with her fabulous local business, 'The Proof of the Pudding'.

Jo Hume – a real-life baking queen, thank you so much for the recipe for the raspberry meringues, and also for the wonderful samples left on my doorstep.

Jenna Brigham – a big thank you for sharing your wedding cake recipe which you made for your own wedding.

And I can't forget all my other friends – glass of prosecco and a chat anyone? Cheers folks.

Food. Food, family and friends, the perfect combination. My enjoyment of food and cooking hopefully shines through in my books. That's why I love to share recipes. Enjoy and happy baking!

This strange new world in 2020. The past few weeks have been very difficult with the impact of the coronavirus crisis. The world has become an uncertain and challenging place. I hope you manage to find a little solace between these pages. Books can be a magical place to escape, to find new adventures and to learn new things. Thank you to all of the above people whose work and support has helped make this book happen, especially at such a difficult time. And warm thanks to you, my readers. A book really is nothing until it is shared and read.

Take care all!

DON'T MISS THE OTHER UNFORGETTABLE NOVELS IN THE PUDDING PANTRY SERIES

Both available to buy now!

'Family, friendships and fabulous food.
The Pudding Pantry is perfect!' Heidi Swain

KEEP UP WITH

Caroline Roberts

For book news, all the latest gossip, giveaways and gorgeous recipe tips, come and pop by online.

THE PUDDING PANTRY IS ALWAYS OPEN!

f/ CarolineRobertsAuthor @_caroroberts

http://carolinerobertswriter.blogspot.com/